CHASING HORSES

Christy Tillery French

AmErica House
Baltimore

First printing

ISBN: 1-58851-259-2
PUBLISHED BY AMERICA HOUSE BOOK PUBLISHERS
www.publishamerica.com
Baltimore

Printed in the United States of America

Acknowledgment:

The author wishes to thank the following people:

First and foremost, my agent, Larry Franklin, for his guidance, counsel, encouragement, and continual faith in this work of fiction;

My mother, Margie Clark, for always being there;

My father, John Tillery, for his creativity and interest;

My "true-blue" friend, Terri Henslee, for being so supportive and encouraging;

Corinne Bell, Ph.D., for her friendship and input;

And last but not least, my husband Steve, for keeping me grounded, my son, Jonathan, for his faith in me, and my daughter, Meghann, for not letting me give up.

CHAPTER 1

"ROY ROGERS IS RIDING TONIGHT"

She was about as nervous as a virgin in a room full of sailors right off the boat. Well, okay, about as excited, too. Her hands were sweaty; her stomach was in knots. Her skin felt greasy. She cleared her throat. "Charlie, I don't know if this is such a good idea," she said, glancing at her companion.

Charlie gave a look meant to shrivel. Ricki straightened up and stared right back. Charlie finally sighed exasperatedly, then said, "All you got is a case of the jitters, Ricki. Once we get inside, you'll be all right, I reckon."

"Did you bring the masks?" Melanie asked from the back, her voice practically in Ricki's ear, startling her a little.

Charlie grinned widely. "Girl, just wait till you see what I have concocted. You'll be so proud to wear it. Knock you flat on your ass, I promise."

They were sitting at a traffic light, in Charlie's Toyota. Ricki had wanted to bring her Sidekick, seeing as how Charlie was such a danger on the highway, but had to reluctantly agree with her other two vigilante partners that a teal-colored mini-jeep with a white canvas top doesn't blend in too well with the scenery. Melanie's car was a sporty white Mustang convertible and hers blended almost as well as Ricki's. So there they sat, nervous, edgy, waiting for the traffic light to change so they could get to their destination and do their dutiful deed. Ricki looked up at the sky, which was darkening quickly. *Good,* she thought. *We need it to be dark. That way maybe, please, God, no one will see us.*

Charlie startled her out of her worries, when she said somewhat reverently, "Lord have mercy, would you just look at that?"

Ricki perked up, thinking that maybe some guy with a nice, tight fanny was walking by, saying, "What? Look at what?"

"Just goes to show ya," Charlie said.

"What the heck are you talking about, Charlie?" Ricki asked, irritably. Shoot, she couldn't understand her carrying on like that over anything other than some gorgeous hunk.

"That Lexus over there, see," she answered, pointing. They all looked. The yuppie-looking driver was boldly picking his nose.

"That is so gross!" Melanie said from the back.

"Like I said, just goes to show ya," Charlie reiterated.

"Show ya what?" Ricki asked, trying not to watch the guy but not being able to help herself. That was so vulgar.

"We are all alike, each and every one of us. Don't matter how rich you are, how poor you are. We're all God's creatures, all made the same, all do the same thing," Charlie pontificated.

"Not me," Melanie said, offended.

"If he puts his finger in his mouth, I'm gonna puke," Ricki said.

They watched as he wiped it on the back of the seat.

"I would advise you never to buy a used Lexus," Ricki told the others.

When they arrived at the complex, it was completely dark and the parking lot was empty save for one car, which they knew to be the owner's, seeing as how they had only staked this place out four days straight.

"Pull into a parking space," Ricki instructed when Charlie drove right up to the door.

"What for? The place is closed. Ain't no point having to walk all that way."

"Listen, Charlie, if, say, the police drive by for whatever reason and see your car pulled up to the front door, don't you think they're going to find that awful suspicious? Don't you think maybe it would look more convincing if we were to park in a slot, like a customer or a visitor?" Ricki reasoned.

Charlie seemed to ponder this a moment, then shrugged her shoulders and pulled into a handicap zone.

"You know what, Charlie?" Ricki fumed. "I am beginning to think you suffer from passive-aggressive, not to mention oppositional defiant, personality traits, acting the way you do."

"What? What'd I do?" she asked innocently.

Ricki gave an exaggerated sigh and rolled her eyes dramatically, shaking her head disgustedly.

Charlie studied her a moment, then said, "Damn, Ricki, I wish you'd get yourself laid so you could settle down a bit, quit with all this psychological nitpicking you keep throwing at me!"

"It's not like she hasn't had the opportunity," Melanie said from the back.

Ricki turned around and gave her the evil eye, which she ignored.

"Yeah, well, if maybe I could meet some guy worth letting lay me, I'd, you know, do it," Ricki said defensively.

8

"My brother wasn't good enough for you?" Melanie asked with disbelief.

"Well, now, I didn't exactly say that, Melanie," Ricki appeased. *Jeez, how do you tell your best friend her brother's about as appealing to you as Popeye?* Okay, maybe Ricki did resemble Olive Oyl, she had to admit that, but only slightly; and this Olive Oyl wasn't looking for no Popeye the sailor man to hoist her mainsails, no thanks. Well, at least not that particular Popeye.

"He is a lawyer, you know, and one of the better catches in Knoxville," Melanie stated somewhat prejudicially.

How could Ricki tell her that was his problem, him being a lawyer? Well, along with arrogance and bias and a need to pontificate on every old thing there is to comment on, which goes with being an attorney. Plus he had this nasal, twangy voice which grated on her nerves like nails on a chalkboard. In addition to which, his legs and arms were hairless, which was about as appealing to her as a dead cockroach. Ricki decided she couldn't tell her all these negative things about her beloved brother, so didn't.

Since Melanie and Ricki had had this same discussion about a thousand times already and it was getting old, Ricki decided to change focus. "I tell you what, being a Virgo is pure, unmitigated hell," she said, looking out the window.

"What's being a Virgo got to do with it?" Melanie sneered at her.

"Well, for one thing, Virgos are only the most loyal people you'll find on this Earth," Ricki answered.

"Says you," Charlie said.

"It's true!" she said. "You just haven't known me long enough to find that out. I mean, look at me with Danny. We've been divorced several months now and I still can't go to bed with another man, much less date anyone seriously, you know, 'cause my loyalty to Danny gets in the way."

"He sure ain't very loyal to you, from what I hear," Charlie observed.

"Yeah, well, let's not get into Danny and the bimbette," Ricki snapped, and in order to waylay the conversation from getting on that topic, said, "Besides which, if my loyalty doesn't get in the way, then my guilt feelings do. That ought to be my middle name, you know, guilt. My whole life is rife with guilt feelings. I live on guilt. I eat, sleep, and dream guilt."

"Here she goes," Melanie said resignedly.

"I tell you what, my next life, if I'm going to come back as a Virgo, I think I'll just commit hara-kiri in utero."

Charlie burst out laughing.

"Tie that dang umbilical cord around my neck, right before I traverse down the birth canal," Ricki declared.

"That's gross!" Melanie said.

"Hey, I'm serious here. You know what I think? I think all Virgos had to have lived a terrible life in their previous ones. You know, maybe we were all murderers or rapists or actors or something. Narcissistic as hell, I'm sure. And to teach us a lesson, make us atone for our bad lives, God said, 'Well, you'll just be a Virgo in your next life, that'll teach you. You'll be condemned to feeling loyal to people you owe no loyalty to, guilt for having normal feelings like, say, happiness.' "

"Will you listen to this crap!" Charlie said.

"Oh, gosh, you think what I just said was blasphemous?" Ricki asked worriedly, ignoring her friend's biased observation. "Was I being sacrilegious? Shoot, now I'll be worrying all the dang-long night about that! 'Cause that's another curse put upon Virgos, you know, we worry all the durn time about every durn thing there is to worry about. And if we don't have anything to worry about, we start worrying over that! It's bad enough we're all about as guilt-ridden as the epitomic Jewish mother . . . oh, shoot, did I do it again? Was that a prejudicial comment? Was I being anti-Semitic?"

Charlie snorted derisively. "Does she ever shut up?" she asked Melanie.

"She always does this," Melanie piped up from the back. "She just doesn't want to talk about why she dumped my brother, so she's trying to make us forget what we were originally talking about by saying all these weird things."

"Hey, maybe it's eldritch . . ."

"Where?" Charlie asked, interrupting Ricki's defense, looking alarmingly out the windshield.

"Where what?" Ricki asked, confused.

"Eldritch."

"Yeah?"

"You said that's Eldritch," Charlie snapped at Ricki.

"Yeah, right."

She sighed dramatically. "Where?"

"Where what?"

Charlie hit the steering wheel with her hand. "Eldritch, damnit!" she half-shouted.

"That's what I said."

"I don't know no Eldritch," she said exasperatedly.

"Of course not."

"Who the hell is Eldritch and where is the man?" Charlie fumed.

Ricki stared at her. "You're kidding, right?"

Charlie gave her a blank look.

Ricki turned to Melanie. "She's kidding, right?"

Melanie just looked confused.

"Jeez, Charlie, you ever heard of a dictionary?" Ricki asked her, somewhat irreverently.

Charlie visibly bristled.

"Hey, we better get inside before the owner decides it's quitting time or someone gets suspicious about us being out here," Ricki said, taking another detour.

"Yeah, right," Melanie agreed, sounding relieved.

They had decided they would don their masks in the car, prior to going into the building. Charlie had wanted to put them on before they left, but Melanie and Ricki managed to convince her that wouldn't be such a good idea, especially if they got pulled over for speeding or a broken taillight or something. After all, they would look suspicious enough, dressed in black sweatshirts, black jeans, and black tennies, and just so no fingerprints would be left, in case anybody got the bright idea to call in the cops, black cotton gloves.

Charlie reached under her seat and pulled out a brown grocery bag, which she opened and began handing out their very crucial disguises. Ricki held hers up toward a street light to get a good look, then laughed out loud. Charlie's concoction consisted of a black pointy hood with two round openings, which Ricki presumed were for eyes, and a slit for the mouth. It kind of reminded her of a dark version of the hood worn by the Ku Klux Klan, that bunch of cowards! "How apropos," she said, looking at Charlie, who grinned, signaling she got this one.

After they were properly disguised, they looked at each other and mutely began exiting the car. "Roy Rogers is riding tonight," Ricki sang, opening her door, ignoring Charlie's, "Say what?" They stealthily approached the outer door of the building, were surprised to find it open, so went on in, being sure to lock it behind them.

He was at the back, in his office. They strolled on in, merry as you please.

The look on his face when he saw them, it was something else. His mouth dropped open, his eyes bugged out, his hands went to his throat, almost like a woman's reaction. *What a sissy!* Ricki thought with disgust.

"Who . . . who are you?" he asked, standing now, trying to look irate. His voice was high-pitched, nasal.

"Who are we? The man asks who we is," Charlie said, sounding just like Whoopi Goldberg in *Ghost*. Melanie and Ricki looked at each other. Ricki could tell by her eyes, Melanie was smiling.

"What do you want?" he demanded, louder than he should have. "If it's money, I don't have any. It's all been deposited."

Charlie laughed, simultaneously moving toward him, reaching out, stopping his arm as he began to open his top desk drawer. "I don't think I'd do that if I was you," she said, her voice threatening. He had to bend his neck back to look at her as she stood towering menacingly over him. *Just like a little kid before a big, bad parent*, Ricki thought, grinning to herself.

"Ouueech!" he yelled as Charlie reached out, grabbed and then twisted his arm behind his back. She put herself in back of him and shoved him forward, raising him up on tiptoes, causing him to do this kind of shuffling dance as she brought him toward her two partners in crime. Ricki couldn't help but laugh. Maybe it was from nerves, but anyway she laughed, thinking that ought to impress Charlie, show her she wasn't any scaredy-cat.

"Who are you? What do you want?" he asked, his voice shrill.

"Honey, we is the lech patrol and we have come to shut you down," Charlie responded authoritatively.

Melanie and Ricki snickered.

"Lech? What the hell are you talking about?" he demanded, trying to make his voice sound forceful.

Charlie didn't answer, looking at the other two, saying, "You know what you gotta do."

Ricki went to his right arm, Melanie to his left. They each tied a lead rope Ricki used with her horses around his wrist, then backed up, forcing his arms straight out from his sides, holding him tight, not giving him leeway.

Ricki took the time to study this little weasel that liked to sexually harass his employees. *Jeez, why are they all such nerdy-looking twerps,* she wondered with irritation, taking note of his balding pate, too-pale complexion, narrow shoulders, wide hips. Then she thought how repulsive it must be trying to fend off the advances of a jerk like that.

Charlie interrupted her perusal as she approached him again, saying, "Mister, we been advised you have been sexually harassing some of our sisters."

"Sexually . . ." he started, but Charlie stuck a rag in his mouth, stopping him. He looked like he was going to gag there for awhile, and Ricki was wondering if they should take the rag out so he didn't vomit. She couldn't stand for someone to throw up. She had an involuntary gag reflex when that happened. He seemed to choke for a minute or two, then calmed back down. Charlie stood, watching him passively.

After he had quieted, she said, "Now, I been wondering to myself, what can I do to help this little man here, stop him from sexually harassing these poor innocent women who work for him, wanting only to make enough money to put food on their table, have a roof over their heads? Well, I reckon the answer is easy enough." She reached into her back pocket and brought out a shiny switchblade. Melanie and Ricki gasped simultaneously. This hadn't been planned.

The man started making high, squealing noises in his throat, struggling against them, but they held him tight. Ricki looked at Melanie and she shook her head like, *I don't know what to do.* Ricki shrugged her shoulders, mutely agreeing.

Charlie reached out, undid his belt, then unfastened and unzipped his pants, and they all watched as they dropped to his ankles. He was wearing boxer shorts. *Shoot,* Ricki thought, *there ain't nothing uglier than a man with skinny, knobby, hairless, ultra-white legs, wearing baggy boxer shorts.* Now she was the one fighting the impulse to gag, seeing that sight!

Charlie then real quick pulled his shorts down. They all stared. Ricki couldn't help it. This was the first nude man she had actually seen up close since her divorce. Well, okay, in real life. And what she saw was one hell of a disappointment. Charlie gave a derisive laugh. She must have been thinking the same thing.

"Well, would you just lookit here," she said, reaching out with the knife, touching his penis, which was all shriveled—from fright Ricki was sure—looking like a tiny worm. It seemed to shrink even more when she touched it with the knife. Charlie looked him in the eyes. "This here is what you been promising those poor girls? This little bitty thing is what you been wanting to put inside them? Sheeeeittt!" she critiqued.

Ricki couldn't help it, but a snicker broke through.

"Why there ain't nothing there," Charlie said, leaning down to get a closer look. "A person would need a pair of tweezers and a magnifying glass just to find the damn thing!"

Ricki lost it at that, trying to cover her laughter by pretending to have a coughing fit. When she had quieted down, Melanie was giving her the evil eye, so she looked at Charlie, who seemed proud of herself.

Then she pressed the button on the knife, exposing the blade. Ricki's eyes widened, but not near as wide as the man's. He started making those squealing noises again.

Charlie came right up to him, held the knife against his groin, began making these circular movements, not cutting skin, but close.

"Now, this is your first and only warning, little man," she said, emphasizing the *little*. "You leave them girls alone. You keep your hands to yourself and your fly zipped. And don't go getting any ideas it was one of 'em that told on you. We have our sources, and it doesn't come from your employees. So I don't want to hear about no repercussions to any of our sisters. You understand?" She jabbed him lightly with the knife, drawing a pinpoint of blood. He squealed. "I don't think I got that," she said, leaning into his face. He shook his head frantically up and down, making himself understood.

"Well, good. Now, if we hear from our sources you been misbehaving, next time, after we get through with you, if'n you get a notion to pee, I guess you'll just have to sit down to accomplish that feat. You understanding me?"

As if in answer a small trickle of urine slid down his leg, making slight plop, plop noises, landing on his shorts.

Charlie watched for a second, then looked into his eyes. "I see you do. That's fine." Ricki laughed again. Melanie shot her a look, which she ignored.

Charlie stopped, pondered a moment, then looked at Ricki and said, "Why don't y'all just bend him over that desk over yonder?" a gleam in her eyes.

He started that damn squealing again.

"What for?" Melanie asked, sounding nervous.

"I figured I'd just leave him with a reminder, so next time he goes to harass one of our sisters, he'll think twice about it."

"Reminder?" Ricki asked, making her voice low.

"Yeah. Like, you know, carve the letter L on his left cheek and the letter F on his right."

More squeals.

Ricki grinned. "L, F?" she asked.

"As in lecherous fart," Charlie replied.

Ricki lost it again, Melanie finally joining in.

Meanwhile, he was going crazy, twisting around, squealing, doing a little dance, peeing some more.

After everybody had calmed down somewhat, Charlie said, "I reckon you're lucky tonight, little man. We've got others to see to and we're running late, so I'm gonna let you off easy. Just remember, if we have to come back, pay you another visit, your wife's gonna wake up to find your tiny little dick on the pillow right next to her. You got that?"

14

He nodded his head frantically.

"Good! Tie him to the chair," she told Melanie and Ricki.

He docilely let them lead him to the chair, shuffling along because his pants and shorts were impeding any wide steps. Well, heck, Ricki wasn't about to pull his pants up. After he sat down in the proffered chair without prompting, they simply pulled his hands behind his back, tied them together, and brought the ropes around to the front.

Charlie watched impassively, then they all headed for the door. Just before going out, she turned, pointed the knife at him, said, "You just remember what I told you!" in a thunderous voice, and they were gone, disappearing into the night. Just like that.

Ricki was hysterical by the time they got to the car, feeling pumped, high, laughing and babbling about what Charlie had done. Charlie drove with a proud look on her face. Melanie sat in the back, looking pensive.

Charlie dropped them off at their cars, saying she had to get home before her husband got there, else he might question where she had been. Before getting out, Melanie voiced the opinion that maybe they went just a little bit overboard with this vigilante thing, maybe stepped over the line. What did they think?

Charlie and Ricki looked at her with disbelief.

Melanie gave them a belligerent look in return.

Ricki sighed. "Look, Mel," she said, appeasingly. "I know when you and I formed the support group for women, it never crossed our mind we would end up engaging in, well, vigilantism."

"And we never even considered it 'till Charlie came along," Melanie said derisively.

"Well, right, but don't forget, you, Charlie, and I decided that for the times WAR couldn't passively handle a situation, the three of us would, you know, step in and handle it our own way, in a passive manner, as well. You were there, Melanie, you went along with it."

"Yeah, well, you two seem to forget WAR is an acronym for Women Aware and Responsive, not a noun for what you want to engage in," Melanie accused.

"Who said anything about engaging in war?" Charlie snapped.

"Okay, okay," Ricki interrupted, knowing an argument was coming. "What we did tonight, Melanie, has nothing to do with engaging in any war, you know that."

"Oh, and a knife isn't a weapon used in a war, I suppose," she said smugly.

"She didn't actually use the knife on him," Ricki said. "It was just a prop, if you will, to, well, scare him a little, let him know we meant business, right, Charlie?"

"Yeah, right, a prop," Charlie repeated a little too quickly.

"Well, I'm sorry," Melanie said. "It's just, what if we had gotten caught in there with that guy, holding him while you threatened him with that knife, Charlie? Damn, why'd you have to bring that thing anyway?"

"Just seemed like the thing to do," Charlie said, shrugging nonchalantly.

"Come on, Melanie, it was fun," Ricki said. "God, I feel great. Wonderful. Alive. Isn't it fantastic not feeling powerless of a situation, instead being in control, doing something to resolve a problem for someone else?"

"I'd like to hear you tell the judge that," Melanie snipped.

"That won't happen, Mel. Come on, girl, you're either with us or you're not," Charlie chided.

Melanie seemed to ponder that awhile, then said, "Okay, I guess I'm in," sounding defeated.

"The Three Vigilantes," Ricki sang.

"More like Larry, Darryl, and Darryl," Melanie cracked.

They checked all the papers the next day but only saw a report about an attempted robbery at that building. Ricki had to admit she was a bit disappointed. Charlie's sister was dispatcher with the police department and Ricki didn't know what ruse Charlie used on her, but she found out that one of the units had been called on a 911 to the place, finding the man all trussed up in a chair *(he had dialed with the heel of his shoe)*, his pants and underwear down. He told the responding patrol that three "black women dressed like the Ku Klux Klan" had tried to rob him, but not finding anything, had simply tied him up and left him there. Said one of them sounded just like that black woman who played on *Ghost*, Ida Mae Brown. When questioned as to why his pants had been pulled down, he gave some vague sort of explanation that they were at one point going to rape him, but he had managed to talk them out of that. "Oh, for Pete's sake!" Ricki said, fighting the urge to gag, remembering the dinkless wonder.

CHAPTER 2

"I'VE GOT A ROMANCE WE COULD CHRISTEN"

Ricki's ex-husband, Danny, and son, Zachary, were taking the dream vacation out West that their little family had planned for so long. Danny, being Danny, had asked Ricki to come with them, but she declined, telling herself this would be a good father-son trip for her erstwhile husband and son, and they didn't need her messing things up. Besides, her goal here was to be independent and live her own life, and she couldn't very well do that by going off on a vacation with her ex.

They had been gone a week and Zachary had called twice, sounding like he was having a great time. So did Danny, for that matter. The last time Ricki talked to Zach, he had asked her to go to the houseboat Danny had occupied since their divorce and get a lens for his camera which he had forgotten to bring along, then Fed Ex it to the hotel they would be staying at the following Friday.

Not having anything particular pressing, Ricki decided to head out the following day, maybe spend the afternoon on the houseboat, getting some sun. When she got there, as she walked down the catwalk, she heard muffled voices from that direction and slowed down, listening carefully. Sounded like a talk show going on. She grew irritated, wondering if someone had taken advantage of Danny while he was away, utilizing his premises, so to speak. Then sighed inwardly, thinking, *knowing Danny, it's one of his down-on-his-luck employees, needing a temporary place to stay.*

She stepped onto the boat heavily, causing it to rock a little, letting the person inside know someone had come to call. When no one came to the sliding doors to peer out, she opened them and boldly stepped in.

She observed a petite blond, seeming enraptured with Jerry Springer, acting right at home, who immediately stood as Ricki stepped inside, looking startled and caught.

Ricki took a moment to study her, knowing full well who this was. Danny's latest and newest, also longest to date. Ricki was not without her sources in Danny's camp, foremost of which was Zachary, followed immediately by Danny's secretary. That woman and Ricki had been friends since she first started working for Danny, a relationship Ricki strove hard for, knowing full well the secretary generally knows as much or more about her boss's life as does the boss's wife.

Ricki didn't actually know a lot about this sweet young thing standing before her, studying her now, somewhat defiantly. Just that Zachary thought she was a real airhead and was incensed his dad had taken up with someone this dense. Just that the secretary had relayed the information on that Miss Stacy had pursued Danny with a vengeance and poor old Danny had finally succumbed. Ricki also knew that her father had once been mayor and politicians abounded in her family. *Therein lay the attraction for Danny*, she told herself.

Ricki had only met Stacy once before, approximately five years earlier, when she was still in college. At that time, she had seemed to be such a mousy little thing. The transformation that had taken place with her body over the next five years was absolutely astounding, as well as calculated. Her once tiny breasts were now round and voluptuous and awfully firm for that size. Her once mousy-brown hair was now long and prettily blond. Gone were the glasses. Ricki supposed she now wore contacts, colored ones by the look of it. She couldn't help but admit to herself that her body was perfect. Well, so was her face.

The fact that Stacy was now a beautiful woman with these humongous breasts did nothing for Ricki's self-esteem and mood. She drew herself up, towering over her former husband's lover, trying for intimidation, feeling like an Amazon. "Who are you and what are you doing on my houseboat?" Ricki demanded, acting as if she didn't recognize her.

Well, it was half hers. Danny and she had agreed that their residence and the houseboat would remain in both their names until Zachary came of age and then they would decide whether to sell the whole mess, split it, or what.

Stacy's eyes glistened at Ricki's irreverent tone of voice. "My name is Stacy Zimmerman, and I'm here as a guest of Dan's," she replied haughtily.

She had this airy, little girl, *I'm so vulnerable and defenseless, won't you please protect me* voice.

Ricki closed her eyes, thinking, *dang, Danny, I thought you had more sense than this.*

She gave Stacy a disbelieving look, then said, "I just talked to Danny and he didn't mention anyone staying here. So, I would suggest you vacate the premises. Like now."

"You're his ex-wife, aren't you?" Stacy asked, emphasizing the "ex," likewise pretending not to recognize Ricki, giving her a disdainful look.

Ricki really hated her then.

"Leave," she said spitefully.

Stacy poked out that bottom lip, pouting. "Dan said I could come here any time I want."

"Well, I'm saying that as long as Danny is not here and I'm apt to be here, you are not welcome and you cannot come here," Ricki snapped, going to the door, sliding it back, thereby indicating, *get the hell out of here.*

"Oh, yeah?" Stacy asked.

Jeez, what a great response, Ricki thought.

"Well, you just wait till I tell Dan what you did!" Stacy threatened.

"Darlin', you do whatever it is you need to do. In the meantime, get lost," Ricki snapped, feeling bitchy and ineffectual to boot.

"You're just jealous!" Stacy snipped on her way out.

"And you are full of shit!" Ricki snipped right back.

Well, her day was ruined. Once she found the lens for Zachary, Ricki decided to head back, after making sure Stacy hadn't disturbed anything. Okay, so she snooped a little. The only thing she found of significance was an almost-empty package of condoms in Danny's nightstand. *Ole Danny has been pretty busy,* she thought. *Well, at least he practices safe sex,* she consoled herself.

Ricki was really down about seeing Stacy, so went home, stuffed herself with goods from her junk food stash, trying not to think about anything in particular but how good all those carcinogens were, then finally sat back, feeling bloated, concluding that now she was feeling really depressed. She sighed, thinking, *the guy I no longer want has himself a main squeeze. A blond all of 25 years. Built just like Barbie: big boobs, small waist, flaring hips, and well-shaped legs. Even got the same voluminous blond hair. Even has the same empty head.* Boy, was Ricki jealous. Not of her. Of him. Because she herself did not have a squeeze.

So she did the stupidest thing she could have: stripped down and took a good look at her near 40-year-old body. *Yep, starting to show age now.* Fine lines around the eyes, butt starting to flatten out, little cottage cheese look on the backs of her thighs. Well, one consolation, her breasts weren't sagging. But then, when you're almost flat, there's not much to sag. *She's got boobs out to there,* Ricki thought, then grew angry. Danny had always told her he liked small breasts when she would bemoan her lack of endowment. "Anything over a mouthful's a waste anyway," he would console, somewhat crudely. And dumb old Ricki bought that hook, line, and sinker. Now here he was with a 25-year-old trophy, with boobs out to there. She sighed.

Now she was majorly depressed. So she closed all the blinds, put on an Elton John CD, got busy doing housework bare-ass naked. If there was anything in this world that could lift her up, it was listening to Elton, and doing housework sort of eased the mental pressure, focusing on rote tasks. Plus doing it naked lent a decadent feel to it.

By the time the doorbell rang, Ricki was harmonizing right along with the main man *(and not sounding so bad, to be honest about it).* Cursing, she went into the bedroom, quickly donned one of her aforementioned ex's frayed dress shirts, which she used to sleep in sometimes and which came down to mid-thigh, went to the door, flung it open, Elton now harmonizing with someone else.

She thought she might be in love, looking into the most gorgeous pair of green eyes she had ever seen. *Whoa!* she thought, *this is surely a gift sent from heaven,* as she eyed the man standing before her, who possessed a masculine face framed by dark-brown, wavy hair, hitting right at the collar. Liking what she had seen so far, her eyes couldn't help but travel downward, checking him out. Great body. Wide shoulders, narrow hips, long legs, nice-size bulge hanging to the right. *Right-handed,* she thought, studying that area.

Realizing what she was staring at and thinking of, Ricki quickly raised her eyes to his and said, "So?" somewhat indignantly, embarrassed at the lazy grin he was giving her back. She surmised he must be used to being given the once-over by women. *Jeez, this guy is really good-looking.* In fact, he was one of the handsomest men she had seen up to this point. He had those nice deep creases in his cheeks, the ones that dimpled when he frowned or smiled. *Hold me back, Jack,* Ricki thought, looking at that gorgeous face.

"Cherokee England?" he asked his voice a deep baritone, to go with that masculine body.

"Yes," she said, somewhat dubiously, studying him further, trying to be as surreptitious about it as she could. That wavy hair, those wonderful eyes framed by dark lashes, bushy eyebrows, heavy beard showing already, nice wide, sensuous mouth, deep crease on each side framing it. She wondered briefly if he had dark hair on his chest and arms and legs. Checked out his arms. Yep.

She was brought out of her reverie when he said, "I'm Samuel Arnold, detective with the Knox County Sheriff's Department," flashing a badge.

Uh-oh, she thought.

Ricki made a show of studying his attire now. Jeans, pullover shirt, name-brand tennis shoes. *Should have known,* she thought. Then panicking, thinking, *oh, God, they've found out about us. What am I gonna say? I'm not prepared for this! Should I call my lawyer*? Trying to cover this up, she said, "So?" again, not so indignant as she wanted to sound.

"I'm investigating a homicide yesterday at the Winn-Dixie in Powell," he responded, giving her a weird look.

"Homicide?" she squeaked, thinking, *what has Charlie done now?*

"Yes. You aren't aware of it?" His voice was professional now and he was not grinning anymore, his look turning skeptical.

Ricki forced herself to calm down. "Well, I heard about a homicide at a grocery store on the radio this morning, but I only caught the tail-end of it." Looked him in the eyes. "Don't tell me it happened at the one I went to yesterday," she said, shocked.

He nodded.

Ricki pondered this a moment. "Can you tell me when it occurred?" she asked, not really wanting to know.

"According to witnesses at the scene, right at 12:30," he replied in a professional tone.

"Well, shoot, it must have happened right after I left, 'cause I was there around 12:30," she gushed.

"Would you mind if I ask you a few questions?" he asked, his voice now interested.

Well, shoot, thought she.

"Uh, sure," she finally got out, then held the door open. "Come on in."

He ambled in behind, Ricki leading the way into the family room, from whence Elton was belting "Funeral for a Friend," her favorite.

She quickly went and turned it down low; irritated she wouldn't get to listen to this one.

Turned back to him. He was looking at her legs, then gave her a lazy grin. "You like Elton?" he asked, as if he knew the guy.

"I love Elton," she effused, pronouncing it El-tahn, her way of honoring the legend.

He laughed a low, manly chuckle. "Yeah, well, don't tell anybody, but so do I," he confided.

That did it. She was in love.

His eyes traveled down her legs again. "Excuse me," she said abruptly and stomped out, remembering she had on no underpants, aware there was no way she could sit down for his little interview without revealing a part of her anatomy she might be willing to, but only if he asked first.

She went into the bedroom, donned a pair of high-thigh, cherry-colored panties, briefly debated putting on more appropriate attire. Then, feeling irritated at his interruption, thinking, *this is my house, I'll dress any way I damn well want to,* and went back into the family room. He was at the stereo, listening.

"Man, I do love that song," he said appreciatively.

21

It was all Ricki could do to keep from lunging at him. So she decided to put him to the test. "That is without a doubt my all-time favorite," she said, nodding toward the stereo.

"Mine, too," he agreed.

Okay. "In fact, this is the song I want played at my funeral," she stated, staring into his eyes.

He contemplated for a moment, then gave a slow grin. "I like that," he said.

He passed! she thought happily. "My husband and son both think that's a little macabre," she went on.

"So you're married?" he asked, somewhat nonchalantly.

"No."

"Well, you just said husband," he pointed out.

Oh. "A slight faux pas," she replied, shrugging, looking into those gorgeous eyes. "I'm recently divorced," she explained.

He nodded, giving her an interested look.

They listened to Elton playing magic on the keyboard.

"Doesn't it just energize you?" she asked him. "Doesn't it make you want to get up off your butt, dance around, make love . . ." Feeling her face redden with embarrassment, she sat down abruptly. "Sorry," she said, grimacing.

He laughed, then sat down across from her.

"So, you were at the Winn-Dixie in Powell yesterday, at approximately 12:30, correct?"

Sounded just like a lawyer. Take away a point. "Uh, yeah," she replied, keeping her knees together, having a hard time. "But how'd you know that?"

"You wrote a check, and we matched the amount of your check against the register's copy of the cash receipt."

She nodded. "Oh, right," she interjected. "They have the time on the register receipt, don't they?"

He gave her a wide smile. "Pretty good," he said.

"Well, I read a lot of mysteries," she admitted.

"Yeah?" he asked, grinning wider. "Me too."

"Oh, come on," she said. "You, a detective? What could you learn from that?"

"Well, I don't. Mostly entertainment, you know?"

She nodded. She did know.

He pulled out a notebook and pen and began scribbling with his right hand (Ricki grinned to herself at this), then looked back up, starting at her legs.

"Did you witness the homicide?" he asked, his voice turning professional again.

"Shoot, no," she said. "I mean, I'm sorry about what happened, but thank God, I wasn't there. I'm sure any witnesses that were present are under a psychologist's care by now, wouldn't you say?"

He simply shrugged. "You were there at 12:30?"

"Well, actually, I left around 12:30."

He nodded. "The register showed you wrote the check at 12:26."

Ricki nodded. "Sounds about right."

"Were you acquainted with the woman who was killed?" he asked, leaning forward a little.

She crossed her legs, watching his eyes go there again, began to feel pretty smug.

"I doubt it. That's not the store I usually go to." Then reading his look, she leaned forward. "Oh, you mean did I talk to her? Maybe. I talked to a couple of women in there."

"Do you recall talking to a Sheila Davenport?"

"I'm sorry, I wouldn't recognize any names. What's she look like?"

"Blond, heavy-set, wore glasses."

Ricki could feel her eyes widen. "Oh, no, don't tell me that's who . . ."

He nodded solemnly.

"I talked to her!" she sputtered. "Oh, Lord, this is terrible. I just talked to her yesterday and now she's dead."

He nodded as if commiserating. "Do you remember what you talked about?" he asked, writing.

"Sure. It was cold in there, and when I made that comment, she started telling me how her ex always liked for the temperature to be hot, and she liked it cold, and I said what a coincidence, it was the same way with my ex, except the opposite, you know, he liked it cold, I liked it hot."

"So how long have you been divorced?" he interrupted.

Ricki stared at him. "Is that essential to your investigation?" she asked suspiciously.

He laughed. "You sound just like a lawyer," he said.

"Well, that's a cut," she drawled.

He laughed again, then gave her that durn grin. "Let's just say, I was curious," he answered.

Ricki pondered this a second, then, "A short while."

He nodded, indicating to go ahead.

"Anyway, we got to talking about how traumatic it is going through a divorce and, you know, I told her I had formed this support group for women

23

who are in problematic relationships and asked her to come one night, see if she might fit in, might want to participate."

"Support group?"

Rut-ro.

"Uh, yeah. You know, just a bunch of women getting together to generally piss and moan about their lives, their husbands, boyfriends, whatever. Nothing interesting," making a dismissive motion with her hand.

He seemed to sit there, contemplating, then, "For women?"

"Yeah. It's nothing, really, just a reason to get together, talk."

He nodded. "No men are members?"

Damn. Why do I always have to open my big mouth? Ricki thought.

"Uh, no. We haven't had any actually inquire, to tell you the truth," she finally answered.

"What about me?" he asked, grinning again.

"You what?"

"Joining your group?"

Shit fire! she thought. "Well, actually, you'd probably feel awfully uncomfortable. I mean, it's just a bunch of women, and, you know, women don't generally talk about the same things men do, sports and the like. We focus more on *feelings*," emphasizing that word.

"Is that a jab?" he asked, his brows furrowing, giving her a suspicious look.

"No, not really," she said, smiling, trying to take the bite off.

"Well, I'm divorced. I could use a little support." He looked her directly in the eyes.

Is this a come-on or what? she thought.

"Don't you have men friends you could, you know, talk to? Or a girlfriend?"

Was she asking this for her own personal reasons or trying to help?

"Not really," he answered.

Ricki decided to give back what he gave out, so eyed him all the way up and down—still hanging to the right, she saw—then looked him boldly in the eyes and said, "I'm a real supportive person."

He grinned lazily.

"But the group is out, no offense intended, of course," she hastily added.

He nodded, looked down at his notebook, got back to business. "So nothing out of the ordinary occurred while you were inside the store?"

"No, nothing," she said decisively.

He looked back up; their eyes locked a few moments. She was wondering, *what the heck is going on here*, feeling some sort of current going back and forth. He leaned forward. "What about afterward?"

She felt herself deflate.

"Afterward?" Gave her time to think. She uncrossed her legs, watching him watch this, then kind of turn his head, as if to see up her shirttail. She decided to tease him with a slight glimpse of the cherry color, then smacked her legs together, planting her feet flat on the floor when she remembered.

"How could I forget?" she said, getting excited now (over what she remembered, not him).

He straightened up, looking interested.

"I was unloading the groceries in the back of my car and I remember this guy pulled up beside me and he sat in his car the whole time I was unloading, and that kind of got on my nerves, not knowing what he was doing, sitting there. I get a little paranoid at times, you know? But then, in this day and age, who doesn't? But anyway, I finally finished, put the buggy in the designated arena . . . I am an honorable and obedient citizen after all," (he grinned at this; she was in love with that grin) "and when I was going back to my car, I looked right at the guy. He had dark hair; I remember that, and a beard. He was driving some sort of a sedan. Charcoal gray. I remember that, 'cause I used to have a car that color. Anyway, he got out, and he was carrying something in his hand, which he slipped into his jacket pocket. I remember wondering why is he wearing a jacket on such a hot day? What do you want to bet that was the gun he put in that pocket?" she asked, speculating.

He kept nodding as he wrote.

Ricki leaned back against the cushion. "Whew!" she said, "this is totally unbelievable," then realized her legs were spread ever so slightly and he was now looking in that direction. Back together they went.

His eyes traveled up to hers, held there. She looked back. Shoot, she was getting turned on just staring at those gorgeous eyes of his.

"Do you think you would recognize him if you saw him again?" Mr. Detective asked.

Ricki pondered. "Maybe. I'm not sure. I could try," she said, not wanting this guy to leave and never return.

"Would you be agreeable to working with a police artist, see if he can come close to the man you saw?"

She pondered, hiding her excitement. Maybe this wouldn't end so quickly! "Sure, I'll give it a try. Although, like I said, he was beside me, and when he got out, I only caught a glimpse of his face before he turned away."

He nodded.

Ricki leaned toward him. "You haven't identified the killer yet?"

"No, but we have suspects."

"Well, what about her husband? I mean, they were divorced, and aren't most crimes committed by family members, out of passion?"

He didn't acknowledge this.

"Didn't anyone recognize him in the store, any of her friends, coworkers?" she asked, not giving up.

"The man who killed her was wearing a ski mask," he responded curtly.

"Oh. Well, then, just show me a picture of her husband, and I'll let you know if that's the man I saw," Ricki suggested.

He frowned, like he didn't like her telling him how to do his job. So, she temporized. "Or the police artist. However you want to work it is fine with me." Gave him her own lazy grin.

Ignoring this, "Anything else you remember?" he asked.

She thought a minute or two. "No, I can't remember anything else," she finally said, disappointed.

He nodded, seemed to ponder, then gave her that grin. She placed her hands on each side of the armchair, forcing herself to remain put.

He rose. She rose. He was a good six inches taller than she was. *He's not short!* her mind caroled. *Shut up!* she told it.

He made a show of putting away his notebook and pen, then fished for a card, handed it to her. "I'll be in touch with you about identification." She took the card, their fingers touching, feeling a slight current, and looked at him, but he didn't seem to notice it. "If you think of anything else, just call me at that number." He reached out, took back the card, then his pen, wrote another number. "And here's my home phone, in case you can't reach me there."

Wow! she thought. "Thanks," she said, trying to act cool, calm, and collected.

He headed toward the door and she followed.

He opened it, turned, looked at her, grinned again. She grinned back, held out her hand, and they shook. It was like a jolt went through her. He seemed to hesitate, as if he might have felt a smidgen of that current, too. They stood there, their hands joined, staring at each other. Ricki released first. Kind of like the old who-blinks-first routine.

"I'll call you," she said, paused, "if I remember anything else."

He nodded, turned, then looked back. "By the way," he said, "could you do me a favor?"

She brightened. "Sure!" she effused.

"Always check who's at your door before you open it," his voice turning stern. "I could have been a mad rapist, for all you know."

Ricki laughed. "I don't think I have to worry much about that," she replied self-deprecatingly.

His eyes traveled from her face down to her legs then back again. "Oh, I think you should," he said, turned, and was gone.

Well! she thought, smiling happily.

CHAPTER 3

"IT'S SEVEN-O-CLOCK AND I WANT TO ROCK"

He called the next day. She had been hoping he would.

"Cherokee England?" he asked in that nice, somewhat gravelly baritone.

Oh, whoa, Ricki thought as she answered, her voice icy cool, "Yes?"

"This is Samuel Arnold."

"I'm sorry?" she asked, pretending not to recognize the name.

"Detective with the . . ."

"Oh, yes, Mr. Arnold. How are you today?" She made her voice warmer.

"Fine. Please, feel free to call me Sam."

"And you feel free to call me Cherokee or Ricki, your preference."

He paused, then, "Ricki. I like that."

"Yeah?"

"It suits you, somehow."

"Thank you, I think."

Low chortle, then, "I was wondering if I could come by and show you a picture of Ms. Dunlap's husband, see if he was the man you saw in the car?"

"Sure, Sam. Come by anytime."

He showed up a half-hour later, this time dressed in a business suit with boots.

"I prefer the jeans," Ricki said when she opened the door.

He grinned at her. "Yeah, well, me too, but I had court this morning."

"Ain't it a shame?" she teased.

He grinned again, giving her the look-over this time. Ricki had hurriedly dressed after his call, throwing clothes hither and yon in her bedroom. She didn't want to look like she had dressed just for him, so finally decided on the casual look: denim shorts on bottom, pale-pink tank on top, leaving her legs and feet bare, trying to give the impression his stopping by didn't call for getting herself all doodied up, although she was hoping fervently she looked good to him.

"You got a few minutes?" he asked.

Honey, I got all the time in the world for you, she wanted to coo. But didn't.

"Sure, come on in."

He entered, glancing around the house again, and said, "Nice place you've got here."

Ricki looked around, ascertaining nothing was out of place, thinking for the zillionth time how much she really loved this house. "Thanks," she replied, somewhat modestly.

"You own all those horses out in the field there?" he asked as she led the way into the family room, feeling his eyes on her butt. Ricki made sure she added a little extra swing, almost tripping herself in the process.

"I own five. The rest are boarders or horses I'm in the process of inseminating," she answered.

Ricki turned, caught his eyebrows raised at that.

"Artificially," she added, giving him a teasing grin.

"That what you do for a living?" he inquired when he stopped laughing.

Ricki shrugged. "Well, when I'm not in class."

He looked at her.

"I go to U.T.," she explained. He nodded. "I think I've become a professional student," Ricki confided. "I decided to go back to school after my divorce and can't seem to decide on a major."

"So, what's the rush?" he asked simply.

She smiled. "Yeah, right, what's the rush? So, you like horses?" she asked.

"Only the powered version," he drawled.

Ricki raised her eyebrows this time.

"I like speed and control," he explained.

"What exactly were we talking about?" Ricki asked, drawing more laughter from him.

She indicated for him to have a sit, then followed suit. Jeez, this guy looked like a dandy cowboy all dressed up and ready to go.

They studied each other a minute. "So," Ricki said, breathing deeply, "Samuel Arnold, the detective with two first names."

He gave her a look like he didn't know how to take that.

"I like it," she said.

"Speaking of names, don't you feel yours is sort of a contradiction in terms?" he asked in a bantering way, leaning toward her.

"More like nationalities," she replied, smiling like an idiot.

He grinned, dimpling. More looks between the two of them.

"So, what's the DanRick stand for?" Sam finally asked, breaking it off.

"Oh, you mean the sign on the gate?" she asked, a little slow on the uptake here.

He nodded.

"Dan, that's my husband, well, ex-husband's name, and Rick, my name. Dan-Rick."

He thought a moment. "Your ex-husband's Dan England?" he asked, looking interested.

"Yeah, right. You know him?"

"The county commissioner, right?" Sam persisted. "Famed businessman?"

"One and only. Why?" she asked, growing suspicious.

"He's an awful popular guy," Sam observed.

Tell me about it, Ricki thought.

"He's got some pretty powerful backing in Knoxville."

"Yeah, well," she answered, thinking, *so what.*

"Rumors are rampant at the courthouse he's going to declare for the county executor," Sam persisted.

Ricki shrugged. "To be honest, Sam, I know nothing about that, but if that's what Danny wants to do, then more power to him. He'd make a good one, I think." She shrugged dismissively. "Do you know him?" she repeated.

"No, not really. Just by sight and word of mouth. It's just, you don't seem to fit within my perception of a politician's wife, you know."

"Well, maybe that's why I am no longer married to the guy," Ricki said, giving him an impish grin.

To get the conversation off that subject, she said, "Could I get you something to drink, Sam?"

He blinked. "No, really, I can't stay long. I just wanted to run this by and show it to you." He fished in his suit pocket for the picture, drew it out, got up, came and sat by her on the couch.

Ricki took the picture, aware of their legs barely grazing each other, glanced over, saw him staring at her feet. *Feet?* she thought wildly, as she forced herself to study the photograph.

The guy depicted was blond-headed and thin as a rail. *Whew, thank goodness.* That meant she'd be seeing more of this detective. She tried to hide her grin as she gave the picture back, saying, "That's not him."

Sam nodded thoughtfully, then said, "Think you could take a few minutes this afternoon, come down, work with the artist?"

Ricki pondered. Hmm, what to do, what with her busy social life and all. Then gave him a smile. "Sure. Tell me the time."

He grinned back. "How about 2:00? I'll meet you there."

"Sounds good to me," she said, rising, not wanting him to go.

He rose, too, stood towering over her. "You got a nice size," Ricki couldn't help but observe, looking up.

31

He gave her the lazy grin again, said, "I was just thinking the same about you, Ricki," his voice sounding like a caress.

Hold me back, Jack! she thought.

Ricki took a moment to get herself under control, then held out her hand. "Well, I'll see you this afternoon, Samuel."

He shook it, holding longer than normal, then said, his voice low, "You can count on it."

What the heck did he mean by that? she wondered, watching him amble on out the door, then frantically running into her bedroom, thinking she had to find something really neat to wear and only had four hours to decide!

Ricki was a few minutes late arriving at the station and Sam was there, waiting for her, not acting irritated at all by her lack of punctuality. She noticed he had changed into jeans. She guessed he noticed she had changed into a taupe colored pair of tailored pants which the sales clerk had assured Ricki—and which she hoped desperately—made her butt look more curvaceous and her legs longer, topped with a white silk shell, accentuating her tan. He smiled at her, said, "Thanks for coming," as he took her elbow and escorted her down the hall.

They sat side by side in front of the computer screen, knees touching, as the artist made this or that change, at Ricki's direction. He finally came up with a real close facsimile to the man she had seen, and everyone grinned with relief as they watched it print.

Sam stood, said, "Well, thanks, Ricki. I hope we didn't inconvenience you."

"Oh, heck, no," she replied. "It was fun watching this guy work," smiling at the artist, who was smiling up at her.

"I'll walk you out," Sam said, frowning slightly, taking her arm possessively.

He followed her into the parking lot and to her car.

"This yours?" he asked, eyeing the Suzuki.

"Yep."

"I drive a Jeep," he offered.

"Yeah?" she asked, thinking, *damn!*

"Wrangler," he said, looking proud.

"Wow!" she effused.

He grinned, then eyed the Sidekick again, nodding his head approvingly. "I like it. It fits you."

Ricki smiled with gratitude. "You don't know what it means to hear someone say that, Sam. Thanks."

He shrugged, watched as she unlocked the door, climbed up and sat down. They looked at each other, and then Ricki stuck her hand out again, said, "Well, I guess my work's done. It's been nice knowing you, Sam. Hope you catch him." She withdrew her hand, started the car.

"Hey, Ricki, wait a minute," he said, stopping her.

"Yeah?" *Oh, please, ask me out*, she prayed.

"Listen, I've been thinking, well, you're divorced and so am I, think we could possibly go out sometime?" looking embarrassed.

God bless his little heart, Ricki thought. She made a show of studying him, not wanting to look too desperate, then said, "When?"

He grinned. "How about tonight? You got anything planned for tonight?"

More studying, then, "What time?"

A wider grin. "How about seven? That too early?"

"Too late," she said, deciding, *what the hey, lay it all out here.*

He chuckled at this, then leaned forward into the car and said, "You feel it too, don't you?"

Ricki shrugged. "How about six?" she asked.

"I'll be there."

"So, are we casual or formal?" she asked, looking into those gorgeous eyes.

"Let's go for casual."

Whew!

She nodded, feeling nervous now, said, "Well, I'll see you at six, then," waved, backed out and left for home, thinking, *oh, God, I've got less than three hours to decide what to wear tonight!*

Ricki made a pit stop at the local Wal-Mart and sat there in the parking lot a good 20 minutes, debating whether or not to go inside and buy something for birth control. The day of her divorce, she had gone off the pill, swearing to herself then and there you'd never catch her back on those vile things again.

Ricki wasn't sure what the proper protocol was in a situation like this. If something were to happen, which she was hoping it would, at a later time, of course, who was the responsible party as concerns the protective measures? Considering the threat of AIDS and who knows what all, in addition to pregnancy, she definitely wanted to utilize something.

Up to this point, Danny was the only man she had ever slept with. Oh, sure, she'd dated some since her divorce, but no one ever really attracted her. Not the way Danny did. Plus, in an inane, incomprehensible way, to Ricki, at least, she still felt loyal toward her ex, still felt bound to him, but this Sam

33

guy was different. The physical attraction between them was a pleasant, very welcome surprise. Ricki was well aware of what was coming, although still feeling guilty, but didn't she regret many times during the latter years of her marriage to Danny the fact that she had never actually experienced other lovers? she asked herself. Well, she wasn't married anymore; she had free rein in that regard. Besides, wasn't she tired of using a machine for any sort of sexual relief; didn't she want a warm body pleasuring her? So, what held her back up to this point? Danny.

Stacy came to mind. *Screw him,* Ricki thought, remembering the condoms in his nightstand, testament to his sexual activity with someone else. She got out of the Suzuki, went into Wal-Mart, and purchased two dozen condoms and a package of spermicides, feeling like everyone was eyeing her disapprovingly as she slunk back out to her car. She wasn't really expecting to use them that night, but just in case.

He arrived in jeans, cowboy boots, and a sport coat. *My own Marlboro man,* Ricki thought, her heart lurching as she looked at him filling up the doorway. *This guy is too gorgeous,* she thought, growing suspicious, all the while giving him a welcoming smile. *He's probably about as vain as a bantam rooster.* But what the heck, she was out for fun, wasn't she? And who better to play with than a really good-looking cowboy detective?

Ricki had finally decided on black jeans, topped by a white camisole and royal-blue blazer. She wore long, dangly earrings at her ears, boots on her feet. "Damn but you're gorgeous," he said, looking at her, sounding like he meant it.

Ricki wanted to cry with gratitude.

"Thanks," she answered, then added, "So are you."

He gave her a disbelieving look. *Huh!* she thought.

"So, you ready?" he asked.

Ricki smiled widely, then drawled, "I was born ready, son," drawing laughter from him, and off she went on what was to be her first date since her divorce from Danny, and subsequently her first man, too.

Sam took her to dinner at a popular Italian restaurant in Knoxville. Sam lit a cigarette after eating, caught her looking. "I like to have a smoke after I've indulged in one of life's more pleasurable activities," he explained, dimpling. Ricki had to bite her tongue to keep from asking if there was any chance that she might be included on that list. By the time dinner was over, she was thinking Sam was one of the most compatible men she had ever met. It seemed they shared a lot of things in common: music, books, politics, movie preferences. Afterward, they went to a new country and western club, one that featured line dancing. Sam was good at this and got Ricki on the floor, showing her the steps, doing the dances with her. She hadn't danced like that in years and it was great. He showed her the Texas Two Step and they did that one time after time after time.

They finally left the club around midnight, drove to a restaurant on the river, shared a decadent hot fudge sundae out on the terrace overlooking the water, telling each other about their lives in general, divorces in specific. Sam told Ricki he had wanted kids but his wife hadn't, and that had led to their divorcing, adding that he wanted a whole houseful one day. She thought that was so sweet, especially seeing as how she felt the same way.

Ricki told Sam about her son. He acted amazed she had a son Zach's age. "Damn, Ricki, you don't look over 30," he said, grinning.

Well, flattery will get you everywhere, she thought, then grew irritated she was so gullible. She leaned toward him and said, "Listen, Sam, I'd appreciate it if you wouldn't use compliments to try to work your way inside my pants, okay?"

He drew back, staring at her, then replied, his voice curt, "If I wanted in your pants, I can think of better lines to use than that. I was only making an observation, for Christ's sake."

Well, dang, now she felt embarrassed and hurt. So, he didn't want in her pants? He wasn't trying to flatter his way in? Ricki could feel her face go red.

"Like, for instance, I could say, shoot, Ricki, you don't look a day over 25," he said, that lazy grin back.

Whew. He does want in my pants, she thought, grinning back, relieved.

He drove her home around two. Just being in the car with him was killing her. He was too close. She could literally feel the friction in the air between them, knowing he was as aware of her as she was of him. Ricki had decided early in the evening she wanted to go to bed with this guy but was still having that infernal internal battle of will, feeling like she was betraying Danny in some way. Forcing herself to remember Stacy, she grew angry with him and decided he didn't deserve any sort of loyalty from her. *He sure doesn't give it to me*, she told herself.

So when Samuel stopped the car in front of her house, she asked if he would like to come in for coffee or whatever.

He looked her in the eyes and said, "Whatever."

Ricki grinned. It was as simple as that.

CHAPTER 4

"AND INNOCENCE ABROAD WAGED A WAR FOR THE UNDERDOG"

She stood before the group, this tall, beautiful black woman Ricki had come to love, the sister she never had, her eyes glistening with tears, her voice strained. As Ricki listened to her story of discrimination, she wanted to kill the man responsible for it. Or at least hurt him a little.

The security firm Charlie was employed by had sent her to a club in Knoxville to interview for a position as security guard. Charlie went to the place, met with the owner for all of ten seconds. "He took one look at me, said I didn't qualify," she huffed. "Wouldn't even let me past the front door!"

"Why not?" Ricki asked, feeling bad for her, thinking she had never seen Charlie anywhere near close to tears.

"Told me I had two counts working against me," Charlie went on, her voice angry, not seeming to have heard her.

Oh, jeez, Ricki thought, knowing what was coming.

"Said unless I had a dick hanging 'tween my legs and lily-white skin, I wasn't even worth talking to!" she spat out.

Ricki felt sick.

"Wouldn't even consider my resume," Charlie said, looking right at Ricki. "Said he assumed since my name was Charlie, I was a man and that's why he had agreed to the interview. Which I didn't get," she snorted.

Ricki stood up, wanting to go kick that guy's teeth in, and said, "We have to do something about this."

Several voices raised up in agreement.

"WAR cannot let that club get by with this kind of discrimination!" she stated dramatically, looking around.

More endorsing comments.

"Charlie should not be disqualified from a job because of her sex or her color or, well, anything else, for that matter!" she declared, somewhat emphatically.

Louder voices of affirmation.

"I say we go picket that dang club!" Ricki half-shouted, getting into this. "I say we show that biased chauvinistic supremacist we are not going to let him get by with that kind of prejudice against women and/or minorities!"

More raised vocal agreement.

Ricki stopped, looked around, then asked, "Exactly how do we go about this?" now feeling confused.

Charlie rolled her eyes.

Melanie grinned.

WAR had a lively discussion that night, finally agreeing on a certain date and time to hold their demonstration. This was to be WAR's first public appearance and everyone was greatly excited about it. Ricki was put in charge of making the placards. Melanie volunteered to do all the organizational duties, making a list of demonstrators, seeing to it that everyone had directions to the club. Charlie was put in charge of calling the participants the night before to remind them about what would transpire on the morrow. Ricki glanced at Charlie, saw the proud look on her face, felt good, productive, powerful. She should have known.

The day of the planned demonstration arrived and Ricki was in some kind of quandary. She knew she couldn't not show up, seeing as how she was the one who had suggested this whole thing, but on the other hand, she didn't want to be recognized, either. She was well aware of what negative publicity could do to Danny's upcoming campaign, and he wasn't above pointing that out at least once a week.

So, she decided to disguise herself. She knew they would be there for hours and wanted to dress comfortably, and after much debate decided on a black denim mini-skirt, black high-tops, and a black T-shirt, reasoning black was a nice, neutral color. She should just simply blend in. Right?

She wanted to hide her hair so as not to be discernible to anyone that might know her, and since she was already clothed in black, decided to stay with that motif. She couldn't find her ebony-colored baseball cap, the one that said "Elton John," so rummaged through her son's closet, finding one that was solid black except for a white "Sox" name on the front. She vaguely wondered if Sox stood for a football or baseball team, or what. Since she didn't particularly care, that little debate skittered out of her mind within two seconds. She finished all this off with a pair of faux Raybans, hiding her eyes and a lot of her upper face.

She stared at herself in the full-length mirror. *Dang, I look like a kid!* she thought despondently, her breasts barely bulging in her T-shirt. *Well, that's good*, she told herself. *No one will notice me this way. Ha!*

Ricki was the one with the placards and, as usual, was running late, so when she got there, had to endure chastisement from Melanie and Charlie about why couldn't she just once show up on time. Ignoring this, she handed out the picketing signs, checking out who was actually there. Noticed they had about 10 women gathered. *Well, that's pretty good,* she thought. She was a little disappointed, though, because she had encouraged everyone to try to bring along members of the opposite sex and none had shown.

After everyone had collected their little signs and marched off after Melanie to get organized, Charlie came up to Ricki, stopping her progress, eyeing her up and down. "You forgot your pistols, Black Bart," she mused loudly.

Ricki laughed. "Tell me the truth, Charlie, can you tell it's me?" she asked, taking off the sunglasses.

Charlie gave her a suspicious look.

"It's just, I don't want anybody to recognize me and all of this to fall back on Danny, you know," Ricki lamely explained.

"What the hell do you care?" Charlie asked, giving her a disbelieving look.

"Well, he is going to run for county executive, and I just don't want what I do to have any sort of negative impact on that, you see."

"Screw him," she chided. "He ain't your husband anymore, is he? Besides, even if he was, what he's doing or what he thinks shouldn't stop you from doing what you feel is right. Shit, Ricki, at least once a week you're telling somebody else that. You gonna have to start practicing what you preach, girl."

Well, she was right and Ricki told her so. Mainly so she'd shut up.

Charlie stood there, giving her this look. "What?" Ricki asked, growing paranoid.

Charlie grinned slowly, then said, "There's something different about you."

"Well, of course there is, Charlie, I'm kind of in disguise," Ricki said feigning exasperation, not wanting to get into that again.

"No, that's not what I'm talking about. There's something different about you, 'bout the look in your eyes. Plus, you're not acting as hyper as . . ." her own eyes widened. "Ricki went and got herself laid," she said, acting amazed.

Ricki rolled her eyes. "Is that so hard to believe?" she huffed at her.

Charlie laughed outright.

"Jeez, Charlie, why do you think the answer to any woman's problems is to go out and have herself a major orgasm?" Ricki fumed at her. "I thought you were above that type of thinking. I thought you were at a higher level than that."

"Major, huh?"

Ricki repeated the procedure with her eyes.

"That good, huh?"

"Let's get this thing on the road," Ricki said, grabbing Charlie's arm, jamming the sunglasses back on her face, propelling her friend in the general direction of the maddening crowd.

Ricki decided to keep her disguise on, anyway, being the chicken she was.

The demonstrating was conducted in what Ricki thought to be a well-organized, passive manner. They simply marched back and forth in front of the club, holding their signs, talking quietly among themselves. It was all an ideal setting—that is, until the TV van pulled up an hour or so later.

Well, foot, Ricki thought, stopping in her tracks, feeling horrified at this. *You would pick a really slow news day to have your damn demonstration,* her inner voice sneered at her. *Yeah, and eff you very much,* she replied.

Ricki took note the van was from a Knoxville station. Her stomach twisted, realizing this was that wacky station that showed all the weird things going on around the East Tennessee area, the station that was such a hit because of that. *Shoot!* she muttered. This short, little guy hopped out of the side door, his dark hair slicked back in that old Michael Douglas *Wall Street* look, wearing gray dress slacks, a white shirt, and red suspenders. He flashed a grin at the group of women as he watched, those teeth reflecting the sun, making Ricki's eyes hurt. Anchorman! She immediately became suspicious. He talked to his cameraman awhile, eyeing them as they went about their march, then came over, microphone in hand, saying, "Anybody care to comment on what's going on here?" Melanie stopped abruptly, causing a domino effect as the person behind piled into her, then the one behind her, and so on and so on. Once everyone was balanced again, all eyes shot toward Ricki.

She glared at them, trying to send the message, *don't look at me! I don't want to be recognized here! That's the last thing on this whole Earth I want today, is be recognized!* But, of course, her sunglasses hid her eyes so they, therefore, did not receive her telepathic statement. Ricki doubted they would have anyway. Hell, she probably could have shouted it and they wouldn't have gotten it.

"Our placards speak for themselves," Ricki answered, her voice low.

He grinned, looking at her. Ricki panicked, thinking he must recognize her. *But how could he?* she thought. *I mean, I am not a celebrity, not even locally. That's Danny's job.*

Just then the front door opened and this tall, portly man came barreling out, yelling, "I've called the police. They're on their way. I would advise you people to remove yourselves from these premises lest you wish to be arrested."

"Lest?" Ricki muttered loud enough for several to hear and laugh at.

Mr. Blubber Gut approached the anchorman. *Well, just what we need*, Ricki thought, *a guy looking for a free promotion for his club.*

"That's the guy," Charlie sneered beside her. Ricki glanced at her, taking note of the angry look on her face.

"You mean the owner, the one that . . ."

"The one and only," Charlie spat, interrupting her.

Ricki nodded, then turned and studied him as he talked to the newsman, swinging his arms around, acting incensed that they had picked his club to demonstrate against. He put her in mind of an aging lawyer, dressed ultra-conservatively in a charcoal-colored business suit, the jacket barely fitting around his waist. He wore wire-rimmed glasses and had thin, gray-going-to-white hair with a balding spot right on the crown of his head, the skin there glowing white in the bright sun, giving him a halo effect. "The avenging angel," Ricki said to Charlie, knowing she would get her gist. She did and started laughing.

Ricki turned her attention back to the portly gentleman, paying more attention to what he was saying. She noticed his crisp, fast-paced sentences, the weird way he pronounced the long "I" sounds. She turned to Charlie, gave her a look.

Charlie glanced at her, then back, seeing that look.

"What?" she asked.

"He's a Yankee," Ricki stated.

"So?"

"Dang, Charlie, what're you doing letting some fat-assed Yankee bigot get by with talking to you the way he did?" she fumed at her. "Shoot, you should have chewed him up and spit him out. You should have wrung him out and hung him up to dry. And I am not speaking metaphorically here! It is your duty as a Southern woman to mentally castrate any Northern foreigner who comes down here espousing any sort of biases against any person."

Ricki noticed it was quiet and everyone was staring at her, some with their mouths open. Okay, she could be tangential sometimes, she had to admit it.

"It boggles the mind, anyway, that the South is the one area of this great country of ours that has been labeled prejudiced and racist and anti-this and anti-that," Ricki continued on. "Shoot. Every Yankee I've ever met is more biased than any ten of us. Plus their prejudicial list runs a lot longer than ours to boot, and top on their list, of course, are Southerners. They all come down here thinking we're nothing but a bunch of illiterate idjits who, when we're not scratching our butts and picking our noses, are copiously and very happily and ignorantly indulging in incestuous fornication."

That drew some laughter.

But Charlie was mad. "Don't you go telling me how I ought to be dealing with this or that person!" she yelled. "I was only here trying to get a job, and here you go, talking that dang old nonsense again, using those stupid long words of yours that don't make no sense to nobody, by the way!"

"Hey!" Ricki said, offended.

"I don't think we came here today to witness you two yelling at each other," Melanie said, stepping between them, glancing toward both men, who were staring.

"Shhh," Ricki said to Charlie, her teeth gritted together.

They made their way over. "Shit, Charlie!" she ranted, louder this time.

"They gonna be eating shit, they mess with me," Charlie said, her voice going redneck.

Uh-oh, Ricki thought.

They came right up to them and just kind of stood there for a moment. Ricki was confused, wondering what they were doing, then finally understood they were waiting for the cameraman to get there and set up.

The older guy took the time to smooth back what little hair he had left, straighten his Republican-looking necktie up, pull his jacket down.

"Your fly's unzipped," Ricki said to him. His mouth formed an O of alarm, his hands and eyes simultaneously going to that very spot. Everyone tittered. Realizing she hadn't been telling the truth, he brought his eyes back to Ricki's, his own glittering. "Gotcha!" she chided and everyone, including the cameraman, burst out laughing. The man's face went red.

"Okay, Frank, we ready to roll?" the supposed journalist asked after the humor had died down.

"Wait a minute," Ricki said. "We haven't agreed to you shooting any of this stuff, and if you think you're going to interview us, you're off your rocker. I told you, our placards state specifically what we're doing here."

"I have something to say here and I want it recorded for the viewing public," Mr. Sagging Jowls stated somewhat lawyerly.

Oh, Good Lord, Ricki thought with great irritation.

Bringing the microphone up to his face, the newscaster began prefacing the interview that was about to take place, leaving out a lot of really important details, foremost of which were who WAR was and the reason they were protesting there today.

He then stuck the microphone in the old man's face, who immediately began ranting and raving about these dykes and lesbians and gays and faggots protesting his gentleman's club and he wasn't going to put up with it. In fact, he had just a few moments ago called the police, who were on their way.

Ricki's mouth dropped open as she stood there listening to his lamentations against them, sounding like the redneckedest redneck there ever was. *Just goes to show*, she thought disgustedly, *looks can be so deceiving*.

Charlie put one hand on hip, a danger signal Ricki well knew. She placed her hand on Charlie's arm, signalling for her to calm down. Realized nothing was going to stop her as she stepped into the man's face and yelled, "You call me a dyke just one more time and I'll plug your dike!" waving the sign under his nose. The look on his face was hysterical; Ricki thought he took her seriously. She burst out laughing. She just couldn't help it.

Everyone looked at her. She cleared her throat, then said, as diplomatically as she could, "Listen, as I stated before you started taping, our placards speak for themselves. However, I would like to point out, for the record, that I find it awfully suspicious that this man didn't seem bothered by our demonstration, didn't even show his face until your television van appeared on the premises."

Everyone looked to the elderly gent for comment. "Hey, I didn't come out here to get into an argument with some lesbian over . . ."

"I think we should leave any sort of sexual aspect out of this, as well as name-calling," Ricki interrupted, trying to sound calm, cool, and collected. "The issue, sir, as our signs indicate, involves discrimination against gender and race."

The journalist gave her an interested look, then asked, "What does WAR stand for?"

"Women Aware and Responsive," Ricki replied somewhat proudly. "Our group was formed in order to make the public more aware of the inequities suffered among the human race. We . . ."

"You're nothing but a bunch of homos trying to get yourself on TV!" the old gent yelled in Ricki's face, interrupting her.

She looked at Charlie, whose eyes said, *go on, girl, give it to him.*

"You're about the dykiest looking of the bunch!" he yelled even louder.

Well, that did it. Now Ricki was offended. She removed her hat, then sunglasses, and gave him her deadliest glare. He didn't even flinch. "For your information, Mr. White Supremist," she snarled at him, "my sexual proclivity is none of your business and has nothing to do with this demonstration. That is not what brought me here today. What we are demon . . ."

"You ain't nothing but a queer, pure and simple," he yelled at her, his voice turning redneck. He then glanced at the camera, making sure it was focused on him, before continuing. "Like every other faggot, you got to get out here and have your queer little marches, protesting any ole thing you can find to . . ."

"Hey!" Ricki yelled at him, her voice overriding his, getting defensive. "I happen to be heterosexual, for your information."

"That's what you say!" he replied, sounding like a juvenile.

Ricki went on as if he had not spoken. "Who just so happened to be married to a real he-man, a male, m-a-l-e, man for 20 years, you geriatric anomaly! A man who on his worst days makes you look like a transvestite on your best days!"

Charlie started laughing. Mr. Curmudgeon's face went red, he began sputtering, but before he could formulate words, Ricki broke in again.

"A man who is all man, a man who I could not have gone into a relationship with as a lesbian, much less come out as one, which I was not and am not!" She nodded her head curtly. Everybody looked confused. She didn't think they got it.

"Um, who exactly is your husband?" the anchorman asked, looking interested.

Ricki ignored him, pointing an accusing finger at the old fart she was facing. "And I will not tolerate you categorizing us as lesbians, when we are here demonstrating against your club's policy for hiring only white, male employees. Whose patronage list I'm sure consists solely of white, probably Baptist as well as Republican for all I know, men."

"And how exactly are you familiar with their hiring policies?" the anchorman broke in, trying to gain some control, flashing his teeth at her.

"Do you find this funny?" Ricki asked him, irritated at his smile. He immediately grew sober.

"Uh, no," he said, giving her a sullen look.

"If you would be so kind as to can the humor, I'll be more than happy to tell you how we have come to know the hiring policies of this club," she said snippily.

"You gonna stand there and listen to that dyke?" the old man broke in, waving his arm at her.

"Hey, I hear that word come out of your mouth one more time, I'm gonna let her do what she threatened," Ricki said, pointing at Charlie, her voice icy. His face went white; he snapped his mouth shut. "Now, if you please, you've had your say, let us have ours," she requested, her voice icky-sweet.

Ricki waited for everyone to settle down, then said to the newscaster, "One of the women here applied for a position with this club. When she was turned down at the door, by this man here, she asked the reason why and was told, and I will paraphrase this—I will not say anything as vile and vulgar as what was said to her—but in essence, she was told that she was not eligible for hiring because her skin was not white enough and she lacked a certain appendage between her legs—a penis if you don't understand what I mean."

"Hey, girlie, this is my club. I have the right to hire who I want to work in my club!" the elderly man snarled at her, his face to the camera.

"First off, my name is Ricki En . . . well, it's not girlie!" Ricki yelled at him, thinking, *oh shit, have I done it now.* "And this is America, after all, and I believe still a democracy, where everyone should have a fair and equal chance for each and every job. Men and women alike. Homosexual and heterosexual alike. Protestant and Catholic and Christian and Jew alike. Republican and Democrat alike. Although you could forego the last one, as far as I'm concerned."

Some of the others laughed.

"Well, this is America, and this is my club, and I got the right to decide who's going to work in my club," he said, sounding insolent.

"We have the right to protest what we feel is discrimination, pure and simple," Ricki said, ignoring him. She turned to the guy with the microphone in his hand, who looked a little befuddled at this point. Maybe he was still concentrating on Danny's sexual achievements, she didn't know. "And until Mr. Aryan to the Extreme came out that door, we were having a very organized, passive demonstration. We were not speaking to anyone outside our group, we were not impeding anyone's progress into the club. We are simply here today to point this gross injustice out to anyone who is not white and male. We feel it should be called attention to and dealt with."

"Well, you can deal with it by getting your sorry butts off my property!" he yelled at her.

"I do not believe an area designated by the city for public access would qualify as your property, Mr. Skinhead," Ricki shouted back.

"Hey, I ain't no skinhead," he countered, looking offended.

"This is a sidewalk, sir. A very public sidewalk. We have not stepped foot on your premises, nor do we intend to. And the one who should be dealing with the problem is you, and you can do so by revising your hiring policies, i.e., allowing women, along with men, of whatever color, etc. to work here . . ."

"That ain't gonna happen," he yelled loudly. "I won't have the likes of you working in my club!"

"First and foremost," Ricki replied, "I personally would not wish to be employed by such an establishment, nor would I care to be a member of same. If it's like any other so-called gentleman's—and I use that term quite loosely here—club, it probably stinks of stale urine, sweat, and cigar smoke, not necessarily in that order!"

"That's a lie!" he yelled, his face red, spittle flying out his mouth.

"And secondly, the very fact that only men are allowed to join or work for your club renders the whole ideal suspect. Could it be that maybe you are what you accuse us of being, sir? Maybe this is a place where, shall we say, closeted men can come and be free to express them . . ."

He lunged for her then. Charlie stepped in front of Ricki, impeding his progress, tripping him in the process. The man went down, lay sprawling on the sidewalk.

There was one huge synchronized gasp as he fell, then stunned silence as everyone stared down at the elderly man on the ground. Ricki noticed the camera was still rolling, and feeling she needed to come across as the good guy here, stepped around Charlie and bent beside him, asking if he was all right.

"Don't touch me!" he screamed at her, slapping her hands away as she tried to help him up.

Ricki shrugged helplessly, then stood, and they all watched as he somewhat arthritically righted himself, then stood.

The police car pulled up then, directing everyone's attention away from what was transpiring in their midst. Two burly-looking guys got out. Ricki was thankful one was black and a minority.

They strode up to the group in that swagger only policemen seem to attain, mumbling, "Let me through here" and "All right, let's break it up," as they came into their midst. You would have thought they were a riotous mob, the way they were acting, the looks on their faces.

They stepped within camera range and only then did they ask what exactly was going on here. *The whole world's a stage,* Ricki thought ironically.

Mr. Nazi and she both began explaining at once. They stopped them, let him go first since he had made the complaint, then it was Ricki's turn.

Both men heard them out, then after conferring with each other to the side, made sure they stepped back into camera range before advising the group to back off from the club about 50 feet.

"Fine," Ricki said, not thinking it was, but she wasn't about to argue with the police while the cameras were rolling. "I think we've gotten our point across anyway," she said snippily as she herded everyone down the sidewalk. The film team, sensing this little scenario had played itself out, promptly packed up and left. That is, after the anchorman tried several times unsuccessfully for Ricki to give him her name along with that of her husband. *Please, please, don't air that on TV tonight,* she prayed, watching their exhaust fumes go off down the street.

So, they demonstrated across the street from the club, pacing off the requisite 50 feet. Every once in awhile the old geyser would come out and stand there, arms folded, glaring. They glared back, but the wind had gone out of their sails, and after a couple of hours, they packed it in.

"What are we going to do now?" Melanie asked as they loaded up the placards.

"Continue demonstrating, the way we planned," Ricki responded. "Have a skeleton crew out here every day, for a couple of hours, to show we're not backing off. You've got the list, Melanie, I'll let you coordinate all that. You know, maybe it would be a good idea to have the newspapers interview you or someone from our group, to help bring this more into focus."

"You just got all kinds of focus from that TV coverage," Charlie responded, laughing.

"Yeah, well, I just hope Danny isn't focused on that station tonight," Ricki mumbled, climbing in her Sidekick, starting it up, and heading home, praying all the way.

CHAPTER 5

"HERE'S A LITTLE HEAT BOYS TO STRAIGHTEN OUT THEM CURLS"

Danny called the night of the telecast, surprising Ricki by asking her to dinner the following evening. After all, she had expected a shouting match. She called her hairdresser the next morning, telling him she needed help, like yesterday, seeing as how she had an important dinner engagement and all. He sighed, and after a lot of pissing and moaning on his part, begging and cajoling on Ricki's, agreed to see her at noon.

Ricki hurried in, a little late as usual, mainly because Sam had called, wanting to see her that night, so of course she had to tell him she couldn't, and when he asked why, she told him about having dinner with Danny, which he didn't like. In the slightest. Then she had a slight tiff with Sam when he told her he wanted her to cancel dinner with her ex and she refused, determined this guy wasn't going to tell her what to do, not like she had let Danny tell her what to do. Who did he think he was anyway? Then their tiff evolving into a major argument when he started questioning her about exactly what did she mean by Danny being a male, m-a-l-e, man and all those comments she made about being married to him? Didn't even have the courtesy to tell her how absolutely totally awesome or terrible or stupid she had been. Just getting into what she said about Danny. No questions about who or why or what or how come the demonstration.

So Ricki sat at her hairdresser's, stewing over Sam and why was he acting so jealous all of a sudden? After making her wait another 10 minutes, being bitchy, she was sure, because she wasn't right on time, her stylist came toward her.

Ricki stood, smiled, gave him a hug, said, "How you doing, Marvin?"

He pushed her in front of him, rolling his eyes at the other customers, who were giving him a puzzled look.

When he had her at the sink, dousing her hair with water, he got down in her face, said, "Hey, Rick? You maybe got PMS or something today? You maybe trying to get back at me for something I don't recall doing?"

"No, of course not," she answered, giving him an offended look. Well, actually, she was a little irritated he had made her wait, but you know, she wouldn't intentionally do something to get back. She wasn't that petty. Honest.

"Then cut the Marvin shit in front of the other customers," he said, letting the spray slip and douse her face.

Ricki sputtered.

"Damn, I wish I'd never told you what my real name is," he hissed at her, the hose slipping again.

It got up her nose this time and Ricki made a big show of getting strangled, taking pleasure at the fact that Marvin—excuse me, Antoine—started to look a little concerned, glancing embarrassedly at the other patrons, who were all focused on them now.

"Hey, Marvin?" she said after she had gotten her nose clear and was no longer hacking, "you maybe got PMS, too? What's the matter, I embarrass you in front of all these eclectic customers you got in here?" waving her hand at three old ladies under hairdryers, one bald and one extremely obese man being serviced by the other hairdressers, two matronly looking women in the waiting area at the front, and one old geezer who appeared to be right on the verge of having a coronary toddling around.

He glared at her.

"Okay, I'm sorry. I forgot, okay?"

More glaring.

"All right, I'll make it a point to call you Antoine, Mar . . . Antoine, in front of everybody, out loud, okay? Although to tell you the truth, you look more like a Marvin than an Antoine, you know? Besides, what's wrong with Marvin, Marvin? It's a good, solid, American moniker. You should be proud of your name, guy, proud of your heritage."

He gave her a reluctant grin. "Yeah, well, you try and get customers into a hair salon called Marvin's," he snipped.

Ricki laughed at this. "Bet you'd get a lot of macho-looking guys," she replied, raising her eyebrows.

He stopped, gave her a look, then, "Damn, why didn't I think of that?" They grinned at each other. "Friends?" Ricki asked.

"For now," he growled, throwing a towel over her head, walking away.

Ricki got up and followed along, drying her hair as she went.

He stood beside his chair, waiting for her to sit. "Thanks, Antoine," Ricki effused loudly. "I just love it when you shampoo my hair, the way you use those magic fingers of yours."

Everyone beamed. Marvin repeated the eye-rolling gesture.

Ricki sat down, studied him as he got out all his little pieces of equipment. He really looked like a Marvin, though. Tall, dark, and handsome, wide shoulders, narrow, tight buns. "You got a nice butt, Marvin, you know that?" she whispered, patting it lightly.

He jumped as if goosed, then frowned widely at her in the mirror. "You know that's taken," he smarted.

Ricki laughed, thinking too bad this guy had gone over to the other side. Marvin's lover was one of his employees, and although Marvin didn't look gay, Anthony did. He had long, blond, permed hair, wore an earring in his ear, gold jewelry around neck and fingers, talked with that lisp you hear in the movies, flung his hands around limply, posed, cooed, and generally acted the part. Anthony's real name was Leonard. Go figure. Ricki wondered what they called each other in private. Marv? Leon? Probably sweet cakes and sugar buns. Now, she didn't personally know how a male homosexual relationship worked, but if it was like a heterosexual's, Ricki would bank on it Anthony was the woman.

She really liked Marvin-Antoine. He became her confidante, her advisor, the times she sat in his chair. Then again, he probably played that role for the hundreds of other rear-ends that occupied that same space.

"So, what are we going to do today?" he asked, scissors held aloft, ready for action.

"I want a new look, Antoine," Ricki said loudly, then lowering her voice, "How about shaving the sides and making it stick up on top?"

He looked horrified. This was one of the few male hairstylists Ricki had ever known who liked long hair on women. She liked to shock him.

"Surely you jest!" he snipped.

She shrugged. "I want to look good tonight, okay? And after much deliberation, I've decided it's time for a different look. I've worn my hair this way awhile now and I'm ready for a change."

He studied her. "How about we layer it a little more, making it wispier? See how that works? What do you think, Ricki?" His fingers flew over her hair, showing her what the result would be.

"Hey, I am completely at your mercy," Ricki said, settling in. "Do with me what you will."

"Oh, my," he drawled, sounding gay.

She laughed.

As he began putting chemicals and who knows what all on Ricki's unsuspecting scalp, he inquired as to who she had a dinner engagement with.

"Danny," she said, watching his eyes in the mirror, which raised to meet her own.

He pondered this a moment. "I see." He nodded, glancing back at his fingers enmeshed in her hair.

Their eyes met again. "He see you on the news last night?" he inquired, his voice sugary.

"Dang," Ricki mumbled.

"Your hair was a horrendous mess!" he chided.

"Well, I'm sorry, but I had that cap on and it kind of messed it up, you know."

"Just do me one favor?" Marvin asked, his voice mocking sweet.

"Sure, Marv, I'll do anything for you," Ricki replied, giving him a bright smile.

"Don't tell anyone who does your hair, all right?"

She stuck her tongue out at him.

He laughed.

"You know who he's been dating?" Ricki asked.

He nodded, raising eyebrows, not commenting.

Ricki sighed despondently. "She's so gorgeous. I'm nothing compared to her," she complained.

Marvin hit the back of her head with the palm of his hand.

"Ow! That hurt," Ricki whimpered, rubbing the injured area.

"Well, can the stupidity," he snapped. Their eyes met again. "She's just a child, Ricki," he said, paused, then, "well, mentally."

She smiled at this.

"Why would you even want to compete with the likes of her? How can she compare to you, you ever think of that? The girl hasn't got a brain. I heard her daddy paid her way through college. Set her up in that little art gallery she has. Probably still pays all her bills, what you want to bet?"

Ricki nodded, then, "But Danny apparently really likes her, Marvin. They've been seeing each other awhile now."

"Yeah, well, Danny's a man and all he's concerned with is having a vestibule to shoot his wad in, seeing as how you're no longer willing to play that part," Marvin said.

Ricki shrugged in response.

"She's had a boob job, you know," he confided.

"Hey, I wondered about that," she said, shifting, looking in his eyes. "I mean, I met her when she was in college, and I swear, she wasn't much bigger than me, and then next thing you know, she looks like somebody put an air hose in her chest and forgot to turn it off."

He snorted. "And I don't care what anybody tells you, a man can tell what's real and what's not," Marvin whispered.

Ricki gave him a look, wondering.

"I know what I'm talking about," he said.

She gave him another look, thinking, *maybe this guy swings both ways.* He ignored her looks.

An hour later, he finally turned Ricki around to see the results of all his labor. Her eyes widened. She liked it. He had given her a tousled, Twiggy-like look with wisps of hair framing her face and the nape of her neck, making her eyes appear larger, darker. She grinned at him.

"Suits you," he said.

"I swear, Antoine, you are without a doubt the best, you know that?" Ricki asked, loud enough for the whole shop to hear.

"Yes, I do," he said haughtily.

She laughed. He studied her a moment, then said, "Come on in the back. I got something you might want to think about wearing tonight."

Ricki pulled off the cape, followed him to where they kept the hot stuff hidden. One of their regular patrons was into shoplifting, and each week she would come into the store, supposedly to say hi, leaving with a list of sizes, colors and specifics, returning a few evenings later, the trunk of her car loaded. Antoine and Anthony then supplied these various and sundry pieces of attire to their customers at a greatly reduced price. Ricki had till this point refused to participate in the purchase of any stolen items, but hey, she was on a quest here to live life to its fullest, to gain new experiences. Seeing as how she had never bought anything hot, she decided this just might be the time.

"Let's see, you're what, a 9?" he asked, eyeing her.

"I can be," she replied optimistically. "If I try real hard," she added.

He pulled out dress after dress, finally deciding on an off-the-shoulder, black, silky one.

Ricki's eyes widened at the sight of this. "It's beautiful," she sighed, as he held it against her, both of them looking in the full-length mirror.

"Perfect for you, dear," he said, sounding like a salesclerk.

"How much?" Ricki asked.

"For you, babe, a hundred will do it," he replied, grinning.

"Will you take a check?"

"Don't I always?"

"Thanks, Marvin," she said as she snatched the dress out of his hands, held it up against her.

He put his hands on her shoulders, turned her to face him, looked her in the eyes, and said, "Knock him dead, babe."

Ricki laughed outright, gave him a kiss, wrote the check, then hurried home, having a big worry fit on the way there, wondering if Anthony and

Antoine got caught with these hot little numbers, could her check be traced back, rendering her an accessory? Then she forced herself to stop being such a scaredy-cat.

CHAPTER 6

"CAN'T CUT THE TIES THAT BIND"

Ricki dressed with care that evening, wearing the black off-the-shoulder dress which landed a couple of inches above her knees. She wore black stockings *(the better to show off her legs)*, a black garter belt, turquoise and silver earrings, black heels, and nothing else. The black of the dress, along with her new do, made her eyes appear dark, smoldering. She liked that.

Ricki was late in arriving at the restaurant. Danny was already seated at a banquette, looking irritably at his watch as she approached. She got the message.

Being the gentleman he was, Danny stood as she came near, bared his teeth at her, which she was sure was meant to pass for a smile in case anyone other than Ricki was watching, but which she knew to be a scowl, waited until she was seated, then sat himself.

"Hey, Danny!" Ricki said brightly.

He studied her hair, then his eyes traveled down her face, dropping to her breasts, then up again. "Looking beautiful, as always," he said, somewhat resentfully.

This surprised her. "Oh, Danny, thanks, darlin', you're so sweet," she cooed.

He frowned long enough for her to get the message, then growled, "All right, let's get to it, Ricki."

"Get to what?" she asked guilelessly.

He gave her a disbelieving look. "That stupid confrontation you got into that was so vividly displayed on TV last night, and by the way, don't play innocent with me, I don't buy it," he stated bluntly, giving her one look she recognized as his reproachful one, the other one she wasn't too sure about. Respect, maybe?

"Oh, that," Ricki said dismissively, not making it easy for him.

"You looked really cute," he said reluctantly, surprising her again.

"Thanks, babe," she said, stunned at this.

Then, of course, "Shit, Ricki!" his voice low.

"Shit, Danny," she replied right back.

The waiter chose that moment to appear at their table, pen poised over his pad, inquiring if they would like anything to drink. Danny stared at Ricki the whole time they placed their respective orders. She ignored him, smiling brightly at the waiter.

"What the hell has gotten into you?" Danny asked when the waiter departed.

"What the hell has gotten into me, Danny?" Ricki asked disbelievingly. "Well, to be frank, it's really none of your business." ·

"Well maybe I happen to consider it my frigging business when your actions reflect back on me, and through me, my future plans."

She leaned toward him. "Danny, we are no longer married. My actions reflect on no one but me, okay? So, don't start on me about this."

"Is that right? Well, you care to explain why I've had to fight the damn news media all last night and all day today, everybody wanting me to comment on what you said and did?"

"First off, dear heart, I didn't do or say diddly-squat. And secondly, I did try to disguise myself, you know. For you."

"You mean from me. You can't fool me, Ricki, you should know that by now."

"Oh, is that a fact?"

"Hell, I knew it was you before you even thought about opening your mouth!"

"Oh, sure," she replied caustically. He scowled copiously. Ricki frowned back, said, "Danny, how in heck could you have known that was me? My face was almost completely covered. Come on, give me a break here."

"Listen, it just so happens one of my favorite pastimes used to be watching your body, watching the way you move in your body, okay? I knew the instant my eyes set sight on you who was underneath that stupid baseball cap."

"Really?" she asked.

He nodded his head curtly.

"Oh, that's so sweet," she said, giving him a smile.

He looked confused. "What are you talking about?" he snapped.

"What you said, Danny, about watching me used to be your favorite pastime. You never told me that before. That's such a nice thing to say, honey."

He looked even more befuddled, then, "Aside from the fact that you didn't disguise yourself from me, you sure as hell didn't disguise that mouth of yours, so the cap and sunglasses were moot, anyway," he hurled.

"Well, how was I to know they'd pick on me?"

"Have you ever heard of the term 'no comment'?" he snapped.

"Yes. I do believe that's your line, isn't it?" she replied haughtily.

He glared at her. The waiter interrupted long enough to set their drinks down, ask if they were ready to order dinner, then scurry off after Danny somewhat irritably said, "Later!" all the while staring at Ricki.

"Come on, Danny," she said appeasingly, "I told them our placards spoke for themselves, you know, when they first approached us. And nothing would have happened if that old man hadn't started calling us those names."

"To which you had to reciprocate, of course," he sneered.

"Of course," she agreed.

His eyes narrowed. "Why couldn't you have just let it go, Ricki?" he railed. "Why'd you let him draw you into a confrontation like that?"

"Hey, if he had called me a dyke once or twice, I would have. But you heard him, the way he was talking. I felt like he was attacking me personally, who I am, and I just couldn't let it pass, you know."

"Hell, no, of course not, but then, you couldn't just leave it at you, could you? Oh, no, you had to go and drag me into it," he snarled.

"Well, shoot, Danny, I made you sound good, so what's the beef?" she asked, giving him a smile.

"You read the paper today?" he inquired, his frown deepening.

"Uh, no," she replied, wondering if he was seguing or what.

"You heard what the press is calling me now, thanks to you?"

"No," she mumbled, thinking, *rut-ro*.

"Male Man Dan," he spat, leaning toward her, murder in his eyes.

"Huh?"

"That seems to be my nickname, Cherokee, instilled by none other than my ex-wife. Male Man Dan."

"Oh."

"Would you care to comment?" he asked, his voice bitterly sweet.

"Maybe not," she said, giving a tiny smile.

His eyes narrowed.

"Well, when you actually consider it, Danny, it's a great compliment. I said male, m-a-l-e, you know. Which you are. Very much so. That is how the papers described you, isn't it? 'Cause if they didn't, I'll call, make them run a retraction." She nodded emphatically.

Ignoring this, he leaned toward her, his voice low, and said, "Cherokee, how do you think this is going to look? I'm going to run for county executive, for Pete's sake, and even though we're divorced, what you do and say still comes back to me."

Ricki grew angry at this. "Is that what this is all about? That I might somehow thwart your wondrous political ambitions?"

"Well, that's the way it sure looks to me!"

She sighed exasperatedly. "In case it hasn't occurred to you, my dear ex-beloved, I think I gave you a pretty good plug. I mean, look at it this way, all the men will think you're this real macho-man, and that ought to draw votes from guys who are still hung up on that, you know, and there are plenty of them out there, by the way. Plus, women will think you're this fantastic lover, and that, I'm sure, will garner additional votes from that sector. So, the way I see it, this all worked out to your benefit." *You are so full of shit,* her inner voice chided.

"That's bull shit," he replied, agreeing.

"Okay, then, Dano, consider this. What would benefit your image more? Being married to a heterosexual woman who, even though she is now divorced from you, still thinks of you as stud duck, or having been married to a woman who, since the divorce, has been labeled gay?" She raised her eyebrows.

"Stud duck, huh?" he asked, trying to suppress the grin playing around his mouth.

Ricki leaned toward him, gave him her most intent look. "Listen, Danny, if you want to become county executive, President of the United States, whatever, I am behind you one hundred percent. I want you to be happy, babe, even if we're no longer married. I do still love you, after all, and I want what's best for you. You know I wouldn't do anything to get in the way of that. For God's sake, I spent 20 years of my life proving that to you."

His looked softened when she said she loved him—that got him every time—and then changed to contrite.

"I'm sorry the media seem to feel the need to come to you for comment regarding anything I might do or say," Ricki continued on. "Shoot, Danny, just feed them some bull, that's all they're after anyway. Tell them, I don't know, that I am so grief-stricken over our divorce, seeing as how you were such a copacetic lover, husband, and father, I've gone looney-tunes. Or tell them I've been deprived of sex for so long, my hormones are going spacy on me."

He reluctantly smiled.

"Or you can tell them it's a midlife crisis, well, pre-midlife crisis, for all I care." Ricki smiled, his faltered.

He stared at her a moment, then tried another tactic. "What about our son, Ricki? How the hell do you think this is going to look to his friends?"

"I hope it looks like Zachary has a mother who is willing to stand up for what she believes in."

"For what you believe in, huh?"

"Yes."

"Well, when the hell did you become such a blatant feminist?" he ranted. "You were never like that . . ."

"I am not a blatant feminist," she spat at him.

"Oh, you're not?"

"I am an egalitarian," she said haughtily.

"Egali . . . you're so full of crap, Ricki."

"I am not! I believe in equality for every member of the human race," she replied indignantly. "Be it man, woman, child, whatever race, color, or religion. Even political persuasion, for that matter," getting a dig in.

He snorted. "I think you believe in trying to embarrass me, is what you believe in," he snapped.

"Why would I ever want to do that?" Ricki asked, her voice sounding offended. "That would never be one of my objectives, to embarrass you."

"Because I am a man, first and foremost," he thundered, then glanced around as if afraid someone had overheard him, "and isn't that the motive behind the feminist movement, to overcome men, in whatever way?"

Well, now Ricki was mad. "Let me reiterate," she hurled at him. "I am not a feminist, I am an egalitarian, but let's talk for a moment about this feminist movement you and every other male on this planet seem so offended by. I put it to you, Danny, that if you men don't straighten your act up, try to understand what women are saying to you, try to understand it is for the betterment of each and every one of us, male and female, separate and apart, you're very well likely to find yourselves considered obsolete one day."

"Obsolete? That's what you think, men will be obsolete?" he asked, his voice rising disbelievingly.

"Ob-solutely," she said, then grinned.

He, for some unfathomable reason, didn't find this funny. "You think women can function without men, is that what you're saying here?" he asked, giving a harsh laugh. "Shit, Ricki."

She tried not to show her anger. "Well, sweetheart, it might interest you to know that thanks to the miracles of modern science, we women now have options when it comes to, let's say, interacting with men," Ricki said snippily.

"Yeah, right," he said, sarcastically.

"Okay, take procreation, for instance. If a woman wants to get pregnant, no need to have some man banging away at you for, what, isn't 10 minutes the national average, if you don't want to go that route."

"Hey, I always lasted longer than 10 minutes," he said defensively.

"Did I say I was talking about you?" Ricki asked him.

He scowled widely at her. Ignoring this, she continued on. "Getting back to the topic at hand, i.e., procreation, today, all a woman's got to do is just meander on down to her local sperm bank and make her own choice regarding her offspring. Just think of it, darlin', this huge sperm pool to choose from." His face blanched. "Consider all the possibilities. You want your child to have a high IQ, choose a donation from an academic. You want your child to be athletic, choose . . ."

"I get your point," he interrupted rudely, then, "but that doesn't make men obsolete. A woman can't become impregnated without a certain, let's call it, contribution from a man."

"Oh, well, that's easy enough. There are, what, millions of sperm in one ejaculation, right? I can just see it, Danny, there'd be these sperm farms set up, kind of like a dairy farm, consisting of men chosen solely for contributing their spermatozoa, and you know, like cows, a select number would be milked at select times . . ."

Danny burst out laughing.

Ricki smiled, said, "I myself would volunteer for a job like that."

He leaned back and had a good laugh at that image. She sat there, grinning, watching, enjoying the sound of his laughter, aware of the more than few curious stares directed their way.

Danny finally sobered, but still smiling said, "Now, I know you're pulling my chain."

Ricki shrugged noncommittally.

He studied her face, then said, "You're forgetting one thing, though."

"Yeah?"

"One aspect of the male-female relationship I would think it would be hard for a woman to do without, Ricki, including you," he said, giving her a smug look.

They both knew he was talking about sex. Ricki gave him a cold smile, said, "Better watch it, darlin', your chauvinism is starting to show."

"You calling me a chauvinist?" Danny ranted, then gave the couple next to them a forced smile when he noticed they were looking their way.

"Well, okay, then, let's talk about sex," Ricki said. "Nowadays, if a woman wants to have an orgasm" (his eyes widened alarmingly, then darted

60

around the room when she said that) "there are machines that can take care of that for her, and much slower and better than you men seem to be able to."

He looked shocked. "Slower, better?" he exploded. "Are you saying I didn't please you, Ricki?"

"Danny," she said, jerking her head slightly toward the room and several pairs of staring eyes.

His face reddened and he forced a smile on his face, for the benefit of the group gathered, but his eyes spoke differently to her.

Oh, jeez, Ricki thought, seeing that look. "I did not say you didn't please me, I never once said that, Danny," she replied appeasingly, her voice low.

"Are you using one of those?" he asked, his look now suspicious.

"One of what?"

"A damn, friggin' vibrator!" he answered, teeth gritted.

"That's of no concern to you."

He gave her a long, ponderous look, then, "Hell, Ricki, you could always call me, you know," now sounding offended.

"No, thanks."

He huffed heavily, studied her, then seguing, said, "You look really gorgeous tonight, babe."

Ricki smiled at him. "Thank you," she said primly, looking across at him, a handsome, powerful-looking man now showing a little gray at the temples, still looking youthful and vigorous, feeling that tug of attraction for him, then, giving him a loving look, said, "You know something, Danny? You're really looking good lately. You've lost weight, haven't you?"

He beamed proudly. "Ten pounds," he said, straightening up.

"Wow!" she enthused. "I tell you what, babe, you remind me of when we first got married, all muscular and strong-looking. The mean, lean, Danny machine," she teased.

He puffed up good at this observation, almost preening.

You nincompoop, Ricki thought to herself. *You're so easy, Danny, it ain't even challenging.*

His look changed quickly. He leaned toward her, gave her his infamous scowl. "You can't fool me, Ricki, so just cut the bull."

Well, heck, she should have known. "I was simply stating the obvious," Ricki replied snippily, thinking, *dang, he's not gonna fall for it this time and am I in trouble now.*

"Let's get back to the demonstration," Danny growled.

"Oh, so, you didn't ask me to dinner just to, you know, see me or talk about some issue with Zach or, I don't know, Danny, be with me. You wanted to talk about the demonstration."

"Just let me have my say about it, then we'll go on to other matters," he said, giving her a shark's grin. He took a deep breath, then he was off, prefacing with, "I can't for the life of me understand why you were there in the first place, let alone allowed that stupid idiotic fart to draw you into that imbecilic confrontation," and then onto the old lecture circuit again. Ricki did what she had always done, tuned him out. After all, she knew Danny. He would have his say whether she wanted him to or not. Besides, the food here was excellent. Plus she was all dressed up and had nowhere else to go.

Ricki sat there, looking at his face, trying to appear as if she was listening, but thinking other thoughts. Like how much she was still attracted to him, then wondering why. She read once it has something to do with the body chemistry of the other person, how their smell affects your olfactory senses. She came to the conclusion that had to have been the only reason she was attracted to this controlling, narrow-minded, somewhat sophisticated redneck sitting across from her.

Ricki looked into his gray-blue eyes, the ones that still sent that tingle up her leg. The ones that told her everything about the man addressing her. She had always thought Danny had the most expressive eyes she had ever seen on a person. As a politician, he had learned how to mask his feelings by maintaining an affable, easygoing facial expression. For the most part, he didn't use that mask on Ricki; she had made known her feelings on that pretty clearly over the years. However, when others were around and the mask was in place, Ricki could look into those two beautiful orbits of his and tell in an instant whether Danny found a situation humorous, frustrating, confusing, worrisome, stimulating, anger-provoking; whether he was feeling happy, sad, melancholy, lusty, tender, passionate, concerned, irritated, mad. She noticed his eyes still held that other look which she now decided had to be respect, one Danny had not favored her with in a long time, it seemed.

He seemed to be only half-hearted about his rebuke, Ricki thought. But knowing him, it had to be said. She squirmed in her seat, becoming aware of her nakedness against the dress. Feeling turned on, watching his eyes, she wondered what his response would be if he knew she was nude beneath this outer shell of clothing.

She decided to test him.

When he wound down, interrupting his tirade to take a swallow from his glass of ice water, Ricki leaned forward, whispered conspiratorially, "Hey, Danny, guess what?"

He eyed her over the top of the glass, said, "What?" disgruntedly.

"I'm not wearing anything under this dress, not one stitch," she said, giving him an impish smile.

He gulped loudly, almost strangling, slowly set his glass down, glanced surreptitiously around, gave her a suspicious look, then said, his voice cracking a little, "Nothing?"

"Nope. Well, not counting the stockings and garter belt."

"Garter belt?"

"Uh-huh."

"What color is it?"

"None of your business," she replied haughtily.

"Jeez, Ricki, at least tell me the color," he implored.

She shrugged, gave him a mischievous grin. "Black. Lacy."

His eyes traveled over her body, slowly, as if trying to see through the dress. He had to lean to the side a little once the table obscured the area he seemed to want to peruse. Ricki smiled at this. Seeming to realize what he was doing, he straightened up abruptly, inquired, "You're not wearing any panties?"

"Huh-uh."

"No bra?"

"Nada."

"Nothing at all?"

"Just skin."

His looked turned angry, he leaned toward her, whispered harshly, "You playing with me, Ricki?"

She gave him an injured look. He instantly appeared remorseful, said, "Okay, sorry. It's just, you never did anything . . ."

"Let's don't start on me the way I am now and the way I was then," Ricki interrupted, her voice brittle. "I'm a little sick of the subject."

The waiter approached with trepidation, and Danny waved him away, sat back, eyeing her again, then said, "So, you trying to tell me something here or what?" His look now turned lecherous.

Ricki gave him another injured look. He sighed heavily. "Once more, I apologize," sounding irritable, then, "Well, what'd you tell me that for, if you didn't have something on your mind? I mean, Jesus, what am I supposed to say to that, oh, wow, that's wonderful, I'm happy for you?" being sardonic.

"No, I just wanted you to know, is all," she said, feeling unsure now. *What the hell am I doing?* she wondered irritably.

He scooted over closer to her, saying, "Want to go somewhere more private?" putting his hand on her thigh, traveling up.

"Stop it, Danny," Ricki said, trying to make her voice sound cold, her body instantly feeling warmed at his touch.

He immediately drew his hand away, now gave her his own injured look. "You used to like for me to do that."

"Yeah, well, that was then, this is now."

He grew angry. "Well, what exactly the fuck do you want me to do, Ricki?" he asked, scooting away.

"I just want to talk, Danny. For once in a very long time, actually talk, okay?"

He pondered this a little, then shrugged his shoulders. "Here?"

"Well, no, it's too public."

"How about the house?"

She didn't want to be in that private a place with him, so just shook her head no.

"The houseboat?"

"I don't think so." Seeing he was getting angry again, Ricki said, "How about we just drive around a little? Talk in the car?"

He immediately waved the waiter over, told him they wouldn't be staying, handed him a $10.00 bill to cover the drinks, told him to keep the change, then stood, held his hand out, helped her up. On the way out of the restaurant, he kept his hand possessively on the small of Ricki's back. She got a little irritated at having to patiently stand beside him as he pumped the flesh with this or that patron. That was Danny for you; he always seemed to know most of the people at a public place like this. *No wonder he's so good at politics*, Ricki thought.

He took her to his car, held the door open. Before getting in, Ricki walked around it. Zachary had told her his dad had bought himself a new set of wheels and this was the first time she had seen them. It was a sporty Mercedes, you know, one of those with letters and numerals included in the name. "So this is your new car?" she asked.

He beamed proudly.

"Shoot, Danny, why didn't you get something sportier than this?" she asked, deflating his bubble. Then temporizing, "Not that it isn't nice. It's just, don't most men your age seem to go for the candy-red Corvettes to go along with their little nympho trophies?" She couldn't help getting that jab in.

He cocked his head, looked at her, then said, "What's the matter, Ricki, you jealous?"

"Of what?" she countered.

Deciding to ignore the way this conversation was headed, he growled, "Get in."

Ricki grinned at him, slid into the seat.

He came around, got in, pulled out of the parking lot. Ricki sighed, leaned back. "Well, it's pretty comfortable, I guess," she reluctantly admitted.

"Anything has to be comfortable over that skateboard you drive," he said.

"Hey, let's not start about my car," she said defensively.

"I wasn't," he answered, giving her a guiltless look.

He put his hand back on her thigh. God, it felt so good there, reminding her of the old days, when even in the car, Danny's hands would be traveling over her body. He hadn't done this in years and it was both surprising and nice. He inched his hand up slightly. Ricki stared down at it. Danny had the biggest hands, square-looking, a worker's hands. They weren't soft, either, felt rough, used. She liked that feel. She put her own over the back of his, rubbed at the curly hairs there. His hand traveled further up her thigh. She didn't stop him. He glanced over at her, said, "Is it okay, Ricki?" before he went where she wanted him to. She sighed, nodded her head.

His hand slid between her thighs, cupping her. It was so warm, so comfortable, so much like coming home. She sighed again. She looked at him, grinned, murmured, "Danny, this isn't like you at all, darlin'."

"I miss touching you," he said, his hand coming back to her dress, inching it up slowly, baring her, constantly glancing from her body to the road. "Oh, man," he moaned, as he uncovered her, ascertaining she truly was naked beneath the dress. "Jesus, Ricki," he whispered, putting his hand back, stroking. She made a low moaning sound. He squealed into a darkened parking lot, went behind the building, stopped, cut the engine off. "I'll have a wreck if I keep driving," he explained.

"Then don't," she answered, closing her eyes, feeling his hand. She lay there, letting him do whatever he wanted to, surprised that Danny would actually do anything sexual in such a public place. During the last years of their marriage, he had been so rigid about this. She wondered if the nympho wasn't maybe good for him, in some way.

Ricki lay there, fighting the urge to just jump right on him and have at it, but made herself resist, determining that if anything happened tonight between them, it would be because Danny pushed it. That way, she could rationalize to herself it hadn't been her actual doing. She could be so stupid sometimes.

"What are you doing, Danny?" she murmured, arching her back for him.

"Remembering," he whispered, his mouth following his hand. She smiled.

He put his mouth to her lips, kissing her, then traveling down. Ricki groaned again. "Damn, Ricki, I'd almost forgotten how beautiful you are, how good you taste, you smell," he murmured into her flesh.

Ricki opened her eyes, stiffened. He raised up, looking at her, said, "What?"

"You haven't told me that in a long time," Ricki said, tears coming to her eyes.

"What?"

"That I was beautiful."

"I haven't?" He really looked surprised.

"No, not in forever. You never said anything, unless it was to put me down," she whispered harshly, the tears falling.

"No, Ricki, that's not true."

"It is, Danny. Why couldn't you have said those things to me then? When I needed to hear them?"

He drew back from her, seeming stunned by this. "I complimented you all the time," he said, sounding offended.

"Only about wifely matters, Danny. Like, 'that was a great meal, Ricki,' or 'this sure tastes good, Ricki,' or 'the house looks great, Ricki,' or telling me I looked nice when we would go out to one of your political wingdings."

"Well, I guess I thought I showed you, through the way I treated you, the fact that I never went out on you, that I stayed faithful to you. You can't say I wasn't good to you." He grew defensive. "You never lacked for anything, especially not sex."

"Yeah, right, every Tuesday and Saturday night, just like clockwork." Ricki studied him, then had to ask it, "Danny, the last few years, didn't you ever just want to, well, bend me over the table, pull my panties down and plunge right in? Didn't you ever have to fight those spontaneous impulses just to give it to me, anywhere but on our bed in our bedroom, the way you used to?"

He surprised her by laughing. "Shoot, yeah, I bet I was fighting that impulse all the time."

Now, she was surprised. "Well, why didn't you do it?" Ricki asked.

"Why didn't you ask me to?" he countered.

They both sighed.

"When did we stop communicating with each other?" Ricki asked him, her voice soft.

He didn't respond.

"You were a wonderful husband, Danny. I never said you weren't. But I needed for you to make me feel like I was special to you. With actions as well as words, the way you did when we were first married, before everything got so dang serious."

He frowned at her, then said, "You really want to know what my problem was with you, Ricki?"

Well, actually, not really. So, what did she say? "I'd like to hear that."

"I was terrified of losing you."

This is a night for surprises, Ricki thought, looking sharply at him. "Jeez, honey, I had the same problem with you," she admitted, her voice weak.

He didn't seem to hear her, saying, "Hell, Ricki, I was the guy from the other side of town. I knew one day you would realize you deserved a classier guy than me."

Ricki laughed.

"It's true. I always felt outclassed by you, in everything. You're smarter than me, you always know the right thing to say, the proper thing to . . ."

"You're full of crap, Danny," she said.

"Hey, I'm trying to open up here, all right?" he said irritably.

"Sorry," she mumbled.

He sighed, leaned back, looked at her. "I don't know, I guess I had you on this pedestal. I thought you were perfect. I thought . . ."

"Well, I'm not perfect, Danny."

"I'm beginning to find that out," he said. He looked at her for a moment. "I just wanted to be the right kind of man for you, Ricki."

"Danny, I loved you when I first met you, when you were the boy from the wrong side of the tracks. I didn't want you to change for me, honey. I wanted you to stay like you were."

"Well, okay, maybe I went overboard on the class issue. Anyway, I guess that's why I stopped doing what you were talking about, Ricki, jumping on you, because I thought, well, that's not the way classy people should act."

"Well, fuck classy people," Ricki snapped.

He laughed again, said, "You sure have learned to cuss good, I'll give you that," bringing his face close to hers. They ended up kissing, tentatively at first, then passionately. Ricki was panting when he got though with her mouth. He gave her his lopsided grin, said, "So, want to talk some more?"

"Hell, no," she whispered harshly, tugging at him.

After a long while, she whispered, "Take me home, Danny, hurry."

When they got there, in the driveway, she put her seat back. He came over onto her, lying on top, settling between her legs. Ricki gently pushed him up, hastily undid his belt, then pants, unzipped them, then yanked them down beneath his butt, along with his underwear. He groaned when she put her hands on him, then lowered himself onto her. She had forgotten how wonderful their bodies were together, how right they could feel. He arched his back, probed, but before he could enter, she stopped him. "Danny, don't you think we need to use a condom?" she asked.

He looked surprised, hurt, a little confused. "Condom?"

"Well, yeah. I mean, you've been with, you know, other women." She wisely didn't advise him she had been with another man. "You know, AIDS and such, it's safer."

"Shit, Ricki, I use the friggin' condoms with them. I don't want to with you. It's different with you."

Ricki hesitated.

"I was tested last month," he said. "I promise, I'm clean. But if you insist, we'll go get a fucking condom."

"That it is," she said.

He grinned at this. They looked at each other a moment, then she shook her head no.

Without any further words, he slid right in. They both gasped. Afterwards, she made moves to get out of the car. He stopped her with his hand. She looked back at him.

"I'm still horny as hell for you," he moaned lowly, giving her the yearning look he used to in their early years.

She smiled.

CHAPTER 7

"WELL I'M OUT OF CONTROL AND OUT OF MY HANDS"

Danny and Ricki had utilized one attorney for their divorce, filing under irreconcilable differences, with the agreement that if things got sticky, one or the other would seek outside counsel. But it was a very friendly, amicable divorce. The attorney they employed was Thomas Leigh, a Knoxville lawyer who had done corporate work for Danny for years. Now, even though Tommy was a lecherous young fart, he and Ricki had become friends during the pending litigation and had kept in touch once his services were no longer needed.

So, when he called Ricki a few days later, asking if she would meet him for lunch, she promptly acquiesced. Besides, he was paying and wanted to meet her at this really expensive, elite club located on the top floor of his firm's building, so who was she to refuse such an invitation.

Ricki made sure she dressed conservatively and presentably, him being an attorney and all, and repaired to meet her lunch date.

They exchanged chaste kisses on the other's cheeks, and being a gentleman, Tommy waved the host away and seated Ricki himself. Tommy was a real cutie, whose only downfall that Ricki could see as pertained to her was his short stature. Ricki's experience with men who are vertically challenged had been dichotomous. Either they hated her or they loved her, right from the git-go. She suspected they were either fascinated by her stature over them or repulsed, maybe intimidated by it. Tommy, thankfully and regrettably, was one of the former.

After they had dispensed with ordering drinks, he said, "You looked real cute on TV the other night."

"Shoot," Ricki said disgustedly. "Is there anybody who didn't see me?" she asked no one in particular.

"Looked like you were in hiding, the way you were dressed."

She shrugged her shoulders. "That was in deference to Danny. And the really ironic thing is, Tommy, that in trying to disguise whom I actually was I only managed to call attention to myself. Go figure."

He smiled. "Did Dan see you?" he asked mischievously.

"Yeah, boy, did he ever," she said wearily.

Tommy laughed at this. After all, he had known Danny before he knew her. He leaned toward her. "And?" he inquired, eyebrows raised.

Ricki studied him for a moment. "You really enjoy this, don't you?" she asked.

"Hell, yes," Tommy replied, leaning back. "It's fun watching you bait the big guy and seeing how fast it takes him to respond."

"I don't bait him," Ricki said defensively.

"Well, let's see, male as in m-a-l-e, man I don't know what you'd call that."

"For your information, Tommy, he was highly offended I referred to him in that manner," Ricki said haughtily, then smiled impishly. "Till I pointed out to him that women of the female persuasion might find that interesting when they go to cast their vote for our next county executive."

"So, he's running," Tommy said, his voice low.

Ricki shrugged. "You know Danny, he can't pass up the opportunity. You know how much he loves politics."

Tommy nodded. "And you don't," he murmured.

Ricki ignored that.

"So, what'd he say about your presence at the demonstration?" Tommy segued, eyes glistening.

Ricki rolled her eyes. Tommy just grinned, waiting. "Oh, you know Danny. I had to endure one of his infamous lectures re: even though we're divorced, what I do reflects on him and ultimately his campaign, etcetera, etcetera." She rolled her eyes again.

"Like that would ever stop you," Tommy laughed.

"Yeah, right," Ricki said, shaking her head.

"That demonstration's one of the reasons I asked you to lunch today, Rick," he said, leaning forward, getting serious.

"Yeah?"

"I thought you might want to consider filing a class action suit against that club, force them into court, force them to revise their so-called policies."

Ricki chewed her bottom lip. "Shoot, Tommy, I don't know. I mean, I thought all it would take to get them to back down would be to, you know, picket their dang club. Seems like all we succeeded in doing was getting their dander up."

"Looks like it."

"Litigation is awfully expensive," she mused.

"All it'll cost is the filing fee," he said, his eyes gleaming.

"Oh, come on, you lawyers don't walk out the door unless there's a dollar on the other side," Ricki somewhat prejudicially stated.

"Listen, Ricki, I've been thinking about this. I'll offer my services to you and your group pro bono, you won't have to pay anything other than the initial filing fee."

She gave him a suspicious look. "And why exactly would you want to do that?"

He shrugged. "It'll get a lot of publicity. That will be good for me and, through me, my firm. I can use it."

She nodded, thinking, *should have known, everybody out for something.*

"So, what do you say, Rick, want to give it a try?" he encouraged.

Ricki contemplated. Danny would be furious, for sure. Well, screw him. He was going to marry Ms. Nitwit 1992. It wasn't any of his business anyway. She looked back at Tommy and said, "I'll have to discuss it with my . . . with the others, Tommy, but it sounds good to me. If they're willing to go along with it, heck, it might be fun trying to put those guys in the hot seat, watch them squirm as they explain their supremacist philosophy to a jury consisting mostly of women and minorities, I hope."

He grinned, leaned back as the waiter approached with their drinks and took their orders. He waited for him to leave, then inquired, "So, how's your sex life, Rick?" somewhat lewdly.

She gave him her own lewd grin and responded, "Interesting, I will say that."

His eyes changed. "I can make it more so. Interesting, that is," he tempted.

Ricki laughed. Ever since she had known this guy, he had come on to her. They had always bantered back and forth about his wanting to get Ricki into bed and her resolve he never would be able to. She had even accused him of trying to live up to the legend of the stereotypical divorce attorney. "Well, a guy's got to do what a guy's got to do," he had answered.

"Tommy, are you going to start that again?" she asked him, teasingly.

"Come on, Ricki, give it a try just once. You'll like it, I promise." He grinned at her.

"For Pete's sake, Tommy, I'm eight years your senior. And if that isn't bad enough, I'm a full head taller than you."

"Why is it you women always automatically assume that short men have short dicks?" he asked exasperatedly. "You just might be surprised at what I got hidden beneath these clothes, Ricki."

"I wasn't even thinking of that, you lech!" she said, laughing, now thinking about the size of his penis.

"Yes, you were," he pouted.

71

"No, really. Actually, Tommy, I was thinking how incongruous it would be if we, you know, made love. I mean, I am so much taller than you are, no offense, Tommy. You're a really great guy, good-looking and smart, but you are shorter than I am, a lot. Haven't you ever thought about it, how asymmetrical it would be? You and me? I mean, take the missionary position, you on top. Shoot, your head would only come as far as my . . ." She stopped, looked down at her breasts. Looked back up. They both burst out laughing.

"I rest my case," he said seriously when Ricki had calmed down.

She laughed again. "What you trying to do, Tommy, dangle the bait a little bit?" she teased.

"Darlin', this bait ain't dangling, at least not now," he growled at her.

They started laughing again; this time drawing suspicious looks from the other ultra-conservative Republican attorneys in the room.

They sat there, grinning at each other. Well, now he had gotten Ricki feeling randy. Shoot, she couldn't get her mind off this little guy on top of her, banging away, his mouth right at her breasts. She squirmed a little, cleared her throat, and looked away from him, trying to distract herself.

"Listen," Tommy said, leaning toward her. "I've got a cabin up on Norris Lake. Why don't I go up Friday afternoon and map out the petition we'll file, if you-all agree to go along with it, and you meet me there? I'll need to get some information from you anyway. Besides, I've got a hot tub. A boat. We can be serious for awhile, then go have some fun."

Ricki gave him a distrusting look.

"No funny stuff, I promise," he said, holding his hands up. "If you don't want to do it, you don't want to do it. But I do like you, I enjoy talking to you, and we need to get started on this suit if we're going to file it."

Ricki thought about it. Well, Zach was spending the weekend with Danny. She hadn't made plans with Sam. *Shoot, it might be fun, going there, relaxing a little, and maybe getting in some water-skiing.*

"You got a slalom?" she asked.

"I got everything, sugar," he said, his voice growing lecherous again.

"Okay," she said. "Give me the directions and I'll come up."

Friday at noon Ricki arrived at the cabin she had been directed to. Tommy was there, waiting.

His place was a rustic-looking log cabin, country, but cozy, nice. He informed her proudly he had built it himself and was still working on it. It was small, one bedroom and one bath, but abounding with large windows all around, with a wraparound deck. Ricki loved it.

They had a light lunch, Tommy asking her questions, initially about WAR and how it had gotten started, subsequently jotting down notes and names as to what had led up to their actually picketing the club, then decided to go play for awhile.

They spent the afternoon on the lake, skiing and sunning. It was relaxing, fun. Tommy had wine coolers in the boat and they sipped on those while they were out there.

By the time they got back to the cabin, Ricki was feeling pretty relaxed, warmed on the outside by the sun, on the inside by the wine, kind of drowsy, really.

"Come on, let's get into the hot-tub," Tommy encouraged, taking her hand, leading the way.

Who was she to spoil the fun? So she followed along.

The tub was on the outer deck, overlooking the water. Ricki stood, watching as Tommy pulled his trunks off, his back to her, thinking how much she envied the male species' lack of modesty about showing their nude body to another person, wishing she could be like this. Tommy turned toward her. Ricki eyes widened horrifically. Jeez, this guy was hung like a horse. She looked back up into his face. He gave her his infamous lecherous grin.

"Surprised?" he asked sarcastically.

"Amazed," Ricki replied.

He laughed.

"'Cause I didn't know you were a true blond, Tommy," she said. "I thought you dyed your hair."

He threw his head back and had a good laugh at this one, then proceeded to get into the tub. Ricki didn't pull her suit off, just climbed in after him.

He reached behind, opened a canister, and pulled out a weird-looking cigarette, which Ricki knew without being told was a joint.

"You're breaking the law, Mr. Attorney-at-Law," she mused, laying her head back, closing her eyes.

"Ever done this?" he asked.

"Shoot, no. I don't need chemical substances influencing my fun," Ricki said, feeling wonderfully relaxed.

He lit up, pulled on it, held it. She watched through slitted eyes. He finally let go, blowing the smoke her way. She breathed it in.

Not bad, she thought. They did that for several minutes, Tommy inhaling, holding, exhaling, blowing Ricki's way, then her inhaling, but no holding.

She began to feel a little hazy, hungry, horny.

She looked at him.

He really is a cute guy, you know, she thought. Real blond hair, sparkly green eyes, still looked fresh out of college, with a compact body except for that one appendage which was without a doubt the biggest her eyes had ever come across. Not that her eyes had traveled across many, you see, but nonetheless, Ricki was pretty astounded. Then the thought of him on her, his head at her . . . *Oh, shit,* she moaned to herself.

He slid over next to her, said, "Why don't you take that suit off, Ricki?"

Well, should she or shouldn't she? Ricki finally determined it wouldn't do any harm if she did. The water felt good but would feel even better without any clothes impeding its contact with her body.

"Sure," she said, stood up, and did so.

"Whoa!" he exclaimed, looking up at her.

"Right!" she replied caustically.

"You've got an athletic body, you know that?" he asked.

"I think I heard that somewhere before," Ricki mused, settling back in the water.

"You're gorgeous, Ricki," he said, his voice soft.

She glanced at him. Well, he looked serious.

"You're just saying that 'cause you want to let the monster loose," she drawled.

He laughed at this, then looked at her. "No, Ricki that's not why I said it. I've got better lines I could use if that's what I was after." Their eyes met.

"You're such a cutie, Tommy," she said, touching his cheek.

"That's not what I wanted to hear," he groused.

Well, now he was sulking. Intending to appease him, Ricki reached out, kissed him gently. Which of course turned passionate when he responded.

She pulled away, said, "Damn," knowing she was getting turned on.

"Let's go into the bedroom," he murmured, heading her way again.

Ricki put her hands out and stopped him. "Wait a minute," she said, trying to clear her drifty head. "Let's think this thing through, Tommy."

"What's there to think about?" he asked irritably. "You either want to or you don't, it's that simple."

"Oh, but you're so wrong," she said. "What about AIDS, what about STDs?"

"I have and utilize the necessary and correct precautions against that," he replied, like a lawyer.

Well, she should have known that.

"You have condoms here?" she asked, this turning her on even more for some reason.

"Rick, I got male condoms, every color and texture imaginable. I've even got female condoms, if you feel the need for that. I'm just as concerned with keeping healthy and alive as you are. I do not take chances. We will not take chances."

Ricki nodded. "But will you respect me tomorrow, Tommy?" she asked him ironically.

He threw his head back, laughed. "That depends on tonight, darlin'," he replied, standing up, giving her his hand.

"Just promise me you won't kill me with that thing," she said, looking down at his tumescence, which was about as frightening as it was exciting.

"Maybe from pleasure," he replied cockily.

"I could believe it," she said.

They both laughed.

They had one hellacious night. Tommy was such a voracious lover, all over her, in her, on her, with a stamina that was amazing. She made him do it the first time just as she had fantasized, the ole missionary position, him riding her, his mouth at her breasts, and she came almost immediately. It was wonderfully exhilarating, intoxicating. Ricki felt she could do this forever and never tire of it. But then again, why not, he was the one doing all the work, which he didn't seem to mind one bit.

Tommy was a playful lover and liked to experiment with different joy toys during foreplay, enhancing the pleasure. Ricki told him brusquely that what with that humongous thing dangling between his legs, he didn't need to worry about any sort of enhancement of anything, but if he felt the need, why, go ahead. He laughed at this. He was even more imaginative than Sam was. Of course, Ricki thought he was a lot more experienced, too.

She had to admit, though, that during that night, she had never seen so much diverse rubber paraphernalia in her life, had not assumed so many different positions, had not had so many novel objects inserted into different orifices of her body. They used assorted condoms, oils, foods, and machines on each other, riding most of the night through, and by morning, Ricki could hardly walk. Tommy wanted her to stay the day, but she knew she wouldn't get any sleep at all, so adamantly refused. But she did request one more ride, the way they started out, just for ole time's sake. He gladly obliged.

Tommy walked her out to the car, his hands all over her. They embraced, kissed passionately.

"Jesus, Ricki, you're a fantastic lover," he murmured into her shoulder.

She laughed. "I'll tell you something, Tommy. You're unmatched, yet," she reluctantly admitted.

He smiled proudly at this. Then, "So, think we could get together soon?"

Uh-oh. Even though the previous night's romps had been a lot of fun, it had all felt, well, sanitized, distanced, and to be honest, cavalier, using each other's bodies for their own pleasure. Ricki thought this out a little, then said, "I don't know if we should, Tommy. Last night was the best time I've had in a very long time, I kid you not, but I think I could get a little addicted to you and the monster machine." He grinned lecherously. "I'm not ready for that, not yet," she said.

He only shrugged his shoulders, said, "Well, you ever feel the need again, Ricki, you know where to find me."

"Do I ever!" she said, getting into the car.

He stopped her before she closed the door. "Oh, Rick, I forgot to tell you, I set up an interview for you with a friend of mine who's a journalist with . . ."

"No way," she said, cutting him off.

"WAR could use the publicity," he answered, frowning at her.

"More like Tommy could use the publicity," she countered.

"Hey, I'll get all the publicity I need once I file the lawsuit," he answered defensively.

Ricki sighed. "Listen, Tommy, have them call Melanie and set it up with her, okay? She's kind of the spokesperson for our group and . . ."

"Whether you believe it or not, after that demonstration, you will be considered the spokesperson, okay?" he interrupted. Seeing her look, "Listen, I've already set the meeting up. You got to have someone hold your hand, take Melanie with you."

"It's not that, it's just, you know, Danny might get upset."

"Are you still married to Dan?" he railed.

Ricki looked at him, remembering very well Charlie having said something like that to her recently. "Well, no, but . . ."

"Then forget about him. Before we file the papers, it'll be good to have some positive publicity for your group, okay?"

She thought about it. "Okay," she said, reluctantly.

"Good," he smiled, told her the time and place, then waved cheerily as she drove away.

Well, she thought, waving back, *there's notch number three to add to my boy-toy machine,* totaling the number of lovers she had experienced in her life. *Jeez, is that all,* Ricki then wondered with disdain.

CHAPTER 8

"GENUINE EXAMPLE OF A SOCIAL DISEASE"

The C's and D's Ricki was pulling in trigonometry were dropping her grade point average big time. She had strived her whole college career, such as it was, to maintain as close to a four-point average as she could and was distressed over her grades in this class. She thought with disgust that the only reason she chose to take the dang class was because it sounded pretty. *Should have known.*

Her real weakness in academics had always been math. When Danny and she were married, he would tutor her in this area, this being his strong suit. And thanks to his help, Ricki had maintained an A or B in these courses. Until now. However, Danny was no longer home and she was determined that she was going to handle this on her own. Besides, she didn't want to see that smug look on his face when she asked for his help.

So, when Ricki received a D on the midterm exam, she felt a conference with her professor was in order.

There they sat in his little cubbyhole of an office, Ricki staring at this guy who put her in mind of a lizard. Jeez, everything about him was long: hair, droopy moustache, face shape, nose, chin, neck, fingers, body. His eyes were deep-set, hooded, sepia cast, appearing reptilian. His skin had gray overtones to it, complementing his hair and moustache, which were pewter in color. Ricki watched as his long tongue flicked out, moistening his colorless lips, then suppressed a shudder, thinking *lizard* again.

He checked his calendar as if to ascertain who had come to call. "Let's see, Cherokee England, right?" he asked, giving her a smile that didn't quite reach those cold, dead eyes.

"Yes, sir," she said, trying for respect.

He pulled out his grade book, ran his finger across the figures on the page, then glanced up. "You're carrying a C minus average, so what's the problem?" he asked.

"The D I got on midterm," Ricki replied, pulling it out, placing it on his desk.

He didn't even look at it, staring her in the face.

"Listen," she tried to reason, "at least half the class failed that test."

His eyes narrowed when she made that observation.

77

"Don't you think you could grade on a curve or something?" Ricki asked, her confidence faltering at the look he was giving her.

"I don't grade on curves," he replied stonily.

"But this class is pulling my GPA down," she complained.

"That isn't my problem," he answered, his voice cold.

"Well, okay, I understand that, but I really need to get my grade up," she said.

They stared at each other. When he didn't offer a solution to her dilemma, Ricki begged, "Isn't there something I can do for extra credit to achieve that goal?"

A smile skittered across his lips.

Good, she thought with relief, misreading him, *this guy is gonna cooperate.*

"You're not married, are you?" he segued drastically, glancing at her left hand.

Ricki blinked in surprise. "Well, actually, I'm divorced."

He nodded, contemplating. "I imagine that's a hard adjustment to make," he mused.

She shrugged noncommittally.

"You must miss certain aspects of a marital relationship," he almost-whispered, his voice sounding like a caress.

"I get by," she said, starting to wonder what his motive was here.

"I presume it must be lonely at times," he offered.

Ricki grew angry. "Excuse me, Professor, but I didn't come here to discuss my social life with you. I requested this conference to specifically talk about my academic life and what I can do to keep my GPA from plummeting."

He took a moment to ponder, all the while staring at her. "I could tutor you," he finally suggested.

"Oh, that would be great!" she effused, inwardly breathing a sigh of relief.

"However, I would expect something in return," he stated, leaning back in his chair.

Ricki stared at him. "Oh, you mean in the way of compensation?"

"You could say that."

"I'd be willing to pay you whatever your fee is."

"That won't be necessary."

"Huh?"

"Perhaps we can work something else out," he suggested.

"Like what?" she asked, growing suspicious.

"Being an obviously attractive, healthy, divorced woman, it would only be natural for you to miss the intimacy of, shall we say, the marital bed," he said, showing teeth.

God, not a lizard, a crocodile, Ricki thought. "Huh?" she asked, biding for time.

"I can help you with that."

"Huh?"

"And in exchange, we will work something out concerning this GPA you feel so strongly about."

Well, that made her madder than the very dickens. Who the hell did he think he was dealing with here, she wondered to herself as she gaped at him. What did he take her for? Some little airhead willing to spread her legs or open her mouth for the price of a higher grade? Not this Jo. So, she decided to get him back. "Just a sec," she said, giving him her widest grin, reaching down into her tote which was beside her chair, palming her mini recorder, the one she used to tape lectures, drawing it out, laying it beside the tote, switching it on, glad the desk blocked his view of what she was doing, then pulling out a pack of chewing gum, offered it to him.

"Want some?" she asked, giving him a big grin.

"I think not," he said, looking offended.

Ricki popped it in her mouth, took the time to break it down, all the while making a big show of giving him the look over. He gave her one right back.

She grinned.

He grinned.

"So, let's be more specific," she said, snapping her gum.

He stared at her, now looking suspicious.

"Just so I'm straight about this, in exchange for an elevated grade in this class, you would expect something back from me as compensation."

He nodded, his eyes glittering.

"Although, as you stated, in this case, compensation does not constitute receiving money from me; right?"

He frowned slightly, then mumbled, "Correct."

"I take it to mean from your prior statements, it would entail somewhat of a sexual aspect, Professor, right?" She smiled lewdly at him.

That long, vulgar tongue flicked out again. Her smile faltered.

Ricki cocked her head, studied him a moment, then said, "How exactly am I to compensate you, Professor Moore?"

He scowled.

Uh-oh, maybe that sounded too much like a lawyer.

"It's just, it's been awhile since I've been with a man," she explained, sending him an embarrassed look. "I'm not sure what exactly you want from me."

He smiled widely. "I knew you were an innocent from the first time I saw you in my classroom," he drawled, looking like he could just eat her up.

"Well, I'm not exactly innocent . . ." she began.

"I can teach you many things in the realm of sexual pleasure," he enticed.

Ricki made her eyes widen. "Really?"

"Oh, yes. I have vast knowledge," he promised, paused, then added, "along with experience, of course."

"Huh!" she said, popping her gum. Then, giving him an intrigued look, "You mean, you and me, maybe engaging in a little sexual exploration?"

"Exactly."

She squirmed deliberately. His eyes brightened considerably.

"And if I do that, I'll receive an elevated grade in this class; right?"

"Correct."

"And you're saying you can teach me different things, about sex?"

"Absolutely."

"Wow!" she effused.

That crocodile grin.

She gave him a coy look, then lied, "You know, the only man I've ever been with in that way is my husband, well, ex-husband."

"Is that right?" he asked, eyes gleaming.

"I really miss that," she said, voice low.

"I can make it up to you," he promised. .

"It's been so long," she moaned.

"Today, if you desire," he encouraged.

"Really?" she asked anxiously, then glanced away shyly. Ricki looked back at him, saw the gleam in those awful eyes, then letting her own travel down to his bulging crotch, said, "Would you mind . . ." letting her voice trail off. She could have sworn she saw that thing twitch.

He studied her a moment, eyes glistening, then stood, came around, sat on the desk, his groin right in her face.

Ricki didn't have to pretend to be embarrassed.

He smiled indulgently at her blush, murmured, "Such an innocent," then undid his pants, slowly unzipped them. Ricki noticed he wasn't wearing underwear as he pulled his engorged member free. She was right, everything about this dude was long.

"Holy cow!" she said.

He grinned lewdly.

She reached out tentatively, but before she got there, withdrew her hand. "Is it all right?"

"Please," he practically moaned, closing his eyes, "feel free to do whatever you wish."

"Really?"

"Of course."

"Cool!" she effused, and as he watched between slitted eyes, reached out as if to touch that vile and vulgar thing, instead grabbing the zipper and yanking upward as hard as she could.

He screamed shrilly.

She pulled on it harder, making sure it was skin that was impeding its further progress. He put his hands on hers, pushed them away, and started trying to work the zipper, making mewling sounds in the back of his throat.

Ricki reached beside her tote, grabbed the tape recorder, held it in front of his face, said, "Now, what say we discuss exactly how I can elevate my grade."

He screamed obscenities at her. She made sure she had that recorded, then said, as sympathetically as she could, "Oh, this must be a bad time for you. Okay, I'll catch you next time," put the recorder back in her purse, sauntered out the door, his screams following her, ignoring the curious stares from the few students wandering the hall.

Ricki's next class was two days later and there he was, walking like he had a corncob stuck up his ass. She had to cover her mouth with her fist to hide her laugh. He made sure not to look at her the entire class, but after he had dismissed the class, as they were heading out, he yelled, "Cherokee England, I need to see you."

Ricki shrugged as if to say *huh!* at her fellow students, broke out of the mass heading for the door, went to his desk, reaching into her tote, turning on the recorder as she did.

He stared at her.

She stared at him.

"What will it take for the tape?" he finally asked exasperatedly.

Ricki cocked her head, made a show of thinking this thing out.

"Grade on a curve."

"I don't do that."

"For everyone, not just me."

"I will not do that."

"Fine, Prof," then sighed heavily. "Let's see, who should I play that tape for?" she asked thin air.

81

His face turned red.

"All right, damn you, I'll grade on a curve," he snapped.

Ricki smiled, said, "Thank you," as nicely as she could.

He held his hand out.

"I'm not shaking with you," she said, looking offended.

"Give me the tape," he demanded, teeth gritted.

"Oh!"

"Now."

"Well, sure." Reached into her purse, pulled it out, gave it to him.

He closed his eyes with relief.

She headed for the door, then turned back.

"Uh, Professor Moore?"

He opened his eyes warily.

"Just so you will be properly apprised, the tape in your hand? It's a copy. I have the original in a safe place and I'm keeping it there to ensure you keep your word."

"You conniving little bitch!" he half-shouted.

"Oh, wow, thanks for the little," Ricki said brightly, then reached into her tote, pulled out her mini-recorder, held it toward him so he could see the tiny wheels spinning through the view window, showing him she had just recorded everything they had said.

His face turned bright red. He looked ready to lunge.

Ricki backed away, out of range, taking note he held his tongue this time. When she got to the door, she glanced back and said, "I'm not some sweet young thing right off the tobacco farm like so many of these other students. So, I'm also holding that tape in case you try on some other unsuspecting female the same crap you did on me." She looked him up and down, gave a big frown, said, "Jeez, kind of makes me feel like puking all over this nice carpet," turned and got the hell out of Dodge.

The next Tuesday night, after everyone had disbanded from WAR's meeting, Ricki told Charlie what had happened, feeling proud of herself. After Charlie had had a good laugh, she asked Ricki to play the tape for her. Since she just so happened to have it near at hand, she did as bid. It was full of static and hard to hear in places, but Charlie got the gist, howling with laughter when he started shrieking. Ricki watched her amusement, a proud smile playing around her lips. That is, till she noticed Zachary standing in the doorway, likewise grinning.

Ricki immediately switched the recorder off, realizing it was now playing nothing but static. When she looked back toward the door, her son had vanished.

Charlie and Ricki got into a big argument over that stupid tape. Charlie wanted Ricki to play it at the next meeting, so everyone could hear how she had handled that particular situation. Ricki refused, her argument being she hadn't actually handled it very well, seeing as how she had used physical violence, such as it was, on the guy. Charlie called her every name she could think of that had to do with coward, but Ricki still refused. Charlie left mad. "Well, tough tootles!" Ricki shouted after her departing back.

She went to find Zachary, who was in the kitchen wolfing down a humongous sandwich he had made.

He grinned at her, his mouth full.

"How much did you hear?" she asked wearily.

"Effrythin," he mumbled around his food, still grinning, his eyes merry.

"How much everything?" she asked, scowling.

He frowned as if he didn't understand.

"I mean, did you hear just the tape, or my preface to what actually happened before I played the tape?"

He held one finger up, masticating, then swallowed loudly. "Everything, explanation and all," he said, grinning again.

Lord, help, thought she to herself. Then, "Zachary, you realize I didn't handle that situation in a really, well, mature manner."

He froze with his sandwich halfway to his mouth, studied her a moment, then said, "Maybe not, Mom, but you handled it, right?"

Ricki smiled inwardly. Well, yeah, she had, actually.

"It's just, I don't want you to think that causing physical pain to another person is the right way to . . ."

"Oh, Ma," he growled at her. "I know all that crap. But a girl's gotta do what a girl's gotta do right?" grinning again.

Ricki rolled her eyes and left, his laughter following her to her bedroom.

She should have known he'd tell his dad.

Danny called a couple of days later, asking if she was going to be home that evening.

"Sure, Danny," she replied, thinking, *uh-oh, he knows.*

But he gave her a big grin when he saw her, light hug, bussed her on the cheek, giving the mistaken impression there was no mission to his visit.

83

They sat out back, drinking iced tea, watching the horses merrily frolicking in the field beyond, enjoying each other's company, Danny telling her about his newest business venture.

After awhile, he eyed her. *Oh, Lord, here it comes,* she thought. But he surprised her, smiling, saying; "I saw the article about your group, Rick. I was real impressed."

So was she. She wondered vaguely how much Tommy had paid the journalist to make them sound so absolutely wonderfully benevolent. "Thanks," she said, smiling back.

"I thought it was just a support group you were involved with. You didn't tell me about any of WAR's altruistic ventures."

"It just kind of evolved," she replied, vaguely.

He segued again, finally getting down to it, saying, "So, who's this professor that was trying to put the make on you?"

Ricki blinked in surprise.

"Huh?" she asked.

He didn't answer, waiting.

"Zachary told you," she stated flatly.

He smiled a little.

"Dang, Danny, I didn't want Zachary to know about that, but he overheard me playing the tape," then inwardly kicked herself when she relayed that little piece of information.

He raised his eyebrows, leaned toward her. "I want to hear it."

"You don't need to."

"Who is this guy?"

"Just one of my professors."

"What's his name?"

"None of your business."

"Ricki."

"Danny."

"What's his name, Cherokee?"

"None of your business, Danion."

"I'd like to go see this guy, have a word with him, you know, man-to-man," he said, leaning toward her, looking intent.

"No."

"Make sure he doesn't bother you again."

"No."

"Damn it, Ricki!"

"Damn it, Danny!"

"Let me deal with him," he insisted.

"Hey, Danny? Guess what? I dealt with him. I handled it, okay? I don't need you coming to my rescue. I took care of the problem."

He sighed loudly, looked out toward the field a moment, then back at her.

"Just let me hear the tape," he said, his voice frustrated.

Ricki studied him a moment, thinking, *well, shoot, why not? It's water over the dam anyway*, so shrugged her shoulders, got up, fetched her recorder along with the infamous tape, came back, played it for him.

He glanced at her when the shrieks started, grinning a little.

Ricki herself flinched. Shoot, the guy sounded in such pain.

After the tape had played out, Danny looked off at the field, nodding. About what, she had no idea. He took his time bringing his eyes back to hers, and when he did, burst out laughing.

Ricki was surprised. So she sat there, watching him, not sure about this.

"Is it all right?" he mimicked her, then lost it, laughing long and hard. Finally not able to contain herself, she joined in.

When he had stopped, Ricki couldn't resist telling him about the way the guy was walking the next time she saw him, this drawing more laughter from Danny.

After he had sobered, he studied her, then said, "You realize you could have gotten into a tricky situation there."

She nodded. "I think what I did would probably be construed as entrapment, don't you?" she asked, growing serious.

"That's not what I'm talking about."

"Oh, well, you mean he maybe could have hurt me," she mumbled.

"Badly," Danny said.

Ricki nodded.

"Damn, Ricki, that hurts just to think about," he said, his voice low.

"Yeah, well you should have been there, darlin'. It was not a pretty sight."

He burst out laughing again, and when he finished, "You perceive this guy as being any kind of threat to you over this?" he asked, looking worried.

Ricki thought a moment. "Not as long as I've got the tape," she replied, grinning.

He nodded. "He gives you any more trouble, Ricki, promise me one thing?"

"Sure, big guy."

"Let me be the one hurting him next time, all right?"

She smiled. Her protector. "Sure, Danny."

They sat there awhile, watching the sun begin its disappearing act over yon ridge.

Ricki looked at Danny, thinking how much she missed times like this with him.

He turned his face, caught her looking, gave her a grin, said, "I really miss these times, babe."

She smiled back, saying, "I was just thinking the same thing, darlin'."

His face quickly changed to anger.

"What?" Ricki asked, growing confused at the sudden transformation.

"Just remember one thing, Cherokee," he snapped, leaning toward her. "You're the reason we don't have times like this anymore."

Oh, dang it all, she thought.

"We would still be sharing memories like this if you hadn't . . ." he started, but she interrupted.

"Yeah, well, I had a good reason!" she yelled.

"I'd sure like to know what it was," he shouted back. "I have yet to figure that one out, Cherokee!"

They glared at each other.

Ricki said, her voice low, "Let me put this in a way maybe even you can understand."

He visibly bristled.

She hurriedly went on. "Essentially, you could say I was sick and tired of playing Aunt Bea to Andy and Opie, that clear enough for you?"

"You comparing me to Andy Griffith?" he yelled, looking offended.

"Taylor. Andy Taylor," she yelled back.

"You're nuts!" he proclaimed.

"Well, you're just like Andy Taylor, Danny. Except you're better looking than he was and you cuss a lot, whereas he didn't. You know," she mused, "I don't think I ever saw one episode where Andy Taylor said anything coming near a curse word. In fact, I guess the strongest word he ever used was darn. And I'm not real sure he ever used that one, to tell you the truth, but . . ."

"Will you shut up?" he snapped.

"I was simply trying to point out . . ."

"I'm nothing like Andy Taylor, so drop it. For Pete's sake, that was a TV character, not even a real person."

"Jeez, Danny, you're just as moralistic and scrupulous as he was. Just as old-fashioned, I guess." Seeing his look, she decided to appease. "As nice and gentle and sweet and kind. Caring. Honest. Plus, everybody just loves you the way they did good old Andy. So don't be offended by my comparing you to him, Danny, 'cause I meant it as a compliment."

"And you're trying to tell me you felt like an Aunt Bea?" he asked disbelievingly.

"Well, yeah."

"Shit, Ricki, you put me more in mind of Barney Fife," he snapped.

She laughed.

He gave her a puzzled look.

"Thanks," she said, grinning. "Barney's my hero."

He rolled his eyes. "I can't recall seeing any one episode where Andy Taylor and Aunt Bea were in bed together."

Ricki shrugged her shoulders. "Well, shoot, toward the end, we might as well have been Aunt Bea and Andy, you know, for all the passion generated between us."

His eyes narrowed; his brow furrowed.

Why can't I ever keep my mouth shut, she wondered to herself for about the millionth time.

"Although now it's a different story," she said hastily, giving him a smile.

His frown didn't falter one whit.

Ricki got irritated over this. "Well, okay, if you can't identify with Andy and Aunt Bea, how about I just throw out some key words, like maybe vicarious and autonomous?" she snarled at him.

He studied her a moment, then shaking his head sarcastically said, "Okay, let me guess. Cherokee felt she was living her life vicariously through, who else, her husband and son, right? Cherokee felt unfulfilled, like she wasn't making a dent in her own little world. Cherokee felt stifled, oppressed, repressed."

"Don't forget suppressed and depressed," she snapped.

He glared at her. She glared back, then said, "Cherokee wanted some autonomy in her own little world, without having to fight for every little crumb of independence she achieved for herself. And even though Cherokee loved her husband more than anyone or anything else in this world, Cherokee felt she had to step out of that relationship, temporarily or permanently, Cherokee wasn't sure which, until, of course, the man she truly loved decided he wanted to permanently end . . ."

"Well, maybe I saw no other recourse than to . . ."

"Oh, pooh, Danny. You were either bluffing me or you really, truly wanted the divorce. And if it was the latter, you are the one responsible for us not having these times together!"

"You're full of crap!" he yelled, standing.

Following suit, she faced him off, said, "Will you ever get it through your head our divorce was the most traumatic, painful thing I have ever been through? Will you please stop blaming me for trying to do what I thought was in my best interests at the time? Maybe I was wrong. Maybe I was right. I have no idea at this point, okay? I am just trying to make my own way, Danny, trying to live my life the best way I know how. But do it on my own, not have you or Joe Blow telling me how to do it. I have to stand on my own two feet. I want to! I need to!"

He straightened, glaring, then said, his voice low; "You were standing on your own two feet when we were together, Cherokee."

"Only when you let me," she stressed.

"Was it worth it?" he asked her. "Was it worth losing what we had, what we shared, for your perceived independence, and I stress the word perceived, Cherokee."

Her eyes teared. She sighed. "Danny, if I had it to do over again, I would try to be smarter about the way I handled it. But that's speaking from hindsight. At the time, I thought it was what I wanted, what I needed, to get out of our relationship. I thought it would make me a stronger person, maybe force me to be the person I wanted to be, force me to grow up. I didn't take into account the fact that I would still love you so much, that I would miss you so much. But understand I did not push the divorce, you did. And now you're ending us through marrying Stacy. So maybe I initiated it, but you're the one responsible for carrying it through, you are the one who is killing us, Danny."

He glared at her, then said, his voice low, "Okay, Cherokee, I admit I pushed the divorce, but not because that's what I wanted. I did it because I thought that maybe it'd force you to come back to me, knowing I wasn't going to hang around waiting. I thought, Cherokee, it'd force you to realize you did love me and you'd come back because you didn't want to lose me."

"Yeah, well, guess what, Danny?" she hurled back at him. "I thought if you really, truly loved me, you wouldn't be insisting we get a divorce. If you really, truly loved me, you'd give me the time and space I needed! So if anybody's to blame for the way things stand at this point in time, Waldo, it sure ain't me!" Before he could reply, she turned and walked into the house, slamming the door behind her, half-hoping he would follow.

When she heard his car start up, she went to her bedroom and called Sam, forcing herself not to cry. She was sick to death of crying.

CHAPTER 9

"YOU HAVE TO CLEAN THE OYSTER TO FIND THE PEARL"

She stood before the group, a chunky woman, everything about her appearing square: glasses, hairdo, jawline, body form. All of 5'2" and about as wide as tall. Ricki listened to her nasal twang and the first thing she thought was, *we got us a whiner here*, as the woman introduced herself. *Donna*, Ricki thought, noting this was the first Donna she had ever met. She perked up a little when she started talking about her husband and this wild affair he was having outright with a woman 20 years his junior. Ricki glanced at Charlie, saw her eyeing her, then focused her attention on Donna.

She described how she had suspected for awhile now but had been so much in love (*you dumb-ass,* Ricki inwardly chided her) that she just wouldn't let herself think he could do something like this to her, but *(and big sigh here)* all the signs were there: mysterious charges on their MasterCard; his clothes smelled perfumery; she would catch him on the phone, talking low to someone, then change his tone as she came into the room; he had to work late two and three nights a week, and when she would try to call him, she would get no answer; a lot of hang-ups at home during the evening when she answered the phone. *Yeah, yada, yada, yada,* Ricki thought irritably.

Donna burst out crying. *Aw, shoot, don't do that,* Ricki thought, sitting up straighter, watching the woman next to Donna comfort her, glancing around, embarrassed.

"I just love him so much!" Donna wailed, losing it again. Ricki felt someone staring, caught Charlie's eye again. She raised her eyebrows like, *Well?*

Ricki shook her head no.

Charlie frowned.

"I just don't know what to do," Donna said, sniffling. She went on to talk about their marriage of 15 years, their two gorgeous little girls, then express her fear that he would leave them for this other woman. Ricki sighed inwardly, thinking, *why are men such slimebuckets?* Then thinking, *why are women such doofuses? Why does she put up with this from him?* Donna finally wound down, acting mortified now, and the next one got up, talking about her ex and his many and sundry affairs. *Lord help, don't expect me to get into this*, Ricki thought.

When the meeting broke up, Charlie pulled Donna aside for what looked like some intense conversation. Ricki watched, feeling her stomach knot.

After everyone had departed but Charlie and Melanie, who were helping with the cleanup, Charlie said, a smile on her face, "We got our next little vigilante sortie."

"Donna?" Ricki asked.

Charlie nodded, grinning widely.

"I think that's butting into someone else's business," Melanie stated, rather haughtily.

"I think she's right," Ricki agreed.

"What the hell were we doing when we went and put a stop to that lecherous asshole sexually harassing his employees?" Charlie asked angrily.

"Well, that was different," Ricki said.

"Yeah," Melanie agreed.

"Ain't no difference whatsoever," Charlie stormed. "We were just trying to right a situation, trying to help a fellow sister. We'd be doing the same damn thing here!"

"Yeah, but, shoot, Charlie, for Donna? I mean, look at her. She doesn't even have balls enough to stand up to him, for Pete's sake, to tell him she knows what he's up to, to try to put a stop to it herself," Ricki stated.

"Yeah, and what about those two little girls they got?" Charlie asked, eyebrows raised.

"Yeah, well, one thing I learned from counseling is past behavior generally predicts future behavior. You stop this little affair, there's gonna be another one. What're we gonna do, go to Donna's rescue every time her horny husband finds a new conquest?"

"Just think of those two little innocent girls," Charlie said smugly, "no daddy at home to help take care of them, their mama all alone, destitute, crying 'cause their daddy went and run off with somebody else . . ." She did the eyebrow thing again.

Ricki thought about it, then nodded back, saying, "What say we pay the girlfriend a visit, donned in our black attire, and put the fear of God into her, in a subtle way, of course?"

"No, no, no, that's all wrong," Charlie said, shaking her head. "What we do, Rick, we pay a visit to the husband, put the fear of God into him!"

Ricki laughed. "Yeah and I bet it involves pulling down his pants at some point," she snipped at her.

"Hey, it worked last time! We haven't heard anymore complaints about that factory owner, have we?"

"Yeah, well, no offense, Charlie, but I don't particularly find it pleasurable looking at a naked man scared out of his wits. Jeez, it's almost repulsive, seeing that thing all shriveled up."

"I think it's repulsive anyway, shriveled or otherwise," Melanie said.

Ricki laughed. "I myself happen to be a great admirer of priapic topography."

"Say what?" Charlie asked, giving her a disgusted look.

"Well, only in regards to a man. Anything else, forget it."

"What the hell are you talking about now?" Charlie asked, irritably.

"I said, I find the male body to be quite beautiful," Ricki answered, haughtily, then, "well, in certain positions. Others, forget it."

"What do you say, Melanie, we go for the man or the woman?" Charlie asked her, ignoring Ricki.

Melanie contemplated, then said, "I think Ricki's right, we go talk to the girlfriend, help her understand this may not be a healthy relationship for her."

They all grinned at this, then proceeded to plan their strategy.

Several evenings later, they were in a residential area of West Knoxville, a few houses up from the one they would be paying a visit to, as soon as it got good and dark and the neighborhood had settled down.

Charlie had informed them the young lady's name was Melissa Dumont. The husband's name was Don, to go with Donna. Seems he was a dentist and had always been a true-blue family man till Melissa came in one day for a checkup. "I bet he didn't confine it to the mouth," Ricki observed.

Charlie grinned, then teased, "How about that dude you're seeing, Ricki, you ever play doctor with him?"

Ricki smiled widely and shrugged noncommittally.

"Yeah, I bet you two play all kinds of little games," Charlie continued.

"Well," Ricki said.

"That is one good-looking man," Melanie observed from her seat in the back.

"And you haven't even seen the best part," Ricki said smugly.

They snickered.

"He is so great," she breathed. "Absolutely fanfuckingtastic. And I mean that literally."

Lewd chuckling from her two vigilante partners.

"So, is he better than Danny was?" Melanie asked.

Rut-ro. Ricki busied herself looking out the window.

When she didn't reply, "Are you going to tell us or not?"

Ricki sighed. "Well, see, it's different, with each one. I mean, with Sam, it's better than it was with Danny during the last years of our marriage, but lately, Danny's, well, with Danny it's like it was when we were first married, you know. It's changed. Don't ask me how, I don't even begin to understand it myself. But it's better. It's really, well, it's just great with Danny. It's . . ." She stopped, flustered, realizing she had just spilled her guts but good.

Was met with stunned silence.

"Okay, so now you know," Ricki said, her voice low. "I slept with Danny. And no, I do not feel bad about it. It was great. It was wonderful. It was like we went back in time somehow." She sighed. "But then there's Sam. He's so good in bed," she moaned, her voice low. More silence, compelling her to dig her grave just a little bit further. "He's so, well, physical. And Danny's so emotional, I guess. They're so different and it's so different with each one. I guess it's better with Danny because I still love him, but when I'm with Sam, it's so intense, so passionate, so carnal, so sexual; and then, there's Danny, and it's so spiritual, mystical, really beautiful." Ricki stopped abruptly, feeling like an ass.

"Well," Melanie said.

"Yeah, boy," Ricki responded.

"You're gonna find yourself in a lot of trouble one day, you keep this up," Charlie said.

"Hey, I'm not married, Charlie, unlike this Don guy screwing around with this Melissa. And unlike Don, I have the liberty to sleep with anyone I want to. Besides which, it's none of your business, all right?"

"Hey, I never said it was," she replied, her voice low.

"Besides, to be honest about it, you want to know who the best lover is, it'd have to be Tommy," Ricki said, shrugging.

"Tommy?" Melanie shrieked. "Good Lord!"

Charlie burst out laughing then said, "Looks like this girl has been having herself some fun!"

"Yeah, boy," Ricki replied.

They sat in silence for a few moments, and then Ricki sighed heavily, thinking of her predicament.

"What?" Charlie asked.

"It's just, my feelings for Sam and Danny are so dichotomous. I'm so confused right now, you know? I wish there was a didactic somewhere that said, if you're feeling this, this and this, then you're in love; but if you're feeling this, this, and this, you're just enamored. The way I feel about Danny is so divergent from the way I feel about Sam. But I enjoy being with both of them. Well, maybe that's what it is, the diversity . . ."

"Excuse me, but are you from this planet or are you just visiting?" Charlie asked snidely.

"What do you mean?" Ricki asked, confused.

"Di this, di that," she ranted. "Shit, Ricki, talk English. Quit spitting out all those stupid di words."

"What's wrong with talking like an intelligent person?" Ricki asked, offended.

"You don't talk intelligent, you talk stupid!" Charlie said.

"Hey, Charlie, at least I talk like I didn't drop out of high school," Ricki snarled.

"I ain't no high school dropout," Charlie said, now offended.

"Ain't no? You sure talk like it."

"A person don't need to be spouting off four- and five-syllable words just to sound intelligent," Charlie observed.

"Says you," Ricki snapped.

"Hey, I am what I am, you got that?" Charlie half-shouted. "This is the way I talk, you understand? This is me. This is who I am. Unlike some people I know, I don't feel the need to put on airs, going around shooting out words so nobody else knows what the hell I'm talking about!"

"You referring to me?" Ricki squealed.

"Why don't you two just shut up?" Melanie shouted in their ears, causing Ricki to startle. "Dang, every time we get together, you-all are fighting over something. It's really getting sickening, let me tell you, having to listen to the bull crap that goes on between you!"

They all got quiet.

"Hey, I wonder what the mistress looks like," Ricki said, going off in another direction.

So, they started a game, visualizing what sweet Melissa would look like.

"Big boobs," Ricki said.

"Blond hair," Melanie said.

"Blue eyes," Charlie said.

"One-digit IQ," Ricki inserted.

"No, two digits, to match her bra size," Charlie revised.

"Red fingernails!" Melanie added.

"Round butt," Ricki said.

"Big butt," Charlie said.

"High butt," Melanie said, and they all lost it.

"Perky as hell," Ricki said after they sobered, picking the game back up.

"This coming from Ms. Perkiness herself," Charlie said irreverently.

"Hey, I resent that!" Ricki snapped, feeling offended.

"Well, it's true," Charlie defended.

"I am not perky!" Ricki declared emphatically.

Charlie grinned.

"Am I, Melanie?" she asked, going for support.

Melanie shrugged noncommittally.

"Okay, I'll prove I'm not perky," Ricki stated forthrightly.

"Go ahead," Charlie said, sounding not interested.

"Well, for one, I don't giggle, Charlie. And as we all know, perky people giggle."

"Yeah, sure," Charlie said sarcastically.

"Well, take Katie Couric!" Ricki hurled at her. "Not one *Today* show goes by she doesn't at some point giggle. And that woman's about as perky as perky gets!"

Charlie gave her a derisive laugh.

"And besides that, my hero, one of the sexiest men on TV, is Bryant Gumble, who also can be a real shit, you know. Heck, that guy's more in the genre of curmudgeon, Charlie, right along with my favorite actor, Tommy Lee Jones. And perky people do neither like nor respect people of that demeanor! In fact, that's more the category I fall into, you know, curmudgeon."

"Says you!"

"Hey, I don't break into song every damn dang chance I get, do I?" Ricki said. "Huh? Not like the aforementioned Ms. Couric or, God help me, the Queen of the Perkies, Kathie Lee Gifford."

"That's only 'cause you can't hold a tune," Charlie huffed.

"Huh-uh!" Ricki half-shouted, even more offended now. "I also hate clowns, Charlie. And perkies like those stupid doofus clowns. Hey, I see one and my first instinct is to cram one of those idiotic monolithic shoes up their butts. That is definitely not a perky instinct!"

"You still haven't convinced me," Charlie said, settling back, grinning at Melanie.

"Well, okay. I also hate mimes, Charlie. Isn't that a perky prerequisite, adoring those stupid white-faced, red-lipped, white-gloved mimics? Shoot, I see one and I want to smear that red lipstick all over their stupid white face. That, my dear, is not a perky thought!"

"Yeah, sure," said Charlie derisively.

"And I see Ms. Queen of the Perkies, Kathie Lee, on those cruise commercials and you want to know what my first thought is, Charlie? Huh?

It's a wish Charlie that she'd fall over the side of that dang boat into that ocean and I'd never have to see her perky face again! Now, you just sit there and call me perky again, Charlie, why don't you just do that?" Ricki shouted at her.

"Ri-i-ick," Charlie said nasally, sounding just like Kathie Lee.

They all cracked up.

"Hey, lookit what we got here," Charlie said, straightening up from behind the wheel. They watched as a middle-aged, balding, slightly overweight man with glasses came out the front door, stopping right in the doorway to give his paramour a big, sloppy kiss, cupping her rear-end with his hands. "I'm think I'm gonna be sick," Ricki moaned, the others agreeing.

They gathered their masks together, got out, tromped up to the house and around back, donned them in the yard, hidden behind bushes, then knocked on the back door.

Melissa answered immediately, stood there giving them a puzzled look, then said, "Can I help you?" in a polite, little-girl voice. She never even seemed concerned about their attire.

Charlie pushed her backwards and they all followed her in. "Who are you?" Melissa asked, that same breathless voice.

"We be from the mistress patrol," Charlie said in that Whoopi Goldberg voice again.

The woman looked at them, then gave a slow smile. "Yeah? Really?" she asked, as if honored.

"I reckon we be needing to talk to you, sister," Charlie said.

"Well, sure. Listen, why don't we go into the living room? We can all sit down and have a nice visit!" She sounded so happy. *What an airhead,* Ricki thought, looking at Melanie, whose eyes seemed to be saying the same thing.

So, they all followed her into the living room and sat down, keeping their masks on, of course. Ricki studied the woman. Yep, she fit the part to a T. Long, blond, curly hair, looking newly permed. Wide, blue eyes framed with dark-blue mascara. Big red lips. A body Ricki would kill for, humongous boobs and all. *Damn,* she wanted to yell at her, *can't you do more with your life and that body than this?* Of course, she kept her mouth shut.

"Would you-all like something to drink?" the little-girl voice asked.

The three vigilantes looked at each other, realizing their strategy wasn't going to work with this one. She was just too dumb. Well, nice, too. So, Ricki guessed, deciding to take the reasoning approach, Charlie led off, ignoring her offer for refreshment.

She got right to the point. "Now, we understand you been having an affair with a married man," Charlie outright accused.

Melissa smiled widely. "Yeah, that's right," she said, bouncing a little, as if excited.

There was a major pause as Charlie pondered this, apparently surprised by her honesty.

"A married man with children," Ricki interjected, making her voice low.

Melissa looked at her. "You got a cold?" she asked.

"Uh, no," Ricki said, trying for the same pitch.

"Well, you sound awful froggy," she said. "Must be the night air." She gave Ricki a bright smile. Ricki found herself smiling back, then made herself stop.

"Girl, what you think you're doing messing with a married man?" Charlie asked sternly.

"With children," Ricki emphasized. Charlie took the time to give her the evil eye. Well, so far as Ricki could ascertain through the slits in the mask.

Melissa got a puzzled look, then seemed to ponder this out a moment, finally saying, "I don't know. He's nice. I like him. We have an arrangement," she finished, flashing a bright smile, as if proud for saying more than a two-syllable word.

"Listen, girl, you got good looks, a good personality, well, at least a bubbly one. What you doing messing around with an old married man?" Charlie asked, not giving this up.

Ricki was going to add "with children," but Melissa interrupted, saying poutily, "He's good to me," her voice small.

"But he's married, girl."

"With children," Ricki interjected again. Charlie turned and made a frantic shushing motion with her hand. Ricki drew back.

"You ought to be out there dating single men, young, single men," Charlie said.

"Without children," Ricki inserted giving Charlie a defiant glare.

Melissa gave them all a blank look.

"Okay, why don't you just tell me what's so great about this married man, with children (this said for Ricki's benefit), that you don't want to give him up?" Charlie asked, exasperatedly.

"Well, for one, he's, you know, good in bed," Melissa said, her voice trailing off.

"Aw, shit," Ricki mumbled.

"Honey, good lovers are a dime a dozen," Charlie said.

"Really?" Ricki asked. Charlie again gave her the evil eye. Well, it was news to Ricki.

"Oh, no, he's really fantastic!" Melissa said. "We make love for hours."

"Honey, every black man I know can go for hours," Charlie said, disgustedly.

"Really?" Ricki asked again. Charlie's eyes glared. Ricki ignored that.

"Which reminds me, is what they say about black men actually myth or truth?" Ricki asked her.

Now Charlie's eyes became slits.

"What do they say?" Melissa asked.

Ricki turned to her. "You know, about how black men are such copacetic lovers," she answered.

"Copacetic?" Melissa asked.

"Excellent, voracious, fabulous," Ricki said, then, added, "not to mention their physique."

"Physique?" Melissa inquired sweetly.

"You know, hung well," Ricki answered her; keeping her eyes on Charlie, whose own were now even narrower slits.

"So, which is it, myth or reality?" Ricki asked her again.

"Oh, I think it's true," Melissa said.

They all looked at her, then back to Charlie.

"So?" Ricki nudged. "What do you think?"

"If a black man's a good lover it's only 'cause of the black woman who taught him how to be that way," Charlie snarled at her.

Ricki thought about that. "Well, I'd say that's generally true for any man, wouldn't you?"

Melanie and Melissa nodded.

"So, what about their bodies?" Ricki asked Charlie.

"Is that all you think about?" she exploded.

Ricki drew back. "What?" she asked offended.

"Sex. That's all ever comes out of your mouth, sex or something to do with it!" she yelled.

"Is not," Ricki defended.

"Would you two just can it?" Melanie shouted.

They sat there, looking uncomfortably at each other, realizing this was not going well at all.

"Well, if you ask me, I think the best lovers are Italians!" Melissa said, smiling widely.

"Huh!" Ricki said, wondering about that.

"They're so passionate," she said, her voice low, her eyes far away.

"Yeah?" Ricki asked.

"Will you shut up?" Charlie yelled, startling Ricki.

"Jeez, you don't have to shout," she said.

"Now, why don't you tell us what the real attraction is?" Charlie asked Melissa, her voice gentle.

Melissa thought, *if you could call it that*, then finally shrugged. "Well, he likes to, you know, do different kinds of things, stuff I like!"

"Different?" Melanie asked, sounding interested.

"Well, yeah." Melissa offered them all a dazzling smile.

"Are you talking about maybe kinky things?" Ricki inquired.

That bounce again. "Well, I guess you could call it that."

"You mean, like S&M?" Ricki asked.

"What's that?" she queried.

"Sadism and masochism?" Seeing that meant nothing to her, Ricki clarified, "B&D?" A blank stare. "Bondage and discipline?" Nothing. "Okay, how about he ties you up and beats you?"

"Oh, no, he doesn't tie me up!" she exclaimed.

They all waited a count, pondering this. "Okay, he beats you," Ricki said.

"Well, not exactly beats me," that little girl voice.

Slight pause while they all thought this one over. "What exactly does he do to you?" Ricki asked, thinking, *good grief, where is her brain located, her little fingernail?*

Melissa's eyes took on a glazed look then she gave a shy smile, doing that little bounce again, like an excited child.

Wait a minute, Ricki thought. *She talks like a little girl, acts like one. And who is she fooling around with? Big Daddy, who likes to spank his little girl, I bet.*

"He spanks you?" Ricki asked, astounded.

Melissa giggled and nodded. Bingo!

Charlie and Ricki looked at each other. "Um, do you by any chance call him Daddy?" Ricki asked.

"How'd you know?" Melissa asked.

Bingo again!

"I bet you didn't have a father growing up," Ricki said.

Melissa's eyes widened. Wow, Ricki was getting good here!

"Yeah, that's right. But how did you know that?" They widened further. "Oh, man, don't tell me. You're psychic, right?"

"Listen, let's not get into the psychology shit," Charlie said, irritably, seeing she was losing ground here.

"Psychol . . . oh, you think maybe that's not a good thing to do. Really, he doesn't beat me. He only uses his hand," Melissa said, in a defensive manner.

Huh! Ricki thought, but didn't voice it. She sat there, trying to imagine this meek, mild, passive-looking character they had seen come out of the house sitting there, with this gorgeous, healthy, vivacious girl-woman bending over his knees, enjoying a spanking from his hand. She bit her lip, trying to keep from laughing outright. Then wondered if he did that to Donna. Why she outweighed him by 100 pounds, Ricki bet. No way she could lie across his knees. Plus, there was a lot of area back there to cover. So, maybe she spanked him. Ricki couldn't help it, but a snicker did escape at this vision.

"Um, how exactly does he do this?" Melanie asked, not noticing the sounds Ricki was making, her own eyes gleaming. Ricki began to wonder about her then.

"Listen, this is really none of our business," Ricki said before Melissa could reply.

"Oh, I don't mind telling you, really," Melissa effused, looking excited.

"Uh, no, now, that's not such a good idea," Charlie said, taking over again.

Melissa smiled widely, folded her hands in her lap, said, "Well," and finally seemed to notice what they were wearing.

"Why are you dressed like that?" she asked, looking interested.

"Oh, you know, your basic black," Ricki said, snidely.

Melissa smiled. "Yeah, right," she agreed. Ricki rolled her eyes. She didn't think Melissa got it.

"Now, listen," Charlie said loudly, giving Ricki an irritated look. "We come here to warn you to stop messing with that dude. He's no good for you. He's got a wife and kids, and they need him."

Melissa stuck her lower lip out, pouting like a child.

"Now, you're a beautiful woman," Charlie quickly went on. "Why, I bet you got guys hot for you all the time."

Airhead smiled at this, nodding in agreement. Ricki sighed inwardly, thinking, *wouldn't it be nice.*

"So, why don't you just drop this Don character, he's too old for you anyway," Charlie suggested. "You need a younger, better-looking guy, someone that will kind of set you off, you know? Someone that looks good with you. A man you won't have to hide your relationship with, you understand?"

Melissa pondered, looking solemn, then gave them all that bright smile. "Okay!" she said, bouncing again.

"And I betcha your next boyfriend spanks better than Don ever thought about!" Ricki said with sarcasm.

Charlie gave her that look again.

"Oh, yeah," Melissa bubbled, looking far away.

Charlie made movements to leave. "Wait a minute," Ricki said, stopping her.

"What?" she asked irritably.

"There's something wrong here," Ricki replied, looking toward Melissa again. "I mean, what we're doing is encouraging her to go out and get some other man to replace the one she has now when we should be encouraging her to stand on her own two feet, you know, not depend on a man to take care of her."

"Hey, we didn't come here to play social worker," Charlie snapped.

"Yeah, but what's going to happen to her when she's older, when she's no longer as attractive as she is now? She needs to learn to fend for herself, not let some man do it for her," Ricki argued.

"Oh, I don't mind, really," Melissa said.

Jeez. Ricki came this close to getting up and going on out that door, but she couldn't just leave her like this. "Did you graduate from high school?" Ricki asked thinking, *I'll just help her find a job, a way to support herself.*

Melissa shook her head. "I wasn't any good in school," she said, sounding remorseful.

"Well, okay," Ricki said, pondering. "How about we help get you into the GED classes, and then once you've gotten your equivalency diploma, we'll help you get a job? That'd be a whole lot better than just lying around the house all day, playing mistress to all these married jerks out there, right?"

"I don't mind, really," Melissa said, looking scared.

"She don't mind!" Charlie snarled at Ricki.

"Really, it'll be good for you, getting your GED, having a career." Ricki got an idea. "Just think of all the men you'll meet out there!" she enticed.

Melissa's eyes lit up. "Well, okay," she said.

"Good. Listen, I'll find out about the classes and give you a call the next few days, help you get started, how's that?"

"Great!" she said.

"You finished now?" Charlie asked, irritated.

Ricki stood.

"I wish you could stay longer," Melissa said, looking forlorn.

Ricki couldn't help it, but she felt sorry for her.

"We'll keep in touch," Ricki suggested. "Make sure you're doing well in school, make sure you get a good job. How's that?"

"Oh, would you?" Melissa said, bouncing again, her breasts doing their own little jig.

"Sure," Melanie said. "We'll call you, catch up with what's going on in your life."

"Oh, that would be great!" she said.

"Now, remember, you tell that old Don to go home to his wife and kids," Charlie instructed.

"I will," Melissa said, nodding with determination.

"And if he don't, why, we'll handle him ourselves, how's that?"

"You're so great!" she oozed.

This is too weird, Ricki thought.

After what seemed like an interminable goodbye, they got out the door, Melissa waving to them as they walked back to the car.

"Dang, I feel like I've just visited the Twilight Zone," Ricki surmised sarcastically, snatching the hood off her head, running her fingers through her hair. Melanie and Charlie simply nodded in agreement.

And after they got in the car, Ricki turned to Charlie and said, "That, Charlie, is perky," pointing in the direction of Melissa's house. Charlie rolled her eyes as she started the car.

CHAPTER 10

"BUT THE RIGHT HAND JUST DELIVERED THE DEVIL IN A SUIT"

She stood before the group, a small, petite woman; her coarse black hair interspersed heavily with gray. She stated right off she was there asking for WAR's help. It seemed her daughter, Angela, a single mother, had been brutally raped and cut, and although she had identified the rapist, he had offered an alibi the police had bought and was now back out on the streets. Her daughter would not leave the house, fearful she would meet up with this man. Even though the rape had occurred over two months ago she was a basketcase; it seemed all she did was cry and sleep. She had lost 20 pounds and wouldn't eat unless her mother forced her to. She couldn't concentrate on her small child and the mother was now caretaker. Ricki quickly began writing down the information on this victim, making a mental note to call a couple of social agencies they had dealt with before to see what kind of help they could get for her.

Charlie started questioning the woman about the rape, sounding like a detective. She found out the victim had identified the man who did it, one Pete Sexton, sole offspring of one of their most esteemed state legislators. The man and his father adamantly denied his involvement and, of course, he had an alibi to go along with it. What sounded like a pretty contrived alibi to Ricki.

Charlie called the next day, telling Ricki she had talked to her sister, the dispatcher for the police department, and learned this guy was no stranger to them, seeing as how he had been charged with rape on two other occasions just this past year. One charge had been dropped rather suddenly, and an alibi had been established for the other. This was starting to sound fishy.

Ricki asked Sam if he knew about the rape since it occurred in Knox County. He said he was aware of it but hadn't investigated, wasn't real familiar with the specifics except that the guy she identified had an airtight alibi. When Ricki advised him this had happened before with the same man, Sam told her to stay out of it, this was police business, they knew all that, they'd handle it. Ricki pointed out to him this was the third time the guy had gotten by with raping a woman, seemed to her like nobody was handling it. He pointed out to her a man was supposed to be innocent until proven guilty;

this was America, after all. Ricki pointed out to him where there's smoke, there's bound to be fire, and someone accused of the same offense three different times sounded awful suspicious to her. Sam told her they were investigating this dude, so just let it go. Ricki dropped the subject.

Charlie had her sister do some digging and they found out all three women were dark-haired, dark-eyed, tall, with a slender build. "I fit that pattern," Ricki told Charlie, watching her eyes light up with interest.

They both paid a visit to the young lady who had been raped, on the pretext of making sure WAR's efforts on her behalf were reaping some results, hoping to gain additional information.

She looked so pitiful sitting in the living room of her mother's small apartment, her body drawn up defensively, eyes darting at every sudden sound, mouth tight. She told them she had met Pete at this bar on the outskirts of Knoxville. She had seen him around town before—it seemed they generally hung out in the same places—but that night was the first time they had ever actually talked to each other. She said he seemed to be a real friendly, real sweet kind of guy. He offered to walk her to her car when she left and, instead, forced her to the back of the building and there raped her, then cut her from her vagina to her anus. She burst out crying. Charlie and Ricki looked at each other and decided just like that if the dang cops couldn't catch this guy, WAR's vigilante core would.

Melanie made a brilliant decision and refused to participate, telling them they could get hurt. "Don't you think you guys are getting too carried away with this vigilante thing?" she asked, giving Charlie and Ricki an intent look. They just shrugged. "You're stepping over the line, you do this," Melanie warned. "You could get into a lot of trouble if you actually do what you're planning to." More shrugs from Charlie and Ricki. "You could get killed!" she implored. Charlie and Ricki didn't think that needed a response. Melanie rolled her eyes.

"Listen Mel, we're dealing with a misogynist here, a man . . ."

"A miss what?" Charlie asked.

"You know, a guy who hates women," Ricki answered impatiently.

"Well why couldn't you just say that?" Charlie snapped at her.

Ignoring her, Ricki turned back to Melanie. "A man who will continue to rape and hurt and maim and butcher if someone doesn't stop him."

"You could get hurt," she stressed again.

"Not the two of us," Ricki said, glancing confidently at Charlie, not realizing until later how awfully stupid that statement was.

Charlie managed to get a copy of the mug shot of Pete from her sister and they studied this, trying to memorize his face, then began frequenting the places Angela had told them about, watching and waiting. They hit pay dirt the fourth night out at a scuzzy-looking bar in Halls, a small community on the outskirts of North Knoxville. They spied him as they came through the door, sitting at the bar, watching a Braves game on the big screen TV. Another guy sat to his left, no one to his right. Charlie went to a table in the back as Ricki sidled on up to the bar and, giving him a sweet smile, asked if the seat next to his was taken.

He flashed teeth at her, shaking his head no, then turned back to the game.

Ricki ordered a glass of white wine, pretended to sip it as she watched the game. He ignored her. She pulled out a cigarette, waited to see if he would offer to light it, which he did not. The bartender did and Ricki sat there, puffing away, inexperienced, trying not to have a coughing fit, pretending to be watching the game while watching Pete. He was an okay looking guy, nothing particularly standout about him. He looked to be around six feet tall, with a stocky build, dark-brown hair, and brown eyes. If there was ever any average way for a man to look, Pete was it. He would blend in, in any crowd.

The pitcher was having a hard night of it, and when Ricki yelled, "Throw the bum out," she finally got a response from Pete as he glanced her way, flashing teeth again. She shrugged as if to say, *sorry.*

They started making comments to each other about the game and during commercials went on to other things, such as names (Ricki gave an alias; he didn't), occupations, etc. Found out they both owned horses and discussed that topic extensively. They, in essence, got along grandly. Ricki could see why Angela had trusted him. He seemed so nice.

She was working up the courage to head on out of there when she got that tingling sensation in the back of her neck, warning her someone was staring at her. There was a mirror along the wall behind the bar and Ricki scanned the room with the mirror, noting this tall guy sitting at one of the tables, watching her. He wore a Braves hat and T-shirt and what she could see of his hair beneath the cap looked dark. It was so dim in that place; his features seemed to blend together into a fuzzy light blur against shadows. The cap was pulled low on his forehead, shading his eyes. *Huh,* Ricki thought, finding that suspicious, what with the bar already being so dim and all. She surreptitiously watched him watch her. There was something familiar about the way he held himself but she couldn't quite place it.

Pete nudged her, said, "You ready for another one?" nodding toward her drink.

Ricki forced herself to look at him, smiled sweetly, answered, "Actually, I think I need to get home."

He looked disappointed, then shrugging his shoulders, said, "Sure. I'll walk you out to your car. Never can tell what kind of demons are lurking about."

Talk about the pot calling the kettle black, Ricki thought, her stomach churning. Trying to override her nervousness, she said, "Great! Just give me a minute to get rid of this drink," as she climbed down off the barstool, grabbing her purse. "Would you watch my coat?" she asked, giving another sugary smile.

"No problem," he replied, looking at her, his eyes dark, unreadable.

Ricki headed for the bathroom in the back, praying to God Charlie would follow so she could tell her she was leaving and this guy was going with her, *so get your butt out there and protect me!* As she pushed the door open, someone from behind propelled her into the room, their hands on her back. Ricki turned around, irritated, thinking it was Charlie. It wasn't. It was the guy with the Braves hat and shirt.

"Excuse me, but I believe this is a women's restroom," Ricki snapped, starting to panic, wondering if maybe this was actually the rapist and everybody had pegged the wrong guy.

He pushed her into the wall, not so gently, his body against hers.

"Hey!" Ricki protested.

He yanked his cap off. Ricki stared into dark green eyes. "Sam?" she asked, her own eyes widening.

"What the fuck do you think you're doing?" he spat in her face.

The door opened and a young woman came into the room, her eyes going from Sam to Ricki.

"We're busy," he snarled at her. She immediately left.

Sam turned back to Ricki.

"What are you doing here, Sammy?" she asked, looking him up and down, "dressed like that?" pointing at his attire.

"Exactly what I wanted to ask you," he fumed.

Jeez, he really looks mad, Ricki thought. "I just came here for a drink with Charlie," she said innocently. "Didn't you see her?"

"You got any idea who you been talking to out there?" he hurled at her, pushing himself right up against her.

"He said his name was Pete," Ricki answered, shrugging, trying to appear guiltless. Her mouth and eyes widened with understanding. "You're on a stakeout," she observed, eyeing his attire.

"Watching you on the make," he spat.

Well durn, she thought. Should she tell him or not? She decided what the heck, she might as well own up to it or Sam would be disinclined to believe her the longer she put it off.

"Well, actually, Sam, I'm trying to catch a rapist," Ricki said, giving him an impish smile.

He drew back, staring at her.

"See, Charlie and I came up with this plan. We figured out this guy is attracted to dark-headed, dark-eyed women, seeing as those are the ones he's raped, so I thought I'd just lure him outside and Charlie would follow us, you know, with her gun, and if he tried anything, then we could . . ."

"Go get Charlie," he interrupted, his face white, jaws gritted together.

Ricki frowned, not liking his tone of voice.

"Now!" he half-shouted.

She gave him an insolent look, then stepped toward the bathroom door, which was opened at that moment by her partner in crime. Talk about timing. Charlie came in, giving Sam's back a dark look.

"Look who's here," Ricki said, trying to smile but failing badly. Charlie looked at his face, then nodded.

"You-all got even half a brain between the two of you?" Sam snarled, showing disdain.

Charlie and Ricki stood there, feeling like two penitent kids called before the principal.

"You realize you probably have blown this whole thing for me?" he raved at them.

Well, no, actually Ricki hadn't. But she wisely made the decision not to say so.

"We've been tracking this guy down for weeks, finally got him right where we want him, our decoy all set to put into place, and who the fuck is sitting at the bar with this pervert, looking ready for action, keeping him away from the person he needs to be with so we can get him? My lover!" he ranted.

Ricki smiled at the word lover. Sam glared. She stopped smiling, casting eyes downward. She heard static, then mumbling. Watched as Sam pulled some sort of radio out of his back pocket, bringing it up to his mouth, saying, "I'm handling a problem in the bathroom."

More static and muttering. Then Sam said, "Don't worry about her, she's the problem I'm taking care of. Get the decoy over there; see if she can get him interested. I'll make sure this problem doesn't interfere anymore," giving Ricki a deadly look.

He signed off, then turned to Charlie, held out his hand. "Give me your gun," he snapped.

"Who said I got a gun?" Charlie asked, glancing guiltily at Ricki.

Sam just stared.

"Why in hell I gotta give you my gun?" Charlie asked, angrily.

"'Cause I am an officer of the law and I am commanding you to," he fumed.

She didn't look too inclined to do what was asked of her.

"Listen, you don't give me your gun, I'm gonna arrest the both of you here and now for interfering with an investigation, for one; obstructing justice, for two. You got me?" now glancing toward Ricki.

"Give him your gun, Charlie," she said.

Charlie glared at Ricki, then reluctantly turned it over.

"Hey, wait a minute," Ricki said. "I thought you worked homicide, Sam, so what the heck are you doing staking out a rapist?"

He scowled at her. Fiercely.

"Just wondering," she mumbled.

Ignoring that, he raved, "What the hell did you think you were doing out there, playing cops and robbers?"

"We were just trying . . .."

"Trying to get your ass raped, then killed," he snapped, interrupting. Then, "For God's sake, Ricki, that guy is a raving lunatic. He goes one step further with each rape, and the next one is murder. That is one of the reasons I asked to be in on this."

"Oh," Ricki said.

He glared at them, then, "You mind telling me how in hell you expected to defend yourself?" he half-shouted.

Ricki fumbled in her purse and pulled out a can of red-pepper mace. "Like this, till Charlie got there," she said, proudly holding it up.

His eyes got big and he breathed in, looking like he was fighting the urge to strangle Ricki, then and there, on the spot.

"I want you two out of here like two minutes ago," Sam snarled at them.

"But Sam, he's watching my coat. He expects me to come back. He wants to walk me to my car."

"Forget your damn coat," he spat.

"Wait a minute," Ricki said, getting an idea. "Since he's already interested in me, why don't I be your decoy? I'll do whatever you want me to, however you say."

His face got red. "You are out of your friggin' mind, Ricki!" he yelled in her face. He pointed to the door. "Get your ass out of here now, or I swear I'll do it for you. You get my drift?"

Ricki straightened up. "Fine, I'll go," she said snippily. "But first, Samuel, I am going to get my coat. It's my favorite one and I'm not going to give it up just 'cause you . . . ."

His eyes narrowed. "All right, damnit, get out there, get your coat away from this guy, tell him you're going, like now," Sam snarled. "Do not, and I repeat not, Ricki, go anywhere with him or I'll save him the trouble and kill you myself."

"But what if he insists on walking me to my car?" Ricki asked.

He huffed loudly. "Take Charlie with you, give him some bull about how you just met up with your long-lost friend and she's invited you to dinner, so you're leaving with her."

"But what if he wants to go with the both of us?"

"Tell him her husband's waiting outside, anything. Improvise. You obviously know how to do that. But I'm warning you, he leaves with you or you blow this for me in any way, I'll be paying you a visit tonight and it will not be pretty. You understand me?" he asked balefully.

"Well, jeez, Sam," Ricki said, sounding like a kid. "If I'd have known you were doing something about him, this never would have happened, you know. But it seemed y'all weren't doing one whit of good, trying to get this guy, so we just . . . ."

"I don't want to hear any kind of rationalizations for doing about the stupidest thing I've ever heard of," he snapped, cutting her off. "Go home, Ricki. Wait for me there. I'm not done with you."

"But Sam . . . ." she started.

"Get out of here now," he flared, "or I will personally take you out and I don't think that's the way you want to be remembered."

Well, was that a threat or what?

Ricki glanced at Charlie, who was giving her a challenging look, and said, "Let's go," ignoring that.

She went to the bar, noticed a dark-haired, dark-eyed woman sitting beside Pete—right where Ricki had—and coming on to him, decided that must be the decoy, went through her song and dance about meeting up with my old buddy, it's been nice, Pete, maybe I'll see you again sometime, and got the hell out of Dodge before Marshall Dillon changed his mind and decided to arrest her.

As Ricki and Charlie walked to the car, they were both silent, not saying a word. Charlie drove Ricki home, still not saying anything. Finally, as she opened the door, getting ready to go inside, Charlie said, "This guy's really into power and control, huh?"

Ricki gave her a confused look. "Who?"

"Sam."

"Well, he was just mad," Ricki said, shrugging her shoulders. "We were kind of intruding on his territory, you know."

"Yeah, well, I'm just glad I'm not the one he's gonna be seeing later tonight," Charlie said, putting the car in reverse.

"Lucky you," Ricki sarcastically replied, wishing it was her Sam would be paying a visit to.

About three hours later, the doorbell rang. Ricki went to answer it, feeling slight trepidation, knowing it would be Sam, knowing he would still be mad.

He pushed it back, out of her grasp, entering, then slammed it shut, glaring at her.

"Hey, Sam," she said, trying for a smile, trying not to let him see her nervousness at his anger.

Without saying a word, he grabbed her hand and started toward the stairs, Ricki in tow.

"What are you doing?" she asked, pulling back.

"Gonna show you what you missed out on," he muttered, going up the stairs, easily bringing her along.

Oh, shit, she thought.

He took her into the bedroom, slammed the door, spun her around, and pushed her up against it, immediately placing his body against hers, pinning her there.

"Sam!" she gasped.

"Okay, Ricki, I'm the rapist," he whispered harshly. "Get away from me."

She struggled mightily, twisting and squirming, but he had her pinned flat against the door. She finally stopped, breathing heavily. "I can't move, Sam, let me go," she pled.

"I am the rapist," he repeated in her ear. "This is my modus operandi. Make me let you go."

Ricki tried to kick back with her foot but his legs were right against hers, molded to hers, keeping them in place. She placed her hands on the door, pushed back with all her strength but didn't budge him an inch. She squirmed again, tried pushing against him with her hands, which he caught in his own.

"Please Sam," she whimpered.

"Please," he snarled, mimicking her. "I don't think that would have stopped him, Ricki."

He raised her arms up over her head, held them there with one hand, and using the other one, pulled her skirt up around her waist.

"Let me go, Sam, don't do this," she begged.

"I am the rapist, Ricki," he repeated, "get away from me."

She fought him again, but to no avail. "I can't," she finally whimpered, feeling fatigued.

His hand came back to her panties and she cried out as he yanked them down, off her buttocks. He shifted back from her a little, and Ricki pushed back with her butt, trying to bring her leg up, trying to kick him. He immediately pushed back into her, using his weight to pin her securely against the door.

"Damn you!" she screamed at him, feeling claustrophobic. "Let me go now, Sam!"

"Make me!" he snarled in her ear.

Ricki struggled again, frantically, panicked from that closed-in feeling, but to no avail. He easily overpowered her. She finally stopped, leaning against the door, breathing heavily.

"I am the rapist," Sam said, inserting one leg between hers, roughly spreading them. She cried out from the pain, from his brutality. Ignoring this, he crudely put his hand between her legs. "This is my dick," he whispered, pushing up with his fist.

Ricki gasped when he did this, struggled weakly.

"This is how he would have done it, Ricki, this is how he would have raped you," he said, his voice tight, gyrating his pelvis against hers in a sexual way. Even though he wasn't inside, it felt like he was.

"Please, Sam, don't," she whispered, starting to cry.

"First vaginally, then anally," he said, ignoring her. "And following his MO, after he was finished, he would have taken a switchblade out, inserted it into your vagina, then cut you wide open, possibly even killed you, and you couldn't have done a damn thing about it!" He pushed his knuckles against her sex.

"Stop it!" she screamed at him.

"Make me!" he repeated.

"I can't," she cried.

"Then you're fucked, literally," he snapped.

Ricki screamed herself hoarse. Sam waited her out, still pinning her to the door, then abruptly released her, stepping away.

Ricki covered her face with her hands, crying, still turned to the door.

He put his hands on her shoulders, turned her around, got in her face, and said, "You were playing with your life, Ricki. That's what would have happened to you tonight if you had left with him. You're damn lucky I was there to stop you."

He jerked her away from the door, opened it, and left. Ricki leaned against the frame, her whole body trembling violently.

She finally pulled her panties up, then crawled into bed, pulling the comforter over her head, fighting the need to vomit, crying into the pillow. Feeling ashamed that she had been so stupid to arrogantly think she could conquer a man who made hurting women his hobby, a man who had had plenty of practice. Feeling anger at Sam for being so crude and rough with her.

A good while later, she heard the bedroom door open, footsteps coming toward her, then weight as someone sat beside her. She prayed it wasn't Zach, prayed he hadn't come home unexpectedly, hadn't heard any of what had happened.

"Ricki," Sam said, his voice gentle. "I made you a cup of tea, babe. Sit up."

Ricki ignored him. He waited a minute, then stood up, came around, and got into bed behind her, putting his arms around her.

She stiffened, tried to break away from him, but he held her tight.

"I had to do that, Ricki. You gotta understand that. You could have gotten yourself killed tonight, babe. I had to make you understand what you would have been up against."

Ricki burst into tears again.

"I didn't hurt you, did I?" he asked, his voice gentle, turning her toward him.

Ricki wouldn't answer him.

"Ricki, listen to me. What you and Charlie planned to do went beyond reckless to just plain stupid. I don't care if she had a gun or not, he would have raped you, possibly killed you after he took care of her. He's a dangerous man, Rick."

Ricki looked at him. "Did you get him?" she asked.

He nodded, gave a grim smile. "Just barely. Had the decoy up against the wall, getting ready to penetrate when we finally caught up with him."

Ricki shuddered.

"And we were professionals, Ricki. A group of trained professionals, going after him. What the hell did you and Charlie think you could accomplish?" His voice turned angry.

She shook her head, not answering.

He pulled her against him, said into her hair, "Jesus, Rick, I care about you. I love you. The thought of that guy, of any man touching you in that way just makes me nuts. It was all I could do watching you talking to him, trying not to blow my cover, trying to find a way to warn you off."

Ricki buried her face in his chest, hugged him.

"Promise me you won't ever try anything like that again," Sam said, putting his finger under her chin, turning her face up to his.

"I won't," she said, feeling ashamed of herself, feeling chagrined.

Sam nodded, watching her, then began kissing her gently. "I don't want to share you with anyone else, babe," he whispered in her ear. "I can't."

The thought occurred to her Sam seemed more concerned with her having sex with the guy than being hurt by him. She told herself, *that's just the way it came out, Sam didn't mean that,* and let herself forget this concern as he traveled with his mouth, closing her eyes, feeling her body respond as it always so passionately and willingly did.

CHAPTER 11

"LET'S GO SHOOT A HOLE IN THE MOON"

Ricki got a phone call from a woman, complaining that a local convenience store located near her house was selling beer, cigarettes, and porno magazines to teenagers. She wanted to know if WAR could do something about it. "Sure," Ricki said confidently.

She presented this at the next meeting, and WAR decided they'd just go picket that dang place.

Till Melanie brought up the fact that maybe they ought to actually check this store out for themselves first, just to make sure this wasn't some kind of crank call.

Oh, yeah.

They knew they couldn't just go hang out at the store all day, so five of them decided to pay visits at different times during the next day. Ricki was the first one in that morning and hung around for 30 minutes, just browsing, till the owner threw her out, telling her if she wasn't going to buy anything, go hang out somewhere else. You'd have thought Ricki was a hooker, the looks she was giving her.

Ricki got a good gander at her, though, as she went out the door, giving her the evil eye, sort of sizing up the enemy, taking note she was a large woman, taller than Ricki, and about as broad as big. She looked to be in her early 50's, maybe, with dyed carrot-colored hair, blue eyes, painted-on brown eyebrows shaped like the Golden Arches. She kind of reminded Ricki of Ma Kettle, to tell you the truth, the way she was built. *A worthy adversary,* Ricki thought, climbing in her car.

Charlie was the last person in and the only one who actually witnessed a teenager buying beer from the same jerk that threw Ricki out.

"We got our proof," Ricki told everyone at the next meeting. "That wasn't a crank call."

"Yeah, but don't you think we ought to have some proof in hand before we go accusing a store of doing something illegal?" Melanie pointed out.

Oh, yeah.

So, after much discussion, they decided they'd just get on film any infractions being committed by the store personnel.

115

Charlie and Ricki volunteered to get the footage they'd need, agreeing to convene after the meeting and plan their strategy.

They knew they couldn't stand around the convenience store all day, camera in hand, waiting for some unsuspecting teenager to come in and buy the required items. That would be too obvious. However, they wanted this on film—prima facie evidence, you might say.

"We need a decoy," Ricki said.

"Yeah, but who?" Charlie asked.

Ricki smiled. "Who else? Zach."

Charlie grinned.

So later that evening, Ricki told her unsuspecting son she needed him to go to the store the next day.

"What for?" he demanded, giving her his why-can't-you-do-that frown.

"Well, I need a pack of cigarettes, a six-pack of beer, and one of those *Playboy* magazines," Ricki replied innocently.

"What?" he asked, an incredulous look on his face.

"I'll go with you," she said. "I just can't be the one buying those things."

His eyes narrowed. He studied her a minute, then said, "Mom, is there something you want to tell me?"

Ricki grinned. She laid it all out for him: their strategy, his involvement. He liked it. Ricki knew he would. However, he refused to pay for the items to be purchased and she ended up shelling out the money.

So, the next day, Charlie and Ricki planted themselves inside the store about five minutes before Zachary was supposed to appear. They had rigged a minicam inside an old book bag Ricki used to carry, cutting a hole in the bag big enough for the lens. Ricki cupped her hand over the hole to cover it until they were ready to begin filming, feeling just like one of those journalists on *60 Minutes*.

She was relieved to see the owner wasn't around when they arrived, the only personnel being a young blond cashier, reading one of those yucky confession magazines. But what the hey, it kept her occupied.

Zachary was late getting there and Ricki and Charlie were beginning to worry they'd get thrown out, from the suspicious looks they were getting from the cashier, so they both breathed respective sighs of relief when Zachary came waltzing through the door. Followed by his best friend, Matt. Ricki groaned. She hadn't wanted Matt in on this. That guy had one big mouth.

Zachary and Matt meandered around the store, every once in awhile glancing at Charlie and Ricki, then quickly looking away, now drawing suspicious stares from the cashier.

Zachary stayed at the magazine stand longer than Ricki felt he should, leafing through some of the magazines. It was all she could do to make herself stay put and not go hit him over the head with one of those durn magazines, telling this kid he had no business looking at that kind of trash. She sighed inwardly, wishing she hadn't included pornography on her list.

He finally picked one out, then went to the back of the store, where the coolers were, and he and Matt got into this real intense discussion about what kind of beer to buy. Ricki looked at Charlie, rolling her eyes. She got busy studying laxatives.

Ricki was headed toward the back of the store to encourage these two nitwits to move it along a little when they finally made their choice and went to the cashier's stand, where the cigarettes were displayed.

Ricki hastily picked up an item off the shelf and got into line behind them, slipping her hand into the book bag, turning on the camera, aiming it upward, praying she had everybody in the frame. Charlie came up beside her, trying to hide Ricki's hand inside the bag.

Zachary quite expertly asked for a pack of Marlboro 100's. Ricki glared at him, wondering if he had done this before. He couldn't resist looking back at her, smiling quickly, then turning back to the cashier.

She gave them all curious stares, frowning widely, then, Ricki guessed, taking to heart the innocent looks they gave back, rang Zach's purchases up, took his money (well, Ricki's money, actually), counted out change, and gave it back to him, telling him to have a nice day as he and Matt went on out the door, which Ricki also made sure she had on film.

It was Ricki's turn now, she realized, feeling the cashier's expectant stare on her. Shoot, Charlie was supposed to take care of that matter of seconds as they were exiting and she was filming. Ricki inwardly rolled her eyes, went up to the counter, laid her purchase down, which she now noticed was a package of Depends diapers for urine incontinence. She frowned widely, thinking, *what the heck am I going to do with these things?* The cashier gave her the same kind of look.

"They're for my mother," Ricki explained, growing red-faced.

She nodded consolingly.

Ricki hurriedly paid for the diapers, then exited the store, dropping the package in the garbage can sitting outside. She made sure she confiscated their evidence from Zachary and his buddy before they got into any of it, telling Charlie she could keep it at her house, then Charlie and Ricki, followed by Zach and Matt, hurried home and plugged the tape into the VCR.

It was grainy and shaky, but Ricki had managed to capture all atrocities on film. They grinned at each other.

The next week, Ricki played the tape for WAR, proving they had what they needed, and they agreed this was the time for Charlie and Ricki to approach the owner, let her know they had proof, get her to commit to stopping these kind of illegalities.

Once she ascertained what they had witnessed and that they weren't paying customers, she threw Charlie and Ricki out, refusing to listen to anything they had to say about anything, telling them to, in essence, stick their proof up a certain part of their anatomy where the sun don't shine. Never even gave them a chance to show her the tape.

WAR decided to go picket the store that very weekend.

So there they were, about 15 of them, marching in front of this emporium, such as it was, placards in hand, receiving curious stares and glares from customer wannabes. They weren't there 20 minutes when the owner came barreling up, demanding to know what the hell they thought they were doing.

Ricki explained nicely and politely what they were protesting against. The owner said they were full of crap, her store didn't do anything like that. When Ricki told her that they had captured the blond cashier on film, then showed her the tape and offered to play it, her eyes narrowed. She went back inside.

Next thing they knew, the nice clerk who had waited on them a few days prior was leaving the store, in tears.

She came stalking up to Ricki. "I just got fired, thanks to you!" she wailed.

Oh, jeez. Ricki felt bad, seeing her cry like that.

Everyone was staring at her, waiting for her to respond. "Well, I'm real sorry you got fired," Ricki said, sympathetically, "but you shouldn't be selling liquor and cigarettes, not to mention pornography, to minors."

"I was only doin' what I was told to do," she whined, blowing her nose loudly.

Charlie and Ricki looked at each other.

"By whom?" Ricki asked.

"The owner, who else?" she yelled, pointing at the store.

All eyes went to that direction, and subsequently the owner, who was standing at the door, arms folded, glaring.

"I'll be right back," Ricki snarled, stalking away.

"She said you told her to sell those items to minors!" she accused.

"Prove it!" the owner snapped at her.

Ricki frowned. Dang, this wasn't going to be as easy as she had thought it would be.

"How can you fire her for doing what you told her to do?" she yelled.

"It's your fault," the owner accused. "You're the one filmed her selling that stuff."

Ricki huffed. "Listen," she said, pointing her finger at her, "just promise me you'll stop selling to minors, okay? If you do, we'll go on about our business and leave you alone. But if you don't, then we're gonna picket this store till you don't have any customers left, you understand?"

"You can't picket me 24 hours every friggin' day," she snapped.

"So you're not gonna stop?" Ricki asked, incredulous.

"Hey, bitch, I'm not gonna let you or any of these other cunts out there get by with telling me what to do, you got that? I will sell anything I freakin' well want to whoever I freakin' well want to."

"Fine," Ricki said, nodding. "I'm sure the police, not to mention the TV stations, will be interested in viewing what we filmed going on in there!"

"By her, and she no longer works for me."

"At your direction!" Ricki yelled.

The owner grinned. "Prove it!" she said.

Ricki didn't know what to do, so stalked back to the protest. After conferring with the others, she went to her car phone, called that wacky TV station—the one that filmed WAR protesting the gentleman's club—asked the reporter why didn't he come on down, seeing as how she had a story for him and all.

About a half-hour later, the van pulled up and the dapper little journalist got out. He sauntered up to Ricki, giving a friendly, "Hey, what's going on?"

Ricki gave him a friendly "hey" back, then explained the whole thing to him and offered to let him have their tape to copy and subsequently show on the news if he felt the need.

He got busy, directing the cameraman to film them having their little march, then his interview with Ricki, during which she detailed what had led up to what was transpiring at the moment, including her home video of the crime in process and subsequent conversation with the owner, who threw them out. He then interviewed the owner, who, of course, came across as Ms. Innocent, declaring she had no idea any of her employees would do something like that and had fired the clerk responsible. "Liar!" they yelled, making sure that got on the film, too.

"When's it gonna show?" Ricki asked as they packed up.

"Tonight at six. Don't miss it."

"You can count on it," she said, forgetting all about one certain Danny England, who would not appreciate at all the fact that she had utilized their son as a decoy.

He didn't offer her the courtesy of a phone call this time, just came barreling into the house that evening at 6:35, right after the news was over, catching Matt, Zachary, and Ricki sharing a Pepsi, congratulating themselves on seeing their mugs on the 6:00 news.

Danny stood in the doorway to the kitchen, breathing heavily, face red, teeth gritted. *Shoot, he must have flown over here*, Ricki thought, glancing at the clock. Matt immediately got the message and stood up, saying as he exited the door, "I gotta get home, see ya later."

Traitor, Ricki mentally willed his way, watching his retreating form.

Danny pointed his finger at her. She rolled her eyes. "You!" he yelled.

"Me?" Ricki squeaked, pointing at herself, trying for levity.

Zachary tried to offer her a consoling smile but somehow couldn't come up with one.

"What the hell do you think you're doing involving our son, OUR SON, CHEROKEE, in one of your little escapades?" Danny roared at her.

"Escapades?" she asked, offended.

"It's bad enough you go flitting . . ."

"Flitting?" she screeched.

" . . .all over this town, petitioning against anything and everything you can find to demonstrate against, getting yourself on TV every other week, not to mention the fact that I have to then put up with the media hounding me about your words and actions, but I will not tolerate you pulling Zachary into this shit!"

"Hey, it was for a good cause, Danion!" Ricki hurled back.

"Good cause? What the hell did you prove? The owner says you only got the cashier and she no longer works for her. So what exactly the hell did you prove here and why the hell did you have to involve Zachary?"

"Well, we needed a decoy, you know, and Zach was, well, he was the right age and everything, and . . ."

"You allowed our son to go into that store and buy beer, cigarettes and a porno magazine, filmed the whole damn transaction, then went and gave the damn friggin' film to a TV crew to show on the friggin' news. Now you'll have the whole world thinking we allow our son to drink, smoke, and read porno. What the hell has gotten into that brain of yours, Cherokee? What the hell do you think you're doing?"

Jeez, he is really yelling loudly, Ricki thought, glancing at Zachary, whose face had a blanched look.

"Well, maybe I should have been more circumspect," she temporized.

"You should have been circumvented!" he roared at her.

"Danny, we were simply trying to stop an illegal act that . . ."

120

"You involved my son in an illegal act," he thundered, "and filmed it to boot!"

Oh, yeah. Ricki hadn't thought of that.

She frowned at him, not wanting to agree, but knowing he was right. Then realizing they were arguing in front of Zachary, a firm rule they had always abode by, said, "Uh, Danny, don't you think we should be having this discussion in private?" making her voice civil, cutting her eyes to Zach.

Danny looked at Zachary, seemed to see him for the first time, pointed his finger at him, said, "You!" and then he was off.

Ricki glanced at Zachary as Danny went lamenting on. His head was down, and he appeared to be studying the small span of floor between his shoes. She bent over a little, studying that area, vaguely wondering if maybe there was a bug down there, then realized Zachary was simply playing hangdog.

She glanced back at Danny, whose eyes had gone to the same area, she was sure, wondering what the both of them were looking at, but that didn't stop his tirade. He went back and forth, Zachary to Ricki, Ricki to Zachary. They both studied the same span of floor, waiting him out.

Danny finally wound down, still pacing back and forth in front of them, catching his breath. Zachary and Ricki exchanged glances, then eyes went back to the floor.

Danny stopped, approached them, and said, "Zachary, I want to talk to your mother alone. Go to your room."

"Yes, sir," Zach said, looking relieved, taking off. *Traitor,* Ricki mentally hurled at this one.

She stole a glance at Danny, who still looked mad.

As appeasingly as she could, Ricki said, "Okay, Danny, I should have thought this out more carefully, I admit that, and I apologize for involving Zachary and then giving the film to that reporter. But he did preface it, you know, saying we were filming the store committing the violation."

He didn't look like he was buying it. So, she deemed it in her best interests to go on the offensive.

"Okay, so you're mad, but why are you so angry with us, Danny? Could it be maybe this might reflect negatively on the almighty campaign to get Dan England elected as grand poopah or whatever the hell you're running for? Huh? Well, if that's where the anger lies then you are out of order, bucko!"

His face got red, his eyes bugged out—in general, he looked ready to explode.

"Just a thought," Ricki said, shrugging her shoulders.

121

"You are so full of shit!" he hurled at her.

"Hey, Danny, I don't have to take this crap from you, you know. So I would advise you to can it, mister!"

"Mister? Did you call me mister?" he roared, face even redder.

Ricki wisely did not reply.

"You listen to me, Cherokee. You involved our son in a crime, and I have the right to say anything and everything I want to say to you about that, you got me? And you will stand there and listen to . . ."

"I don't have to . . ."

"Shut up!" he yelled, overriding her.

"You shut up!" she yelled right back.

They stared at each other, breathing heavily.

He really looked furious.

"Maybe you ought to come back when you're not so mad," Ricki said, trying to appease him.

"Maybe you ought to just shut that friggin' mouth of yours, Cherokee," he snarled.

"Okay," she said, giving him a mock smile.

He glared. She quit smiling.

He paced some more.

Ricki watched.

He finally gave one of his life-is-so-burdensome sighs, came up to her, studied her face for awhile, then said, his voice low, "Keep our son out of whatever the fuck you and that WAR group are involved with, you got me?" pointing his finger at her.

Well, that finger made her mad, but she tried to control her temper. "Didn't your mother teach you pointing is rude, Danny?" she asked caustically.

He bristled. She pointed her finger at him. *Well, like gets like, okay?*

"Listen, Danny, I have apologized to you for involving Zachary. I won't do it again, okay? But don't come in here, treating me like a child, telling me I can and can't do this . . ."

"I am not treating you like a child," he said, voice tight.

"Well, that is the way I perceive it," Ricki snipped. "I concede, okay? I was wrong, okay? Well, about involving Zachary. Not about proving what the store is doing and continues to do."

"Says you."

"Says the owner. She stood right there, grinned at me, and told me to prove it."

He rolled his eyes.

"And whether you want to believe it or not, what I do, what my group does, is for the betterment of our community, and through that, helps your campaign, you know. After all, look at all the free publicity you get."

"Leave the campaign out of it," he snapped.

"Well, it's true. Come on, face it: I've done more for your campaign than anyone," Ricki said smugly.

He got that look again. *Uh-oh.*

"Well, okay, maybe some of it hasn't been so great, but most of it has."

"I said leave the friggin' campaign out of it!" he snapped at her.

"You brought it up the first time!" she yelled at him.

His eyes bugged out again. *Damn,* she thought.

"Okay, we'll drop the dang campaign," Ricki said.

A staring match ensued.

This time Ricki blinked. *Jeez, isn't this guy ever going to calm down?*

Danny stood watching her some more, then finally came up to her and said, his voice low, "I want your promise you won't involve our son in anything else, Cherokee. I understand I have no control over you, over what you do or say, but I do my son. So, promise me no more involving Zachary."

Ricki gave him a benign smile and said, "Sure. No problem."

He looked relieved. She felt relieved.

He frowned again. *Uh-oh.* "What'd you do with the stuff?" he asked.

"What stuff?"

He rolled his eyes.

"Oh, you mean the purchases Zach made? Charlie has those. She's keeping them as evidence, in case we need them." Looking into his eyes, she said, "Lord help, Danny, I am not so stupid I'd bring that stuff home with Zachary and Matthew here. For Pete's sake, give me a break, why don't you."

"Okay," he said, nodding his head as if to say, *well, that's taken care of.* Then, "I'm going to go talk to Zach," heading out of the kitchen.

"Whew!" Ricki said loudly after he had departed.

The phone rang. It was Charlie. "Well, what are we gonna do now?" she asked.

Hmmm, Ricki thought, looking toward the stairs, just in case Danny was coming back down and might hear any strategic planning on their part.

"You got any ideas?" she whispered.

"How about doing something vigilante?" Charlie said.

Oh, dang.

"Such as?" Ricki asked carefully.

"Stuff that tape up her rear, for one," Charlie clipped.

123

Ricki laughed.

"I'm serious, Ricki."

"I knew you were."

"You gonna let her get by with outright lying like she has?" Charlie asked.

Well, that got Ricki's dander up. The woman did blatantly lie. No one should get by with that.

"No way," she said firmly.

"All right!"

Someone knocked on the back door. "Somebody's at the door, Charlie, I'll call you back," she said, hanging up before she could reply.

It was Sam.

"Samson!" Ricki said brightly, glancing behind her, aware Danny was still there.

He gave her that lazy smile. Oh, shoot, there she went. She was grinning like a maniac when he got through with her mouth.

"Saw your demonstration on TV," he drawled, following her into the kitchen.

"Yeah?" Ricki asked, giving a grimace more than a smile.

"Didn't do you much good."

Ricki shrugged.

"Where's the tape?"

"The reporter has it." She thought a minute. "Can't y'all use that tape as evidence or something?" she asked.

"Well, the way I see it, the owner could possibly end up paying a fine for what the clerk did, but as you heard, Ricki, she's claiming no responsibility whatsoever. In fact, she seems to think she's exonerated herself by firing the clerk."

"Has she?"

Sam shrugged. "I'm no lawyer. It would have helped if she had been the one on tape."

Ricki fumed. "Dangit, Charlie saw her selling beer to a minor. She as much as admitted it to me, off camera."

"Well, unless you can get a witness to testify the owner actually sold him beer, some sort of evidence in that regard, you can't actually prove anything against her."

"Shoot!" Ricki said.

"And seeing as how y'all made such a big production of the whole thing, she would have to be pretty durn stupid to turn right around and do it again."

"Well, pooh!" Ricki said. She looked at him. "I want to see her put out of business, Sam. She has no business corrupting our children the way she does and getting by with it!"

"I agree."

"Can't y'all at least put your own decoy in there, try to get her yourself?"

"Maybe."

"But?"

"That's awfully expensive, sending in people undercover, trying to catch her, when we could be out going after the more hardened criminals," Sam said, noncommittally.

Well, fine, we'll just get her ourselves, Ricki thought, then shrugged, deciding to drop the subject, stepped into his arms and said, "What about me, you consider me one of your hardened criminals, Sam?" teasingly.

"You're criminal, all right," he said, putting his mouth on hers.

"You gonna come after me?" she whispered.

He frowned. "Is there a sexual pun in that question or what?" he asked. Ricki laughed.

Which was interrupted by Danny stomping down the stairs. Sam and Ricki both turned and looked toward the entranceway, through which Danny stepped, seeming startled at seeing Sam there, much less his ex-wife in his arms.

He and Sam gave each other grudging nods. "Ricki, you care to walk outside with me?" Danny asked, his voice tight.

"Sure, Danny," she said, brightly, making a face at Sam.

Danny was silent all the way to the car, then stopped before opening the door, giving Ricki a look she couldn't decipher.

"What?" she asked.

"You and that Sam character . . ."

"Danny, his last name is Arnold, not character."

" . . .you getting serious or what?" he continued, ignoring her.

"Just enjoying each other," Ricki answered snippily.

"I see," he said, giving her a hard look, nodding. "Well, if I recall right, Ricki, you once upon a time seemed to enjoy me." His voice was bitter.

Ricki looked him in the eye, replied, "I still do, Danny, don't you know that?" turned on her heel and went back into the house, to Sam.

CHAPTER 12

"SOMEBODY HELP ME 'CAUSE THE BUG BIT ME"

The vigilante group was in a quandary about what to do concerning the storeowner. Charlie wanted them to put on their little black suits with their little black hoods and go pay that woman a visit she'd never forget. Melanie and Ricki both told her they needed to try other avenues first.

"Like what?" Charlie asked.

Ricki had no idea.

Charlie pointed out rather strongly that this time, she would not partake of anything through the justice system, seeing as how WAR's class action suit with the gentleman's club was still ongoing and they had not as of yet been inside a courtroom and, according to Tommy, were still months away.

Ricki agreed.

So, they decided to go on protesting, which proved ineffectual. Ricki realized they couldn't be there 24 hours of every day, as the owner had so rightly pointed out.

So, they canvassed the houses around the store, talking to each teenager they came across, trying to find just one witness who would testify the owner had sold them beer, cigarettes, or pornography. The innocent ones, of course, couldn't. The ones who looked guilty refused. And why shouldn't they, Ricki thought. She was sure they continued to make the illegal purchases, as long as WAR wasn't around.

Of course, Charlie and Ricki and most of WAR knew they couldn't go back into the store, seeing as how they had been so public with the demonstrating. The owner knew their faces well by now. Besides which, they were all sure she'd be hyper-vigilant concerning any large totes, which might appear suspicious, like maybe carrying a video recorder inside.

Charlie and Ricki finally decided to mount their own private campaign against this lady and her little business establishment. They spent all of one day painting signs, and that night, when it was dark and no one was around, put on their black sweatshirts, black jeans, black pointed hoods and planted those signs all over the parking lot and along the front of the building, warning anyone and everyone that came near that this store illegally sold alcohol, tobacco, and pornography to minors. They decided not to include

Melanie since it seemed lately all she wanted to do was question their real reasons for engaging in vigilantism. She, for some unfathomable reason to them, had decided Charlie and Ricki were only in it for the excitement. They kept telling each other Melanie was so wrong. Maybe they should have listened to her.

Ricki's and Charlie's little foray into enemy territory made the news the very next day. Ricki didn't know what it was about showing it on television, but instead of looking like a lot of signs being tacked here and there, it appeared somebody had done a good bit of vandalizing. She called Charlie and asked her if she had seen the film. She said, "That ain't all."

Uh-oh, Ricki thought, then, "What?" she asked with trepidation.

"I just got off the phone with my sister, you know, the police dispatcher," Charlie said, her voice low. "Seems there's a witness, says they saw two figures dressed all in black, wearing these pointy hoods, doing all that damage."

"But there's no damage really!" Ricki half-shouted into the phone. "Just a bunch of signs. Shoot, Charlie, that TV report made it look like vandalism."

"Tell me about it." Then, "It gets worse."

"What?" Ricki moaned.

"The owner's blaming us, told the police WAR threatened her we were going to put her out of business."

"She lies like a dog!" Ricki expelled.

"To quote her, prove it," Charlie snarled.

"Well, what are we gonna do?" Ricki whined.

"Beats me!"

"How profound!" Ricki said snidely.

"Hey, Ricki, you gonna get bitchy, I'll talk to you later," Charlie said, hanging up.

"Well, fuck you very much!" Ricki yelled at the phone.

Danny called. Without any preambles, any amenities whatsoever, he said, "You by any chance got a black, pointed hood in that closet of yours, Ricki?"

"A what?" she asked, trying for innocent.

"You heard me."

"What do you need a black, pointed hood for, Danny?"

He sighed heavily. "There something you want to tell me?" he asked, his voice low.

Ricki thought a moment. "I don't think so," she replied, forcing her voice to sound bright.

"I would advise you, Cherokee, you got a black, pointed hood laying around somewhere, go burn it."

"Well, shoot, Danny, what would I be doing with a black, pointed hood?" she asked him, quickly determining she better get rid of that thing, like now.

"I never thought for one minute you'd be the sort of person that would resort to vandalizing a place of business!" he said, his voice angry.

"Vandalizing? What are you talking about?"

"I'm talking about that convenience store we recently discussed, the one that got vandalized last night. I saw the news, Cherokee, and find it awful coincidental you're picketing the place one day, it's vandalized the next."

"You accusing me of vandalizing, Danny?" she shouted at him.

"I'm asking you, Cherokee, since you won't tell me. I did give you the chance to tell me."

"Hey, bucko, I do not vandalize, you got that? Now, if you had asked me did I maybe go tack up a bunch of signs, that would have been a different matter, but I did not vandalize!"

Oh, shoot, she thought, grimacing, realizing she had just spilled the beans.

He paused, thinking the same thing, Ricki was sure.

"Jesus Christ, Ricki," he moaned.

She rolled her eyes.

"Uh, Danny, I have to go, there's something I gotta do like yesterday," she said, hanging up the phone, running out to the car, grabbing her hood, going into the garage, getting a shovel, then running into the field, burying the hood underneath a maple tree, telling herself this was the last of it, she wasn't going vigilante anymore, no matter what Charlie said.

When she got back to the house, all dirty and sweaty from her laborious feat, Samuel was standing in the driveway, waiting.

"Sam!" Ricki said, giving him a bright smile.

He raised his eyebrows.

"Hey, I do not vandalize!" she said, cutting him off at the pass.

"How come you're so dirty?" he asked, giving her the look-over.

"I've been working in the field," she replied, giving him a challenging stare. Well, it was true.

He sighed. *Dang,* Ricki was beginning to hate all these sighs she kept getting from people.

"Ricki, I need to talk to you," he said, his voice low.

She nodded. "About the store, right?"

"Right."

"Hey, Sam, I will repeat, I am not into vandalizing anything, okay?"

"Did I accuse you?"

"Well, no, but Danny sure has."

"Have you seen it?"

"Only on TV."

"Somebody spray painted graffiti all over that store, Ricki, painted the windows black, threw a brick through one."

"You're shitting me!" she said, shocked.

"Now, I've been thinking about this," Sam said, his voice mild. "It's real obvious the handwritings on the signs are different from the handwriting on the building. Not to mention whoever did the graffiti can't spell worth a flip. Makes me wonder if actually two different incidents didn't occur last night."

Ricki smiled widely. "You are one hell of a detective, Mr. Arnold," she said, as reverently as she could.

"I've been wondering if maybe the guy who reported seeing the black hooded figures didn't figure out once they had left he could get in a little vandalizing of his own, seeing as he had two others he could blame it on."

"Hey!" Ricki said, this time feeling real reverence.

He nodded.

"You talked to him yet?" she asked.

"On my way," Sam said, giving her a look. Then opening his car door, he turned back and said, "You know, Ricki, whoever that was dressed up in their little black outfits, little black hoods, ought to be more careful next time."

"Fer sure," she agreed.

"They also might want to consider getting rid of those outfits. Might behoove them to."

"Yeah, I'd think so," she said.

He studied her face, nodded, climbed in, and left.

Damn, why am I so dang transparent to everybody on this earth? Ricki wondered despondently, going into the house to shower.

While therein, she was thinking she had done the right thing, burying that durn hood. *But what about the black jeans and sweatshirt?* her inner voice sneered.

Okay, she reasoned, *a lot of people wear black jeans. But what about black sweatshirts? Well, yeah, that too. But how many people actually own both black jeans and a black sweatshirt?* Okay, she'd just get rid of the black sweatshirt, seeing as how the jeans fit her so well and, besides, the shirt was the cheaper of the two.

Ricki leaned her head against the tile, dreading the thought of going back out into that field, digging another hole. It hadn't rained in awhile and that ground was hard as rock.

Wait a minute! She'd just dye the thing. Well, no, it was black, that'd be too hard to do. Okay, she'd bleach it, she thought as she dried off, got dressed, and headed for the laundry room off the kitchen.

Ricki put the shirt into the washer, poured about two cups of liquid bleach on top and started it up, thinking, *that takes care of that.*

While the bleach was doing its thing, she dialed Charlie's number and when she answered, said, "Hey, Charlie, I resign as of now, you got that? I am out of this vigilante crap. One ex-husband, not to mention one present lover qua detective has already identified me. And I am calling to pass on the advice as passed on to me: get rid of anything black you might happen to have in that closet of yours, especially anything pointed," then hung up before she could answer.

She next dialed Melanie, asking her if she had a good alibi for the previous night, advising her she might want to consider getting rid of her black hood.

"I just knew that was you!" she yelled at Ricki.

"Now, I'm not saying it was and I'm not saying it wasn't," Ricki offered.

Melanie, who hardly ever cussed, let loose with the likes of which Ricki had never heard before from her.

She stared at the receiver a minute, then putting it to her mouth, shouted "I can't hear you!" into the phone, hanging up on her.

When the washer stopped, Ricki pulled the shirt out, held it up to observe her handiwork. *Jeez, it looks awful splotchy,* she thought, then decided that must be from irregular water absorption. She threw the shirt into the dryer, turned it on, and stood there thinking about that black hood.

She could imagine a whole bevy of police officers invading her home, in search of that stupid thing. She could see them tearing the house apart, going through her bedroom, her lingerie drawer, and grew panicked, wondering if she had anything holey in there, making a mental note to check that out like real soon. She could see those officers stretched out along the field, inspecting the earth for signs of any recent diggings.

Well, forget the panties, holey or not; I have to get out there, make sure that grave doesn't look fresh! Ricki thought, heading out.

She walked around, thinking it did look pretty recent to her. She pondered a moment, finally going and chasing her horse Boomer down, then walking him over that filled-in hole at least a thousand times, stomping the earth down, making it look trampled.

When they finished, Ricki stood back and observed their handiwork. Now it looked like someone had tried to pack the earth down in this one particular spot. *Shit!* she thought, leading Boomer around the tree about another thousand times, trying to make it look like this was his hanging-out spot.

The whole time she led that stupid horse around that stupid tree, he was using her back and side and front as a scratching post for his muzzle, covering her with dust and dirt and who knows what else.

By the time Ricki stopped, she was wiping sweat from her brow as she studied the earth, which now looked trampled but not just in one area. She backed off about fifty feet and looked again. Seemed to kind of blend in from there.

Okay! she thought, heading back to the house. The dryer rang its little bell just as she came into the mud room, so she went on through into the laundry room, noticing her dirty, sweaty attire.

Since Zachary wasn't due home for another three hours or so, Ricki stripped down in the laundry room, throwing her dirty clothes in the washer, thinking she'd just wear the sweatshirt upstairs, then take another shower.

After she washed the dirt from her hands, arms, and face, Ricki pulled the shirt out and looked it over before she put it on, making sure there were no black spots thereon.

It looked like some sort of animal skin, going from dark gray to almost white. Okay, maybe an animal with the mange. Or maybe like somebody had tried to do one serious bleach job on a black sweatshirt. *Dang, can't I do anything right?* Ricki asked herself, then shrugged, thinking she'd worry about getting rid of this thing after she got upstairs and put some clothes on.

She slipped it over her head, glad it came down to mid-thigh and not waist, seeing as she had nothing on beneath, and started into the kitchen, heading for the stairs, when who should come barreling through the door but the big Dan, scaring the very dickens out of her.

"Danny!" Ricki squealed.

He stopped short, glaring.

"You scared me to death," she said, patting her chest.

He scowled at her, took the time to look her sweatshirt over, and then inquired, "What the hell happened to your shirt?"

Ricki looked down as if seeing it for the first time. "What do you mean?" she asked innocently. "This is the way I bought it."

He looked at it, then her, then back to the shirt.

"You don't like it?" she asked.

He frowned widely.

Shoot.

"How come you're wearing a sweatshirt on such a hot day?" he asked, his look turning suspicious.

Ricki gave him this long spiel about how she'd been out in the field with Boom-Boom, and you know how he likes to use me as a scratching post, Danny, so I took my clothes off downstairs and put this on to wear upstairs.

He kept giving that shirt these looks, so meaning to sidetrack him, Ricki went to the refrigerator, opened it, bent over just far enough to make him wonder what exactly she had on underneath that thing, and while in that position, asked over her shoulder, "You want something to drink, Danny?"

"Uh, no," he said, and when she straightened up and looked back, he glanced quickly away.

She smiled to herself, pulled out a carton of orange juice, went to the cabinet, opened the door, had to reach way up to get the particular glass she wanted to drink from, showing Danny just a fraction more skin this time, turned back to him, gave him a smile and said, "You sure?"

He scowled copiously. Ricki turned back around and said as she reached up on tiptoe again, this time flashing him for just a second, "Well, I'll get you a glass in case you change your mind."

She got one, came back, and poured juice into both glasses. He watched all the while, not saying a thing.

"Why don't you have a seat?" she asked politely.

He plopped onto one of the high stools at the breakfast bar.

Their eyes met.

"You going to tell me about it or not?" he asked.

"About what?" Ricki asked, giving him a guiltless look.

"Did you or did you not just admit to me over the phone, Cherokee, that you were involved with . . ."

"Hey, I will repeat for the last time, Buster Brown, I do not vandalize, okay?"

"You said . . ."

"I said I did not vandalize, Danny, so stop accusing me of it."

"Hey, I'm not accusing you of anything, I just want you to . . ."

"Well, then, case closed," Ricki snapped, cutting him off.

"Cherokee," he said, giving her a look.

She stepped close to him, stared him in the eye, and said, "You think I'd do something like that, Danny? You think I'd go spray graffiti all over a

133

building, throw a brick through the window? Huh? You telling me you think I'd get down to that kind of level?"

He didn't look so sure.

Ricki gave him an intense stare, leaning into him, and said, "Look me in the eye, Danion England, and tell me you think I would commit that sort of a criminal act."

They had a short staring match, which he broke by glancing away, then back. "Well, no," he admitted, "but I didn't think you'd do some of the other things you've . . ."

"We're talking vandalizing, Danny, harming property, not possibly harming myself."

They stared at each other for about ten seconds. He finally said, somewhat defeatedly, "No, Ricki, I don't think you'd do something like that."

"Thank you," she said in a polite way, straightening up. "Now, while we're on the subject, let's get something straight, something I thought you were aware of, and that is that I do not lie to you." Then she remembered she had just lied to him about the shirt, but that was a small matter that didn't count, so she revised, "About important things. You have something you want to ask me, ask me. Don't accuse me; don't come storming in here asking me if I have anything I want to tell you. 'Cause half the time, I don't know what the hell you're talking about."

He chewed on that one for a minute, then said, "Okay, let's talk about the signs."

She told him what Charlie and she had done, told him they had simply put signs on the property, that was all, then advised him of Sam's theory on what had happened.

When she finished, he sat there nodding for a few seconds, then surprised her by saying, "So did you mean what you said the other night?"

"Huh?"

"The last time I was here."

Ricki seemed to ponder. She knew what he meant. "Gee, Danny, I've slept since then, refresh my memory," she finally said.

He gave her another one of his suspicious stares. She just looked back innocently. "About still enjoying me, Cherokee," he finally replied, irritably.

Ricki stepped between his legs, resting her hands on his upper thighs, looked him in the eye, and said, "Didn't I just tell you that I don't lie to you, Danny?"

He nodded. "Well, which would it be, then, you enjoy me more than that Sam guy or less?" he asked, looking embarrassed.

Ricki cocked her head, gave him a mischievous grin, and answered, "More or less."

He surprised her, throwing his head back, having a good laugh. She stood there, grinning.

He put his hands on her legs, slid them up, and cupped her bottom. She tried not to shiver.

"You enjoy that?" he asked, his voice husky, his eyes turning that smoky color, telling her he was feeling passionate.

"You know I do," she said, giving him a challenging stare.

He brought his hands around to the front, to her breasts, rubbed each thumb over a nipple. She let out a low moan. "How about that?" he whispered

"Yes," she sighed.

He pulled the sweatshirt up, then nuzzled his head under and put his mouth to her breasts, eventually pulling the sweatshirt off, his mouth following its trail. He drew her right against him, then onto her knees on the stool, straddling him, his mouth at her breasts again. "Oh, Danny," she murmured, cradling his head with her arms, kissing his hair. She was breathing heavy by the time he released her, stood, and started hastily undoing his tie, then unbuttoning his shirt.

Ricki slid off the bar, put her hands on his belt, undid it, then his pants, pulled them down, along with his underwear, knelt before him, and paid a little homage.

They thrashed around on that floor for a good while, doing some vocalizing to go along with their physical juxtaposing, and finally, sated, lay there, entwined, sweating, panting, drifting. They looked at each other, grinned like idiots.

You really love him, Ricki's inner voice whispered. *Well, of course I love him,* she answered back. *No, you're in love with him,* that stupid voice insisted. *There's a difference, and you know it.* Ricki felt like she'd just been buried under a pile of bricks. She stopped grinning, feeling kind of sick, couldn't seem to catch her breath.

Danny's look changed to one of concern. "Ricki, you okay?" he asked, putting his warm hand to her face.

Somebody startled the both of them by pounding on the back door.

"Oh, shoot, it's probably the cops," Ricki whined.

Danny sat up.

"Go upstairs, get dressed while I see who's here," she whispered.

As Danny ran around, gathering his clothes. Ricki found the sweatshirt, pulled it over her head, hurriedly got a paper towel and mopped body fluids off the floor, then went to the door, and seeing Danny's naked butt heading up the back stairs, opened it, her eyes widening to see Sam standing there.

"Sam!" she said brightly, trying to breathe normally, trying to act glad to see him.

His eyes traveled over her perspiring face, down her body. "How come you're sweating when you're inside?" he asked.

Uh-oh.

"Well, I just got in, and it's as hot as Hades out there for this time of year," Ricki said, looking away.

He stepped in, giving her the look-over.

"What happened to your shirt?"

"My shirt?" she asked, looking down. "I bought it like this."

He gave her one of Danny's suspicious looks.

"Don't you like it?" she asked.

He ignored that, asking, "How come you're wearing a sweatshirt on such a hot day?"

So Ricki went through the same song and dance with Samuel she had with Danny.

"That Dan's car outside?" Sam asked.

Yikes.

"Uh, yeah."

He gave her a questioning look.

"Danny's looking for some sort of paper he thinks he left here," she said, lamely.

She felt something hot and sticky traveling down her leg. *Oh, shoot,* she thought, realizing she was leaking, *I should have thought about this before I opened the dang door.*

Ricki crossed her legs, stopping the progress of the slide.

Sam frowned at her and said, "How come you're standing like that?"

"Oh, well I'm just glad to see you," she teased.

"You look like a kid needs to go to the bathroom," he said, grinning.

Ricki smiled with relief. "Yeah, real bad. Uh, would you excuse me a minute, Sam?" she asked, heading into the bathroom off the laundry room, doing a quick cleanup with toilet paper, stopping by the washer on her way back in, digging her panties out, putting them on, going back into the kitchen.

When she came back in, Danny was coming down the stairs. "Hey, Danny, did you find what you were looking for?" she asked before he could say anything.

He looked at Sam, then her, blinked, and said, "Naw, I must have left that on the houseboat."

"Oh, well," Ricki said, glancing at Sam, giving him a little smile.

Danny came toward them, his face still red and sweaty-looking, his hair damp around the forehead and nape of his neck, a self-satisfied smirk on his face, looking like a guy who had just indulged in one major fuck, gave Sam a polite nod, then Ricki as she opened the door for him.

He stepped through, then stopped, turning to her, reached around, slid his hand up beneath the sweatshirt, felt the panties, gave her butt a friendly pat, kissed her on the lips, answered her fierce scowl with a wide grin, and said, "I enjoyed it, babe," before heading out.

Ricki slammed the door. Hard.

Sam's eyes were narrowed. "Enjoyed what?" he snapped.

Ricki rolled her eyes. "He's just playing with you, Sam, trying to make you jealous. Honest." Then seeing his look, "Hey, I had just come in when you got here. I'd been out in the field, remember? You can see how sweaty I am!" *Uh-oh,* she thought, inwardly grimacing, *that last remark could get me in a lot of trouble.*

He studied her, looking suspicious. *Dang, I wish I'd left those panties off,* Ricki thought, thinking this guy was even easier than Danny to sidetrack. Well, no, that wasn't such a great idea, seeing as how Danny had left a deposit as evidence he had been there first.

Sam finally nodded, as if believing her, and said, "I just came by to tell you what's been happening."

Whew!

Ricki opened the door, looked outside, then back at Sam. "Where's the cavalry?" she teased, giving him a mock grin.

He smiled back. "Headed 'em off at the pass," he drawled.

"Thank the good Lord, and you," Ricki said, meaning it.

Sam told her that he had interviewed the guy who had reported seeing the two dark figures, a teenager of about 17, and after a little persuasion (Ricki didn't ask what kind), he had admitted that all he had seen the figures doing was planting signs all over the property, and yes, he had been the one to do the vandalizing.

Sam added it hadn't hurt that he had found a garage full of spray paint cans, some of which matched the colors on the outside of the store.

"So what about the owner?" Ricki asked, thankful for a friend like Sam.

"I think she's disappointed your group wasn't involved with doing all that damage. Still insists you-all put the signs there."

Ricki didn't say anything, wondering if that would be considered actually committing a crime, placing signs around an establishment.

They looked at each other.

Don't ask me, she prayed.

"You look real cute, all sweaty like that," Sam said, segueing.

She blinked in surprise.

"I've got some free time," he encouraged.

Rut-ro.

He pulled her toward him. She put her hands on his chest, stopping progress, wondering if he could, like, smell Danny on her.

"Uh, Sam, I'm all sweaty and dirty, let me shower first," Ricki said, pushing away.

"Just to get all sweaty and dirty again?" he teased.

She grimaced, said, "Yeah, but I smell like a horse."

"I like the way you smell, horsey or otherwise," he muttered, his voice low.

"I'll be through in two shakes of a lamb's tail," Ricki promised, moving away, heading for the stairs.

She showered quickly, growing excited at the fact that never in her life had she experienced two different lovers within one day.

Sam was already undressed and waiting for her when she got out. Ricki made sure she locked the bedroom door, knowing Danny's tendency to just come on in, then joined Sam on the bed.

He was playful at first, then seemed to grow serious, Ricki guessed, wondering why she wasn't as energetic as usual. Or maybe why she couldn't climax. He changed positions constantly, placing her here or there, and she docilely let him. *I must be more tired than I thought,* she determined, not really able to get involved with Sam in lovemaking as she normally would. *Or maybe you're just feeling sated from Danny,* her inner voice sneered. *Shut up,* she commanded it.

He finally lay her across two pillows and entered from behind, and when she felt her body responding, not realizing it, she moaned, "Oh, Danny," into the sheet.

He froze.

Shit! Ricki screamed at herself.

"What'd you say?" he asked.

She sighed.

"Did you say Danny?" he demanded, his voice pressured.

Ricki looked back over her shoulder at him. "Danny? No, Sam, I said, 'oh, daaang,' " drawing the word out, trying to make it sound like Danny. "Whatever made you think I said Danny?"

He looked at her for a long time. She tried to look back as innocent as could be. Which was kind of hard, to tell you the truth, the position she was in.

Intending to encourage things along, she said, "Why'd you have to stop for, Sammy, I was real close to going off."

He shook his head a little, then mumbled, "I guess I misunderstood," before getting back to business.

Ricki sighed with relief, then trying to take his mind off what had occurred, began moaning and moving around a lot, trying to get into it.

He turned her back over, and as she lay there, watching his beautiful sweaty face above her, feeling that magnificent body in her, the thought occurred to her that she would never love this man, not like she loved Danny. Ricki felt herself grow rigid with this observation. He stopped, gave her a funny look.

"I kind of got a twitch," she apologized.

He grimaced more than smiled and quickened his pattern, thrusting into her harder.

I wish Danny was here, Ricki thought, then closed her eyes, feeling tears come. *I want Danny,* she thought, then told herself to stop this nonsense. She didn't have Danny; she had Sam. *And look at him, he's gorgeous, a great lover . . .but he's not Danny!* her inner voice screamed at her.

Ricki squelched it. For the time being.

CHAPTER 13

"I MAY USE A LITTLE MUSCLE TO GET WHAT I NEED"

She stood before the group, a woman in her 40's, dark hair showing streaks of gray. Her face bore the marks of tortured motherhood: circles under the eyes, wrinkles on the forehead, deep lines from her nose to the outer corners of her mouth. As Ricki watched her, she could see the pain and hurt in her face, hear it in her voice.

Her son attended a high school in West Knoxville. Had been an A-B student all his academic life until this past year. Until he met up with the drug dealer that stood on the outskirts of the school grounds, enticing the kids with free samples, getting them hooked, then selling his wares to them.

Her son had been a school jock till he met up with this piece of trash. Now her son didn't study anymore, didn't play sports anymore, rarely went to school anymore, didn't do anything anymore except visit this dealer and stay stoned all day. She started crying.

"Exactly what school is it and what does this guy look like?" Ricki asked, glancing at Charlie, who nodded at her.

She told them.

The group discussed what WAR could do against this dealer. They finally decided they'd just pay him a visit as a group, placards in one hand, cameras in the other, video and otherwise, get a little footage of his action, try to intimidate him, try to force him away from this school. Ricki also made a mental note to call Sam, give him this info, and see if he couldn't do anything about it.

About ten people showed up for the planned demonstration against the dealer. They didn't have any trouble locating him and simply set up their march around him. He watched with an amused expression, not seeming too irritated by their presence. But as the afternoon wore on and no one showed up to buy any of his wares, he grew angry, finally threatening to call the police if they didn't get out of there.

"I've got a cell phone you can use," Ricki offered.

He made a vulgar motion involving one hand and one extended finger.

After about another half-hour, he sullenly left, offering the group a whole list of various sexual activities they could do with their signs and cameras.

The next day, the minute he saw them, he was out of there.

The third day, he wasn't there. *Well, that worked,* they thought, and Ricki climbed back in her Suzuki, feeling smug, then slammed on the brakes a couple of blocks away when she saw he had set up shop on another corner.

Everyone was gone by then, leaving just her. She stopped the car, climbed out, grabbing her video camera, and stayed back, filming as what looked to be a student approached. As they stood there, apparently dickering, Ricki got closer with the camera. The minute the student saw her, he took off. Ricki got that on film, then turned to the dealer, who was stomping toward her, and before she knew it, he had jerked the camcorder out of her hand, opened it, removed the tape, and dangled it in her face, offering suggestions of what she could do with it, calling her some pretty terrible names as she jerked the camcorder out of his hands; but hey, Ricki wasn't offended. She knew from whence the source came.

When he saw her go back to the car and place another tape inside the camera, he left quickly, offering more expletives. *Jeez,* Ricki thought, listening to him. This wasn't all for naught, she was learning some really good cuss words.

The rest of the week, several members of WAR drove around the school a few times a day, trying to find this guy, but he was nowhere to be seen. Ricki felt proud that they had handled this situation in a mature, passive, successful way without having to resort to vigilantism.

Should have known.

A couple of weeks later, the woman was back, this time telling WAR the dealer had set up shop in an apartment which was a couple of blocks from the school. She found this out by following her son there over the weekend.

Dang, Ricki thought, glancing at Charlie, who was looking at her. She raised her eyebrows. Ricki nodded her head slightly, then looked at Melanie, who rolled her eyes.

After the WAR meeting, the three vigilantes conducted another, private one.

"Did you ever talk to Sam about this guy?" Charlie asked Ricki.

"Yeah. He said since it was inside the city limits, it would fall under the jurisdiction of the police department, so he was going to pass the information on to them."

"And?"

"All he's told me to date is they've got him under surveillance. Although, to tell you the truth, the times we were surveilling I didn't notice anybody else doing the same, did you?"

Charlie and Melanie shook their heads.

"I guess it's up to us," Ricki said.

Charlie grinned. Melanie sighed.

They quickly decided they'd pay that nasty ole drug dealer a visit, donned in black attire, and convince him it would be in his best interests to get the hell out of Dodge. And while there, confiscate any drugs he might have along with the names of the slimebuckets he got his wares from, then turn them over to the police. Anonymously, of course.

"Now, listen," Charlie said, giving her cohorts an intent look. "This is a different type of person than we've been dealing with, so we're going to have to go in there prepared."

"What do you mean?" Melanie asked.

"Well, he's into drugs," Charlie explained. "You can count on this guy having guns, weapons to defend himself."

Melanie and Ricki looked at each other.

"So, I'm just warning you, I'm taking mine," Charlie said dramatically.

Ricki stared at her. "Your what?"

"My gun."

"Well, what about us?" Ricki asked. "I mean, it's not fair you get to hold a gun on the guy, keep him from shooting you, but what about us? We just supposed to stand there, say, 'here, we're not armed, aim at us'?"

"You do what you feel you gotta do," Charlie replied, shrugging.

Ricki thought about the gun Danny had bought for her, the one he had put in the nightstand, over her protests, the one that had never been removed from there, but nixed that idea. She hated guns. So, she thought some more, then smiled.

"I've got an idea," she said, getting up and leaving the room.

She came back a few minutes later, carrying a pistol in each hand. Well, a toy cap pistol.

She handed one to Melanie, showed the other to Charlie. They had belonged to Zach years ago and Ricki never liked them because she thought they looked so authentic.

Charlie held it up, turning it this way and that. "It's a toy," Ricki said.

"I know that," she replied snippily.

"Well, I think it looks real," Ricki offered.

Charlie slowly nodded. "Maybe from a distance. Okay, you two use these, just don't put them where he can get a good look at 'em."

"Great!" Ricki said, grinning, hefting her gun, then pointing it at the wall, mock-shooting that mean ole druggie. Charlie and Melanie both rolled their eyes.

Several nights later, they were parked two blocks over and one block down from the dealer's apartment, waiting for darkness to descend. As usual, they had on our black jeans, sweatshirts, and tennis shoes. Their masks were stuffed down their shirts.

Since Ricki had been with Danny, her mind wouldn't let go of her feelings for him. She sat, lost in her futile attempts at analyzing just exactly where and when and why she had fallen back in love with her ex. Charlie startled her, saying, "What's wrong with you, Rick, you're awful quiet tonight."

Ricki shrugged her shoulders noncommittally.

"How're things going with that Sam dude? You haven't said much about him lately," Charlie asked.

Ricki looked out the window, away from her. "Fine. Things are fine," she said curtly.

"But?" Charlie nudged.

Ricki could feel their expectant stares.

She sighed. "But I'm in love with Danny," she said, biting her lip, wiping at her teary eyes.

You could have heard a pin drop a mile away, that car was so quiet.

"Did she say she still loves Danny?" Melanie finally asked Charlie.

"Yep."

Ricki could feel their eyes on her, waiting.

"I guess I'm over that infatuation stage with Sam," she explained, watching a homeless man drastically weaving down the alley, a bottle clutched in one hand. "I mean, sex is still great with him, you know, but it's . . .Sam's not the one I want anymore. I want Danny," Ricki said, her voice cracking.

"Shit fire," Charlie mumbled.

"Yeah, boy," Ricki agreed.

"What the hell did you divorce the dude for, if you were gonna fall back in love with him?" Charlie snapped.

"Well, I just didn't have healthy feelings about the relationship," Ricki explained lamely.

"But you do now?"

"Yes. No. I don't know. It's just, things are different with Danny now. We actually communicate our feelings to each other, something we haven't done in years. I mean, we argue all the time, it seems, but I'm not afraid to stand up to him and he doesn't pull that withdrawal shit on me like he used to. And the sex, Lord, the sex is fabulous. Somehow we've found all that passion we used to have for each other, Charlie." Ricki turned teary eyes on her, gave her a weak smile, and said, "Go figure."

Charlie rolled her eyes.

"Well, I think it's great," Melanie said from the back.

Ricki gave her a grateful smile.

"So, how's Sam taking this?" Charlie asked.

"He doesn't know."

"You gonna tell him?"

"Why should I? I mean, Danny's marrying Stacy . . ."

"Wait a minute, just hold it. He's still engaged to that bitch, yet he's sleeping with you?"

"Well, yes," Ricki answered, her voice small.

"So, what's it gonna be, Rick, he marries her and the ex-wife becomes the mistress?"

"No," Ricki sighed. "I'm going to end it."

"Why don't you tell Danny how you feel?" Melanie asked. "I mean, apparently he still loves you, Ricki, or he wouldn't be sleeping with you, you know."

"No," Ricki said, pointedly. "I want Danny to be the one to make the decision that he really loves me and wants me. I'm not going to influence his feelings in any way. He has to comes to that conclusion on his own."

"You're so full of shit," Charlie muttered.

"Yeah, well," Ricki answered.

"So, what are you gonna do about Sam?" Charlie asked her.

Ricki shrugged. "I'm not sure." She sighed. "It's just not the same with him anymore. I guess I'm starting to see all the flaws now."

"Yeah?" Melanie asked from the back, sounding happy at this.

Ricki ignored her. "He's so possessive," she explained to Charlie. "He's jealous of Zachary and I hate that. He wants me to commit and I can't. He smothers me at times, you know? When we first met, I thought we had so much in common, but now I wonder if he wasn't just agreeing with what I like, to get whatever he wanted from me. And when we're together, we never do anything, really, except have sex. We don't talk about much except what's going on at the time. I've been doing a lot of thinking about us lately, and I think the attraction I have to Sam is his propensity to be so, well, physical."

"You mean violent?" Charlie asked.

Ricki shrugged.

"He been violent with you?" she asked, sounding mad.

145

"Well, no, not really. I mean, sometimes he gets kind of rough, you know, but he's never actually hurt me."

"You are one sick puppy, you know that?" Charlie railed.

Ricki rolled her eyes. "Shoot, Charlie, how many times you gonna tell me that?" she asked her hatefully.

"You need to get out of that relationship," Melanie advised.

"Well, that's easier said than done," Ricki defended, then to force conversation away from that topic, opened her door and said, "Come on, let's go get us a drug dealer."

They stood outside the door to the dealer's apartment, quickly donning their masks, anxiously aware they were in the open here, easily visible to anyone within the next few moments.

Charlie took out this little black leather case, opened it, and drew out what looked like two small picks. Ricki watched in awe as she worked the lock on the door and within a couple of minutes simply turned the knob and it opened.

"Where'd you learn to do that?" Ricki whispered as they went through.

Charlie motioned for her to keep her mouth shut.

They stepped into the apartment and closed the door silently behind them. All three huddled there, listening, trying to let their eyes adjust to the darkness so they could see better.

Ricki guessed Charlie determined that wasn't going to happen, because she reached out, felt along the wall, located a switch and flipped it. A lamp immediately came on, giving off a soft light, offering just enough illumination to tell them they were standing in what was apparently a sparsely furnished living room.

They simultaneously heard a low moaning noise coming from somewhere else, all six eyes going to a closed door across the room from them.

"He's got to be in there," Ricki whispered, pointing.

Charlie nodded.

They listened to louder moaning sounds.

"Dang, Charlie, sounds like he's having sex," Ricki muttered, disgustedly.

"Well, let's go see," she said, heading that way.

Ricki reached out, drew her back. "Listen, I have no desire to witness two people screwing," she whispered harshly. "Let's wait out here till he comes out."

Charlie looked at Melanie, who nodded, then back at Ricki, shrugging as if to say, don't make no difference to me.

146

After a minute or two, Charlie said, her voice low, "Why don't you two get on either side of that door? When he comes out, Mel, take your pistol and put it upside his head. Ricki, you check the bedroom, make whoever's in there join us out here."

Sounded good to Ricki. She hefted her little old cap gun out of her jeans waistband, holding it in the air, feeling just like a cop, crossed the room, and stood outside the door, listening, waiting.

After what seemed like an eternity, the low moans increased somewhat, then stopped altogether. They waited and waited and waited. *Dang, he must have gone to sleep*, Ricki thought irritably. She finally looked over at Charlie and mouthed, "What do we do?" to her.

"What?" Charlie mouthed back.

Ricki rolled her eyes and sighed heavily. She lightly tapped on the door, listened for a second, then knocked louder. When she heard the bed squeaking, she nodded at Melanie as if to say, get ready, as they heard movement on the other side of the door.

Which was opened rather quickly, startling Ricki, who jumped back a little, her movement catching his peripheral vision. He turned his head toward Ricki, and Melanie, as slick as could be, placed her cap pistol on the side of his head, and her voice low, said, "Step on out here."

As he did that, Ricki molded herself to the outer wall, then as quickly as she could, just the way they do it on TV, stepped around and into the room, going down into a crouch, making a sweeping motion with the gun, aiming it anywhere and everywhere.

A small boudoir lamp but nothing else lighted the room. Shadows were everywhere. Ricki cast her eyes from side to side, up and down. No one was standing or sitting that she could determine. She saw a pale lump on the bed, rose slowly, her gun trained on that lump, and said, "Okay, just get up, slowly."

The lump didn't move one whit.

Huh! Ricki thought, advancing toward the bed, holding the pistol in both hands as is properly shown on each and every cop show each and every week.

She approached the lump with trepidation, saying, "Just do as I say and no one will get hurt," wondering why whoever was on that bed didn't do or say anything.

Finally reached the edge, peered thereon, and wanted to laugh and throw up at the same time.

There was one of those inflatable women dolls on that bed, the kind you see in those sex catalogues.

"Oh, my God, I don't believe this!" Ricki said out loud.

"What?" Charlie called.

"He was using one of those inflatable dolls," she moaned, trying not to look at it but having a hard time of it.

Ricki turned and went back out into the room, as Charlie was saying to the dealer in Whoopi's voice, "Whatsamatta, you so hard up you can't get it up with a real, live woman?" snickering.

He glowered as fiercely as he was able to, standing there in nothing but baggy undershorts.

"Tie him up," Charlie instructed Melanie and Ricki.

"How does that thing work anyway?" Ricki asked, curious.

He turned his glare on her.

"I mean, does it feel like a real woman? Although to tell you the truth, I can't see as how something cold and rubbery could feel as good as soft, warm skin," Ricki rambled on.

"What is your problem?" Charlie snapped at her.

"What?"

"We didn't come here to discuss kinky sex," she hissed.

"Kinky?" Ricki asked. "Actually, I would think that would be perverted more than kinky." She turned to Melanie. "What do you think?" she asked.

"Just drop the damn sex thing," Charlie snarled at her.

"Well, shoot, I'm only curious. I mean, I've never met anybody that's used one of those things before and I was just wondering . . ."

"Shut up!" she yelled.

"You shut up!" Ricki yelled back at her.

"Both of you shut up!" Melanie shouted. "For Pete's sake, did you forget why we came here?" she asked, leaning toward them, pointing toward her prisoner.

Before they knew it, he grabbed Melanie's hand, the one with the gun, the one she was pointing at him with, wrenched her weapon out of her grasp, and was now standing behind her, pointing it at her head.

"Yikes!" Ricki said, forgetting for a moment that it was a toy.

"Let her go," Charlie said.

"Put your guns down first," he said, pressing the one in his hand against Melanie's temple.

"Shoot her," Ricki said.

He gave her a blank look.

"Go on, shoot her," she repeated.

"Would you just shut up?" Melanie hissed at her.

"'Cause you can't actually harm her, you shoot her," Ricki went on, "seeing as how all you've got is a toy pistol."

He stared at her for a moment, trying to determine if she was playing with him or what, slowly pulled the gun away from Melanie's head, studied it, then threw it down disgustedly.

"Now, this here is not a toy," Ricki said, holding her own gun up, lying through her teeth. "Shall I demonstrate?" she asked, pulling the hammer back, pointing it at his chest.

His face paled.

"And hers is more real than mine," Ricki said, waving her pistol in Charlie's direction. "Show him your gun," glancing at Charlie. She raised it up. *Damn, that thing looks lethal,* she thought.

Melanie wrenched out of his grasp, bent down, retrieved her play weapon, and backed away.

"Tie him up," Charlie instructed again.

Melanie tucked the gun in the waistband of her jeans, then pulled out the rope, jerked this little twerp around, and began tying his hands behind his back. He was more than cooperative, standing there docilely in nothing but his underwear, letting her bind him. *What a weenie,* Ricki thought disgustedly.

"Okay, what do you want?" he asked, starting to sweat here.

"Your source and your stash," Charlie replied.

"Your life," Ricki said, snorting.

Charlie and Melanie looked at her.

Ricki shrugged. She didn't know what it was about holding that pistol in her hand, real or not, but she could feel this change coming over her. She felt powerful, mean, bad, like she could rule the world, especially this little peon.

Melanie went into what Ricki supposed was the dining area, seeing as it contained one of those maple-colored tables and four matching chairs, pulled one of the chairs out, dragged it over, and indicated for him to sit, which he quite promptly did.

Charlie approached him, took her time studying him as they bound him to the chair, then said, "Okay, where do you keep your stuff?"

"Hey, lady, I don't know what the fuck you're talking about," he snarled at her, trying to look mean.

Now Ricki approached, feeling meaner than he looked, took her toy gun, stroked his cheek with it, and watched him recoil in fear. Felt so big and bad. "Doesn't look to me like he's real willing to cooperate," she said, her voice low. "Let me persuade him a little."

"There's no need to get violent here," Charlie admonished her, playing along.

"Come on, I won't kill him. Just shoot him somewhere not real vital. Just one shot." Ricki looked at her. "Please," she pled.

"Yeah, that's what you said last time," Charlie replied, sounding just like the good cop playing to the bad cop. "And lookit what happened, I never seen so much blood in my life."

His eyes were frantically darting from Ricki to Charlie, then back again. It was all Ricki could do to keep from laughing out loud.

"Well, it's not my fault my sights were off," she whined. "Dang, I never knew shooting somebody in the gut would make their insides just come out of their body like that, did you?" she asked, watching the weasel turn even paler. Sweat broke out on his upper lip. He let loose with a small whimper.

"Now, listen, you promised me you wouldn't get trigger happy here," Charlie chided.

"Just one shot," Ricki begged. "I've had my sights fixed. I've been target shooting. I'll get him where I aim, I swear. Come on, how about the kneecap? There won't be much blood that way. I've heard it causes excruciating pain. I want to hear him scream. I love to hear them scream!" she said orgasmically.

"Don't let her shoot me!" their vicious little drug dealer begged, looking frantically from Charlie to Melanie. Melanie made choking noses, turned around, walked away.

Ricki ignored this. "Plus that ought to put this scumbucket out of commission for awhile, not being able to walk, minus a knee at least, a leg at worst."

"Please, don't let her shoot me!" he pleaded, right on the verge of tears. "I'll give you anything you want."

Ricki ignored him. "Shit, this guy don't even deserve to live," she said, her voice growing angry deliberately. "What positive influence does he have in this world? Of what value is he? None, I tell you. What difference is one less drug dealer in this world gonna make? Huh? Nobody will even grieve for this piece of shit, you know that. Come on, let me kill him. We can find his stash. We can find his source. We don't need him telling us."

"Oh, pleeeaaaase," he wailed to the ceiling.

"All right, now, we didn't come here to commit murder," Charlie said, her voice mild. Ricki could tell she was smiling.

"I'll leave," he promised somewhat frantically. "I'll get out of Knoxville. I swear."

"Says he," Ricki snarled. "Shoot, he's just a friggin' drug dealer. You gonna take his word for it? Come on, if you're not gonna let me kill him, at least let me shoot him. I didn't come here just to talk, you know!"

"You can't let her shoot me!" he screamed.

Ricki ignored him again. "Let me have him," she pled with Charlie. "Please, just let me put one bullet in him. Just one. I'll use my silencer, I'll put the gun right up against the skin, you won't . . ."

"I'll tell you whatever you want to know," he interrupted rather rudely, sweat running down his face. "I'll give you whatever you want, just don't let her near me," turning fearful eyes upon Ricki.

Man, she felt so bad.

"We'll listen to what the man has to say," Charlie stated authoritatively.

"Shit, man, don't do that," Ricki said. "It's been awhile since I've shot anybody. I was all geared up for that and he has to go and ruin it by playing coward. Damn, can't we find anybody willing to stand up for anything?" she lamented.

Charlie didn't say anything. Ricki surmised she was laughing to herself. Melanie still had her back turned. Ricki guessed she was doing the same thing.

"I keep a book with the names of all my sources in the bedroom!" he yelled. "My stash is in there too. Please, just don't let her shoot me. Oh, God, I don't want to die."

The stupid idiot was outright sobbing now.

"Don't you have any principles?" Ricki yelled at him. "Don't you have any scruples at all? Hell, if you're gonna deal drugs, then you got to be strong here. This is your life, man; this is what keeps a roof over your head, food on the table. Don't tell her what she wants to know! Tell her to go fuck herself!"

He looked confused.

"Let me shoot him, please," Ricki begged, her voice a harsh whisper.

"In my closet, under a loose plank in the back, you'll find everything!" he cried.

"Damnation!" Ricki yelled, stalking angrily away.

Charlie went into the bedroom.

Ricki came back to him, stroked his cheek with the gun again. He whimpered, drew his head back.

"It ain't over till it's over," she whispered to him.

He started bawling like a baby.

God, how Ricki hated a crybaby. Especially if it was a man. There was nothing more revolting to her than to see some big galoot crying his eyes out over nothing. So she watched him, feeling disgust for him, pride for her. She was thinking she might just look into joining the police force when Charlie came out of the bedroom carrying several cellophane bags, some containing white powdery stuff, some what Ricki recognized to be marijuana, others different-colored pills, and a little black book.

They heard a commotion at the door, then a loud banging, followed by, "This is the police, open up."

Charlie, Melanie, and Ricki all looked at each other.

"Help me!" he screamed before Ricki could clamp her hand over his mouth.

"There's a window in the bedroom, we'll go out that way," Charlie said, taking one of the bags and stuffing it in his mouth. Leaving everything behind for the cops as evidence, they ran for all they were worth, could hear a loud banging on the door as they raised the window up, and all three climbed out, thankful his apartment was on the ground floor, thankful there weren't any police officers lounging about outside the window. They quickly took off the masks, stuffed them down their sweatshirts, and at a rather brisk pace, appearing to one and all to be three women out for a midnight walk, exited the alley, encountering two officers heading toward the back of the apartment. They kept their heads down, the better to not see them, don't you know. Ricki gave a silent prayer of thanks that it was dark out and no lights were on back there to make them discernible to anyone who might be interested. Then another prayer of thanks the officers had been too stupid to question what they were doing back there.

After they exited the alley, they ran for Charlie's car, piled in, and took off, laughing excitedly.

The next morning, the only thing Ricki was wearing was her favorite necklace, the one with the gold cross with the diamond in the center, the one Danny had had made out of the small engagement ring he had given her, before they could afford anything at all, really, the necklace she never took off.

Sam picked it up, studied it a moment, then giving her a look she couldn't decipher, asked, "Don't you ever take this thing off?"

Ricki shook her head no, wishing he'd get on with it, then to encourage him a little, nuzzled into his neck, kissing, licking, and traveling.

He stretched a little, offering more area, then said, "Remember that dealer you told me about, the one at the school in West Knoxville?"

"Uh-huh," she mumbled, mouth against skin, starting to grow nervous.

"KPD arrested him last night."

Ricki raised up, looked at him and smiled. "That's great, Sam. I hope they can keep him off the streets," then continued on with her mouth.

"Found him tied to a chair, a bag of cocaine stuffed in his mouth."

"Whoa!" she said, mouth against skin. "That could be dangerous."

"He told them he had just been paid a visit by three women dressed in black," Sam persisted, ignoring her efforts.

Uh-oh.

Ricki stopped what she was doing. "Yeah?" she asked, then making herself start up again.

"Said they all wore these black hoods over their faces, kind of like the Ku Klux Klan."

"Hmmmm," said she.

"Claimed one of the women was wearing a necklace with a gold cross, had a diamond in the center."

Rut-ro.

Ricki stopped, raised up, gave him her most innocent look, and said, "Well, that's a coincidence."

She didn't think he bought it, so she did what she deemed in her best interests, proceeded to travel down his chest, toward his abdomen, hoping to short-circuit any thought processes going on, but he was having none of it.

"Said one of the other women was wearing a Mickey Mouse watch," Sam went on, his voice mild.

Ricki didn't respond, wildly wondering if Sam knew Melanie wore a Mickey Mouse watch.

"Reported one sounded just like Whoopi Goldberg."

Eeeck.

She raised up, smiling like she thought this was funny. "Really?" she asked.

He scowled at her.

Damn, she thought.

"Claimed the one with the cross was acting half-crazy, waving a gun around, threatening to shoot him. Said she would have if the one that sounded like Whoopi Goldberg hadn't stopped her."

Ricki sighed. "Come on, Sam, I didn't get naked just to hear you talk about some spacey drug dealer."

"Look at me, Ricki," he commanded.

She ignored this, traveling on down, getting frantic here.

He reached down, grabbed her arms, and pulled her up to him, face to face.

"These women, Ricki, are starting to tread dangerous waters," Sam said, giving her a serious look.

"So?" she asked.

"So, I think these women need to be aware that the cops have connected them to what happened with that garment factory owner a couple of months ago. Not to mention the business at that convenience store WAR got involved with. And highly suspicion there are other incidents involving these women we don't know about. Yet."

Ricki shrugged noncommittally.

"Maybe these women feel they're doing their civic duty, maybe they think they can accomplish something by taking the law into their own hands," he went on, shaking her slightly, getting angry.

"You're hurting me, Samuel," she said, teeth gritted. His grip loosened, but not by much.

"Maybe these women, Ricki, have got it in their heads they can do anything they damn well want to, hiding behind those little black hoods of theirs."

Ricki tried to squirm out of his grasp but he held her too tight. "Yeah, and maybe these cops, Samuel, are so damn territorial they can't stand to think that three women—women, Samuel—can accomplish what those doofuses have failed to for so long."

His eyes narrowed. "Maybe these women, Samuel, are tired of feeling powerless, inconsequential, not important enough for those cops to pay any attention to their problems. Maybe these women are doing what they can to help their fellow man, put things right for once."

"And just maybe these women are going to find their pretty little asses sitting in jail one of these days," Sam snarled at her, bringing his face close to hers. "Maybe they ought to heed my advice and stop things before they get out of hand or they get caught."

They had a staring match. Ricki finally shrugged, said, "Well, jeez, Sam, if I knew who to tell that to, maybe I would."

He rolled his eyes, released her. She immediately started to get up. He reached out, pulled her back to him, studied her a moment, then said, "You got a reckless streak in you, Ricki, and, for the most part, I find that to be an awfully appealing characteristic."

She smiled sweetly said, "Thank you, Sammy."

He scowled at her. "But sometimes, reckless people can get carried away, go beyond reckless to just plain careless and stupid."

Ricki cocked her head at him and frowned like she didn't quite follow.

He sighed heavily. *Oh, jeez,* she thought, *not another Danny, with the sighs.* "I really care about you, you know," Sam said forcefully, shaking her slightly again.

"Don't get physical with me, Samuel," she said, growing angry. He looked surprised.

"Don't shake me again," she snapped.

He released her. "I'm sorry," he said, looking it. "It's just, you could find yourself in a dangerous situation, Ricki, you keep this up."

She gave him a befuddled look. "Are we talking about me, Sam, or those three women?" she asked.

Now he looked confused.

Don't ask me, she plead silently. *Please don't ask me if it was me.*

He studied her face, then nodding his head, reached out and said, "Okay, let's just forget it for now," giving her that lazy grin, the one she had a real problem resisting. "Come here, baby, I am in dire need of some of your special kind of loving," he murmured seductively.

Ricki looked away, saying, "No, I don't want to," sounding like a kid.

"Come on, Rick," he begged.

"No," she pouted. "I'm not in the mood anymore."

"I can get you in the mood right quick," he enticed.

"I said no," Ricki declared firmly, proceeding to get up.

He grasped her arms again, brought her down on the bed. She wrestled with him, trying to get out of his grasp. He easily overpowered her, began kissing her, holding her down. She felt her body responding. He raised his head up, and in a smug way, said, "Tell me no now," before putting his mouth on hers again.

Ricki kissed back, feeling sick at herself in a small corner of her brain, sick at the realization that she had wanted him to overpower her, that it had excited her when he had.

CHAPTER 14

"GET A LOAD OF HIM, HE'S SO INSANE"

When Ricki arrived home from class, Sam was there waiting for her. He had that wild look in his eyes she was more than familiar with now. The look that told her he had been on the scene of a grisly homicide, the look that said he wanted to expunge that memory from his mind, while proving his own existence on this earth. The look that said her body was the tool he would utilize for this purpose. She felt her lower stomach cramp slightly, then a shooting sensation down to her ankle. Knew she was aroused already.

He never talked during these times, and neither did she, understanding he only wanted physical contact, no verbiage of any kind exchanged, till later.

Ricki smiled at him, opened the door, and held it. As soon as they were inside, he was on her, kissing her, pushing her up the stairs toward the bedroom. She smelled liquor on his breath, realized he had been drinking in the middle of the day. This was a first for Sam, and it was unsettling to her.

Ricki broke away in the bedroom, said, "Sam, you've been drinking. Maybe this isn't . . ."

His mouth was on hers, roughly kissing her, fondling her over her clothes. She felt her body responding to his hands, despite her tentativeness.

He kicked the door shut with his foot, maneuvering Ricki to the bed, starting to undress her.

He roughly removed her blouse and skirt, then yanked her bra and panties off and turned her over on her stomach. She lay there, tingly with anticipation, as she listened to him undress, then straddle her as he put the condom on.

He didn't indulge in any foreplay, raising her hips, roughly entering her. Ricki cried out as he did, from pleasure, from pain.

He pounded himself into her, pinning her with his weight. Ricki put her face into the pillow, biting it as she climaxed. He eventually stopped, turned her over onto her back, and began thrusting again. She lay there, watching his sweating, grimacing face, thinking, *this is wrong. This is not right. I don't need this. I don't want it. I've got to end it.* She was stunned to feel relief at that last thought.

157

When he was finished, he rolled off, got up, went into the bathroom, and flushed the condom. Ricki lay on the bed, still on her back, feeling a little sick at herself, at her body for its betrayal during this sort of assault.

He came back to the bed, lay down beside her.

"Was it that bad?" she asked.

He glanced at her, threw one forearm over his eyes.

"You've been drinking, Sammy. That's not like you," she said.

"God, Ricki, it was hellacious," he moaned.

Ricki lay there, letting him deal with whatever he'd been witness to.

He finally turned, studied her, and said, "No one has ever understood me the way you do, Ricki, the way I need to, to, well, go away from it, forget for awhile," giving her a respectful look.

Ricki smiled slightly, thinking, *I've been fighting my own dark demons for years, Sammy, no sweat.*

He reached out, stroked the side of her face, then surprised her, saying, "We've got to talk."

"Sure," she said, weakly.

"Ricki, we've been seeing each other awhile now . . ." he started.

Oh, please, don't do this, Ricki thought.

" . . .and I think it's time we made some sort of a commitment," he finished, giving her an intent look.

"Sam, I don't think this is a good time to get into that kind of conversation," Ricki said, glancing at the clock.

"Why not?" he asked angrily.

"Well, it's just, Zachary will be home soon and you know how I feel about us being up here when he comes home."

"He's a 17-year-old, for Christ's sake!" Sam exploded. "Jesus, when are you going to stop protecting him? He knows about sex, right? I'm sure he at least suspects you and I are engaging in sex. So, why in the hell does it bother you so much for that fact to be confirmed?"

"It's just, he loves Danny so, and he doesn't really understand our relationship, you know, and I don't want him to feel like you're taking Danny's place in any way, Sam."

"Fuck him."

"Don't do this," Ricki said, angry.

"You're just using him as an excuse to keep from talking about us, anyway," he accused.

She didn't answer, knowing he was right.

"Why won't you commit to me?" he demanded. "Why is it so friggin' hard for you to state your true feelings for me, Ricki?"

She sighed, sat up. "I don't know. I guess it's because I just came out of a 22-year relationship, and I don't want to tie myself down right now."

"That's what you call it, tying yourself down?" he asked, giving her an incredulous look.

Ricki moved to get up, away, saying, "Well, that's probably a poor choice of words, Sam. I'm just not ready to com . . ."

He reached out, grabbed her arms, threw her back on the bed, and hovered over her.

"No, maybe you won't commit to me because you still love Danny," he snarled, shaking her slightly.

"I've told you I love Danny," Ricki answered, tersely. She squirmed, trying to get out of his grasp. "Let me up, Sam," she said, feeling claustrophobic.

"Exactly how much do you love him?" he asked, his voice mild, belying the feel of his body pinning her down.

"Get off me. I'm not going to talk to you like this," Ricki said, her voice tense, struggling against him.

"Answer my question, then," he snarled at her.

Ricki stopped squirming, staring at him. His grip on her tightened as he studied her face. "You've been fucking him?" he raved. She didn't know if he saw something in her eyes or if he was guessing or just being an accusing bastard. She didn't particularly care at that point, her anger with him overriding anything else. She just barely managed to hold her tongue, glaring at him.

"Answer me!" he shouted, his eyes narrowed.

Ricki stared at him, opened her mouth and said, "Yes."

He backhanded her. She didn't even see it coming.

Tears sprang to her eyes. Her hand went to the side of her face, which felt hot, burning.

"I'll give you that one, Sam," she said, forcing her voice to remain calm, "'cause just maybe I deserved it. But that's the last time you'll ever lay a hand on me. Now get off me."

"When? How many times? How long has this been going on?" he yelled, shaking her roughly.

"Is that really relevant?" she asked, spitefully.

"I'll teach you to think you can fuck around on me, you bitch," he snarled, raising his arm up to strike her again. As he did, Ricki recognized with dread the malicious, malevolent gleam in his eyes, a look she had not seen for years, a look she knew all to well: the look her mother's eyes had held before the beatings would begin. She wondered why hadn't she seen that before, then wondered if maybe she had.

She felt her body respond as it had in the past, as his hand made the sweeping gesture toward her face: passively accepting the forthcoming pain, her legs and arms weakening, a cold, damp feeling of apathy and surrender traveling through her veins; and when the blow landed, her ears ringing from the force, her mouth tasting blood, her inner voice whispered, *you don't deserve this, you don't have to take this, you are stronger than this.*

"No!" she screamed, and before he could do anything else, brought both hands up, clenched into fists, and using the knuckles of each index finger, jabbed him in his eyes.

He immediately covered them, yelling with pain, shifting off her slightly.

Ricki brought her knees up, squirmed out from beneath him, then with the heel of her right foot, kicked him in the crotch as hard as she could.

He screamed in agony.

It felt great. *Good girl!* her inner voice sang. "Yes!" she agreed.

As he lay there, hands now covering his genitals, eyes bugged out, making a gagging noise, Ricki rolled off the bed, opened the nightstand, and got the gun out. The one she hated. The one Danny had insisted she keep there. The one he said would protect her. The one that would now.

"Get out of here," Ricki hissed at him, turning and glancing out the window, afraid her son would be coming.

He moaned loudly.

She went and got his clothes, threw them on the bed, keeping the gun pointed at him, having a hard time keeping it from waving violently in the air, she was shaking so.

"That's the last time you'll ever touch me, you bastard," she snarled, watching him drag his clothes on, seeming to stay stooped over as he did this.

"I'm not through with you," he said, his voice raspy, glaring at her.

"Oh, but you are, Sammy," she said, looking out the window. "And if you don't want a bullet where I just kicked you, I'd suggest you get out of here, now, through those doors," indicating with a gesture of her head the ones that led out onto the upper deck.

He gave her a baleful look as he gathered his shirt, socks, and shoes up, then approached the door, but before he went through, promised, "This isn't over."

"Oh, but darlin', it is!" Ricki shouted after him, then locked the door behind him, praying that Zachary wouldn't come till after he had left.

She waited until Sam drove away, then got into the shower, scrubbing him off her body, and stayed there until the water ran cold, her tears mingling with the water.

Zachary was home when she came downstairs, sitting at the breakfast bar, eating oatmeal cookies and drinking a big glass of milk.

His eyes widened when he saw her face. Ricki had tried to cover the red marks which were already beginning to bruise with makeup, had told herself Zachary never actually looked at her, he looked through her, he wouldn't see it, but when she saw the expression on his face, she knew they were more visible than she had convinced herself they were.

"What happened?" he asked, getting up, coming toward her, gingerly touching her left cheek.

Ricki gave him a wry smile. "I was trying to deworm Boomer today, and you know how he hates the taste of that stuff, so we had a fight, and as you can tell, I'm afraid I lost." She shrugged as if to say, *it's nothing.*

Her son studied her face like he didn't believe her. Ricki stared back, praying he would.

He finally sighed and said, "Jeez, Mom, you know better than to get in the way of a horse."

"Well, if I didn't before, I do now," she replied, grabbing a cookie and trying to act normal.

She didn't think he bought it.

Ricki stayed home the next few days, giving her face time to heal, keeping to her bedroom, telling her son and friends she was feeling bad, wanted time alone. Which was true—she was feeling bad. Not about Sam, about her. Her thoughts kept turning to her childhood, to what had transpired between her mother and her. She wondered if that had any bearing on her attraction to Sam. Maybe she saw in him the same flaw she had seen in her mother. Maybe the little girl who always felt she must have deserved the punishment or else she wouldn't be getting it had zeroed in on Sam, intuiting in some way that violent aspect of his nature. She didn't know. She did know that she wanted to be healthy, mentally. She wanted to put her mother behind her. She wanted to put Sam there, as well.

Ricki kept the answering machine on, screening her calls, or using Zach when he was there. Sam kept calling, apologizing to the machine but not to Zachary, saying they had to talk. "Not on your frigging life!" Ricki yelled at the phone more than once. Each call was more demanding, and about the fifth time he got the machine, he threatened to turn Ricki and her friends in if she didn't talk to him.

She picked the phone up.

161

"Thought that'd get your attention," he snarled.

"What do you want?" she asked, her voice hard.

"I just want to see you, Ricki, talk to you," he answered, his voice soothing.

"You're talking to me, but you won't see me," she snapped.

"Listen, I apologized . . ."

"Yeah, and it is not accepted, Sam. I won't forgive you for what you did, you understand? You had no right."

"I had every fucking right in the world!" he shouted at her.

Ricki sat there, shaking, listening to his angry breathing over the airwaves, then said, "Okay, Sam, let's forget the violence aspect and get on to the threat you just made."

"Threat? What threat? Just bear in mind, Ricki, I know all about you and your two . . ."

"I don't care what you think you know or what you think you don't know," she broke in. "But let me tell you something, Sam, you try to turn me and my friends in for whatever fabricated lie you come up with, I'll be sure and turn you in for physically assaulting me, and I've got the bruises to prove it. Now, where's your proof?"

He was silent.

"I thought so," she snarled, and hung the phone up, cutting on the answering machine.

Zachary finally asked why she kept the machine on and wouldn't talk to her boyfriend, saying that word snidely, and Ricki told him she had broken up with Sam.

His eyes narrowed. "He give you those bruises?" he asked.

She put a shocked expression on her face. "No," she said, sounding surprised he'd think such a thing. "This happened after I broke up with Sam. Shoot, Zachary, you don't think I'd let a man beat up on me, do you?" she asked, staring at him.

He looked uncomfortable, then said, "No, Mom, I'd never think that."

"Good," she answered.

"But for what it's worth, I'm glad," he said. Ricki looked at him. "That you broke up with Sam," he explained. "I never did like him."

She gave him a smile. "You always were a good judge of character, Zee. I guess I should have listened to you."

"Oh, well," he said, looking uncomfortable again.

An air of sad despondency seemed to settle around her, like a diaphanous shroud, and no matter how much she tried to shake it off, she couldn't. Zachary seemed worried about her, checking on her when he was home, asking if he could do anything for her, get her anything. Ricki was sure he thought she was grieving for Sam. She wasn't. She was grieving for that confused little girl.

She felt apathetic, soporific, lethargic. She felt angry, confused, hurt. She felt sick inside.

Danny had called every day, several times. Ricki strongly suspected their son had told him about her face. He usually got the answering machine or Zach if he was home. Ricki was sure he got mad she wouldn't talk to him. She didn't care.

He came by a few days later, while Zach was at school. As was his wont, he just used his key and came on into the house. Ricki was in her bedroom at the window seat, absently petting Bruce, who seemed to hover near her lately, listening to her favorite Celtic instrumental disc, and staring out at nothing, really, feeling numb, then startled when he opened the door and stood there, watching her.

She glanced at him, then back out the window.

She heard his footsteps approach, felt a stir in the air as he stood beside her. He didn't say anything, just stared, she guessed.

He finally moved away, sat down on the other side of the window seat, and turned to face her.

"Ricki," he said.

She was glad the side of her face that was practically healed, the one without a visible bruise when covered with makeup, was turned toward him.

"Yeah?" she asked, looking out.

He didn't answer, instead reaching out with his hand, gently placing his fingertips underneath her chin, and turning her face to his.

"Jesus," he muttered.

"More like Boomer," she said, giving him a grin that wasn't heartfelt.

"That Sam guy do that to you?" Danny asked, glowering.

"No," she lied.

"'Cause I'll kill that son-of-a-bitch, he laid one hand on you," Danny said, sounding mad.

Ricki gave him a gentle smile, thinking, *thank you, Danny*, then said, in a teasing manner, "You think I'd let some man do something like that to me?"

Their eyes locked. Danny finally grinned a little and said, "No, babe, no, I don't."

"But a horse, now, that's a different matter," Ricki said, shrugging.

He frowned again, giving her a puzzled look, then said, "Zach told me you broke up with Sam."

163

She nodded, not able to look at him anymore, turning her gaze out the window.

"You all right?" he asked.

She shook her head no, tears springing to her eyes.

"You want to talk about it?" he asked, his voice gentle.

No again.

"It might help, honey," he nudged.

No.

He was silent for awhile, watching the tears stream down her face. Ricki sighed hitchingly, then said, "It was my decision to break up with him. I want you to know that."

He drew his head back and looked at her. "You did the right thing, Ricki, I hope you realize that," he said.

She nodded.

"He wasn't good enough for you, not by a long shot."

She snorted.

"But then, I can't think of anyone who would be, you know." Ricki glanced at him. "Good enough for you," he explained.

She smiled weakly and noticed Bruce, who had gone to stand by Danny now and was gazing adoringly at him as Danny scratched behind his ears. "I should have listened to Bruce," she said.

Danny looked at her.

"He hated Sam." She shrugged. "Well, for that matter, so did Charlie and Melanie and you and Zach."

"Well, concerning Zach and me, as well as Bruce, anybody you'd choose to be with, I hate to tell you, babe, but I think there would probably be a problem in that regard."

She nodded, smiling slightly.

He cocked his head, listening to the CD playing. "Celtic?" he asked, looking back at her.

She nodded.

He listened a moment more, then said, his voice low, "You used to listen to that a lot during our latter years."

She nodded again.

"I'm sorry it hurts," he whispered.

Ricki drew her head back, looked him in the eye and said, "I'm not crying over losing Sam," her voice hard.

He cocked his head at her.

"I'm just trying to deal with me, Danny. I'm trying to get my head together, you know. I've been doing a lot of soul-searching, I guess, a lot of introspection. It's been a real painful process."

He nodded.

"I've been thinking about going back into counseling," she muttered, laying her head against the window.

He didn't reply.

"I'm so tired of chasing horses," Ricki said, feeling tears well again, wiping at her eyes.

He waited a minute, then said, "Chasing horses?"

Ricki looked at him. "You know, if you want to catch a horse, the last thing in the world you do is chase him, right?"

He nodded.

"Well, that's how I've been going about facing my problems, my life," she muttered. "Chasing at everything that comes down the pike, not trying to approach it, reason it, resolve it."

"Oh," Danny said, nodding his understanding.

She looked at him. Their eyes locked. *God, I love you so much*, she thought. He smiled gently as if he had heard this.

"You're right," she whispered. "He wasn't good enough for me."

CHAPTER 15

"I'M STARTING TO FEEL A LITTLE MUSCLE AGAIN"

Some journalist named Mitchell Elliott had been calling at least twice a week for a month now, leaving messages on Ricki's answering machine, each one a little more insistent than the last, that he needed to talk to her about a pending lawsuit. Well, it didn't take a genius to know what the dude wanted to discuss. That stupid demonstration and subsequent confrontation and class-action suit, which was still ongoing. So, Ricki did what she deemed in her best interest: ignored the calls even though he had one of the sexiest voices she had ever heard, sounding just like a deejay. Ricki realized with some sense of relief that the mental detritus left behind, such as an intense hatred for the male species, excluding Danny and Zachary, was beginning to dissipate.

Ricki should have known sooner or later he would catch her at home, and the somewhat lyrical tenor voice should have told her who had called, but she was in a rush and didn't connect it at the time when he asked, "Cherokee England?"

"Yeah?"

"This is Mitchell Elliott, I'm with . . ."

"I know who you are, or who you purport to be," interrupted Ricki, somewhat angrily.

"Listen, I'd like to talk to you about . . ."

"I do not think so," she interrupted again, rudely.

"You didn't even give me a chance to fin . . ."

"Let me tell you, Mr. Mitchell Elliott," Ricki started, then paused, thinking, *another man with two first names, what is this?*

"Tell me what?" he asked, his voice almost caressing.

"This involves that dang gentleman's club, am I right?"

"Well, yes, but . . ."

"It's been nice talking to you, Mr. Mitchell Elliott. See ya, bye," and Ricki hung up the phone, cutting on the answering machine.

Charlie called the next day, informing her she had set up a meeting with a journalist by the name of Mitchell Elliott for the next evening at . . .

"No way," Ricki snapped.

167

"No way what?" she snapped right back.

"Listen, Charlie, I am not talking to anybody associated with the media, okay? Like I told you before, I want to stay in the background, not be any more publicly involved than I have been with that situation. You and Melanie go talk to the guy and give him whatever information it is he's after, explain our . . ."

"That's not what he wants," she interrupted.

Ricki sighed heavily, took the time to sit down, prop her feet up, then said as wearily as she could, "Okay, what exactly does he want?"

"A list of the members of the club," Charlie answered, her voice sounding hush-hush.

"So?"

"He needs our help."

Ricki sat up. Oh, well, this was different. "How?" she asked, growing suspicious.

"That's what he wants to have a meeting with us about."

Ricki thought a moment. "Well, shoot, Charlie, why us? Why not just him or somebody he knows? I mean, I don't know how we can help him with this. I myself would like to get my hands on that dang list, you know that. Even Tommy wants to see it, but there's nothing we can do that we're not in the process of actually doing." She paused. "Well, legally, that is," she added, thinking, *uh-oh*.

"What we can do is go listen to what the man has to offer," Charlie suggested.

Ricki hemmed and hawed a moment.

Charlie finally sighed, then said, "Listen, Rick, don't you think you've holed up in that house, crying over Sam, long enough?"

"Hey, I'm not crying over that bastard," Ricki snapped at her.

There was silence on the other end, then Charlie asked, somewhat exasperatedly, "You ever gonna tell me what happened between you two?"

"I told you, Charlie, I deemed it was in my best interests not to continue the relationship," Ricki said, snippily.

"Yeah, but something happened to make you come to that decision, didn't it?" Charlie asked, her voice low.

Ricki didn't answer.

After several seconds, Charlie said, irritably, "Okay, forget it."

"I will," Ricki answered, her voice cool.

"Now, about that Mitchell guy . . ."

"Forget it," Ricki snapped.

Charlie threw the gauntlet down, saying, "Whatsamatta, Ricki, you scared Danny's gonna get mad 'cause you're not doing what he wants you to, staying out of this mess you helped start?"

"Hey!" Ricki said, offended.

"Well?"

"Danny doesn't tell me what to do!" Ricki defended.

"Yeah, right," Charlie snorted.

"Okay, give me the time and place and I'll be there!" Ricki commanded. Charlie did, her voice sounding smug.

They were to meet at a popular restaurant in downtown Knoxville, right on the river. Charlie and Ricki sat waiting for Mitchell, who was late, playing a guessing game as to what he must look like.

"He sounds sexy as all get-out," Ricki said, taking a sip from her glass of iced tea.

"Don't he, though," Charlie agreed.

Ricki grinned. "Black hair."

Charlie grinned. "Dark eyes."

"Maybe blue."

"Sexy lips."

"Bushy eyebrows."

"Heavy beard."

"Tall."

"Athletic build."

"Tight ass."

"Tube-sock-sized bulge," Charlie said, snickering, and they both started laughing, which was interrupted by this big bear of a man standing at their table, staring at them. They stopped laughing just like that, looking way up at what Ricki perceived to be the largest, ugliest, hairiest man she had ever to that point come across.

"Cherokee? Charlie?" he asked, looking at Ricki, then her companion. Ricki snapped her mouth shut as she nodded in the affirmative.

"I'm Mitch Elliott," he stated in that deep, almost sonorous voice, holding this huge hairy paw out, shaking with each of them as they introduced which was which, before sitting down.

Charlie and Ricki exchanged a quick glance, thinking, *damn! Were we ever off?*

Ricki turned back to Mitchell and studied him as he ordered a beer from the waiter. *God, he is beyond ugly!* she thought. Well, they had been right about one thing: his hair, which was black in color, shoulder-length and which he wore loose; small, beady, chocolate-colored eyes under big black bushy eyebrows; a full beard and moustache which seemed to flow right into the hair. He was close to Sam's height, maybe a little taller, and had to weigh every bit of 300 pounds, with this big barrel chest and humongous belly, the largest set of shoulders Ricki had ever seen, and arms and hands to go right along with them. His thighs reminded her of two tree trunks. She deliberately dropped her napkin, then bent down to retrieve it, taking the time to look at his feet (yep, big there, too) and then up to his groin. *Dang,* she thought, her eyes widening, then raised up, giving Charlie another look, trying to send the thought, *hey, lookit what he's got down there!* which she blatantly ignored.

Mitchell glanced at Ricki, giving what she took to be a grin beneath all that hair. "So, where's your Sox cap?"

"Real cute," she replied dryly, not appreciating the humor.

He studied them a moment, then got down to business. "So, you got any idea how big a can of worms you guys have opened up?"

Charlie and Ricki looked at each other, then Mitch. "I'm afraid I'm not following you," Ricki said, giving him a blank smile.

"The club you picketed?"

"What of it?"

"The one you filed the class-action suit against?"

"So?"

He leaned conspiratorially toward her. "I got an anonymous phone call the other day informing me that there are a lot of highly connected politicos who are members of that club."

Ricki's eyes widened. "No shit?" she asked.

He nodded affirmation.

"You think the phone call was legit?" she asked suspiciously.

"Whether it was or not, I think it bears checking out, don't you?" he asked back.

Another look between Charlie and Ricki. Charlie's asked, *are you interested?* Ricki's said, *yeah, boy.*

Ricki turned back to Mitchell. "So, what kind of a club do you think this is?" she inquired.

He took his time answering, finally saying, "My guess is you're dealing with a bunch of white supremacists."

Ricki shook her head. "Nah, I think it's probably some kind of secret gay club." She turned to Charlie. "Remember how the owner lunged at me when I suggested that?"

Charlie nodded, saying, "Yeah, I think Ricki's probably right."

Mitchell shook his head. "I'm pretty sure we're talking supremacist," he said smugly.

Ricki thought about it. "Well, how about supremacist gays?" she asked teasingly. Neither Charlie nor Mitchell saw the humor. She shrugged, then said, "You know, this just doesn't make sense to me," staring at Mitchell. "If they're supremacists, gays, whatever, and if politicians are involved, why are they fighting us so openly and publicly? Why is that stupid doofus of an owner so visible, you know? Why did he get into that exchange with me the day we picketed? Why does he keep giving those stupid interviews? I mean, my feeling would be, if they have something to hide, they're not acting it by being discreet or subtle about that wretched club."

Mitchell pondered, then said, "Unless they do have some pretty heavy political influence. If so, what have they got to worry about?"

Charlie and Ricki looked at each other. *Bingo,* Ricki thought.

"How can we get the roster?" she asked him.

He smiled.

They worried this issue for about an hour, till Mitchell let slip the name of the security firm who provided protection.

"I used to work for that firm," Charlie said.

His eyes lit up. "My source says the guard on duty at night is a guy by the name of Russell Headrick. Happen to know him?"

Charlie grinned widely. "Know him? I went to school with that idjit!"

More haggling about how to get the roster. Mitchell finally suggested that Charlie get in touch with Russell, offer him money to leave the back door unlocked and turn his head one certain night within the very near future while Mitchell stole into the office and looked around for the roster.

Charlie was reluctant at first. Ricki thought it was a great idea, so encouraged her about as eagerly as Mitchell did, but what did she have to lose? She wasn't actually involved at this point. *Planning a break-in isn't literally doing one,* she told herself. *You can be such an idiot at times,* her inner voice sneered at her, which she chose to ignore.

Charlie finally acquiesced, saying, "You'll need help, though, when you go in."

Mitchell thought a minute, then replied, "Just a couple of lookouts. I can handle the search myself."

Charlie and Ricki looked at each other, then at Mitchell, who grinned.

It was decided as simply and as stupidly as that.

After all plans had been made, Charlie left abruptly, saying she had to get home before Eddie or he'd be wondering where she was. Ricki sat there, staring at this hairy ape, wishing he looked as good as he sounded.

He studied her openly, then said, "Looks like we're about to be partners in crime," teasingly.

171

Ricki grinned uneasily. *Jeez, that is true.*

"So, what say we extend that on out to partners in a more amorous way?" he asked, giving her a lewd grin.

Ricki gave back a shocked look.

He favored her with an innocent one in return.

"I hardly know you!" she practically gasped.

"That's what makes it so great," he said, smiling around all that hair. "Just a few hours of physical fun, nothing more, nothing less."

Well, shoot, Ricki had never actually had a one-night stand with someone she didn't really know. It would be an experience to reflect back on in her old age, and it had been awhile since Sam. Well, for that matter, anyone. The last few weeks, she hadn't even let Danny near her. She studied Mitchell. *Huh-uh, no way.* This guy was just too unattractive to her. *I'd rather be caught dead than lying in his arms*, Ricki thought, giving him a fake smile, saying, "Your idea of fun is my idea of death," getting up, making movements to leave, half-afraid she'd change her mind if she stayed.

"Okay, okay, it was worth a try," he said, offering a conciliatory grin.

Ricki gave him a suspicious look.

"Look, we probably ought to legitimize this meeting," he said, glancing around.

Ricki wasn't sure what he meant.

"If anyone sees us, I need to have a reason we were together," he explained. "Like interviewing you for an article about your group. That way, when the roster comes up missing, you and I can each say this meeting was the interview, not you and I planning a break-in at the club. That is, if anyone asks."

Ricki thought about that. "You could have interviewed Charlie," she finally said, "or Melanie, call her. She's our official spokesperson."

"Melanie is not your official leader," he stated.

"Well, neither am I," Ricki said.

"Maybe not, but you are the perceived leader," he replied, indicating with a wave of the hand for her to sit back down, which she did.

"You were the one who had the confrontation with the owner of the club, you're the one who always seems to be making the statements at the demonstrations your group is growing so popular over. So, as long as we're here, let me interview you. You can speak for WAR—that's the name, isn't it?"

Ricki nodded.

He drew out a tape recorder.

"Wait a minute," Ricki said, holding her hand up. "Just one thing, Mitch. Anything I tell you off the record is off the record, okay? Not that I actually have anything to say that would be, but in case I decide it should be, off the record, that is, you will abide by what I request, right?"

"Sure," he said easily.

"Okay," she said, "go ahead. Ask away. Just remember one thing, though, we're in this little roster thing together, so it would behoove you to put us in a really good light, all right?"

He grinned, switched the recorder on.

The article came out in the following Sunday's paper. Ricki was impressed. Mitchell had managed to convey exactly what it was WAR was trying to accomplish, presenting them as caring, involved women who were making an effort to bring awareness to the public what they felt were inequalities against men, women, and children. He made them sound like the most benevolent group of women you'd ever want to meet, citing some prime examples Ricki had given him, like helping to find housing for an indigent mother and child; hospital care for a homeless old man with cancer; a shelter for a battered wife; medical care for an indigent AIDS victim. He made sure to stress that their group operated solely without any sort of cash flow; everything they engaged in was given and done voluntarily. The thing Ricki didn't appreciate about the article was the focus on her, making her sound like head honcho, and to make matters worse, he also brought out who her ex was and the office he had declared for. Ricki groaned when she read this part, knowing Danny would be pissed, but Danny surprised her, calling that afternoon, telling her how much he liked the article, praising her for her involvement in the group, acting hurt Ricki hadn't let him know all the good work they were doing.

You wouldn't be saying that if you knew about the three vigilantes, Ricki thought to herself, while saying, "Oh, well, you know how it is," somewhat modestly, then, getting off, thinking ironically Danny was probably pleased because of the free publicity he got out of it. *Couldn't hurt his campaign any,* she thought resentfully.

The article did do WAR some good, though. Their membership doubled the first week. Several social agencies called, volunteering their services to anyone in need, adding to their resource list. A local channel called, asking a representative of their group to appear on their morning news show. Of course, the number being called was Ricki's, and since she was the one answering, she was the one dealing with all these people, perpetuating the myth even further of her position as leader of the clan, which she kept telling herself she wasn't. Really.

CHAPTER 16

"AND THE NIGHTTIME IS A TIME OF LITTLE USE"

The night of the planned soiree, Charlie and Ricki met Mitch at a Wendy's close to the club. They had an hour before they were supposed to rendezvous with the guard, so decided to get something to eat and drink as they finished planning out their strategy.

Ricki watched with amazement as Mitch put away a double with everything, fries, side salad, chili, and a Frosty. Even though she had only eaten a couple of hours before and wasn't really hungry, Ricki, being the glutton she was, got a single with cheese, fries, and a large iced tea. Well, she just happened to really love their hamburgers, okay? Besides, she was extremely nervous, and when she got nervous, she either got sick at her stomach or the munchies. Tonight, it was the latter.

They had agreed beforehand that Mitch would be the one to actually go into the club while Charlie and Ricki acted as lookouts. Charlie would be at the front, Ricki at the back. This really sounded good to Ricki, as she breathed an inward sigh of relief, rationalizing to herself she wasn't exactly doing anything wrong. She wouldn't be the one lifting the roster, she wouldn't be the one actually going inside and committing any crime. She was just, well, in essence, along for the ride. *You're bullshitting yourself*, her inner voice warned and she told it to shut its frigging mouth.

They left 45 minutes later, all piling into the front seat of Mitch's pickup truck. Charlie made Ricki sit in the middle and she was more than aware of the body heat emanating from this grizzly next to her. They were packed so tight in there, Ricki was right against Mitch, shoulder to shoulder, and jumped slightly the first time his upper arm brushed her breast. She glanced at him to ascertain if that was intentional or not, but he was simply staring at the road, singing beneath his breath to an old Bob Dylan cassette he had plugged in, looking innocent. The next time he did it, Ricki knew it was intentional, *but what the hey, he's just a man,* she thought. Besides, he liked Bob Dylan; he couldn't be all bad.

Ricki was excited and scared out of her mind. The closer they got, the more scared she got. She started babbling about maybe we shouldn't be doing this and maybe we ought to just forget this and maybe Mitch ought to let me out right here, till Charlie told her to shut her mouth or she'd shut it for her, then had to go and remind her no one forced her into the damn truck in the first place. *She must be as scared as I am, talking to me like that,* Ricki consoled herself, giving Charlie a hurt look, which she ignored.

They slowly drove by the club, the three of them staring at the front. All the windows were dark. It looked vacant. The only light shining was the security one over the door. Mitch went down the block, turned to the right, took the next right, and they were behind, cruising slowly. The back was dark, as well, looking deserted.

"Where's the guard?" Ricki asked Charlie.

"Probably asleep," she said, sounding distracted. Then she glanced at her. "Don't worry, he'll be there. He knows we're coming."

"You're sure he can be trusted?" Ricki asked for the millionth time.

"There you go flogging that same old dead horse again!" Charlie railed. "Shit, Ricki, I done told you a hundred times already, he's cool. I will vouch for him personally, okay? Not to mention the fifty dollars Mitch is gonna be passing him. If nothing else, that'll keep that boy quiet, believe me!"

"Well, I just don't want to have to explain to my son why my butt is in jail if this guy isn't who you say he is!" Ricki said.

"Will you listen to yourself?" Charlie said, giving her a disgusted look. "Damn, girl, you're one of the whiniest white bitches I've ever seen, I tell you what."

"Okay, okay, I'll shut up," Ricki said, feeling chagrined. She peeked at Mitch, saw the smile playing around his lips.

They drove by twice more, just for good measure, then went down another block over, parking in a metered zone, making sure there were other cars around theirs. Mitch reached behind the seat, threw this rubbery thing in Charlie's lap, one in Ricki's, keeping one for himself. Ricki lifted hers up, looked at it, burst out laughing. "Richard Nixon!" she said, studying the mask. "My hero," she effused, causing Mitch to guffaw. She reached over, picked up Charlie's, which was Jerry Ford, then Mitch's, which was Lyndon Johnson, big ears and all. She cracked up. Mitch sat, watching her laugh, grinning widely, looking kind of proud of himself. Charlie just looked vexed.

After Ricki had calmed down, she gave Mitch her own appreciative look, said, "Whoa man, you're deeper than I thought," and they both went off.

"Okay, already," Charlie said, sounding mad. "Let's get going here. We ain't got all night, you know."

They stuffed their masks down the front of their dark sweatshirts, got out of the truck and, keeping to the shadows, approached the club from the rear.

They stood in a cluster of bushes on the outskirts of the alley behind the club, donning their masks. Ricki started laughing at their disguises and wished she had a mirror to see hers. Charlie and Mitch both told her to can it; this was serious business. Ricki forced herself to calm down, taking note she had to pee bad.

She put her hand on Mitch's arm. "I hate to tell you this, Mitch, but I need to, uh, use the bathroom," she said, her voice low. "I don't think I can hold it till you get in and then out. Think we can go back to the truck and go to a restaurant or something real quick?"

"Sheeeeeet fire," Charlie exploded.

"Well, I'm sorry, Charlie," Ricki said. "I shouldn't have drunk that big glass of iced tea. That happens to me every time I drink tea. It just seems to go right through me, you know."

"Well, no wonder. Tea's a diuretic," Mitch submitted.

"You know, I think I read that somewhere," Ricki said. "Must be what, the caffeine?"

"When you two pieces of trash get through discussing what does and does not make you have to pee, I would suggest we get on with this B&E we're about to engage in here," Charlie snapped at them.

"But . . ."

"Damn, Ricki, you got to go that bad, use the bushes," she spat.

"That's primitive," Ricki said, offended.

"Well, then, you're just gonna have to hold it, 'cause there's our man."

They looked toward the back door and saw it opening, letting a yellow sliver of light out.

Charlie left quickly, heading toward the front. Ricki followed Mitch to the rear.

The guard stepped outside as they came up.

"You Mitch?" he asked, rather stupidly, Ricki thought. The police could have been lurking around somewhere and here this guy was, using Mitch's name. She prayed Charlie hadn't told him hers.

Ricki glanced at her partner in crime, wondering if he was aware the guard knew his name. He didn't seem particularly bothered by it as he nodded and held out his hand, and Ricki watched as the money went from his palm to the other man's.

"Just so you know, there's two security cameras," the guard said, jerking his head toward the building. "One's in the office, the place you need to go."

177

"Shit," Mitch swore.

"Yeah, well, don't worry about it. They told me this afternoon it was acting up, so they shut it down."

"What a piece of luck!" Ricki said.

Both gave her a look, not saying anything.

"Sorry," she mumbled.

"Where's the other one?" Mitch asked.

"Back toward the front, in the foyer area, pointing into the hallway, but don't worry, that's away from the direction you're going."

Ricki stood there, shifting weight from one foot to the other, and half-listened as the guard told Mitch to go inside, down the hallway, take the first left, and the room he needed was the first one on the left.

Mitch turned to her as he donned thin driving gloves and said, "Wish me luck," his voice muffled behind the mask, and they both disappeared.

Ricki turned her back to the door, peered out into the yard. It was hard to see anything with that dang mask on. Plus it was hot as Hades in there. She drew it away from her face, then peeled it up slightly and peeked out real quick, pulling it back down when she heard movement, afraid it was Charlie, who would give her hell for not being properly disguised.

A spasm hit her bladder and Ricki bent over, scared she was going to pee all over herself. *Damn, there's no way I'm going to make it till he gets back,* she thought, feeling awfully uncomfortable. She was troubled by the fact that she was having such a hard time controlling herself. *Must be nerves,* she decided.

The door opened and the guard came out.

Ricki sighed with relief. "I've got to use the bathroom real bad," she said, shifting weight again, fighting the urge to hold herself, like a child.

"There's one inside, near the end of the hall, on your right," he said.

"Great. Thanks!" said Ricki as he held the door open for her, and she went in, forgetting all about gloves and the like in her haste.

Ricki ran down the hallway, shoving the door open with her palms, breathing a great sigh of relief upon seeing the line of urinals against the opposite wall.

She went to a stall, pushed the door open, danced around as she very hygienically put toilet paper down on the seat, and then wrestled her jeans and panties off her hips, groaning loudly as she sat and felt the relief of the release.

After she had done her business and washed her hands, wrinkling her nose with distaste at the messy sinks, then being the neat person she was, wiping the water off the sink and faucet she had utilized, Ricki finally went back out into the hall.

"Mitch?" she whispered loudly.

No answer.

She decided to go find him. She stood facing back the way she had come, trying to get her bearings. *Let's see, the guy said down the hallway, turn left, which would make it her right. But which one? First, second? Durn.* She looked to her right, saw an entranceway, stepped over, peered in, more out of curiosity than anything, and found herself looking right into the foyer at the front. *Uh-oh,* Ricki thought as she glanced up and saw the video camera aimed right on her.

Shit! she mentally screamed.

You stupid ass, her inner voice whispered.

You got that right, she answered.

Ricki stared at the camera for a moment, frozen, then thinking, *well, shoot, the damage has been done, might as well leave your mark,* put both hands up and made the V sign, mimicking good ole Tricky Dick. Then she backed up, still waving her victory sign, grinning like a maniac behind the mask, turned around and took off, flew down the hallway and out the door, which was standing wide open.

Mitch was outside waiting on her.

"What took you so long?" he asked.

"Did you get it?" she asked, ignoring his question, not wanting him to know what an imbecilic thing she had just done.

"Man, did I ever!" he said, sounding excited. He held an envelope up, then reached out, hugged Ricki to him, and they jumped around excitedly in each other's arms.

Mitchell released her, pulled the mask up past his mouth, put two fingers therein, and whistled shrilly. Charlie came running a few seconds later.

"Got it!" he proclaimed proudly.

"Good going, man. Now, let's get our butts out of here," Charlie whispered, heading into the bushes.

They ran for the truck, removing their masks as they went, Mitchell and Ricki laughing like two little kids.

When they got there, they all piled in, throwing the masks behind the seat, and took off.

They went back to Wendy's, Ricki babbling all the way about how fun and exciting that had been, Mitch and Charlie ignoring her for the most part, then sat in the truck in the parking lot, looking excitedly at the large manila envelope in Mitch's hands.

He showed the outside to Ricki and Charlie, which said, "Membership."

"Oh, God, that was fantastic," Ricki said, feeling high now. "Absolutely fanfuckingtastic."

He laughed.

"Open it up," Charlie said, ignoring her. Ricki gave her friend an irritated look, wondering what was wrong with her. She acted like she did this sort of thing every day. But then again, maybe she did. Ricki looked at Charlie again, who caught her staring and raised her eyebrows questioningly. Ricki turned back to Mitch.

He carefully opened the envelope and slid out a legal-sized sheet of white paper. They couldn't see too well in the dimness of the parking lot, so he turned on the overhead light. Ricki looked at the roster, blinked, looked again. It was in code. She burst out laughing.

Charlie and Mitch gave her an irritated look.

"I knew it was too easy," Ricki said, shaking her head.

"Jesus, girl, you are getting on my fucking nerves," Charlie snarled, shoving her slightly.

"Hey!" Ricki said, offended.

"Break it up," Mitch said mildly, studying the list.

"Listen at her, carrying on like she just been to some kind of party or something," Charlie snapped.

"Hey!" Ricki said again, for lack of a better retort.

"That's enough," Mitch snapped. Charlie and Ricki exchanged deadly glares, then settled back down, turning their attention to the roster.

"You think you can decode it?" Ricki asked.

He glanced at her. "I doubt it, but I know somebody that probably can," giving them a secretive smile.

"See, there's nothing to worry about," Ricki told Charlie.

She rolled her eyes, opened the door, and said, "I can't take any more of you, Rick."

"Hey, what'd I do?" Ricki said.

"What ain't you done?" she snapped. She looked at Mitch. "Remind me, next time, leave this bitch at home," then slammed the door, stalking toward her car.

Ricki turned to Mitch, who was watching Charlie march off. "What'd I do?" she asked.

He grinned.

Ricki grinned back.

Half an hour later, Ricki found herself doing the very thing she had promised herself she'd never be caught dead doing, i.e., at Mitch's apartment, in his bed, in his arms, having their own little celebratory party. She guessed it was because she was still feeling so high from all the excitement, nervousness, anxiety over their little escapade, she didn't know. She just didn't want to go home and do nothing, not after all that excitement. She needed a way to vent all this adrenaline pumping away in her system.

When Ricki had finally wound down, laying there naked as a jaybird, hidden in this big bear's arms, she felt ashamed of herself. *You slut, you whore,* her inner voice chided, but she was feeling too excited to really care. Besides, they hadn't actually done anything yet but get bare-assed.

Ricki squirmed her way out, sat up, breathing heavily, and looked down at his body. Jeez, this guy was covered with hair from head to toe. She had never seen such a woolly person in her life. He could have been a caveman, all that fuzz covering him. Even his rear-end had dark down on it. The only bare spot she could ascertain was his male organ, which looked like a nice-sized salami roll in some sort of bristly nest, ready to burst at any moment.

He was such a big guy, barrel-chested, massive stomach, huge thighs, arms, actually close-up appearing more muscular than fat. Ricki was surprised at this. In fact, the only really soft part she could ascertain so far was his abdomen, which wasn't that soft. His heinie was small, tight. She liked his butt, and reached out and patted it gently. "You got a nice ass," she surmised.

He laughed and said, "It's nothing compared to yours, Ricki, that's for sure."

Ricki smiled at him and went back into his arms. There was something comforting about this, like being enveloped by a huge, fuzzy teddy bear. She snuggled in closer, feeling that immense body heat, wondering how the hell she was going to get out of this situation, then wondering if she really wanted to.

He lay there, holding her, waiting for her, she guessed. *Well, are you going to do something or what?* she thought irritably, wanting him to push it, the better to rationalize her behavior with, don't you know. *But dang, this isn't bad,* she thought, rubbing her body over all that soft, downy fuzz. She nuzzled her face in his chest, then her breasts, turned over, rubbed her butt against his fuzzy stomach, causing him to laugh. She wondered what it'd feel like making love to this man-bear.

Ricki went into his arms again and kissed him. His beard and moustache were soft; they tickled her face and then her body as he moved his lips over her. She wanted to laugh. She wanted to sigh. She wanted to close her eyes and let him do whatever he wanted with those lips, that tongue, all that hair. And so, she did, idly wondering what it would feel like for him to be on top of her. *He could crush you!* her inner voice warned. *Yeah, but honey, what a way to go,* Ricki thought, as he came back up to her lips, started doing some serious kissing, this time utilizing his tongue in a more advantageous way.

He finally stopped, looked at her and said, "Well!"

"Yeah, boy," Ricki said, smiling lazily at him.

He grinned.

"So, you want to get serious here or what?" he teased.

"I just got one piece of advice, Grizzly Adams," Ricki said.

"Yeah?" he asked, grinning like the Cheshire cat.

"You better git while the gittin's good!"

He laughed and proceeded to.

"I've got condoms if you don't," Ricki suggested, almost immediately stopping any real progress.

"I've had a vasectomy," he offered.

"Yeah, well, that's just one of the reasons condoms are used," she replied.

He sighed. "I'm clean, Ricki, no disease of any sort. I swear it."

"Famous last words," she chided.

"Man, I hate those things."

"Well, you got your choice, Teddy, them and me or nothing but maybe your hand."

He studied her, then, frowning, said sarcastically, "I've got my own supply, thank you very much," rolling over and reaching into the nightstand.

Ricki watched him cover that big ole thing surrounded by all that hair, then when he came to her, said, "Would you mind being on top?"

He gave her that grin, like he knew what she was thinking behind the request, and said, "No problem."

And there wasn't. He real quickly established a soft, slow rhythm and Ricki sighed inwardly, thinking what a mundane lover he was going to be. She was used to Sam's restless energy or Danny's intensity in bed, but not so with Mitchell. He kept the pace the same till the end, when he came. At first, she tried different maneuvers to encourage him to speed it up a little, tried to force him where she wanted him, but to no avail. He simply overpowered her, all the time giving her that knowing grin, and as it turned out, the guy knew what he was doing. He had her yelping by the time he was through with her.

Afterward, he looked at Ricki and she looked at him and they both said, "Well," simultaneously, then cracked up.

"I'm starving," Mitch said, getting up, going into the bathroom, flushing the condom, then heading for the kitchen and throwing a popcorn envelope into the microwave.

Ricki sat up in bed, still breathing heavily, thinking, *what the?*, wanting to shout, *hey, come on back here*, but of course, being the lady she was, she managed to restrain any outward display of frustration.

She gave one of Danny's sighs, got up, went into the bathroom, made sure to urinate, hopefully flushing out any unwanted bacteria that might be traveling upward toward her bladder, did a quick cleanup, then still nude, followed Mitch into the kitchen.

She watched with amazement as he ate this huge bowl of popcorn, talking on the phone to whoever his secret decoder was. After they agreed to meet the next evening, Mitch hung up, looked at her, and said, "You sure you don't want anything to eat?"

"God, no," Ricki said, moaning. Her stomach was still full from that hamburger.

The knowing grin again, then he got up, went into the bathroom and started brushing his teeth.

After years of conditioning, Ricki found herself cleaning up this guy's mess, fussing at herself inwardly all the while; but she couldn't help it, she just hated dirty dishes and crumbs.

She was leaning over the table, wiping it off, when she felt him up against her, gyrating against her butt with his pelvis. She wondered what it is about guys and women who just happen to be bent over at the moment. Every man she'd been with (what few there were) had never seemed able to resist her bending over, clothed or unclothed. *What is it?* she wondered. She didn't understand it. The sight of a naked man bending over did nothing for her. In fact, it kind of grossed her out, to tell the truth. She asked Danny about it once and all he did was laugh. So she hadn't asked again. Maybe she should.

Anyway, liking this, Ricki bent further over, till she realized the guy was getting serious and he didn't have a condom on, so she straightened up quickly. He laughed like he knew why she did that, then turned her around, threw her over his shoulder, and like a caveman toting his woman, carried her to the bed, depositing her thereon. She giggled as she landed.

Ricki got on top this time. This guy was so big, she almost had to do a split to straddle him. She closed her eyes as she rode him, pretending she was Fay Wray laying King Kong. It wasn't a bad fantasy.

Ricki was worn out when they finished, and he put those big, hairy arms around her and she snuggled in and drowsed for a couple of hours before making him take her to her car.

By the time they parted, she was starting to feel guilty about what she had been involved with that evening, at the club and then at Mitch's apartment. They parted with a kiss, Mitch saying he would call her tomorrow. Ricki wasn't sure she wanted him to.

When she got home, thinking now she had her own teddy bear, she put notch number four on her fun-gun.

CHAPTER 17

"CALL OUT THE GUARDS, TURN OUT THE LIGHT"

Ricki had been at the stables all morning, working with the orneriest horse she had ever come across, trying to force her to take a bit into her mouth, which she time and time again refused to do, slinging her head around as much as the tie-off would let her and refusing to open those dang teeth of hers, even when Ricki pinched the hell out of her upper lip. She was standing in the kitchen, mentally cussing that durn animal while pursuing what was contained in the refrigerator that she could put together for a quick lunch, when the phone rang. She snatched it up, wanting and not wanting it to be Mitch. It was.

"What the hell did you think you were doing going into the foyer?" he yelled at her.

"Huh?"

"And what's with the stupid victory sign?" he shouted.

"Aw, shit," Ricki mumbled.

"Damn, Ricki, what the hell did you think you were doing?" he asked, his voice calmer.

She sighed. "I was trying to find you, Mitch, after I went to the bathroom, and don't ask me how, but somehow I got turned around and found myself standing there, right in front of that dang camera. I don't know what got into me, I was so excited about being there and what we were doing, and well, in essence, I guess I was just thumbing my nose, you know."

"Yeah, well, you're gonna be doing a lot of thumbing your nose in the county jail!" he snapped.

She groaned.

"Damnit, Ricki, you've blown the whole thing."

"Wait a minute. How do you know I did all that?"

"I got a call from a friend of mine at one of the local channels, wanted to give me a lead on a story for the paper. Seems that friggin' guard forgot to lock the door after us last night, so this morning when the owner shows up, he gets suspicious and goes hunting for the roster. When it comes up missing, they pull the tape out of the camera, and there your sweet ass is and was on all the local stations during the noon news."

Yikes, Ricki thought, realizing that Danny always watched the local news at noon. *Please let him be doing something else,* she prayed vehemently, then, remembering Mitch, "How the heck did it get on TV?"

"You were right about the old geezer who owns the club; looks like he's after all the publicity he can get. Instead of turning it over to the police, he called a press conference and ran it for the media."

"Dangit all to hell! I swear, Mitch, if it wasn't for bad luck, I'd have no luck at all."

"Luck had nothing to do with your stupidity," he snarled.

"What about the guard, is he talking?" she asked, thankful the only name he couldn't give in this little illegal act was hers.

"I got his number from Charlie, called him just now, and he told me the owner fired him as soon as he found the door unlocked, so he's not telling anything to anybody. Besides, he knows he's gotta protect his ass; he's just as guilty as we were."

You were, Ricki thought, but didn't relay that.

"So what are we gonna do now?" she asked.

"Nothing. You had the mask on, you weren't recognizable. I wore gloves . . ."

"Uh-oh," Ricki mumbled.

"What?"

"I didn't have gloves on, Mitch, and I touched the bathroom door and the faucet."

Now he was the one doing the groaning.

"Oh, God, I'm going to go to jail," she said, tearing up.

He sighed this time. "Well, now, let's calm down for a minute and think this thing out, okay?"

"Okay," she whimpered.

"First off, have you ever been fingerprinted, 'cause if you haven't, the whole point is moot anyway, you know."

"I have been," Ricki sighed. "Back when Danny and I first got married, I applied for a civil service job . . ."

"Okay, so you didn't have gloves on, you left fingerprints. Now, if they dust for prints, I'm sure they'll lift dozens, not just yours. So, maybe they won't have a clear enough print to determine whose is whose, you know. Besides, why would they dust the bathroom? They'll probably stick to the outer door and office, wouldn't you think?"

"Yeah, right," Ricki said, feeling relieved.

"So, let's just sit tight, Ricki. Don't say anything to anybody. Act innocent, go about your business, and see if it doesn't blow over."

186

"Yeah, but there's one problem," she said despondently.

"What's that?"

"I will be a suspect, Mitch. You know that. I was involved in the durn demonstration. I was the one that got into that verbal exchange with the owner. I'm one of the principals of the class-action suit. You know they'll look to me."

"Oh."

"They'll probably come get me and take me down to the station and book me, just like in the movies!" she said, panicked.

"Well."

"Well? Well? Is that all you can say, Mr. Breaker and Enterer?" Ricki yelled.

"Hey!"

"Well, you're the one who actually committed the crime, Mitch. I was only there for the fun of it. I only went inside 'cause I had to use the bathroom. I didn't do anything wrong."

"Oh yeah? Then why were you wearing a disguise if you don't think you did anything wrong?" he snarled at her.

He had her there. "Maybe 'cause I thought it was cute," she answered, sounding childish.

He snorted, then said, "Listen, Ricki, if they do come aft . . . talk to you—now, I'm not saying they will, but if they do—you're not going to, well, implicate me, are you?"

"Huh?"

"Well, the way I see it, they don't have actual proof you took the roster, so if you were to keep quiet, tell them you don't know anything about anything, I really don't see how they could, you know, book you for breaking and entering or whatever the charge would be."

"Screw you!" Ricki screamed at him.

"Why throw me to the wolves?" he asked, his voice sounding whiny.

"Because you committed the crime!" she shouted at him.

"Ricki, listen to me. This is a real coup for me. This could get me a big promotion, maybe even a better job with a bigger newspaper. Don't do this to me, Ricki."

"You're full of shit, you big weenie!" she snapped at him. "And to think you reminded me of a teddy bear. You're more like Winnie the Pooh, you big old bellyaching coward!"

"Hey!"

"You, Mitch Elliott, are lower than a snake's belly in a wagon rut, you flabby old jellyfish!" she yelled.

187

"I resent that!" he yelled back.

"You put the word man to shame, you pusillanimous douche-bag!" she screamed into the phone.

"Now, wait just a min . . ."

"You're welcome," she said and hung up the phone.

It immediately began ringing. Ricki picked it up, slammed it down, cut the answering machine on.

He called five more times, threatening each time to come see her, they had to talk about this. "You just try it, bucko," Ricki shouted at the phone. Of course, he didn't hear her.

Charlie called. She was laughing, not acting at all upset there was a good chance by that evening Ricki's butt would be occupying a place at the county jail. Irritated by her lack of concern, plus the fact she seemed to take it for granted Ricki wouldn't involve her, Ricki told her to perform a certain act that she, being a woman and all, would have found impossible to accomplish. "Wait a minute," Charlie said, stopping Ricki's hand's advance to hang up the receiver.

"What?" she asked, vexed.

"I just wanted to tell you, girl, what you did took balls. I liked that victory sign you gave the camera."

"Yeah, well, you be sure and tell the media that while my ass sits in jail!" Ricki yelled and hung up on her.

She turned on the TV. The news was over by then. One of the stations ran those five minute news-of-the-hour updates every 60 minutes, so she stayed glued to the set till that came on, and there she was, waving her stupid fingers in the air, looking like a slender, smaller Tricky Dick with tiny breasts. She disgustedly turned the TV off.

Man, was she nervous. The tape playing on the news kept rolling in her head, over and over, like some ludicrous nightmare. *Good Lord, what have I become?* Ricki chided herself. *There I am on camera, caught in the act of committing a crime!* She made a note to tell Charlie this was it, she wanted out. *No more. Forget it. Huh-uh. No way.*

She prowled the house, frustrated, angry, pissed at herself. "You'll be laughing at this in a few years," Ricki tried to appease herself. No dice.

She came upon the pack of Virginia Slims someone had left at their last meeting and thought, *what the hey.* Hadn't somebody once upon a time told her they were good for your nerves? Well, hers were a jumble right now, thank you very much. Ricki stared at them, contemplating. She had always thought cigarettes were a nasty vice, but, shoot, she needed something and she needed it now.

So, she pulled one out, placed it in her mouth, then began the search for something to light it with. Finally found the extended lighter for the fireplace, almost burned the end of her nose off when she lit up, mumbling, "You deserve it, you stupid idiot!"

She inhaled, had a coughing spasm, tried it again. Paced and puffed. Paced and puffed. Started feeling a little mellow, slightly high. Inhaled. Exhaled. Not wanting the house to smell like cigarette smoke, she walked outside, carrying the cigarettes and a small crystal bowl which served as her ashtray.

She sighed heavily, sat down on the lounge by the pool, lit another cigarette off the one she had been puffing on, then ground that one out and lay back on the lounge, watching the movement of the pool water, pondering her situation and what she was going to do about it.

Ricki had almost finished her second one when she heard first one, then two car doors slam.

Oh, shoot, she thought, remembering Zachary's truck wouldn't start that morning and Danny was supposed to bring their son home from school.

She stuffed the cigarette in her mouth, for lack of a better place at the moment, her eyes watering at the smoke trailing upward, reached down, grabbed the ashtray and cigarettes, looked frantically around for a hidey-hole, and finally crammed them underneath the cushion she had been lounging on.

She heard voices in the house, heading this way, and managed to put the cigarette behind her back just as Zachary opened the French doors, leaned out, and gave her a big grin as he yelled, "Hey, Mom, I'm home!" before he went back in, for food, she was sure.

Oh, wow, that was close, Ricki thought, starting to bring the cigarette around front, the better to put it out with, when who should appear at the door but her dear ex-beloved.

"Danny!" she said, surprised, sneaking the cigarette back around.

"Cherokee," he snapped, coming toward her, a fierce scowl on his face. *Uh-oh,* Ricki thought, hearing her full moniker.

He came up to her. She felt like a kid caught smoking behind the barn who was about to get it but good, then felt resentful Danny brought these feelings out in her. So, she frowned back at him.

He sniffed audibly and said, "I smell smoke."

Ricki looked around innocently, then replied, "I don't smell anything."

"What's that behind your back?" he asked, looking over her shoulder, from whence a thin wisp of smoke was curling to the sky.

"Nothing," she said, flipping the cigarette into the pool behind her.

The hiss as it made contact with the water and was snuffed out was audible to the max.

Danny took the time to glare, then stepped around her, peered into the water. Throwing a look of disgust her way, he went and got the net and fished it out.

"This yours?" he asked, picking the soggy butt up, holding it in front of her face.

"Might be," Ricki said, haughtily.

"So now it's cigarettes?" he asked, incredulously.

"I just had . . ." Ricki began, then stopped herself. "Hey, it's none of your business whether I'm smoking cigarettes, pot, cocaine, whatever the hell, okay? Stop making me feel like a kid, Danny. I don't need that."

"I'll stop when you quit acting like one, Cherokee," he fussed at her.

"I am not acting like a child," she said defensively.

"You ever heard of second-hand smoke?" he asked, still holding the wet cigarette, which was coming apart in his hand. "If it isn't bad enough this shit can kill you, it's even worse the harm it can do to our son!"

"Zachary wasn't here, Danny. I wouldn't do that around him."

He gave her a disbelieving look. "Really, Danny. I swear I only smoked two, and that was today, this afternoon. I was feeling kind of nervous, you know, and I heard somewhere cigarettes are good for calming you down. They aren't even my cigarettes, Danny. Honest. Somebody left them here from the meeting." Jeez, she sounded just like a kid trying to talk her parent out of the spanking she knew she was in for. Ricki grew sick at herself over this revelation.

"Where's the other one?" he asked sternly.

Ricki meekly went to the lounge chair, pulled the cushion up, retrieved the ashtray, and gave it over. "See, Danny? I hid it from Zach. I didn't want him to see it."

"Where's the pack?" he asked, snatching the ashtray out of her hand.

She sighed, went back to the lounge, retrieved it, and brought it to him.

He made a show of taking her stash and throwing them in the garbage, giving her another disgusted look. Ricki sighed again.

He came back to her, the initial scowl back on his face. *Eeeck,* she thought again.

"Sit down, Cherokee," he commanded.

Well, who the hell did he think he was? So what did she do? She folded her arms and stood there, glaring at him.

"Please," he said, making this sound like anything but a request.

Ricki gave him the evil eye, turned on her heel, flounced over to the table, and sat down in one of the chairs adorning it. She tried to look bored, picking at a cuticle.

Danny came over, pulled a chair out, placed it right in front of her, sat down, and leaned toward her.

Ricki felt kind of like somebody about to be interrogated for murder, the look he was giving her, the way he was acting.

"So, what's up?" she asked, giving him a smile.

"You're going to be sent up if you don't cut out this shit," he snapped.

"Up where, pray tell?" Ricki asked, looking away.

He leaned back, stared at her till she reluctantly brought her eyes back to his. *Oh, Lord, he knows,* Ricki thought miserably.

"So where'd you get the mask?" he asked, his teeth gritted.

Zachary came out onto the deck then, a banana in one hand and a bowl of ice cream in the other. Danny and Ricki both looked at him. He stared at his mother, then his father, and then back at Ricki, his expression growing puzzled. Danny said, "Zachary, your mom and I are discussing something kind of important. Can you give us a minute?"

He looked from his dad to Ricki again, then shrugged his shoulders, said, "Sure, Dad," and headed back in.

Ricki looked back to Danny, who was staring at her again. She didn't feel like playing any games with him, not anymore, but gave it one last try.

"What mask?" she asked, her voice squeaking a little.

His eyes said, *don't play this shit with me, Ricki.*

She sighed. "How'd you know it was me?" she asked, resignedly.

Now he sighed. "I know the way you move, Cherokee. I know your body, your actions."

"Oh come on, Danny. A lot of people move like me, act like me. I bet millions do. You can't convict me on that."

He leaned toward her again. "I wouldn't bet on it. No doubt about it, that's you in that film."

Ricki threw her head back, stared at the sky, and mumbled, "Dang."

He waited for her eyes to again find their way back to his. "I'm not going to ask you why, I'm not going to demand to know what the hell has gotten into you. I will simply tell you, Cherokee, you have stepped over the line with this one. Not only did you commit breaking and entering, but burglary as well. Not to mention criminal trespassing and who knows what other counts. I hope you're proud of yourself."

Her eyes teared, but she forced herself to look him square in the eyes, and said, "I can't tell you how badly I feel about it, Danny. I know better than

191

you that taking the roster was against the law. I'm just sick over it. But I didn't steal it, Danny, really. The only thing I'm actually guilty of is complicity, I guess. I was there, and the door was open, but I only went inside to use the bathroom and then got lost. That's how I ended up on camera, but I do know who took it. I know what happened. That's why I was smoking, trying to calm myself down so I can decide what I need to do. I'm scared, Danny. I don't know what I should do!"

He shoved his chair back, stood, leaned over her, and said, "You're the one says they want to be independent, Cherokee, be responsible for themselves, so you handle it." He walked away abruptly, leaving her looking after him.

"But I don't want to handle it," she mumbled to herself.

Ricki sat there a good fifteen minutes after Danny left, chewing her bottom lip, pondering.

Zachary came out and called, "Mom, everything all right?"

She startled, then looked at him, gave him a shaky smile and said, "Sure, honey, everything's fine," lying through her teeth.

She got up, went inside, called Tommy, and groaned to herself when the receptionist put her through to his secretary, signaling to Ricki Tommy wasn't there or was screening his calls and, either way, she had a better chance of having a sit-down meeting with the big guy upstairs than talking to her attorney.

"Hey, Sarah, is Tommy there?" Ricki asked, her voice as sweet as it could be.

"Whom may I ask is calling?" she droned, sounding like Bela Lugosi, Ricki thought. Come to think about it, she favored him a lot, too.

"It's me, Ricki England," Ricki said, as brightly as she could. "I need to speak to Tommy for just a second."

"He's unavailable at the moment, may I ask him to return the call?" Sarah inquired, her voice grating.

Jeez, this woman had always hated Ricki, and she didn't know why. Ricki sat there, as she always did when she came up against Sarah, fighting the urge to ask what was so terribly wrong with her. Okay, Ricki had to admit it; she was one of these people who wanted everyone to love them. Well, with the exception of the future Mrs. England. That was a different matter.

"Please, Sarah," she begged, "it won't take but a minute, I swear, but I need to talk to him."

"I'm afraid that's impossible at the moment," she answered, sounding happy at denying Ricki what she needed. She probably was. Ricki imagined sending a thin, steel cable running through the telephone receiver, coursing through the wires, coming out through her handset, ramming itself into her ear, then her brain, grinned happily as the blood ran and she screamed horribly.

"Do you wish to leave a message?" Sarah asked somewhat impatiently.

"Uh no, don't bother, just tell Tommy I'll let Danny handle it," she said, knowing that was the only way she'd get through at this juncture.

"Please be sure and tell Mr. England hello for us," Sarah said, her voice now sounding warm.

"Yeah, and fuck you, too," Ricki whispered, then quickly hung up the phone, feeling like an adolescent.

Ricki gave her 10 minutes, then called back, this time disguising her voice, trying for a British accent, but sounding speech-impaired, saying, "Tommy Leigh, please, Danny England calling."

"One moment, please," Sarah answered with great reverence.

"You old battle-ax," Ricki spat at the phone. "What the hell is wrong with me that you won't let me talk to Tommy? Is Danny England the magic word or something?" she asked the air snidely. "I mean, what am I? A nothing? A nonentity, unless as pertains to the most esteemed Danny England him . . ."

"Hey, Dan, what's going on?" Tommy broke in.

"Tommy, it's me," Ricki said.

She could literally see him rolling his eyes. "Hey, what's with you using profane language with my secretary?" he huffed.

"Well, what's with her being so mean to me all the time, Tommy?" she said. "Shoot, she acts like it pleases her to no end to tell me no, I cannot talk to you."

"She's just doing what I told her to," he snapped.

"Oh, not letting me talk to you."

"No, holding my calls until I can get my desk straightened out. You ought to see the mess in here. Jeez, I go to Chattanooga for half a day and it's like everybody and their brother panics 'cause I'm not here when they want me."

Ricki listened to his complaints about the woes of being an attorney till he paused to draw breath, then asked if she could meet him like a few minutes ago.

"I've got dozens of phone calls to return, Ricki, and it's close to five now. How about tomorrow?" he asked.

"You read the paper today?" she asked.

He paused, then said, somewhat warily, "No."

"Listen, I don't want to go into it over the phone but I think maybe I'm in need of a good criminal lawyer," she said. Tommy, being the nosy butt he was, told her to come on down.

Ricki dressed carefully, not sure what one wears to one's arrest. She finally decided on a knee-length straight skirt, topped with a long jacket, thinking she could pass for a secretary or business exec.

She grabbed her tote, told Zachary she had an appointment, see you soon, baby, kissed him, turned her face to hide her tears, and left.

When Ricki got to Tommy's office, she surmised he must have read the paper while waiting on her, seeing the angry expression on his face as he met her in the hallway.

"It's that damn roster, isn't it?" he railed at her, in front of his stone-faced secretary, who for some unexplainable reason was shooting daggers at Ricki with her eyes.

Ricki hurried into his office, Tommy following her in, slamming the door, and before he could go off into a tirade, explained to him what had happened.

They went round and round about what Ricki should do. She insisted she had to turn herself in. He insisted that wasn't so important. After all, Ricki was innocent of stealing the roster.

"But I know who did it, Tommy! I was there. I was involved. An accessory, isn't that the word you guys use? Not to mention the fingerprints I left behind."

He lit a cigarette and pondered as he smoked. "Give me one," Ricki said, grabbing his pack.

He gave her a funny look, watched her inexperience puffing away, then said, "Look, Rick, I can only advise you on what I think you should do, and I'm going to do that as a friend, not an attorney, okay? 'Cause if it were me—and bear in mind, I didn't actually say this to you—if anyone should ask, I'd just sit on it for awhile."

"No."

"Hey, they could arrest you for this."

"I'm well aware of that."

"Come on, Rick, show some sense here."

Ricki stood. "You coming with me or what?" she asked.

He gave her a withering gaze. She stared back impassively. He finally shrugged his shoulders, said, "Okay, already. Give me a minute, we'll go down. But I'm warning you; I don't normally practice criminal law. If they arrest you, I think we should call in another attorney."

"Whatever."

"You want me to call Dan?"

"No."

"He has a lot of influence down there, Rick. He can help you."

"No!"

"You're making a mistake if you won't accept help from whomever is willing to give it," he warned.

Ricki looked him in the eye and said, "I have depended on Danny for my entire adult life. I feel it's time I stood up for myself, Tommy, and that's what I'm going to do."

"Yeah, well, you sure picked a hell of a time to decide that," he snapped, grabbing his briefcase, escorting her out.

CHAPTER 18

"I"LL TAKE MY WOUNDED PRIDE, I'LL TAKE IT ON THE CHIN"

Tommy was a friend with one of the detectives on the vice squad, and an hour later; they were closeted with this guy, who questioned Ricki intensely, growing angrier and angrier as she refused to disclose who had actually stolen the roster.

When he threatened to arrest her right then and there, Ricki offered her own solution.

"What if I get in touch with the person who actually has the roster in hand, the one who took it, and tell that person if he . . . they hand it over, say, to me, so they won't incriminate themselves to you, they won't be charged?" She shrugged nonchalantly, then continued, "I'm the only one who at this point can lay hands on it for you." He visibly bristled at this. "Listen, I know that's not proper protocol or actually going by the book, per se, and if you would rather arrest me, go ahead. Do that if it makes you feel better. That, however, will not get that roster back to the owner of the club, which will ensure the names on that roster do not get into the media. Which is going to happen if I don't get it back. And I think if you talk to the owner, you're gonna want to make sure those names don't get leaked," she said, somewhat overconfidently, not knowing actually what the hell she meant by that, but pretending as if she did.

"Who the hell do you think you are, dickering with me over whether or not to arrest you?" he asked, incredulously.

"I am the person who is trying to put this right," Ricki said, indignantly.

Tommy rubbed his jaw. Ricki could see the humor in his eyes. He winked at her. She didn't wink back.

"I can arrest you for obstructing justice, right here and now," the detective threatened.

Ricki leaned toward him, said, "If you want to charge me, go ahead. You have the right. You have the grounds. But I'm what, Tommy, a first-time offender? My only crime was that I entered through an open door and used the premises, then got lost. My fingerprints will prove that out. You know that. So what can you charge me with other than obstructing justice and is that gonna fly anyway? Criminal trespassing? You think I got the roster, go find it." Seeing his look, "Okay, so I had the mask on. I'll give you that. That incriminates me more than anything does. But Tommy here's a good attorney. He can find some logical reason I had that mask on, can't you, Tommy?"

Tommy grinned outright this time.

Ricki shrugged. "And can you actually prove that's me underneath that mask?" she asked the detective.

"You just told me it was you!" he ranted at her.

"Oh, yeah, and I killed Kennedy, too," she said, smirking.

Tommy laughed.

Mr. Detective drew back, giving her a baleful look.

"As for the fingerprints, shoot, I was there the day we were demonstrating. Who's not to say I didn't have to use the bathroom then?" she asked loftily.

Tommy snorted happily.

The detective somewhat grudgingly and angrily informed them he had to call the D.A.'s office, the owner of the club, and probably God for all he knew before he would agree to anything.

Tommy and Ricki were standing in the hallway, Tommy smoking, Ricki feeling dazed, waiting for the detective to confer with the Assistant DA and the owner of the club. Their eyes met. They grew uncomfortable looking at each other, so glanced away, simultaneously clearing their throats. Ricki was wondering why it was that they had been as intimate as any two people could be, had engaged in numerous physical acts together, yet that closeness had only made them feel unsettled when their eyes met. *Love must be the key*, she was thinking, 'cause she knew for dang sure if they loved each other, after a night like Tommy and she had shared, they wouldn't be glancing away from each other but would be sharing these long, heated, passionate looks.

"So, how are you and Dan getting along these days?" Tommy asked, interrupting Ricki's musings, his gaze going to the window.

Ricki turned and looked too, shrugging her shoulders.

Tommy stared at her.

"What you said is true, you know," she said, tracing a dirt pattern on the pane of glass with a fingernail.

"Yeah?"

"Yeah. You were right, Tommy. I egg him on. I tease him. Keep him riled enough to keep the interest up, I guess."

"I knew it!" Tommy declared.

"But he's engaged to Stacy and I've got to accept that and get on with my life," she said, her voice sounding mournful.

"I'll tell you what, Rick," Tommy said, putting his hand on her arm, looking up into her eyes. "All you got to do is crook your finger at the big guy and I guarantee he'll drop Stacy in a minute and come running."

Ricki snorted at this.

"He would," Tommy insisted.

She rolled her eyes, turned away from him, and thought, *speak of the devil,* as Danny came strolling in. Ricki glared at Tommy, who simply shrugged his shoulders.

My protector, she thought ironically, turning back around and watching Danny as he approached, stopping every few feet it seemed to shake hands with this or that law official, smiling that fake smile, his eyes coming to her every chance he got. Looking into his eyes, she could still feel that pull to him. *Damn, why did I have to pick this guy to fall in love with,* she wondered irritably to herself.

He came up to them, and Ricki and Danny commenced to have a staring match. Danny finally gave a sigh of defeat and said, "Can I do anything, Ricki?"

"No," she answered curtly.

"Come on, Rick, this isn't the time to pout."

"Pout? Who's pouting?" she asked belligerently, glaring at him. "How'd you know I was here? Who told you?"

His eyes shifted to Tommy then quickly back to her. Ricki turned and glared at her so-called attorney.

"Thanks a hell of a lot, Tommy," she snapped at him.

He shrugged those shoulders again. *And I slept with this weasel,* she thought disgustedly.

"So, what's going on?" Danny asked, his voice now directed toward Tommy.

Ricki stepped away to the window and stood half-listening, staring out at the parking lot as Tommy filled Danny in on what had transpired up to this point.

After he finished, she felt movement at her side, focused on the reflection of the window, and saw Danny looking at her again. She turned slightly, giving him her back.

"If it counts for anything, you did the right thing, coming here," Danny said, his voice low.

Ricki didn't respond.

He sighed again. *Shoot, I wish he'd quit with those damn sighs,* Ricki thought. "Look, Ricki, Tommy told me you insisted on doing it this way, the hard way. I got to tell you, I respect you for that."

She glanced at him. Well, he looked serious.

"I wouldn't have turned you in, no one would probably have ever known," he continued, his voice quiet.

Ricki turned toward him now. "Yeah, but the thing is, Danny, I knew and you knew and I knew you knew. Besides, I felt bad about it and I'm fully cognizant of the fact that it was wrong. I was aware of that when we were there, but I just got so caught up in it, the excitement and everything, you know?"

He looked like he didn't.

"Well, anyway, what's done is done," she said lamely.

He nodded.

"So, Danny, you think I ought to tell Zachary about this?" she asked.

He pondered, then said, "It's your choice. I won't tell him, I promise you that."

"I don't know whether I should," Ricki said, then shrugged. "Well, if I get charged, I won't have to worry about that, I guess," then turned back to the window.

She heard someone call Danny's name and watched his reflection in the window as he moved off down the hall, conferring with some guy in a dark business suit.

Ricki felt movement beside her, and thinking it was Tommy, glanced that way. Sam was standing there, watching her. She looked away quickly.

He moved close, leaned against the window, still watching her, and said, his voice barely audible, "Ricki, we've gotta talk."

"I don't have anything to say to you," she answered tersely.

"Come on, Ricki, I've apologized a dozen times. I just lost my temper, that's all. I'm sorry. It won't happen again."

"Oh, but I think it would," she mumbled.

He leaned toward her. "Tell me what to do here. Tell me what it'll take for you to forgive me," he whispered.

Ricki turned, looked him in the eye, and said, "I'll never forgive you, Sam. What you did was reprehensible, and you know it."

He opened his mouth.

She leaned toward him, interrupting before he could respond. "I wonder how many other women you've told it won't happen again."

"Ricki, I was drunk, I . . ."

"No, Sam. You weren't that drunk. The issue is that you hit me. I'll never let you do that to me again. I'll never let you touch me again. You understand?"

"You betrayed me," he said, glaring. "You betrayed us."

"But the point is, when I was with Danny, I never felt like I was betraying us, Sam. So what does that tell you? It's over, okay?"

"I won't accept that," he snarled.

"Listen to me, Sam. I don't like the way I respond to you. I don't like the way we are together. It's not healthy and I don't think it's in my best interests to have anything more to do with you."

His eyes narrowed. He moved closer to her.

"So, what, you've gone running back to Danny?" he snarled, glancing Danny's way.

"If I had, you wouldn't be standing here, or anywhere else for that matter," Ricki said, somewhat smugly.

"So, can I take that to mean you're not gonna report me?" he asked, trying to appear nonchalant, but she could tell from the gleam in his eyes this was a real threat to him.

Ricki thought a minute, then looked into his eyes and was glad she wasn't attracted to him anymore. "I really liked you, you know," she said, throwing him off balance. He blinked in surprise. "You're basically a good man, Sam, but you just seem to have all this anger inside that you need to deal with. Listen, I'll make a deal. Get help, go for counseling, and I won't do anything. I swear. Otherwise, I'll force you to."

"It'll be my word against yours," he growled, growing angry again.

"True, but the thing is, Samuel, we both know what happened. No matter what you say to the contrary."

"I'll turn you and your friends in," he threatened. "I know you're part of that vigilante group. I've known for awhile."

They stared at each other.

"Do whatever the hell you need to do," Ricki said disgustedly. "I've never physically harmed another person, so I would think you would have a higher price to pay than me."

His eyes narrowed. He stared at her, then nodded. She nodded back.

His look softened. He surprised her by pleading, "Come on, Rick. Give me another chance. We were good together, you know that."

"No," she answered her voice firm. "It's finished."

His eyes gleamed. He leaned so close their faces were almost touching, said, his voice low, "The one needs counseling is you, Ricki. You liked the rough stuff just as much as I did and you know it."

"Just leave me alone," she said, stepping back, feeling sick.

She noticed Danny standing there then, wondered uneasily how much he had overheard.

Sam's eyes followed hers, and Ricki watched as he and Danny glared at each other for a moment, the animosity clear. Then Danny came to her side and said, "I believe the lady asked you to leave her alone."

Sam glared at Danny a moment, then shrugged his shoulders, put a fake smile on his lips, and said, "I have every intention of doing that."

Ricki watched him walk off, aware of his anger by his posture.

Danny said, "What'd he do to you, Ricki?"

She glanced at him, then turned back to the window. "Nothing I didn't let him," she answered.

Danny put his hand on her elbow, turned her to him, and stared into her eyes. "What the hell did he do to you?" he asked, his voice low, angry.

"Only proved to me how really messed up I was," Ricki said, looking away, her eyes tearing.

"Aw, babe," Danny said, pulling her against him.

Ricki stepped back, not letting him comfort her, cleared her throat, and blinked hard to clear her eyes. "Danny, I'm sorry about all this. I hope this doesn't negatively affect your campaign. I'll do whatever it takes to see to it that doesn't happen."

He put his fingers on her lips, stopping her, then said, "To hell with the campaign, Ricki. You're more important than that."

She was surprised at this, stared into his eyes to confirm his veracity. He looked serious. She stepped into his arms, gave him a slight hug, and said, "Thanks, Danny. Thanks a lot."

Tommy came up then, said, "Here we go," and led the way back into an interrogation room.

A young woman was sitting there, a briefcase before her, and beside her the owner of the club, who was staring angrily at Ricki. Next to him was a heavyset, middle-aged man, with these little Porky Pig eyes, his graying hair combed in such a way it was clearly discernible to any and everyone that he was trying to hide his ever-widening bald spot.

Tommy shook hands with the woman and introduced her as Elizabeth Emory, ADA. She had short, blond hair, ice-blue eyes, and was small and petite. Ricki smiled vaguely at her nod, watched Danny make it a point to shake hands, and then sat, Tommy on one side, Danny on the other. The ADA then introduced the man next to the owner as his attorney, Billy Joe Whitehead.

Rut-ro, Ricki thought, hearing that name. *This guy had a reputation as a killer attorney, available only to the mucho-rich or mucho-politically connected.*

Before they got started, the ADA questioned Danny's presence. "I'm Ricki's husband," he said stonily.

"I want Danny here," Ricki said, taking his hand, not correcting him.

The detective sat down, began questioning Ricki again, same old song, same old dance.

She refused repeatedly to disclose who actually had the roster. The ADA took over, same tune, different words. Ricki still resisted. She threatened arrest. "Fine," Ricki said, "but first prove that's me on camera."

The owner of the club got his two cents in, saying he'd see to it that Ricki's butt sat in jail till she rotted. "Maybe," Ricki said, agreeably. Danny squeezed her hand at this.

Finally the detective and the ADA looked at each other and then at the owner of the club, who was looking at his attorney.

"I want the roster back," he said.

"I'll get it," Ricki said.

"Wait a minute," Tommy said. "One proviso. She gets the roster for you, I want the agreement that she doesn't get arrested for whatever charge you guys dream up."

More looks between the three. "I want it back, now," the owner insisted.

Billy Joe leaned over and had a huddle with the ADA, who finally nodded her head curtly, then said, "Agreed," looking at Ricki. As she rose, she wondered what was so dang important about that roster it could influence the DA's office to let her get by with a criminal act.

"You can call from here," the detective offered.

"No," Ricki said.

He glared at her.

"The phone is what, wired, tapped, trapped? I don't know the lingo but I don't want you tracing the call."

Simultaneously, Danny, Tommy, and the ADA pulled out their cellular phones, offering them to Ricki. She couldn't help but grin at this sight, went to Danny, took his, then retreated to the farthest corner of the room, her back to them as she punched in the number for the newspaper and whispered the extension into the phone, which wasn't answered. She sighed, dialed Mitch's home phone, after taking a minute to remember it. Shoot, all she needed to do was dial information and ask for the number of Mitchell Elliott. There went everything down the drain; she gave the detective that information. Ricki prayed silently as it rang, then cursed silently as the answering machine clicked on. She waited impatiently for the tone, then said, "This is Ricki. I'm calling from a mobile number, call me back like right now. ASAP!" and after providing the number, hung up. Then remembering he had given her his beeper number, she dug in her purse, glanced at it, trying not to let anyone see what she was doing, aware of the silence in the room, everybody trying their hardest to listen to what she was saying, she was sure, then rang the beeper, punched the number in.

Ricki turned back, held up the phone and said; "It'll be a few minutes." Everyone nodded. The detective and Tommy leaned back, got comfortable, lit cigarettes. Danny sat watching her, his look unreadable. The owner glared at her. Billy Joe picked at his fingernails, humming beneath his breath. The ADA got up and left the room, returning a few minutes later with something in a Styrofoam cup. Ricki grew a little irritated no one was offering her any refreshment. *Well, you are the suspect here. Why should they worry about your comfort?* her inner voice reminded her. *Can it*, she inwardly snapped.

The phone rang, startling them all. Ricki immediately hit the button, saying, "Yeah?" turning her back on the group gathered.

"Ricki?" Mitch's voice asked.

"We've got to talk," she said.

"Well, it's about time. I'm home, come on over."

She returned the phone to Danny, asked to borrow his car keys, said, "I should have it within the hour," and left, feeling everyone's stares right through her back.

When she got there, without any preambles, nothing, Ricki said, "I've talked to the police. They've agreed not to arrest anyone concerning the roster if you turn it over."

"You turned me in?" he squealed.

"No, Mitch. I wouldn't give them your name. I simply told them I knew where it was and I would go get it. They're waiting on me now. Give it to me."

His eyes darted behind her. "Did anybody follow you?" he asked.

Ricki rolled her eyes. "No, for Pete's sake, I wasn't followed."

"You're sure?" he asked worriedly.

"Mitch, just give me the dang thing so I can give it to them and we can get on with our lives, okay?"

"Sure," he said, grinning.

This is too easy.

"Wait a minute," she said, getting suspicious, looking into his eyes. "Don't think for a minute, Mitchell, that the copy you made of the roster is yours to decode and then disclose. If you do that, I'll tell them it was you, I swear it."

He grew angry with this. "Damnit, Ricki, I need this."

"Yeah, well, you should have thought of that before everything got all bungled up," she snarled.

"You're the one who fucking bungled it up!" he spat at her.

Ricki studied him. "Partly, yeah. But you didn't do a whole lot of thinking here, did you, Mitch, in your great quest for the mysterious roster. What do you think would have happened once you disclosed the members of the club? The police would have been on you in a minute, you stupid idiot."

"Well, I had that covered," he said, sounding offended.

"Yeah?"

"Sure. I was just gonna tell them I bought it from a source, you know. And then claim my amendment rights when they asked who the source was."

"Yeah and then still got your ass thrown in jail till you revealed the name of the supposed source, of which there isn't!" she snapped. "I happen to watch TV, too, you know."

His eyes lit up. "Oh, man, that would be perfect! Think of all the publicity I could get off that!"

"You're so full of shit," Ricki hurled at him. "Plus lazy as hell."

"Hey!"

"You should have done it the hard way, Mitch. You should have earned the right."

"Oh yeah? How's that?"

"By staking out the club, day and night, taking pictures of who enters and exits, matching those pictures up to faces. Or go through the court system, force them to disclose their membership list. Might have taken a lot more time than it did to steal the roster, but it sure as heck would have been legal, wouldn't it?"

They glared at each other. He turned, went into the bedroom, came out with the envelope, and threw it at her.

Ricki opened it up and peered inside. Looked legit. She stared at him, then said, "I want the copy, too."

His face grew angry. "I mean it, Mitch. You don't give me the copy, I'm going to tell them who has it."

"Since when did you decide to get so all-fired ethical?" he yelled at her.

"Since my butt is the one got put on the line," she snarled.

"You put it there!" he stated with disbelief.

"After I asked you to haul it down to a restaurant so I could use the premises!"

They glared for a few minutes, then he went back into the bedroom, came out with the copy, and threw that at her, as well.

Ricki turned to go, then turned back. "Hey, Mitch? Did it ever occur to you last night to simply take this list, place it on the Xerox machine, make your copy, then put the original back and leave with the copy? Would have saved us all a whole lot of anxiety here, you doofus. Would have gotten you what you wanted, too, you Neanderthal!"

His eyes changed. *And I slept with this idiot,* Ricki thought, making a hasty retreat in case he came after her.

She headed back to the police station, thinking Mitch there would be a good match for Ms. Stacy. Miss Vacuous and Mr. Vapidity.

Ricki was back within 45 minutes. After she parked the car and was rushing toward the entrance, her dandy little journalist friend, who was loitering around outside, stepped in front of her. "I thought you might show up here," he said, flashing ivories.

Ricki stopped, manila envelope in hand, and somewhat lamely explained she was only meeting a friend who worked there.

He eyed her for a moment rather suspiciously, then asked if she had any info for him.

"About what?" she asked.

"Well, let's see, how about a missing roster for starters?"

"Shoot, isn't that the stupidest thing you ever heard of?" Ricki asked, giving him her most innocent look. "I mean, who would be so dumb as to break into a place, steal a roster, go parading before a security camera, making sure they got their picture taken, then forget to lock the back door behind them?" She shrugged. "Sounds kind of contrived to me."

He grinned at this. "Hey, that's an angle I hadn't thought about," he said.

Then to take the conversation in another direction, Ricki told him about an upcoming march WAR was holding against a car dealership in South Knoxville that had been proven to overcharge women for sales and service. He grew excited over that fact, busily writing down the specs as she spat them out. "Be sure to bring your cameraman," she called after him as he headed toward the news van.

After he left, Ricki stood there, staring at the manila envelope, thinking, then went inside and ducked into the first bathroom she could find. She removed the lists, stuffed them in her tote, resealed the envelope, then went into the interrogation room, where Danny, Tommy, the ADA, the detective, the owner, and his attorney were still waiting, everyone but the owner having a good laugh over something as she came in the door. Their faces sobered as they stared at her.

Ricki took the envelope to the owner, but before giving it to him, said, "I have one more provision to make, well, actually two."

Someone in the room groaned loudly. Ricki glanced around, saw Danny and Tommy exchanging amused looks, the ADA and Billy Joe looking vexed, the detective rolling his eyes. She thought he was the one who groaned.

"Now, wait just a minute, we've already made a deal here," Billy Joe said.

"Maybe you ought to listen to what she has to offer," Tommy suggested.

Ricki turned back to the owner. "I give you the list, you swear to me you'll keep anything about how you got this list back or who had access to it out of the media. I don't so much care for myself, but my hus . . .Danny's running for public office, and I don't want anything I'm involved with that might besmear his campaign to get out."

Ricki snuck a glance at Danny, who looked like he didn't appreciate that. *Huh*, she thought.

"And I have my own provision to make," the owner snarled at her. "I don't go to the media if you drop your suit against my club."

"Not unless you revise your policies and agree to hire minorities," she shot back.

"That ain't gonna happen," he said, going back to his redneck voice.

"Well, this ain't gonna happen," Ricki said, waving the envelope under his nose.

He snatched it out of her hand, said, "Think again," as he opened it. Then threw it down in disgust when he saw it was empty. "I can't believe this shit!" he raved at his attorney.

"Oh, yeah, Tommy, did that guy from the ACLU get in touch with you?" Ricki lied, turning to him.

The room grew still.

Tommy gave her a puzzled look.

"I guess not," she answered herself. "Anyway, he's coming in from Atlanta next week, says the ACLU wants to get involved in our case."

Billy Joe swore under his breath. Ricki grinned to herself.

"Oh, yeah, and he's gonna have a guy from the NAACP with him from New York," she went on happily. "Once they found out Charlie was black and a woman, they decided they wanted in on the action."She then grimaced and said, "Oh, shoot, Tommy, maybe I shouldn't have let them know that," inclining her head toward Billy Joe.

"Too late now," he said, frowning widely at her with his mouth, but his eyes were laughing.

Ricki turned to the owner, smiled at him and said, "Oh, well, forewarned is forearmed, I guess."

He glowered at her.

Billy Joe, who now had a blanched look, stood and said, "If y'all will excuse us for a few minutes, my client and I need to confer," steering the owner out the door.

Ricki turned, looked at Tommy. "You are one bad woman," he said respectfully, shaking his head and grinning.

Ricki grinned. Till she saw Danny frowning at her.

So she went and somewhat meekly sat down beside Danny, waiting. The room grew quiet as everyone tried not to look at anyone else. Danny finally got up and said, "Ricki, I need to speak to you for a moment," as he headed for the door.

She shrugged her shoulders at Tommy, got up, and followed him out.

They stood in the hallway, Danny scowling at Ricki, she giving a puzzled look back.

"What?" she finally asked.

"You don't need to protect me," Danny huffed.

"Huh?"

"I'm a big boy, I can take care of myself," he said, his voice quasi-angry. "So don't go trying to make deals for me, all right?"

Ricki studied him. "You think I'm trying to protect you?" She pondered this a minute. "Well, I don't know, maybe I am. I mean, I don't want you to lose the race because of me, Danny." *Wait a minute,* she thought, *why am I explaining myself for doing what I thought was a pretty darn nice thing for him?* She grew angry. "What is this, some sort of macho threat to you?" she spat at him. "What the hell is wrong with me trying to protect you? You try to protect me. But do I get mad at you when you do? Hell, no, I appreciate it. I thought that was one aspect of loving someone, you know, trying to protect them."

They stared at each other. She could see he was thinking over what she said. He finally glanced away, then back. Ricki watched his eyes change from angry to conciliatory. "Well, okay, maybe I misunderstood," he mumbled.

"No, maybe you didn't. Maybe you need to understand I'm as capable of protecting you as you are me." Ricki paused. "Well, now, I'm not speaking physically, of course," she revised. "I might have a little problem in that regard."

He smiled. She smiled.

They went back inside.

After they were seated, the owner and his attorney made their appearance. The owner stepped up to Ricki, said, somewhat belligerently, "Okay, we've got a deal."

"Really?" she asked, not making any effort to hand over the list.

"Give me the list," he demanded, holding out his hand.

"I want you to specify exactly what kind of deal we have here," Ricki insisted.

Tommy snorted. Danny grinned.

The owner rolled his eyes. "It might behoove you to watch the body language," Ricki said, her voice low. "After all, I've still got the upper hand here." This time, the detective snorted.

"Okay, damnit, you drop the lawsuit, I'll revise my policies, I won't go to the . . ."

"In what way?" Ricki asked sweetly.

"What way what?" he shouted.

"How exactly will you revise your policies?"

He turned and glared at his attorney, who seemed to nudge him with some sort of eye signal. "I'll hire minorities from here on out, all right?" he snapped, gritting his teeth.

Ricki nodded her head.

"I won't go to the media about any of this, I'll simply issue a statement the roster was misplaced."

Ricki nodded again.

"Now give me the damn list!" he roared.

She turned to Tommy, said, "Can we get something in writing here?"

"Sure," Tommy said, grinning. "I'll draw it up first thing tomorrow."

"Give me the list," the owner snarled.

"Can I trust this guy, Tommy?" Ricki asked her attorney.

Tommy seemed to ponder. "You've got an awful lot of witnesses here, and I don't think it would be in his best interests to renege on any sort of agreement reached in front of three attorneys, a detective, and our next county executive."

"Okay," Ricki said, reaching into her tote, drawing the original of the roster out, and handing it over, deciding to keep the copy, just in case. As she gave it to him, she said, "I'm really sorry this happened. You have my word it won't be disclosed. If it is, I'll tell you who's responsible."

The old gent stood up to his full height, looked her in the eye and said, "This gets out, you'll pay for it. I'll see to it."

"Darlin', I have already paid for it," Ricki said, staring him down.

Tommy and Danny rose, both shaking hands all around, after which they left.

Once outside, Danny told Tommy he'd take Ricki to her car, which she had left in the parking garage in Tommy's building. On the way, she asked him what everyone had been laughing about when she came in.

He grinned and said, "Tricky Dick giving the old V for victory sign." Ricki smiled a little.

He reached over, squeezed her hand and said, "I'll say this for you, Rick, if you were a man, you'd have balls the size of Seattle."

Ricki laughed.

Her car was parked on the top floor of the garage, in a deep, dark corner. Danny pulled into the space beside it. Theirs looked to be the only two vehicles on the whole floor.

Ricki reached over, kissed his cheek and said, "Thanks, darlin', for everything."

He smiled.

"Well, I guess I better get home," she sighed, clutching the door handle.

"Ricki," he said, reaching out, staying her with his hand.

"Yeah?" she asked, turning back to him.

They looked at each other. She could see the desire and need and want in those wonderful eyes of his, and wondered what he saw in hers. As they slowly grinned at each other, Ricki decided it must have been the same thing.

They collided into each other, kissing frantically, and her mouth on his, she straddled him, reached down, and pushed the lever, sending his seat back.

He laughed. But not for long.

For a time, the whole world was blotted out as they pleasured each other, oblivious that if anyone drove into their corner, what they were doing would not be considered for public display. As far as they knew, though, no one saw them. It reminded Ricki of when they were dating, the way they used to go at each other in his truck, and that seemed to make it all the more special to her. And when she finally climbed out of his car, skirt askew, pantyhose grabbing at her crotch because she'd pulled them up wrong, her panties feeling sticky and wet as his seminal fluid leaked back out, her shoes clutched in her hand, she bid him goodbye the way she had those long 20+ years ago, kissing the tips of her fingers, turning them to him, watched him do the same to her, smiling happily, then got into her car and headed home, feeling so wonderfully good inside. Till she walked in and found the house empty, Zachary having gone out with a friend, and realized her ex-husband, now lover, probably had gone home to Miss Dumb-butt of the Century, the future Mrs. Danny England. *And look at me, all alone and lonely, the erstwhile Mrs. Danny England,* she thought.

CHAPTER 19

"OH AND WE MUST HAVE GOTTEN LOST"

Ricki hadn't talked to Charlie since the day after their break-in incident, simply because she was half-afraid Charlie would try to get her to go off on another sortie and Ricki deemed it in her best interests to stay away from that sort of stuff. At least for the time being. Okay, Ricki had to admit she was the one that pushed Charlie on the roster thing, but shoot, she had never been inclined to do anything like this before Charlie came along. She was beginning to think her good friend might be a bad influence. Never occurred to her that Charlie might be thinking the same thing about Ricki.

The following week, after their usual Tuesday night WAR meeting, Charlie talked Ricki into going out for a "bite to eat" the next Saturday. *Well, I can't get into too much trouble just eating*, Ricki thought. Besides, she didn't have anything else to do.

They went to a nice restaurant in the Old City and who should they run into but Ricki's hairdresser and his gay lover. Who were on their way to the grand opening of a new nightclub, and why didn't they go with them? You'll enjoy it, they promised, giving each other wicked grins. *Well, why not*, Ricki thought, *can't get into too much trouble if I just stay away from the alcohol.*

When they walked into the nightclub, Ricki's first impression was that everybody excluding them seemed to be wearing nothing but black leather, studs, and chains.

"Is this a biker's convention or what?" she asked Marvin, who grinned slyly.

The room was smoke-filled, hazy. Ricki looked around, squinting her eyes, which widened at the sight of men dancing with men, women dancing with women. She glanced at Charlie, whose eyes appeared larger than her own.

"You didn't tell me this was a gay club," Ricki snapped at Marvin.

"You didn't ask," he snipped back.

Charlie and Ricki looked at each other. "Let's leave," Charlie said.

Ricki wasn't really sure if she wanted to. She guessed she was more curious than anything. She'd never been in a gay club before, didn't know what went on. And wasn't her quest in life to live it to its fullest? Didn't that include engaging in experiences outside of what she would consider normal for herself? Like partying with gays?

"Let's stay," Ricki encouraged, "just for a few minutes. Just to be polite," whispering this last part.

Charlie glared at her.

"Aren't you curious about being in a bar like this?" Ricki asked her. "Haven't you ever wondered what happens at gay clubs?"

"Do I look like a faggot to you?" Charlie asked insolently.

"Well, no," Ricki answered, looking around with alarm, hoping no one heard her and would take offense.

"Then why the hell do you think I care or, for that matter, want to know, what goes on in a place like this?" Charlie snarled, glancing around somewhat angrily.

"Come on, Charlie. We'll stay with Marvin and Anthony. No one will bother us. We're safe. Besides, if they do, we'll just pretend we're together," Ricki whispered.

Charlie's eyes narrowed when Ricki said this.

"Please, Charlie, do it for me. I'd like to just be able to say that during my lifetime I have had the experience of going to a gay nightclub," Ricki implored.

"Yeah? And who exactly would you care to say that to?" she asked snidely.

Ricki shrugged, not really knowing. "Just one drink, then we'll go," she promised, ignoring her friend's irritated look.

They made their way toward a table near the bar and all sat down, a really good-looking, Marine-type coming over to take their orders for drinks.

This guy was really cute, with great buns. "You think he's gay?" Ricki asked Marvin, who rolled his eyes at her.

The music in the place seemed to consist of nothing but a heavy, thudding, erotic-sounding bass. People were everywhere, in different degrees of being stoned or drunk. Ricki liked to watch this human species we are a part of, so settled back, observing all the activity. The thought occurred to her that the group gathered seemed freer than the straights, maybe not as restrained in showing affection. Or maybe more exhibitionist, she didn't know.

Ricki felt like she was in another world, watching the dancers on the floor. There wasn't one man dancing with one woman out there. They danced close, with a lot of touching, a lot of affectionate groping. She couldn't help but close her eyes when she caught sight of two guys giving each other tongue.

"Oh, gross," Ricki said, mock shuddering. Marvin and Anthony exchanged an amused look.

Charlie borrowed a cigarette from Marvin and sat puffing, impatiently drumming her fingers on the tabletop. Their table companions seemed to know a lot of people in the room and someone was constantly stopping by, making conversation. Ricki listened and watched in fascination at the exaggerated laughs, poses, and sexual innuendoes.

Her mouth literally dropped open when her dentist made a stop at their table, giving her a secretive smile. Ricki had never suspected he was gay, and as she gaped at him, she thought how awful narrow-minded that thought was.

"Ricki," he cooed, "I didn't know you were one of us!"

"Uh, I'm not, actually," she said, giving him an embarrassed smile.

He looked from Ricki to Charlie, then back, nodding as if he understood, giving her a wink. She rolled her eyes, leaned toward Charlie, and whispered, "And I let that guy put his hands in my mouth!"

She burst out laughing.

"Just think where he might have had those hands, Charlie," Ricki said.

"Nowhere yours haven't been," she reminded her.

Oh.

The nape of Ricki's neck tingled slightly, the way it always seemed to when someone was staring at her. She glanced around, noticed this really tall, heavyset woman with short, blond hair eyeing her from the bar. She wore jeans and a white T-shirt, rolled up at the sleeves. Ricki wondered if she had a pack of cigarettes tucked within the folds and a wallet stuck in her back pocket. Ricki did try not to categorize or stereotype people, but this was the sort of woman she had always assumed were lesbians. The ones that looked, well, masculine. And she did. To the extreme. *I bet she plays the man's role in the relationship*, Ricki thought, beginning to wonder exactly how they did it.

Ricki looked away but could still feel the woman's stare, and when her eyes met Ricki's again, she gave her a smile, nodding her head. *Uh-oh,* Ricki thought, as she nodded back, that being the polite thing to do and all.

"Charlie, that woman's staring at me," she whispered, jerking her head in the direction of the bar.

She followed the movement of Ricki's head, then grinned. "Maybe she thinks you're cute," she said, snorting.

Their drinks finally arrived. Ricki sighed with relief, sipping her mineral water with lime, thinking maybe Charlie and she ought to head on out of there. She was just about to make that suggestion when movement to her side caught her eyes. Ricki looked there, then up, to see the woman at the bar standing beside her chair.

Marvin and Anthony were engaged in what seemed to be a delightful conversation with some of their friends. Ricki lightly kicked Charlie under the table to gain her attention.

"Hello," the woman said, her voice sounding surprisingly feminine to Ricki.

"Hi," Ricki said back, glancing at Charlie, who was grinning again. She really hated her sometimes.

"I'm Melody," the woman said, again surprising Ricki. She had also stupidly thought they all adopted masculine names.

"Well, hey, Melody. I'm Ricki," she said, her face growing red, "and this is Charlie," realizing they were the ones who had the masculine-sounding names and were apparently the only two straight women in the vicinity.

"Nice to meet you, Ricki," she said, holding out her hand. Ricki shook limply.

"I've been watching you," Melody offered, giving Ricki the look-over.

"Oh? Really?" she said, not sure how to reply.

"You got really great legs and a nice ass."

Well, talk about subtlety. Ricki looked harder at her face and could tell by the laxness around the mouth, the glassy expression in her eyes, that she was either drunk or well on her way. "Well, thank you so much for saying that," she muttered, glancing around in alarm.

"So, Ricki, would you care to dance?" Melody asked, giving her an intent look.

"Uh, thanks, but no," Ricki replied, once more glancing at Charlie.

Melody frowned slightly. *Oh, dangit all to hell*, Ricki thought miserably.

"Any particular reason you don't want to dance with me?" she inquired, sounding offended.

"Well, it's just . . ." Ricki stammered, then the lightbulb went on. "I'm with her," she said, placing her hand on Charlie's arm, squeezing ever so possessively.

The look she received from Charlie was clearly discernible to her, i.e., *get your hand off my arm or you're gonna find it crammed into a certain orifice of your body and you don't want to know which one.*

Ricki immediately withdrew it.

Melody stared at Charlie a moment, then, "You care if your girlfriend dances with me?" she asked her.

Charlie, looking offended, said, "Hey, she ain't my girlfriend. You want to dance with her, go right ahead."

Ricki sent Charlie the evil eye, which she ignored.

"Go on, Ricki, dance with the woman," Charlie encouraged, giving her a fake smile.

I hate you! Ricki's mind screamed as she glared at Charlie, but she didn't seem to catch that.

"So, let's dance," Melody encouraged.

"Well, actually, I just don't feel like it right now," Ricki said, giving her a wimpy smile.

"Whatsamatter, there something about me you don't like?" Melody slurred, her voice growing angry. "I mean, there any particular reason you don't want to dance with me?" she asked, rather disbelievingly, Ricki thought.

"Well, actually, no, you know," she said, shrugging, kicking Charlie's shin under the table. She promptly and quite firmly kicked back.

Damn you! Ricki mentally screamed at her. She missed that one, too.

"Or maybe you don't want to dance with me 'cause my skin's the wrong color," Melody said snidely, getting in Ricki's face, glancing menacingly at Charlie.

What is this, Ricki thought, *a lesbian racist?*

"Maybe I'm not black enough, is that it?" Melody snarled.

"You got a problem with that?" Charlie asked her, getting mad.

"Uh, no, that's not the reason," Ricki said, trying to waylay a riot here.

"Well?" Melody asked.

"It's just, well, to tell you the truth, I'm not one of you, you know," Ricki said lamely.

Melody's eyebrows went up.

"Well, I mean, actually, I am one of you, meaning I am a woman and all, but, you see, I'm not one of you."

Melody's look was incredulous. "One of me?" she asked, pointing at herself.

"Uh, yes."

"One of whom?" she asked suspiciously.

"Well, I'm afraid I prefer men to women," Ricki said, feeling like she ought to be apologizing here. Seeing her look, "Now, please, no offense, it's just, I'm not, well, I'm not homosexual. I like men, well, I like being with men, you know, sexually."

Melody's brow furrowed.

"I mean, there's nothing wrong with you being who you are, with you preferring women. If that makes you happy, well, then, I'm happy for you." Ricki heard strangling sounds to her left, looked to see Charlie choking on her drink. She started to kick Charlie again, but her shin was still hurting from her last physical assault thereon in response to her very tender one, so determined it to be in her best interests to delay that action.

"And I have the utmost respect for people of your, well, persuasion," Ricki stammered on, trying to be as politic as possible. "I feel empathy for you, for your cause; and I also feel, you know, it's your decision, it's your life, and whatever you do with whomever you choose to do it is not my business or anyone else's for that matter, except, you know, you and who you happen to be with."

Ricki noticed it seemed awful quiet around their table. She looked at Marvin and Anthony, who were staring at her.

"Help me out here!" she said.

They did nothing but smile. Woodenly.

Ricki turned back to Melody, who still didn't seem to get it. "And I assure you, if I were one of you, I mean, if I were a les. . .if I were homosexual, I would be more than happy to dance with you. I'd be proud to be seen dancing with you. But I can't because you're, you know, not a man."

Oh, please, God, make her go away and leave me alone, Ricki prayed silently, watching Melody process what she had just stated.

"So, you're saying you're straight, right?" she asked.

"Yes," Ricki said, with relief.

"Then what are you doing here?" Her look was smug.

"I came with them," Ricki answered, pointing to Anthony and Marvin, who quickly looked away. She willed some pretty heavy profanity their way, but for some reason they didn't pick up on it. *They must be on the same nincompoop wavelength as Charlie,* she thought disgustedly.

Melody stood there, studying Ricki like an insect under the magnifying glass. Her heart stopped. "You ever been with another woman?" Melody asked, cocking her head.

Uh-oh. "Well, no, actually, I haven't. Haven't really ever felt the inclination to, to tell you the truth," Ricki said, then added, "No offense. Like I said, I find nothing at all wrong with it, it's just, well, that's just not me." She nodded.

Marvin and Anthony snickered. Charlie had a coughing fit.

Ricki glared at them all. Didn't phase them one bit.

"I could change your mind," Melody enticed.

"I'm sorry?" Ricki said, giving her a sick smile.

"About lesbianism." Melody leaned her hands on the table, stared her in the face. "I bet you I could pleasure you a hundred times more than any man you've ever been with," she challenged.

"Uh, I don't think so," Ricki mumbled.

"I'll prove it to you."

"Well, actually, I'd prefer not," Ricki said, sounding strangled.

"You know what I think?" Melody asked her.

Well, to be quite honest about it, Ricki didn't really give a shit, but she couldn't tell Melody that, seeing as how she got so easily riled and all, so instead, answered, "Uh, no, no, I don't."

"I think the fact that you're sitting here in this bar with these people indicates that maybe you're at least a little bit interested in the gay lifestyle."

Ricki was starting to get irritated here but tried to squelch it. She gave Melody a glassy smile and said, as firmly as she could, "Listen, Melody, I came here by mistake. I didn't know this was a gay club, okay? I'm not interested, no offense. I like men, all right?"

Melody smiled lecherously.

Ricki sighed heavily, wondering what it was about her that she had to deal with people she was not attracted to in the least coming on to her, and never in a subtle way. *It has to be a look about me,* she thought for the thousandth time. *Maybe I look, well, sexually hungry. Desperate? Please, God, don't let me look desperate,* she prayed silently. She swore to herself then and there that as soon as she left this place, she was going to seek out the nearest nunnery.

"I can promise you an experience you'll never forget. I can introduce you to different feelings within yourself," Melody said, going for enticing.

Well, Ricki sure wasn't about to try to find that out. So what did she respond with? Only the worst thing she could have possibly, but only because she didn't know what else to say. "Really?" she asked.

"Why don't we leave?" Melody asked, leering at her.

Ricki glanced at Marvin and Anthony, who now appeared to be busy in conversation with each other. Upon seeing her look, Charlie said, "I think I need to make a phone call," rising from her seat.

You're gonna die for this, Ricki screamed mentally at her.

"I'd rather stay," Ricki answered, turning back to Melody, idiotically wondering if there had ever been a case of a woman raping another woman. This Melody looked like she could just eat her alive. She was not helping Ricki's self-esteem.

"Come on, let's go," Melody said, jerking her head in the direction of the door, reaching out with one beefy hand, and helping Ricki up out of her seat.

Ricki was mad Charlie was making haste to leave her at such a traumatic time as this, a time when she desperately needed her help, so decided to get her back, clamping her left hand on Charlie's arm as she began to turn to leave, looking Melody in the face and saying, "Well, actually, all that I just told you? It was a lie. I only said it because I didn't want to offend you. The real reason I won't dance with you is because I have feelings for this woman right here, and I do prefer my women the same way I do my coffee: black," feeling awful smug at taking a dig at all those male chauvinist pigs out there she had heard use different variations of this line.

Marvin and Anthony immediately got up.

Charlie jerked her hand out of Ricki's arm, saying, "Damn you, Ricki."

"Well, she asked," Ricki explained.

"What the heck has she got that I don't have?" Melody asked, looking really angry.

"Black is beautiful, or haven't you heard?" Ricki mocked.

"You mean to tell me you prefer a nigger over me, one of your own kind?" Melody snarled, and Ricki immediately stepped back, giving Charlie room to lunge.

It seemed like within a fraction of a second, all hell had broken loose in that nightclub. Charlie, of course, started the physical violence, going for Melody's face and hair. For no reason at all, people just seemed to start fighting. It was the weirdest thing Ricki had ever seen. She looked around for Marvin and Anthony, saw them exiting the door. "You spineless amoebas!" she yelled at them, then darted for the bar, crawling over it, hiding behind as bottles and chairs and articles of clothing flew through the air.

Ricki would peek up from time to time, trying to pinpoint Charlie and Melody, but they were nowhere to be found in all the hullabaloo. Shoot, she didn't know what to do. She wanted to get out of there but couldn't just leave Charlie, right in the middle of this huge fight. She might be hurt. She might need someone to take her home or to the hospital. More pertinently, Ricki was well aware of the fact that if she left her friend, she would track her down and she'd probably never see daylight again.

So, Ricki crouched and cringed.

In a matter of minutes, she heard a lot of masculine voices shouting, and the whole melee seemed to break up quickly. Ricki breathed a sigh of relief, standing, coming face to face with an officer of the law.

They stared at each other for a few seconds, then Ricki said, somewhat frantically, "Listen, officer, you've got to help me. I didn't know this was a gay club when I came here, and then this huge fight broke out, and it's just been the most terrible experience of my life. Please, could you help me get out of here?"

He gave her an icy grin and said, "So, you want to leave?"

"Oh, yes, please," Ricki begged.

"Fine, then, just come with me," he commanded, helping her over the bar and, keeping his hand on her elbow, leading her out.

"Oh, thank you so much, officer," Ricki effused, trailing along, stepping over various and sundry debris, not to mention a couple of prone bodies. "I promise you, I won't forget this. I'll pay you back in some way for your kindness, I swear. I'm just so glad you came along. I didn't know what I was going to do . . ." Her voice stopped as he pulled her outside and practically threw her into a paddy wagon.

What the, Ricki thought to herself, looking at everybody looking at her. Well, they were actually doing more than looking; they were glaring, to tell you the truth.

"That's the bitch that started it," Ricki heard a familiar voice say, squinted toward the front and saw Melody.

"Oh, hey, Melody," she said, trying for friendly. "You seen Charlie?" she asked, then screamed as Melody got up and came toward her.

If the door hadn't been jerked open at that very moment, in order that another body could be thrown inside, Ricki was sure she would have been DOA by the time they got to the police station. Thankfully for her, the body deposited by hers was Charlie's. Once Melody saw who was beside Ricki, she calmed down somewhat, going back to her position on the bench, glaring sullenly.

It seemed to take forever to process them through, Ricki all the while proclaiming her innocence, receiving a deaf ear in return from all present. Except from Charlie who, after telling her she was no longer her friend, advised Ricki to can it or she would for her.

The one phone call Ricki was allowed she placed to Tommy, who answered, sounding out of breath. "Hey, Tommy, this is Ricki," she said, wanting to cry.

"Ricki? Uh, Rick, I'm right in the middle of something, let me call you back hon," he said.

"No way, Tommy. I am in dire need of your services tonight."

"Come on, Ricki, don't do this to me," he whined.

221

"Tommy, you've got to help me. This is the only phone call they said I could make," Ricki begged.

He took a minute, then, "Where are you?" sounding suspicious.

"At the police station," she sniffled.

"Aw, Rick, what the hell have you gone and done now?" he demanded, not sounding like a lawyer at all.

"I am completely innocent here, Tommy," Ricki proclaimed.

"Famous last words, Rick."

"Well, it's true!"

"What do you want?" he asked wearily.

"I need you to come bail me out."

"Tonight?"

"Well, yes. You can't let me spend the night in jail, Tommy, come on."

"I think that'd probably do you a whole world of good, spending the night in jail."

"Please, Tommy. I won't live through the night, you leave me here, I'm serious."

"I'm busy, Ricki."

She glanced around, lowered her voice to a whisper. "Tommy, there's this lesbian who has it in for me and there's a good chance they'll put me in the same cell with her. Now, you've got to get me out of here. She's liable to kill me good if you don't."

"I'm sure she has just cause."

"Tommy, don't do this to me."

"I'll call Dan for you."

"No!"

"Listen, Ricki, I didn't take you to raise, okay? You got yourself into some trouble? Fine, get yourself out. I've got plans."

"Tommy!" she wailed but he had hung up on her.

Ricki made a mental note to demand Danny no longer retain the services of a certain Mr. Tommy Leigh. Well, after she got out of this mess.

They put them into holding cells. Thankfully, Melody wasn't in the one with Ricki, but regrettably, Charlie was. She, for some unexplainable reason, was blaming Ricki for this whole mess. Ricki pointed out rather emphatically to her that she could have left the premises with Marvin and Anthony, those cowards, before the police arrived, but no, being the true-blue friend she was, she had stayed in case Charlie needed her. She tried helping Charlie understand if she had stood by Ricki when Melody was hitting on her, like any real friend would have, she wouldn't be sitting in this jail cell at this very moment. And besides, Charlie, who threw the first punch? When she threatened to throw the next one at Ricki, Ricki got up and moved away from her, deeming it to her advantage to stay away from trouble.

Charlie really made Ricki mad though when they came and told her her husband had made bail and she could leave. Being her friend and all, Ricki assumed she would have looked after her, too. Ricki would have done it for her. But no way. Charlie strutted on out that door, Ricki's progress through being stopped by the guard. Ricki watched her retreating form, calling, "Charlie?" which she ignored. Ricki finally yelled, "Charlie, you're not gonna leave me here, are you?" to which she replied, "You bet your sweet ass I'm leaving you there, Ricki. And I hope they keep you!"

"Hey, Charlie?" Ricki screamed at her. "I won't be in here forever, and when I get out, you're gonna regret what you did. You're gonna rue the day you ever met me, Charlie!"

"Hey, I been ruing that day from the first," she hurled back, turning to glare.

"Yeah, well, no more than I have!" Ricki yelled, then wondered if that sounded like she rued the day she met Charlie or like she was agreeing with her, that Charlie rued the day Charlie met her.

"I'm beginning to think you ain't nothing but a bad influence," Charlie snapped over her shoulder, as the officer led her through the outer door.

"Yeah, well, I didn't want to tell you, Charlie, since I'm such a nice person and all, but I've been thinking the very same thing about you!" Ricki yelled after her departing back, more than aware that everyone had fallen quiet and was watching this little exchange. "In fact, I was thinking it way before you thought it!" she yelled, rattling the bars of the cage rather fiercely, she thought.

Charlie retaliated with a vulgar, "Fuck you!"

Ricki was really pissed she said that to her and raised such a ruckus the guard told her to pipe down or she'd see to it she stayed there a good long while. So Ricki slunk to a corner of the cell, keeping to herself, trying to look mean in case anybody got any ideas.

CHAPTER 20

"IF I ONLY COULD TELL YOU, IF YOU ONLY WOULD LISTEN"

Ricki had resigned herself to spending the night in jail when an officer came to the door and unlocked it, calling out her name. She sighed with relief, thinking Tommy must not have been serious after all, then followed him out of the cellblock and into this room, where who was waiting to take her home? Danny England. Mr. Protector.

He scowled at her. She scowled back, thinking, *damn, can I not do one wrong thing in my life without this guy finding out about it?*

Danny waited patiently as she was given back her "personals" and signed the receipt for it. She glanced at him from time to time, taking note of the looks he was giving her: perplexed, angry, befuddled, and worried. She guessed whoever had called him had gotten him out of bed. He was dressed in jeans and a pullover shirt, tennis shoes on sockless feet. His hair was tousled, giving him a little-boy look. Since Stacy, Danny had taken to dressing in a dapper fashion, but this was the way Ricki preferred him, casual. She finally approached him, feeling guilty as hell and about as resentful.

"Who called you?" she asked.

"About half of Knoxville," he snarled.

"Oh, Danny, I'm sorry."

"Yeah, you're sorry, all right," he agreed.

"Hey!" Ricki said, offended.

He ignored this, led her out to the car, and was gentleman enough to open the door, then climbed behind the wheel, not saying a word.

They rode home in silence. Ricki was kind of glad but surprised. She had steeled herself for Danny to start yelling or something and his taciturnity was a little unsettling to her, being something she wasn't used to from him.

He pulled into the driveway and stopped the car.

"Thanks, Danny," Ricki said, opening the door. "I'm sorry whoever called you did. I was going to handle this on my own, without getting you involved. I just hope this didn't do anything to harm your campaign. Believe me . . ."

"Ricki, shut up," he growled.

"Sorry," she mumbled.

He gave one of his sighs, then, his voice low, said, "So, is there anything you want to tell me?" giving her a strange look.

"Tell you?" she asked, puzzled.

"About tonight. Where you were."

"Oh, I was at this nightclub and it seems this brawl sort of . . ."

"I know all that. I'm talking about why you were at a gay club."

"Oh."

"Right."

She looked at him, realized what he was getting at. "Danny, if you're asking me if I've gone over to the other side, the answer is no way, Jose. I still very much like and prefer men."

"Thank the good Lord," he sighed.

She stared at him, not sure if he was serious or not, then decided *well, heck, the guy bailed me out, he does deserve an explanation.* So she told him the whole thing, from when they met Marvin and Anthony to how she had come to be arrested. He laughed when she told him about how the fight got started, surprising her.

"I guess I'm actually the one responsible for the fight," Ricki admitted.

"Well, maybe in an indirect way," he agreed.

"So, shouldn't I pay restitution or something, Danny?" she asked, starting to worry now maybe she'd be going to jail for inciting a riot or something.

"Shoot, Ricki, that could be thousands of dollars," he answered.

"Well, I'm good for it. I can, like, pay a certain amount down, then monthly payments. They'd have to accept that sort of payment schedule, wouldn't they?"

He sighed heavily. *Dang,* she thought. "Listen, I've got some influence where it counts. Let me see what I can do," he offered.

"No."

"Ricki!"

"I started the whole mess, okay? I have to make amends in some way, and I'm not going to let you just ride in here on your white steed and make all my problems go away. I have to be responsible," she insisted.

"You're so full of shit," he moaned.

"Well, that's the way I feel."

"Okay, listen, I'll call Tommy tomorrow, we'll go talk to him, let him advise you on what you're facing here. Although, actually, I don't think there's any way they can prove who started the fight. You weren't involved in it physically." He paused, eyed her, then, "Were you?"

Ricki smiled. "No, darlin', I wasn't," she said, kind of wishing she had thrown one good punch, just to see what that felt like.

"Well, okay, then. You just kind of got caught in the middle of it," he finished, sounding relieved.

Ricki decided what the hey, let him think what he wanted, she'd just handle it on her own. Danny, being Danny, wouldn't like it, but tough tootles. *Wait a minute,* she thought. *If this thing gets in the papers and it comes out that I was arrested during an altercation at a gay bar . . .*

She looked at Danny. "Uh, maybe it wouldn't be such a bad idea if you used whatever clout you might have to see to it that my name doesn't get into the paper, Danny."

He grinned warily. "That part's already been taken care of," he said, somewhat smugly.

Whew, she thought with relief.

Danny put his head back and closed his eyes wearily. Ricki looked at him, feeling that old attraction reach out. He finally turned his face, gave her a reluctant grin, then said, "Well, that Melody was right about one thing, babe."

"Yeah?"

"You do have a great butt and legs." He gave her one of his lecherous looks. "Well, great everything, to be honest."

Ricki smiled. "You know something," she said, musing. "I was watching those men with men and women with women tonight, and I have to tell you, I just couldn't understand it. Now, don't get me wrong, I think the female body is beautiful, wonderfully put together, but there's just something about you men that I don't see how a woman could, you know, replace. At least not for me."

He turned his head and looked at her.

"I like the way you guys look. The way you're put together. The way you move. Your deep, rumbling voices. Stubble on your cheeks. Hair on your chest, arms, and legs. The way your body feels hard, tough." Ricki started feeling embarrassed, wondered why since their divorce she kept opening herself up to this guy when she hadn't been able to the last decade they had been together. She noticed Danny was giving her an ironic grin.

Well, shoot, she'd started, so why not finish. "I like the fact that you're so simple, you know? Men seem to see things more starkly, more in black and white. With women, everything is so much more complex, so much more shaded."

"Wonder why that is," Danny mused.

"Well, I guess men are more ruled by basic emotions than women are."

"Yeah? Like what?" he asked, his voice low.

"Well, love, for one. Fear of harm to yourself or your family. Aggression. Domination."

"Don't start, Ricki," he griped.

"No, that's not what I'm saying. It's just, I've thought about this a lot, you know, and I'm trying to tell you, it's not so bad, the way men are. Now, I'm speaking in generalities, Danny, not about any one specific man. Of course, there are men who function at a lower level, others at a higher level. I mean, take you, you're one of the best men I know, well, actually darlin', the best."

He stared at her.

"I'm trying to say, I think a lot of my perceptions about men, a lot of the way I feel toward men, the fact that I like men so much is because of you, Danny."

Their eyes met. He reached out, hugged her to him, and gave her a tender kiss. "You say the damndest things," he whispered.

Ricki grinned, reached down, took his palm in her hands, brought it to her mouth, kissed it warmly, hearing his intake of breath, and somehow it found her breast and they were at it again.

Ricki came up for air long enough to realize they were in the car, which was in the driveway, which was clearly discernible to anyone looking out of any front window like, say, their son.

She pointed this out to Danny. "Let's go inside," he said, breathing heavily.

"Zachary and Matthew are in there, Danny, they might hear us," she whispered, trying desperately to come up with a fast solution, fearful once his thought processes traveled north again, he'd change his mind about what was about to transpire.

"We'll leave," he said.

"No, let's go to the stables, get a blanket, go out into the field, make love under the stars."

He stared at her.

"Come on, Danny," she urged. "Just like we used to."

He opened his door, got out, came around, helped her out, and they both walked toward the stables, arms around each other, groping each other, got a clean blanket out of the tack room, took it out into the back field, away from the house and anyone who might be looking that way, and threw it down, hungrily kissing. There was a full moon, giving them enough light to see each other. Ricki pulled back from Danny, feeling mischievous, thinking,

I'm not gonna make it that easy for you, big guy, began playing with him, backing up, unbuttoning her blouse, watching him come for her.

She made him chase her around a little, but not too much. She didn't want him to get winded. And when he caught her, he kissed her so passionately, it took her breath away. She placed one leg around his waist, then the other, and he carried her back to the blanket, kissing her all the way.

Out there, in the cool night air, the stars glistening in the dark sky above Danny and Ricki, two tiny beings in this bucolic setting, it seemed they made enough noise to raise the dead. Well, at least some dogs from somewhere were howling like wolves. Afterward, they lay there, entwined still, sweating, breathing heavily, coming down, laughing lazily at the baying sounds of the dogs.

After awhile, Danny turned on his side, stroking her body lightly, then asked, "So, you ever going to tell me what happened with that Sam character?" surprising her.

Ricki stiffened slightly. He stopped stroking, watching her.

"It's over," she said, her voice sounding strained.

Danny paused a moment, then, "Want to talk about it, Ricki?"

She smiled. "No. No, Danny, I'd rather not."

"Sometimes it helps to talk," he said, mocking the very words she used to say to him.

She laughed a little, reached out, put his big warm hand back on her body, and snuggled closer. "In essence, we weren't good for each other," she said. Then, "Well, not at the end. It wasn't the kind of relationship I want or need to have."

He nodded, then surprised her again, saying, "I never could understand you and him together, Rick. He was way out of your league." She didn't respond to this. Then he asked, "What was it, was he a great lover or what?" smiling, trying to belie the seriousness of his question.

She studied Danny a moment, then decided, *what the hey, I'll just tell him.* "Danny, you know I don't lie to you, and don't take this the wrong way, but yes, he was a fantastic lover."

His face shut down.

She sighed this time and lay back, looking at the sky, telling more than she wanted. "He liked to experiment, do different things. I enjoyed that. But that wasn't what was so great with him. He made me feel alive at first. I had felt so dead for so long. And he came along, so good-looking, and he kept telling me how gorgeous I was, how smart I was, how much fun I was, what a fantastic lover I was." She shrugged, saying, "I was so gullible, Danny. He dangled the bait, and I bought it hook, line, and sinker."

His face came close to hers, and his voice tight, Danny said, "He only told you the truth, Ricki. Don't ever think otherwise."

She shrugged.

He watched her, his face changing. She wondered what he was thinking, then he said, "Did I do that to you, Ricki? Did I make you feel unattractive, dead?" his voice sounding hurt.

She shook her head. "No, honey, I did it to myself."

He lay back, looking at the sky. "You know, babe, I've done a lot of thinking about us since our divorce."

"Don't feel like the Lone Ranger," she intoned, dryly.

He turned his face to look at her. "I knew you were unhappy for a long time, Ricki, way before you told me, and it scared the shit out of me."

She blinked in surprise.

"I was terrified you'd decide one day you didn't love me anymore and would leave me. Sometimes you seemed almost like an automaton. Even in bed. You did everything you could to please me, babe, but you just weren't there. Not at the end. Ricki, I wasn't insensitive. I could see it, feel it. But I was scared. That's a lousy excuse for the way I treated you, but it's the truth. Even though I knew you were unhappy, I couldn't bring myself to say, 'hey, babe, tell me what's wrong, tell me how to fix it.' Mainly because I was afraid you'd tell me and I wouldn't be able to. And when you did start trying to talk to me about what was wrong, I shut you out. I didn't want to hear it confirmed, I guess. So I tried to make you depend on me more, tried to make you feel like you needed me in your life. I admit I was too controlling with you, too domineering. I didn't see it so much then as I do now, Rick. I'm sorry I didn't ask the question I should have asked. I just couldn't bear to hear the answer, I guess."

"Oh, sweetie," she said, rolling into his arms, kissing him. After awhile, she looked at him, said, "You didn't let me finish telling you about Sam, Danny."

He didn't reply.

"Like I said, he was a fantastic lover. He knew all the right words to say, all the right buttons to push, all the right things to do. But being with him wasn't the same as being with you, darlin', even during the bad times. With Sam, I felt like there was something missing, some gaping part not being filled when we made love. When I'm with you, whether I climax or not, whether it's great sex or not, it's just enough, being with you. Feeling you near me, smelling you, touching you, kissing you. You make me feel complete, Danny, you make me feel part of you. With Sam, it was two individuals engaging in a pleasant physical act. With you, it's two people

230

molded, sharing, pleasing, loving." She lay back again, sighing. "Maybe it's love, I don't know. Anyway, what it comes down to is he didn't measure up to you in any way," saying the words she knew he wanted to hear, but they were sincere, too.

He pulled her to him, kissed her hungrily.

A long while afterward, they were on our backs, staring at the sky again, holding hands. Danny turned his head to her and said, "You know what you were saying about Sam, Ricki? It's been the same for me. I mean, with other women."

She smiled slightly. "What do you mean?"

"Not a one, Rick, fit me the way you do. I'm not speaking just physically, but also mentally, emotionally."

She felt herself tear with emotion. "That's exactly what I was trying to say to you," Ricki whispered.

He closed his eyes, then looked at her again. "This is hard for me, you know," he said.

She smiled, nodding.

"I'm not used to, well, opening up like this, Rick."

"I know," she whispered.

Seeing he was caught now, he continued, his eyes glistening. "None were as beautiful as you, none as exciting. None as intelligent, open, warm, nurturing. You're my best friend, babe, you always will be. I love talking to you. I love telling you about what goes on in my business and the way your face lights up if it's good news or falls when it's bad. Anyone else, I just get these blank looks." He shrugged.

"Is that why you dated all those different women, Danny? Shoot, I thought you were just out having fun, sewing wild oats, I guess."

He laughed. "Don't I wish." His face turned sober. "Naw, Ricki, I think I was trying to find someone who could usurp your place in my heart, my mind, my body, my soul."

Oh, God, I love this man so much, she thought, looking at him. "Really?" she asked.

He nodded.

"And it didn't work?"

"No," he replied his voice low.

"Not even with Stacy?" Ricki inquired, really wanting to know.

He shook his head no.

She propped myself up on one elbow. "Then how can you want to marry her?" she asked, her voice growing angry.

He sighed again. "I like being married. I like the security of marriage, the stability."

"You've got years to remarry, Danny."

"Listen, she will be the perfect wife for me, okay? She loves me very much, she . . ."

"Do you love her, Danny?"

He didn't respond.

Ricki grew angry. "Listen, Danny, I told you about Sam when you asked me. I think you owe me the courtesy of reciprocating, okay?"

He thought a moment. "Well, I don't love her the way I do you, Ricki. But I feel affection for her, I care for her. And eventually, maybe I will love her in that way."

"That's not enough."

"It is for me."

"She's not right for you, Danny."

"Well, politically speaking, she's perfect. She comes from a political family, knows all the ins and outs of politics. Knows who to know and who not to know. She's been a great asset to me during this campaign and she will as my wife. She will be a good wife for me, Rick."

"You make being married sound so cold and calculated, Danion!" she snapped.

He visibly bristled. "Hey, Cherokee? Guess what? The first time around, I married the woman I felt was my true love. My life mate, if you will. Only to have that woman, you, Cherokee, 20 years later pull my world out from under me by telling me you no longer wanted to be married to me, you no longer wanted me." He abruptly stood and began angrily gathering his clothes.

"What are you doing, Danny, playing it safe this time?" she taunted him.

"I won't set myself up for that kind of pain again," he growled, stomping around.

"You're being a coward, Danny!" Ricki yelled at him, beginning to cry.

"I will not endure that sort of pain again!" he roared, jabbing his finger angrily at her. "It was unbearable. I couldn't breathe sometimes it hurt so much. YOU hurt me so much. I will never cry or pine for another woman like I did you, Cherokee, I promise you that," he snapped, turning and marching off.

"Hey, Danny, you're nothing but a spineless piece of shit!" she yelled at his departing back. "You know what I'm seeing now, Danny? I'm seeing a big yellow stripe down your back, you big old coward!"

"Yeah, well, you're the one that put it there!" his retreating voice said. "Let me take it off," Ricki said. But he was gone.

CHAPTER 21

"I SAW A LIE IN THE MIRROR THIS MORNING"

Ricki knew in her heart that she was pregnant. However, she refused to entertain that thought for very long in her mind, convincing herself time and time again her symptoms signified some other problem. A gynecological problem. *You're full of shit,* her inner voice snarled. She squelched it, thinking, after all, she wasn't any Fertile Myrtle here, you know. She was well into her 30's; therefore, not prone to become pregnant as easily as when she was younger.

So there she sat, in the office of her gynecologist, waiting for him to get off the phone talking to some other patient about some sort of yucky old discharge, so she could explain what her symptoms were and they could go from there, which always led to Ricki lying naked on the examining table, legs spread, feeling embarrassed and uncomfortable and resentful, to tell you the truth, at having to be in that position for a man she did not wish to be.

She sat waiting, feeling nervous and edgy, thinking this guy knew every intimate detail of her life, from when she conceived Zachary to when she stopped having orgasms with Danny. She shifted, tried to take her mind off why she was there, focusing on Dr. Hutchison, who she had called Hutch forever, it seemed. He put her in mind of a penguin, with his salt-and-pepper hair, black bushy eyebrows, small, dark eyes, rather portly build. Ricki smiled to herself, thinking how offended he would be to know she thought of him in this way.

Hutch concluded his conversation, then favored her with a big, warm smile. She tried to give one back, but feeling it falter, gave up rather quickly.

"So, Ricki, how are we today?" he asked in his big, booming voice.

"What do you mean we, kemosabe?" she teased, watching him chuckle at this. She bet they had said these same lines half a million times to each other. She sighed. He raised his eyebrows, waiting expectantly.

"I think I'm going through menopause," Ricki stated forthrightly.

His eyebrows went up further.

"Maybe pre-menopause, maybe an early one, who knows," she said, shrugging. "I mean, I know I'm kind of young for that. But hey, Hutch, I've read it can happen to a woman in her late 30's."

Hutch nodded, flipped open her file, studied it, frowning slightly. Raising his head, he inquired, "So, what are the presenting symptoms that lead you to this conclusion, Dr. England?"

Ricki stuck her tongue out at him. He grinned. She rolled her eyes. He grinned wider and settled back, watching her.

"I'm serious here, Hutch," she said.

"I never thought you weren't," he replied.

They eyed each other a moment, Ricki wanting him to tell her the exact symptoms of menopause so she could say yes, yes, that's it. He apparently wanted her to tell him exactly what she was experiencing, which she thought was kind of unfair, seeing as he was the doctor and knew infinitely more than she did, but unable to stand the silence any longer, she gave all the symptoms to date. "Well, for one, I'm so emotional anymore, Hutch. I mean, I cry at the drop of a hat. I feel like I'm on some sort of emotional roller coaster, you know? Plus, I'm sick at my stomach all the time, and I've been having these awful hot flashes lately. All of a sudden, for no reason, it feels like there's a fire going up my face, I'm not kidding you, like it's being enveloped in a flame from the neck up, and I can feel my face go red, and I feel so hot and break out in a sweat. That's one of the symptoms, right?"

He didn't reply, just nodded his head slightly, watching, indicating, go on.

"During menopause, your body goes through this hormonal change, or at least that's what I've read, and, well, that would make you prone to be teary and sick at your stomach 24 hours of every frigging day, wouldn't it?"

Still no response, but she had his attention now. He leaned forward, looking interested. So she continued.

"I wake up at night, sweating like a pig. Sometimes I'm so wet I have to change nightgowns. That's also a symptom. I read that, you know," Ricki said, nodding emphatically.

He made a temple out of his right and left index fingers, resting it against the bridge of his nose.

Uh-oh.

"My breasts are tender, my lower back feels like it's gonna break in two, and I keep feeling like I'm going to start, but I never actually do. Plus, I have to urinate more than usual, so maybe I'm getting a bladder infection on top of all that other crap." Ricki settled back, waiting. He didn't say anything, staring. She grew uncomfortable, racked her brain for something else. "Oh, yeah, and I'm, well, I'm somewhat late for my period." He didn't even blink. "Anyway, I just thought maybe you could give me some sort of shot, you know, I've heard about those, to get me started and then everything will be all right."

He frowned.

"Well, I've read doctors do do that," Ricki stated defensively.

His frown grew deeper.

"Hey, I'm not asking you to do anything illegal here," she said. Jeez, the look he was giving her, you'd have thought she'd asked for an illegal drug or something.

He picked up his pen, began writing, and then asked, "When was your last period?"

"About two months ago," Ricki mumbled.

He seemed to be watching her face awfully carefully, she thought, so she looked away from him.

"How long since you were due to start the next one?" he asked, his voice sounding professional.

"I don't know, a couple of weeks maybe," Ricki answered, sighing.

Their eyes met.

"Hey, it's not what you're thinking, Hutch," she said, really getting worried here.

"That being?"

"I am not pregnant, so just get that dang thought out of your mind, okay?"

"I didn't say you were, Ricki," he said, his voice soothing.

"Okay, I concede, the symptoms are much like when I was pregnant with Zachary, but that is not the case here. This is all menopausal or pre-menopausal, like I told you. Nothing but a hormonal imbalance, probably. So, just give me the damn shot or some pills or whatever to give my body, you know, like a jump start, and everything will be fine," she said, rather frantically.

He leaned back, pondering.

"And I'm telling you here and now, Hutch, I have given you all my symptoms, so I see no need to go into that examining room and take off all my clothes and get up on the table and put my feet in those cold stirrups. Jeez, I bet if I came in here with a splinter in my little finger, you'd still have me in there, naked, supine, legs elevated, doing a dang pelvic."

He laughed.

"What is it about this specialty anyway that would make a man like you—a really nice guy, Hutch, by the way—want to spend all day with his head between a woman's knees, eyeing her genitals? It boggles the imagination."

He grinned lewdly, waggled his eyebrows. "I like women," he said.

"I can't imagine a worse profession, to tell you the truth," she stated rather opinionatedly. "Well, no, I guess a urologist would be an even worse field than this. Imagine having to look at men's penises all day. I think I'd get rather sick of the sight."

"You think that's bad, how about a proctologist?" Hutch asked. Ricki couldn't help but give a reluctant laugh at this.

"Shoot, I don't know how you do it, Hutch, seeing naked women all day. How can you go home and make love to your wife? Don't you get sick of looking at a woman's body?"

He smiled widely. "I love the female anatomy," he said, raising eyebrows lecherously.

Ricki snorted.

"I am a connoisseur of the female body," he said.

"I always knew you were a lecherous old fart," she huffed.

He laughed just like one, and when he had finished, gave her a serious look and said, "Ricki, go into examining room 3, take off all your clothes, get up on the table, and put your feet in the stirrups."

"I knew it!" she fumed.

He grinned.

She did as requested, well, everything except put her feet in the stirrups. Her little act of rebellion. Hutch came in, chart in hand, writing busily, then eyeing her over the top, said, "Did you give us a urine sample when you came in?"

Ricki rolled her eyes. "Hutch, I cannot walk through your front door without having to hand over a urine sample. What do you guys do with all that stuff, sell it on the black market? Maybe extract some unknown protein and sell it overseas as a youth chemical? I mean, I cannot understand why every time I come into this office I have to pee into a cup as well as get up on this table and let you look at my most private parts!"

He raised his eyebrows, then said, "You are definitely not your usual perky self, Ricki."

"Hey, I am not perky!" she railed at him. "Don't ever call me that, Hutch, you hear me? I take great offense at being called perky."

He ignored this, busily writing, then said, "I take it you've had sex within the past two months."

"Yes, but that has nothing to do with this," she said haughtily.

He eyed her, then said, "Unprotected sex?"

Well, shoot. Ricki hung her head in shame and mumbled, "Yes."

When he didn't reply to this, she looked at him, saw his anger, and before he could lambaste her about the dangers of unprotected sex, said, "It was with Danny, and he's clean, you know that, Hutch."

His eyes widened with surprise. "Did you say Danny?"

"Yes," she said, somewhat petulantly.

"As in Danny England?"

"Yes," she said, looking away.

"I thought you were having a problem with Dan sexually; I thought that's one of the things that led to your divorce," he reminded her.

"Well, yeah, but that was then. Lately, we've, well, shoot, Hutch, I don't know, things have happened between us and when we're together, it's fantastic. It's the way it was when we were first married, you know, passionate, lustful, exciting."

He gave her a dark look and then said, "Well, explain something, Ricki. How come while you were married to Dan, you didn't feel this way, but now that you're divorced from him and he is going to marry another woman, I understand, all of a sudden, sex with Dan is the greatest thing on earth?"

She shrugged. "Go figure."

He rolled his eyes this time.

"Hey, this is none of your business anyway," Ricki said defensively.

"Thank God," he replied somewhat nastily.

He buzzed for the nurse, then once she arrived, proceeded to do the pelvic examination, feeling around on the inside with one finger while prodding on the outside with fingers of the other hand, saying "uh-huh" and "hmmm" all the while.

Ricki clutched at the sheet covering her, staring at the acoustical ceiling, ignoring him.

He finished and told her she could sit up. As he removed his rubber gloves, Hutch conferred with the nurse in whispers near the door, and after she exited, gave Ricki a look she couldn't read.

"What?" she said, growing worried, adjusting the sheet tighter around her body.

"Ricki, I'm pretty sure I know what your problem is, but I want to confirm something first. I'll know for certain as soon as the nurse gets back."

"What?" she said, voice faltering.

"Let's wait," he urged.

"No, Hutch, tell me now," she insisted.

"Well, speaking from the symptoms you're described and the pelvic examination I just conducted, I would say that you're . . ."

"I am not . . ."

". . . pregnant," he said.

". . . pregnant," she finished.

They looked at each other.

Hutch came over, held her hand.

"This is horrible," Ricki said, breaking into tears.

"Pretty wonderful, if you ask me," he said, giving her a paternal look.

"Yeah, well, you can say that, Hutch. You're not an unmarried woman in her late 30's with an almost-grown teenage son, in love with the man I used to be married to, who is now engaged to marry Ms. Dumb-Ass of the Century!" she wailed.

"That I am definitely not," he conceded.

The nurse came in, glancing at Ricki, then conferring with Hutch, who nodded his head, shut the door behind her, turned back to her and said, "I was right, Ricki."

"What am I gonna do?" she sniffled.

"Tell the father," he replied.

"No way," she replied.

"Who I would assume is Dan."

"I'm not gonna do it, Hutch," she wailed.

He frowned at her. Ricki wiped at her eyes, then took the Kleenex he offered, blowing her nose.

She sighed dejectedly. "I can't tell Danny," Ricki said, her voice small and shaky. "He was so adamant while we were married about not having another child. Remember? You and I talked about that. He'd go ballistic if he found out about this."

"It's only fair you tell him," Hutch counseled.

"I'll handle it," she said.

"And how exactly do you intend to handle it?" he asked, his voice firm.

"I'll have an . . . I'll have the pregnancy terminated," she said, crying again.

"Not from me you won't," he snapped.

"Well, fine, Hutch, if you won't help me with my problem, I'll go to that women's health clinic downtown. They do abortions. I'll let them do it."

He scowled at her, then said, his voice low, "Ricki, do me something before you hightail your butt down to that clinic. Think this thing through, all right? You're upset right now and that's understandable, but it's not the end of world. Besides, I know how much you love kids, how much you wanted more when you were married to Dan. So don't deprive yourself of something you may want because of what he might say or people will think, all right?"

She nodded, thinking, *anything to get out of this office.*

He eyed her as if reading her thoughts, then said, "I'll let you get dressed. Stop by my office before you leave, Ricki; let's talk further about this."

"Sure, Hutch," she said, climbing off the table, but she didn't stop by his office. She left, heading for home, telling herself this was her decision, no one was going to influence her over this. When she got there, she looked up the number to the women's health clinic, dialed the phone, made an appointment the following day to talk to a counselor, then went upstairs to cry.

CHAPTER 22

"BABY YOU'RE THE ONE"

Zachary's first tournament game was scheduled for the following Thursday evening. The distaff had easily trounced their rival and was still on the floor when Ricki arrived, waiting to offer high-fives and encouragement to the boys when they made their appearance on court. This was the beginning of what their community hoped would be a long line of tournament playoffs for the high school basketball teams, and even though Ricki felt like crap, she wanted to be there for her son, this year's star player. Without looking around for Danny, she began climbing the bleachers, went to the highest one, the light here being dim, sat down on the farthest end, in the shadows, and scrunched down a little, trying to become invisible.

Danny had called earlier that day, asking if she was going to Zach's game, then telling her he would be there, wanting to know if they could "talk" afterward. His voice sounded courteous, quasi-warm, and yet unreadable. Not able to keep her mind off her appointment the next day, what was going to happen, Ricki didn't want to have that talk, afraid if Danny ended them, she wouldn't be able to cope with two major losses in such a short time, so was in essence "in hiding."

She clutched her stomach as a nauseous wave hit, rode it out, almost gasping from the effort. Her attention was called to the court when the crowd began cheering and clapping, some whistling shrilly.

Ricki watched Zachary come out with his team, a big grin on his face. She couldn't help but smile at this. He seemed to really come alive out there, she thought. Every bit the athlete, just as his father had been.

She couldn't take her eyes off this boy who was now as tall as his dad and built just like him. *He's going to be have a few inches on Danny before it's over*, she surmised, taking note of his young age.

She watched Zachary warm up, his ponytail slinging with his movements, and grinned ironically, thinking of the big fight Danny and she had had over that. *One I won,* she thought smugly.

Nausea hit her again. She closed her eyes, willed it away, and opened them to see Zachary looking up into the bleachers, searching. His eyes finally found her and he gave her a bright smile, flashing teeth. Ricki smiled back and gave him a half-wave, hoping Danny wasn't somewhere down on the floor and would track her from his son's gaze.

Zachary watched her a moment, his smile fading, looking concerned, then went back to the warm-up. Ricki noticed he would glance at her from time to time, a worried scowl on his forehead, just like his dad.

She clutched her stomach, leaned forward a little bit, and wondered if this was morning sickness or just her nervousness about what was going to transpire the morrow. *Don't think about it,* she chided herself, feeling the tears well up.

But she couldn't help but think about it. *Watch Zachary,* she mentally told herself.

He was such a good-looking boy, with Danny's hair and her eyes, and that great big athletic build, but his beauty was deeper than that. *He's such a special kid*, she thought, thanking God for about the zillionth time for blessing her with Zachary. She watched his body maneuver so fluidly, this guy who was always tripping over his own feet at home, much less anyone else's, moving like a dancer on the court, the ball right along with him.

He stopped, looked up at her again, cocked his head, and mouthed, "You okay?"

Ricki grinned and blew him a kiss.

He nodded and went back to what he was doing.

"My miracle baby," she muttered to herself, clutched her stomach harder, feeling tears form in her eyes.

Ricki's mind wandered back to her predicament. How ironic it seemed. Almost 40, going around acting like some hormonal adolescent, managing to get herself knocked up.

I can't have this baby, she rationalized to herself, for about the millionth time, the next day looming in her mind. *I've already raised one child; I don't need to start all over again. I'm past all that. I should be a grandmother, not a mother.*

Ricki remembered with a pain that tore through her how she had once upon a time pined for another child with Danny. She had literally begged him to have another one. He had been so adamant, though, that Zachary would be the only child their marriage would produce. Danny was so afraid of raising a child, terrified of repeating the mistakes his parents had made, and although he went overboard in many ways, Ricki thought he was the best father she had ever seen, but never could convince him of this. She had at one point gone off the pill, defiantly telling Danny she was going to have another child, and he had punished her, staying away from her, not touching her, not even kissing her until she conceded. *Oh, God, why didn't I just trick him then*, she moaned to herself. *You tricked him now!* her inner voice screamed at her.

Did I? she wondered. *By not telling him I wasn't on the pill, which he must have assumed, since I had used them while we were married? By having unprotected sex with only Danny, insisting with Sam and the others that we use a condom? Did I subconsciously trick him?* she asked. *You know you did,* her inner voice sneered. *Well, I don't have to tell him*, Ricki mentally spoke back, sounding petulant. *I'll just go to the clinic tomorrow have the abor - have the procedure done, and no one need know the wiser.*

But that's not what you really want to do! her inner voice chided.

Yeah, well maybe it's time I grew up, acted responsibly, and did the logical, mature thing here, Ricki defended.

You're not being fair to him; you're not being fair to yourself! that inner voice snarled.

Shut the fuck up, she mentally told it.

Ricki looked back to Zach, her baby, her son, and thought about all the wonderful times they had had together. He was such a fun kid, had been from an infant. *Such a miracle,* she thought, watching him, amazed he had come from Danny and her. She sat up straighter, placing her hands on her stomach, stroking, as her inner voice said, *What about the other miracle you got from Danny, the one inside you now?*

She caught the sob as it escaped her throat, turned it into a cough, ducked her head so no one would see the tears rolling down her face. She bit her lip, trying to gain control over her emotions. Damn. It seemed all she did anymore was cry. All she had done for a long time was cry.

Ricki got up abruptly, started making her way down, feeling the need to get out of there before she had one huge crying fit or threw up all over somebody, calling unwanted attention to herself either way.

She caught sight of Danny as she worked her way down, standing on the floor in front of the bleachers, his back to her, looking up, searching for her, she knew.

Ricki turned her back to him, stepped down faster, reached the floor, everything a blur through her tears, and left the gymnasium on the opposite end from him.

She cried all the way home, having to pull over from time to time to try to gain some sort of marginal control. When she got there, she hurried into the bathroom, threw up violently, then stumbled to the bed and curled up there, crying again, wondering miserably if this was hormonal or pain and grief over what was going to happen the next day.

Ricki lay there, thinking how awfully ironic it was. She had always been one who straddled the fence when it comes to abortion. She sincerely believed each and every woman had the right to make any decision she deemed necessary as concerned her body, including abortion; however, she had always felt abortion was murder, pure and simple. So, while she would laud that right for other women, she would deny it to herself. Until now.

She must have fallen asleep because the next thing she was coherent of was the front door banging shut and muffled voices in the house. Ricki opened her eyes, glanced alarmingly at the bedside clock, grew panicked when she realized this must be Danny and Zachary home from the game, then quickly shut her eyes, snuggled deeper into the comforter, hiding her face, trying to appear as if she were sleeping.

The door opened with a slight clicking sound. Ricki heard movement coming toward her, then Zachary's worried, "Mom?"

She didn't respond, praying they would think she was sleeping and go away and leave her alone.

He whispered, "She's asleep, Dad."

She heard movement coming closer, felt Danny's warm, dry hand on her forehead.

"She must be sick," Zachary whispered, his voice full of concern. "Mom never lies down during the day, not unless she's sick."

Danny pulled his hand away, tucked the comforter around her more, and said, "Why don't we leave her alone, son. If she's sick, sleep's the best thing."

She listened to them both tiptoe out, then shut the door quietly behind them, felt the tears come anew, and rolled onto her back, wiping angrily at her face, frustrated she couldn't stop. She didn't want Zachary to see her like this. She knew her eyes would be swollen, red, just from the previous crying stint. She didn't need anything making it worse.

The door came open again. Danny stood there, watching her roll back onto her side, bury her head.

He shut the door, came into the room, sat beside her on the bed, his weight forcing her to roll a little toward him.

"Ricki," he said, his voice low.

She didn't answer.

"Come on, Ricki," he growled. "I shared a bed with you for 20 years and I can tell when you're actually asleep."

A sob escaped her throat again.

She felt him stiffen.

He leaned down, pulled the comforter away from her face, and said, "Babe," his voice concerned.

Ricki tried mightily to hold it back, but a fresh torrent began again.

"Ah, Ricki," he said, patting her back, his voice miserable.

Ricki cried like she had never cried before, violent-sounding sobs, her whole body shuddering.

"Oh, Jesus, baby," he said, pulling her up into his arms, holding her against him, rocking her a little.

Ricki clutched him, cried into his shirt, feeling it grow sopping wet beneath her.

He held her tight, making comforting sounds to her.

She finally wound down, chest hurting, nose running, making hiccuping sounds.

"I, I'm sor-sorry," she said, moving away, feeling embarrassed.

Danny grabbed her back and said, "Don't apologize to me for crying, Cherokee," sounding mad.

He released her abruptly, got up, went into the bathroom, came back, and handed her tissue.

Ricki wiped her nose and turned her face away from him. She was so ashamed of herself, of how she must look.

He stood there a moment, watching her, then walked across to the rocker, plopped down on it, giving Ricki her precious space, and waited for her to look at him.

She finally turned her head his way, allowed a quick glance at him, and then dropped her gaze to her hands, which were shredding tissue.

He rocked a little, staring at her, waiting.

Ricki cleared her throat. "How'd the game turn out?" she asked, voice cracking, building a small mountain out of tissue, afraid to look at him, afraid of what she might do.

He sighed, then said, "It was real close there at the end, but we won, 54 to 52."

"That's great," Ricki whispered, meaning it.

"Our son was high point man again," Danny stated proudly.

"Just like his dad," she said, smiling slightly.

He didn't answer.

Ricki sighed hitchingly, looking at him, and burst out crying again.

"Rick," he moaned, then held his hands out. "Come here, honey," he said, his voice gentle.

She went to him, curled up on his lap, crying into his neck. *Just like a little girl,* she chided herself. *Is that so bad?* her inner voice snapped. *Every once in a while, is that so fucking bad?*

Danny held her tight, rocking her comfortingly, waiting her out. Her outburst quieted shortly. She nestled her face into his neck, savoring the feeling of his strong arms around her, his sturdy legs beneath her, smelling his scent, loving him. She sighed, thinking Danny was the only person she had ever known who made her feel especially cared for. *Yeah, and isn't that all that matters,* her inner voice yelled, *someone caring for you, you caring for someone back?*

He finally stopped rocking and said, "Want to tell me about it?"

She shook her head.

"Maybe I can help," he offered, his voice tender.

How ironic, Ricki thought.

He pulled his head away from her. She could feel the coolness on her forehead as his warmth left, could feel his eyes on her. She wouldn't look at him.

"Talk to me, Ricki," he said. "Tell me what's got you so upset."

"You'll hate me if I tell you," she said, tears falling again, but managing to keep her voice under control.

"Damn, Ricki, I could never hate you," he replied, his voice sounding pained. "Don't you understand that? I love you, more than anything. I'll never love anyone the way I do you."

She sighed, hitching, leaned back, looked at him, said, "Danny, have you ever wanted something so badly you couldn't stand it, yet for some reason that certain thing was deprived to you and . . ."

"Yes, you," he said, his eyes blazing.

She paused, then continued, "And then, when you do have the chance to have what you wanted for so long, the timing just isn't right?"

"God, I hope not," he whispered.

He stared at her, waiting. She looked away from him, toward the window, toward anything, and finally not able to stand it, back.

He studied her face, then said, "Zachary tells me you haven't been feeling too well lately."

Ricki shook her head.

"Says you're sick at your stomach a lot, tired all the time." He raised his eyebrows questioningly.

She wouldn't meet his gaze.

"Ricki?"

She reluctantly brought her eyes back to him.

"You want to tell me about it?" he asked, his voice low, gentle.

You have to tell him, her inner voice whispered. *I know,* she answered. She looked back at Danny, couldn't help it as her face scrunched and the tears started again as she said, "I'm pregnant, Danny," her voice barely decipherable.

He stopped rocking, giving her a stunned look now. "Holy Mother of God!" he declared, his voice unreadable.

"Not hardly," Ricki replied as sarcastically as she could muster.

He gave her a reluctant grin.

Their eyes locked.

The tears started again. After she calmed, still sniffling, she said, "It's yours, Danny. I've been off the pill for awhile and I should have told you, I guess, but when we were together, I, I guess I just was afraid if I told you that, we wouldn't, you know, be together." She stopped herself from rambling, then looked into his eyes and said, "Please don't be mad at me 'cause I got pregnant with your child. I know how you feel about having anymore children and I'm going to take care of it, Danny, I've made all the arrangements. I've got an appointment tomorrow at the abor . . . I'm going to go have it taken care of. It's just, I'm having a hard time right now, dealing with that."

"You're sure?" he asked, giving her a strange look.

She nodded. "I went to Hutch last week, had the test done, and he confirmed it."

"No, Ricki, I mean, are you . . ."

"Oh, about you. You're the only one I had unprotected sex with and you're the only one I've been with since my last period, Danny. You're the only possible one."

"I didn't mean that, Ricki, for Christ's sake. I meant, are you sure you want to do that? I thought you didn't believe in abortion."

"I have to," she answered, crying again.

"Shit!" he said.

"I knew you'd be mad," she said, starting to get up.

"No, honey, I'm not mad," he stated, pulling her back. He looked into her face, gave her a wide grin. "I think I'm kind of glad. Well, that you're pregnant. I also think we ought to talk about your decision concerning the abortion. That doesn't look to be what you want, babe."

Ricki closed her eyes and lay her head against him. "I don't know what I want, Danny," she whispered.

He stopped rocking, gave her a stern look, and said, "I think it's time you figured that out, don't you?"

She shrugged her shoulders.

"Or maybe you already know what it is, just won't admit it to yourself?" he asked, giving her an intent look.

She abruptly got up off his lap, went to the window, and stood looking out, her back to him.

She knew, all right. She had known all along. She turned back around to face him. Danny was watching her, but she was already aware of that. Their eyes met. She went to him, knelt between his legs, placing her hands on his arms, and staring into those beautiful eyes of his, whispered, "I want you. I want us, the way we are now, the way we were once upon a time, before things changed between us."

"That's exactly what I want, babe," he said.

She smiled at this.

He grinned. "Damn, a baby!" he said, his voice sounding happy. Then sobered, seemed to ponder, leaned forward, looked into her face. "Ricki," he said, seriously, "if you want to go ahead with the abortion, I understand that's your decision."

She studied his face. "Wait a minute, is this the Danny England I was once upon a time married to?" she asked, teasingly.

He grimaced and said, "If I learned anything from our divorce, it was you've got to make your own decisions, make your own way, however you deem best. But if you'll allow me any sort of input, I'd like for you to have this baby, for us to have this baby. It can be a new start for us, Ricki, a new beginning. But don't worry, I won't push you about marrying me and making everything all legal. That's your decision, as well."

She was surprised at this, especially considering Danny's own illegitimacy.

"But what about Stacy?" she asked.

He grimaced. "That's what I wanted to talk to you about today. I'm not going to marry her. I broke it off yesterday." He looked away, then back. "I couldn't marry one woman loving another, Rick. I never stopped loving you."

She went back onto his lap, snuggled against him, and said, "I want this baby, Danny. Badly. One of the reasons being it came from you. You've already given me one miracle, I'd like another one."

He smiled.

"And maybe a few more," she said teasingly.

"We could work on it," he said, his voice low.

She grinned at him. "Have you noticed, darlin', how in my quest to become grown up and independent, I've managed to act like an irresponsible, terribly narcissistic child?"

He smiled. "Well, now that you mention it," he said.

She laughed.

He kissed her forehead, then surprised her again, saying, "But if anyone was due a childhood, it was you, Rick. I wish I had realized that sooner."

"Well, I did find out something."

"Yeah?" he asked, his voice rumbly.

"It's not so bad to need someone, especially if that someone is you, and I need you in my life, Danny. I really, truly love you," she sighed into his neck.

"And I really, truly love you, babe," he replied.

She raised her head and looked into those eyes, the ones that still could make her cream her pants, the ones she would love forever, above all others, and said, "Danny, would you marry me?"

She never could remember whether he ever actually verbally responded to her question or not. He was too busy kissing her, then taking her to bed.

Well, that was answer enough.

CHAPTER 23

"OPEN UP YOUR HEART AND LET YOUR FEELINGS FLOW"

Danny and Ricki came downstairs the next morning, goofy looks on their faces. Zachary was waiting in the kitchen. He shot the both of them a repulsed look when they came into the room, then apparently not able to contain himself, said, "Well, I hope you two got it out of your system last night. I couldn't sleep for all the noise you were making."

Oh, shoot, Ricki thought.

"You're really disgusting, you know that?" he fumed.

Danny and Ricki looked at each other, feeling chagrined, like two little kids caught doing the nasty by a parent.

Danny finally gave one of his infamous sighs, then said, "Zach, your mom and I want to talk to you."

"Yeah, and I want to talk to you," Zachary growled, sitting at the breakfast table, indicating with a wave of his hand for them to follow suit. They did, giving each other an amused look.

He leaned toward them, then said, "First off, did you use protection?"

Ricki couldn't help it; she cracked up at that. Danny joined in, his laugh prolonging hers. Zachary sat there, scowling, not appreciating their humor. When they had finally quieted down, Ricki looked at her son and said, "No, Zachary, I'm afraid we neglected to consider that."

He rolled his eyes.

"But there's a reason," she offered.

"Yeah, and what reason could there possibly be?" he snarled.

Danny gave him a big grin and said, "Well, because your mom's pregnant."

Zachary's face blanched. He looked at his father, his mother, his father, then back at his mother, raising his eyebrows questioningly.

"It's true," Ricki said, grinning widely.

Her son asked the question his dad never actually had posed to her, the question his father had every right to ask, i.e., "Who's the father?"

Ricki glanced at Danny, then put her hand in his and said, "It's your dad's."

Zachary looked like he didn't believe this, then said, "But you've been divorced longer than . . . you're not big yet, so you can't be too far along, and you and Dad . . . how can that possibly be?"

"I've been with your father since the divorce," Ricki said, quietly.

Zachary sat there, studying her, then his dad, then her, then said, "Is that so?"

"Yes, honey, that's very much so."

"And you're sure he's the father?" Zachary asked.

Ricki sighed, leaned forward, said, "Zee, if you want, I'll have the blood work done to prove it to you, but your dad's the only man I've ever had unprotected sex with, and more importantly, the only one I've been with since my last period, the only one it possibly could have been."

Zachary leaned back and studied the ceiling a minute. Danny put his arm around Ricki and kissed her temple, drawing their son's attention back to them.

"You going to keep it?" he asked Ricki.

"Yes."

"I'm 17, Ma."

"I know that, Zee. I'm sorry we waited so long to give you a baby brother or sister, but better late than never, huh?" She smiled at him. He didn't smile back.

"I'll be 18 when you have it."

"True."

"How do you expect me to tell my buddies my mom is gonna have a baby?" he said, his voice angry. "They'll know what you've been doing, for Christ's sake."

"We haven't done anything their parents don't do, Zee."

"Jeez, pregnant at your age."

"My thoughts exactly."

He studied her again, pondering, chewing his bottom lip, then addressed his dad. "I hope you're going to do right by her, Dad."

Danny smiled at this and said, "I intend to, Zee."

"So, you are going to get married?" Zachary asked, confirming.

Danny and Ricki smiled at each other, then both said, "Yes" simultaneously.

"To each other?" Zachary asked.

"Yes," together again.

He leaned toward them and said, his voice dead serious, "I would advise you to make it as quick as possible, guys. I'm sure some people are gonna be counting once the little tyke gets here."

Danny and Ricki laughed at this, then Danny said, "Plans are for this weekend, Zach."

Zach leaned back, folded his arms and nodded. "Good. That's great. I'm happy for you." He got up, kissed his mom on the cheek, shook his dad's hand, and said, "I'll stand with you for this one, Dad."

Danny grinned, got up, gave his son a hug and said, "Thanks, Zee, it means a lot to me that you do."

"Yeah, well, next time make sure you're married to the lady before you go knocking her up," Zachary chastised, kissed his dad's cheek, and left.

Ricki and Danny cracked up, and after they had calmed down, went back to bed, foregoing breakfast.

Danny left for the office around eleven, after they made plans to start moving his stuff back in. Even though they had hardly slept the night before, Ricki felt elated, content, at peace for once. She ate half a piece of dried toast before finally giving up. Her stomach just couldn't seem to settle down. Melanie called, wanting to come over and show Ricki the logo she had come up with for WAR. Ricki told her to come on ahead, she had great news she wanted to share, then headed out to the stables to check on the horses' feed and water.

When she came back, she noticed a florist van in the drive. Ricki approached the deliverer, who was standing there watching her come toward him, a bouquet of pale pink roses in his hand. She surmised they must have been from Danny.

As she got near, he asked, "Cherokee England?"

Ricki nodded, feeling a slight tug of recognition, but not able to place him.

He held the roses out and said, "Delivery for you, ma'am."

Ricki smiled as she reached him, took the roses and buried her face in them, searching for a card. When she raised her face up, she was staring into a dark hole surrounded by a chrome-colored barrel. Her eyes widened along with her mouth. *What the?* she wondered to herself, then trying for levity, said, "I take it that means you're expecting a big tip?"

He gave her a grin and said, "Real cute."

"I thought so," Ricki said, looking at him, then, "What exactly do you want?"

He grinned again, then leaned toward her slightly. "Don't tell me you don't recognize me," waving the gun at his face, then back to her.

Ricki studied him, once more feeling that tug, then shrugged her shoulders. "No, I'm afraid not. Maybe you've got the wrong person, whoever it is you're looking for."

255

He turned to the side, tilting his head back a little, offering her his profile, still grinning. "What about now? Recognize me now?"

Uh-oh, she thought, finally knowing this was the guy at the Winn-Dixie that day, the one who had gotten out of the car, the one who had supposedly shot and killed the cashier.

He turned back to her.

"Uh, no," Ricki said, trying not to let her nervousness show. "I have no idea who you are and, actually, don't care to. Now, if you'll excuse me, I've got . . ."

"Huh-uh," he said, waving the gun, stopping her, then giving her a disbelieving look. "You mean to tell me, you got half the state out looking for me and you don't know who I am?" he asked, now appearing offended.

Well, shoot, Ricki thought, *how do I play this?* Not knowing, she said, "Afraid not," trying to appear nonchalant.

"You only gave my description to the cops, got them to do a drawing of me, got it shown on the TV and everything," he proclaimed proudly.

"Really?"

He rolled his eyes and stepped closer. *The better to see me with, I guess.* "It's me," he said, stupidly pointing the gun at himself. Ricki wished it would go off. "The guy at Winn-Dixie that day. You know, the one that . . ."

"No, it's not," she argued.

He looked hurt. "No, really. It's me. I'm the one. I was in the car, the one you saw get out of the car and go inside. That was me!" acting smug.

"No, that wasn't you," Ricki said. "The guy I saw had darker hair and looked pudgier than you do. Plus he had a beard."

"Well, I shaved it off," he pronounced, "and I was wearing a jacket that day, I guess that made me look pudg . . .heavier."

"No, you don't even look like the same guy," she continued arguing.

"Hey, it was me!" he said, sounding angry. "I ought to know whether I shot that girl or not. I ought to know whether I was the one in the parking lot or not, okay?"

They both stopped, pondering this little confession. *Well, shoot, why did he have to go and tell me all this for,* Ricki thought, watching his eyes, as he seemed to realize this at the same time she did.

He pointed the gun at her, said, "Let's go."

Ricki threw the roses in his face, turned and started running.

"Hey!" she heard him yell behind her.

It was at that moment her stomach decided to empty its contents, and for those of you who have not tried, it is downright impossible to run and vomit at the same time. So, Ricki stopped, bent over and threw up in the yard.

He was beside her within a few seconds, then, "Shit!" he yelled, seeing the mess she made. "Damn! What'd you have to go and do that for? Man, I can't stand this!" acting like she had done something bad to him.

Ricki remained bent over, clutching her stomach, trying to get control, trying to bide for time, trying to think.

He jerked her by the arm, started pulling her to the van. Bruce came bounding around the side of the house, tongue lolling, drool falling.

"Sic him, Bruce!" Ricki yelled. The kidnapper stopped short, Ricki running into him.

Bruce stopped, eyed his owner, the guy, then came and joined them, wagging his nubby tail and grinning happily.

"He's hurting me, Bruce, kill him!" Ricki yelled.

"Nice doggy," the murderer said, his voice coaxing, holding out the hand with the gun.

Bruce gave a happy bark, came up to the man, and allowed himself to be petted.

"Damn you, you stupid dog!" Ricki shouted as her nemesis started pulling her toward the van again.

Now Bruce looked hurt.

"Where are we going?" she asked when they got to the van.

"Somewhere it'll take them a long time to find you," he said, trying to act mysterious.

"Come on, why don't you just leave?" Ricki asked him. "I didn't recognize you. I couldn't possibly identify you in court, if I didn't then. I couldn't say it was you I saw."

"Well, maybe before you made me tell you it was me actually done it," he said, placing the blame on her.

"I wasn't listening," she tried. "I don't know what you told me. I didn't want to hear what you were saying."

"You heard me, all right," he snarled, getting a rope out of the van. She tried pulling away from him. He yanked her back, then one arm around her throat, pointed the gun at Bruce.

"You try getting away one more time, I'm gonna kill that dog," he snarled in her ear.

"You'd shoot a dog?" Ricki asked disbelieving. "What kind of a person are you, killing a poor, defenseless dog? For Pete's sake, you gonna shoot something, shoot me!" Then she thought, *oops!*

"Hold still," he commanded, jerking her arms behind her back, the gun waving violently in the air as he bound her. Ricki prayed if it had to go off, it'd go off in his damn face. Bruce sat there, watching all this, tongue hanging out, looking like he was grinning. He probably was.

"Go get help, Bruce," Ricki yelled as the killer shoved her into the van.

Bruce cocked his head, as if to say, *you talking to me?*

"Okay, I'm sorry I called you stupid," she apologized.

Bruce grinned as if to say, *that's okay, don't worry about it.*

The killer started the van up, directing Ricki's attention back to him. "What are you going to do to me?" she asked, scared now.

"Make sure you don't ever testify against me," he said, being mysterious, but they both knew what he meant.

He put the van in gear, went down the drive. Bruce stayed where he was, wagging his tail and barking as if to say, *bye, see ya, have a good time.*

Ricki went from frantic to angry, thinking, *shit, the one time I try to do my civic duty, try to do the right thing, and where does it get me? In a van with a maniac, on my way to get killed and deposited by the side of the road somewhere.*

Melanie was turning in as they were turning out. She gave Ricki a questioning look as the van went by. Ricki silently mouthed "Get help, Melanie!" to her.

She cocked her head questioningly, furrowed her brow, and mouthed, "What?"

"Get help!" Ricki yelled loudly before he clamped his hand over her mouth, the one with the gun. Ricki saw Melanie's eyes widen. He stopped the van.

"Get out of here, Melanie!" Ricki yelled and watched breathlessly as she put her car in reverse, backed out into the street, and took off. The stupid idiot maniac killer stood in the middle of the road, firing shots at her departing car. Ricki prayed he was too ignorant to aim for the wheels. Thank God he was.

He got in the van cussing and screaming at Ricki, reached over and slapped the fire out of her. She watched the dust settling after Melanie's departing car, ears ringing, cheeks burning, tears sliding down her face, praying she'd go somewhere and call 911 quick.

He took off at great speed in the opposite direction, still cussing at Ricki. She ignored him, concentrating on her stomach, which was heaving again. She kept telling herself she had to protect this baby, had to make sure he didn't hurt her and through her the baby. Feeling sorry for herself because she had let so much time go by with Danny, then mad that they had finally worked things out and everything looked all bright and rosy and along comes this pistol-packing jerk to go and ruin it all, Ricki burst out crying. He hit her in the mouth. She tasted blood.

"Shut your fucking mouth!" he screamed at her.

Ricki forced herself to stop crying, forced herself to sit there quietly, docilely, working at the rope on her wrists, trying to free herself. She had read somewhere that rope stretches. She worked that rope every way there was to work it and all it did was get tighter. She looked in the side mirror, noticed what looked like Melanie's car coming up behind them. *Oh, God, please don't let that be her,* Ricki prayed. *Please don't let her think she can play cops and robbers, not today, not with my life at stake.* Ricki was scared he'd notice the car behind them, so decided to get his attention, and started rocking herself against the door, as if trying to force it open.

"Hey!" he yelled, reaching over, grabbing hold of her arm, forcing her to stop.

Ricki glanced at the side-view mirror again. Melanie was right on them. *Damnit, Melanie, go call a real cop!* she wanted to shout. She turned her head, bit his hand.

"Shit!" he screamed, letting her go.

Ricki began kicking the door. He pulled to the side. *Oh, please, Melanie, go on, go call the police,* Ricki prayed. Melanie pulled around them, took off. He never seemed to notice her. *She must have been getting the license plate number,* Ricki thought, thankful Melanie had the foresight to think of that.

He hit her hard enough to daze her this time. Ricki forced herself to stop moving, cowering against the door.

"You do that one more time and I'll shoot you dead right here in this van!" he yelled at her. "Shit, it don't belong to me, don't make no difference to me if it gets all bloody and messy."

Ricki believed him.

He took off again, heading for the interstate. Ricki sat there, frantically trying to think of another diversion, half-afraid he would do what he had threatened to. She knew if he got on the interstate, chances were they could go clear to Canada and no one would know the wiser. She kept looking in the side-view mirror, hoping to see a white car with a red and blue bar across the top. None ever appeared.

He pulled onto 75, going north. *He's heading for the state line,* she thought, wondering if that would maybe pull the FBI in, if he went into another state. She thought it likely would. *You'll probably be long dead by then,* her inner voice said, sounding scared. *You're right,* she sighed inwardly.

They hadn't gone far when Ricki felt bile start rising in her throat again. She kept swallowing, trying to fight the urge to vomit, then knowing it was useless, looked at him, said, "I have to throw up. If you don't want to get it in the van, you're gonna have to stop."

He gave her a disbelieving look, but she must have looked like crap, because he immediately swerved over to the side, got out, ran around, opened the door, and pulled her out. Ricki landed on her knees, vomited there at his feet.

"Damnit, lookit my boots!" he yelled, dancing back. "I swear to God, I should have shot you dead back there at your farm. Don't know why I didn't!" as he went into the grass, started rubbing the boots with leaves, trying to get the vomit off.

There Ricki was, on her knees, on the side of the road, her hands obviously tied behind her back and at least 20 cars went by. Everybody was rubbernecking but not one damn single person stopped to offer assistance. *Well, this is America, the land of the free, the land you love*, her inner voice chided. *Fuck you very much*, she snapped back.

Ricki tried to get to her feet but was too dizzy, so turned around to stare out at the interstate and any car passing by, mouthing, "Get help" or "Help me" and once, "You friggin' coward" to this little old man who slowed down, then took off real quick when he saw the maniac waving the gun around.

He came over to her, pulled her up, threw her in the van, got in the other side, and off they went on their little adventure.

An hour and a half later, he crossed the state line into Kentucky. Ricki had half-expected to see a state trooper's car sitting there or something.

Ricki kept asking where he was taking her, but he wouldn't answer. She begged him, pleaded with him, to no avail, then finally hit on an idea and said, "You know my husband's a really rich man, don't you?" embellishing here.

He gave her a sideways glance, trying not to look interested, but she could tell he was.

"He's Danny England," Ricki said, proudly.

He gave her a suspicious look. "So?"

She inwardly rolled her eyes, seeing he had no idea who Danny was. *So much for your beloved politics and all the fame that carries, Danny*, she thought.

"You know, the county commissioner," Ricki said. Seeing that didn't mean anything, "The guy who's running for county executive."

Still nothing. "Well, anyway, you could make a lot of money, thousands of dollars, if you held me for ransom," she intrigued.

He pretended not to hear but Ricki knew better.

"He loves me very much. He'd pay anything to get me back. I promise you that."

Another sideways look.

"Look at it this way. They've already got you for kidnapping; you've crossed the state line. So, whatever you do to me, that will also be part of the charge, and kidnapping's a federal offense, you know. Plus, if you kill me, you're facing the electric chair in the not-so-distant future. My husband is very well connected politically, and I swear to you, he'll see to it. I take it your assets are limited, right? You got nowhere to really go, right? Now, the way I see it, you could offer me back to my husband, you know, for say, what, fifty thousand?" She kept it low, in the event he decided to negotiate.

He smiled a little at this. *Bingo,* Ricki thought.

"Offer me for fifty thousand, tell him to meet you somewhere, no cops, and you'll exchange me for the money, then you can be on your way, a lot richer. Think of all the places you could go with that kind of money, all the places you could hide out. They'd never find you."

She could see by the smile playing around his lips that he was stupid enough to buy this.

They sat in silence for awhile, then, "So you're telling me this guy loves you enough to pay that kind of money?" he asked.

"Hey, listen, I know he does. You saw where we live. He's got it. He can pay it to get me back. And he will. If not for himself, for our son."

He pondered this a little, then, "Might not be such a bad idea," he said.

About an hour later, he pulled off the interstate into one of those cheap little motel units, the vacancy sign on the verge of fizzling out. He forced Ricki onto the floor of the van as he went inside and booked a room in the back. Single, of course. Then pulled around to the room, made her wait till the way was clear, then ushered her out and inside.

Talk about cockroach hotel. That place not only looked bad, it smelled worse. Ricki gave him a look. "You're about to be fifty thousand dollars richer and this is the best you could do?" she wisecracked.

"Hey, you don't shut that smart mouth of yours, you're gonna be dead ransom," he snapped.

Ricki didn't doubt it.

He sat her in the chair by the wall, the only one in the whole room, then put another rope around her, tying her to the chair.

"Okay, I need a number I can reach your old man at," he said, pulling out a pencil, licking the end.

You're such a shit, Ricki thought. She gave him Danny's number at the houseboat, at the office, his mobile cellular, and their home phone. She told him if somebody else answered, tell them he was calling about the babe and Danny would know this wasn't a bogus call. He grinned knowingly at this. *You jerk, you shit, you stupid asshole,* Ricki railed at him. In her mind, of course.

He went into the bathroom, got a washcloth which looked unclean, came back, stuffed it in her mouth, almost gagging her, and tied another rope around it, securing it. Where he was coming up with all this rope, Ricki didn't know. "I'll be right back," he said, giving her a grin and going out.

Ricki immediately scooted her chair back further against the wall, turned around and leaned forward, placing her ear against it, trying to ascertain if anyone was in the room next door. She heard a bed squeaking, a moaning sound. *Dang!* she thought, *If they're doing what I think they are, they won't be paying attention to anything but what they're doing!*

She kicked the wall with her foot, a steady, continuous beat. She did that for a good five minutes before she finally heard someone let out a loud, "Oh, God!" amidst furious bed squeaking, then it grew quiet in there. Ricki quit momentarily, giving them time to come back to Earth, then started the kicking again.

She heard mumbled voices after a couple of minutes of this, then the bed squeaking again. *Oh, please, don't start that up again*, she prayed.

But then someone slammed a fist against the wall, right at her head, startling her. Ricki jerked back.

"Hey, hold it down in there!" some redneck jerk yelled through the wall.

Ricki started kicking the wall again.

"Hey!" she heard through the wall. "I said hold it down in there or I'm gonna call the manager."

Well, that didn't stop Ricki. She kicked for all she was worth, the guy on the other side retaliating by hitting the wall with his fist. Ricki kicked with first one foot, and when that tired, switched to the other. She was thankful the stupid idiot that had brought her there hadn't had the presence of mind to bind her feet. Finally, feeling slightly dizzy and out of breath, she stopped for a brief respite, heard a woman's soft voice, something about come on back to bed, lover, then the bed start squeaking again and those sex sounds start up. They grew louder and louder and Ricki started up again, growing louder and louder, bolder and bolder, as if they were in competition with each other. Finally realizing they were into it and she wasn't going to stop them at this point, Ricki gave her feet a rest again and sat there, listening.

Her stomach was heaving and she grew panicked, realizing if she threw up, the washcloth would prevent anything from coming out of her mouth and she very well could drown in her own vomit. Her stomach seemed to grow queasier and queasier, thinking these thoughts. Ricki forced herself to calm down, breathe as deeply as she could through her nose, and she tried visualizing a calm, serene stomach. Finally, it seemed to work. She sat there, listening to the sounds in the other room, trying to take her mind off her nausea. After a few more minutes, she heard a woman screaming some unintelligible name, along with fulminative bed-squeaking noises, then a man grunting loudly, and knew this tryst was over, at least for a few minutes. *Man,* she was thinking, *I hope I never have to hear any other two people make love again.* She had had her fill of it by then.

After the bed noises had died down for good, Ricki started with the kicking again.

"God-damn it!" she heard from the other side of the wall, then a woman's consoling voice. Ricki figured the guy was really mad by now, so kicked louder and harder. She heard him open his door, then he was at theirs pounding hard, threatening if they didn't stop this shit, he was gonna make them, every other word a cuss word. Ricki continued to kick. He tried the door, but stupid had locked it behind him, and Ricki heard footsteps retreating, then going inside again. She kicked frantically now. "Fuck!" she heard the guy yell, then footsteps outside, going away.

Please, go get the manager, she prayed.

He did. A few minutes later, there was a rather firm knock at the door and Ricki heard a muffled, "This is the manager, open up," come through.

"I would if I could," she said around her gag but he didn't hear her.

"I said, open up," he commanded.

Ricki kicked the wall again, loudly, fiercely, at a fast pace. She saw the knob turn, then stop, heard a key being inserted, then the knob turned again, and the door was opened. There stood the manager cautiously peering in, master key in hand, Mr. Redneck behind him, looking over his shoulder.

Ricki made frantic noises around the gag. They finally looked her way, their eyes widening at what they saw.

The manager turned around, said, "Go call the cops," and came toward her.

"Help me!" Ricki screamed through the gag.

He studied her for a minute, as if unsure what to do with her. Maybe he was debating whether he would be tampering with the evidence.

263

"Help me!" she screamed again.

He blinked, as if startled, then came around and pulled the rope down and the gag out.

"Please, help me get out of here before he comes back," Ricki said, crying with relief.

The manager knelt behind her and started working with the ropes. He was about as nervous as Ricki was and seemed to make them tighter rather than undo the knots. She could feel his hands shaking, hear his mumbled profanities. She kept glancing toward the door, frightened she would see her kidnapper standing there. The rope finally started to loosen and they simultaneously breathed a sigh of relief. Ricki looked up toward the door and there he stood, looking very unhappy.

"Hey!" he yelled.

The manager jumped, stopped what he was doing, and came around, half-stepping in front of Ricki, protecting her. She loved that man in that moment more than I can tell you.

"What the fuck do you think you're doing?" Mr. trigger-dick asked, waving the gun around.

"The police are on their . . ." the manager started but this was interrupted rather rudely as a bullet was fired into his chest.

Ricki screamed with horror as blood and tissue and she didn't know what landed on her face and chest, as she watched the manager crumple at her feet, a large hole in his back. She glanced at the shooter, saw the barrel coming to aim on her, knocked herself sideways, tipping herself over, feeling a hot, tearing sensation in her shoulder as she landed.

Ricki lay there, playing dead, hurting like hell, hoping all the blood from the manager, not to mention hers, would convince her assailant that she was no longer on this earth. She heard him coming toward her, held her eyes closed as he stood over her, breathing heavily, then heard the soft snick as he pulled the hammer back.

Dear God, please protect this baby, she prayed, waiting.

"Police! Drop your gun!" someone yelled from the doorway.

Ricki wanted to cry but forced herself to remain still.

"Freeze, you fucker! Put the gun down! Now!" the voice said, more authoritatively this time.

Ricki felt a shift in the air as her maniac killer turned from her. She heard the gun land softly on the carpet and burst out crying. She opened her eyes, turned her head, and saw one officer jerk the shooter over to the wall, making him assume the position, snapping handcuffs on, and another one approaching her. He stepped over the manager's body, giving him a quick glance, not even bothering to check him for a pulse, came to Ricki, looked into her eyes, and said, "Jeez, lady."

Ricki thought he was thinking she wasn't long for this world. "We need an ambulance, stat," he said, his eyes looking scared, worried. The other one mouthed something into an object resting on his shoulder.

"Help me," she whispered, her voice harsh.

"Help's on the way," he said.

She felt weak, dizzy, like she wanted to throw up. She looked at her shoulder, could see blood pumping out, glanced around, and saw blood on the wall behind her, on the carpet beneath her. She couldn't tell whose it was, hers or the manager's. She looked back at the policeman, who appeared sick now. He probably thought it all belonged to her. "Shit," he muttered, under his breath.

"I'm pregnant," Ricki said.

"Oh, God," he moaned.

"Be sure to tell that to the paramedics, okay? Don't let them do anything, give me anything that will hurt my baby. Please. Promise me that," she said, her voice growing weak.

"Sure, lady, sure," he said, consolingly, reached out, took her hand, and held it.

"And could you please call my husband for me? Danny England, Knoxville, Tennessee? Please? I think he's probably looking for me."

"Danny England?" He turned to his partner. "Hey, this is Cherokee England, this is the lady we've been looking for."

His partner glanced at Ricki, his face pale, blanched.

"And tell Danny I love him, tell him I'll always love him," Ricki said, feeling the blackness closing in, settling over her, pulling her down.

The next thing she was aware of, Danny was yelling at her, screaming at her, "Damnit, Cherokee, you're not gonna do this to me! You're not gonna take yourself away from me again, you hear me, Cherokee? Damnit, you listen to me, Cherokee, I won't let you do this! Please, Ricki, I love you!"

She opened her eyes. His beautiful face swam before her, a bright white light right behind it.

"Jeez, Danny, you don't have to shout. I can hear you."

His mouth dropped open. Ricki heard frantic movement around him.

"Ricki?" he asked, tears falling down his face.

"Who else do you think it is?" she said, trying for sarcastic, feeling so tired.

"Oh, God, baby," he said, sobbing loudly.

Hands were pulling him away from her. "Danny?" she asked as his face disappeared from view and masked ones took his place. "Danny, what about our baby, Danny? Is she all right? Danny?" but he wouldn't answer.

The blackness took her away again.

Ricki was underwater, down in the inky depths, struggling to get to the surface, watching the liquid color change to lighter shades of blue as she went up, fighting, trying to get to the sun and the air. She could hear muffled, mangled voices around her, seeming to be talking to her, but she couldn't understand what they were saying. She sensed something was wrong with her body, something was missing from her body. As she broke the surface, opened her eyes, saw the pebbled acoustic tile on the ceiling, and heard Danny say, "Ricki? Babe?" she placed her hands on her abdomen and screamed out, "No! Please, God, no!"

EPILOGUE

"OH, I'VE FINALLY DECIDED MY FUTURE LIES . . ."

Ricki was in the hospital a week and then got to go home. Danny stayed with her the whole time, rarely leaving her side, sleeping in her room. Zachary came up and stayed, too. She really loved these guys.

She lost the baby. Danny cried when he told her what she already knew. The doctor explained it was from loss of blood, shock. He said they could try again in three months, that there was no reason they couldn't get pregnant again. "But it won't be the same child," Ricki replied, sobbing.

The motel manager died on the scene. Ricki cried when Danny told her this. He left behind a 10-year-old son and not much insurance. The governor of the state proclaimed him a hero, and Danny pledged to send monthly checks to help support his widow and son, in appreciation for what he did. Ricki only wished he had lived. She wished she could tell him thanks. She wished he hadn't lost his life for her.

Danny and Ricki were married a month after her release from the hospital, after she had gotten her strength back. Since they had eloped the first time, Ricki insisted this time they do it right, have the real thing. Their wedding was held at Danrick, outdoors. The weather cooperated with their plans and gave them a nice, sunny, warm day. Ricki wore a long, white, traditional wedding gown. A gown she used to dream about when she was a teenage girl. A gown she would keep for their daughter to be married in, if they were so lucky to have her, and she so opted. Charlie and Melanie were her matrons of honor. Zachary was best man.

Danny and Ricki went on a Bahamian cruise for their honeymoon, the honeymoon they never got to take the first time around. It was fantastic, full of fire and passion and lust and love, like when they were younger. Whatever it was they had lost in their latter years, they found again.

Sometimes, now, Ricki watches Zachary and his girlfriend Brooke interacting, their playfulness with each other like little kids at times, the innocent passion they share, the giddiness they display, and thinks, somewhat longingly, *ah, sweet youth*, remembering Danny and her at that time of their lives, but then Danny comes home and she watches him greeting their son and probably future daughter-in-law, watches the way his eyes dart around the room, searching, then stopping when they land on her, watches the light come into his eyes, becoming aware of her own eyes changing, the silly smile on her face, the tingling in her body as he breaks away and comes toward her, takes her in his arms. Listens to him tell her he's been wanting to hold her all day, or he's been waiting to see her all day, or God, she feels so good, any several of a hundred sweet things he murmurs to her as he holds her, and more times than not, then saying, somewhat loudly so Zachary and Brooke will hear, there's something we need to talk about, Ricki, and smiling inwardly as she always answers, "Let's go upstairs," then catching the smiling looks passing between Brooke and Zachary, knowing they're not fooling them one bit, but it has to be done, she guesses.

Then going up the stairs hand in hand with her husband, into the bedroom, where they have their own special conversation, not so much with words as with their bodies, hands, mouths, speaking volumes to each other in their own special way.

Ricki's continued on with WAR. Danny's always there and sometimes she sees him at the meetings in the background, listening. Zachary still hangs around. At times, she sees her son and husband exchange this kind of amused look, but Ricki takes that as a defensive posture. She thinks the meetings are good for these two guys, maybe sensitize them to what it is WAR is trying to accomplish, and they do create some pretty heavy discussions between the three of them. That's something Ricki appreciates.

Charlie and Melanie and Ricki have disbanded their vigilante group. They wisely decided they were going in the wrong direction with that, but sometimes Ricki looks at Charlie and she looks at Ricki and they both know all it will take is a nod from either one of them. Maybe . . .

Ricki's happier than she's ever been. She just had to find out who she was, what it was she wanted out of life, and she has. She's back where she started: wife, lover, mother, friend . . .and she's Cherokee England, too. She's made her way now. She no longer feels like she's stumbling down this narrow corridor, bouncing from one wall to the other. She knows what her strengths and weaknesses are, what she likes and dislikes. She knows what she wants to do with her life and also how to attain it and not be so god-awful afraid to take a risk or stand up for herself. Plus, she likes herself now. She respects herself now. That counts a hell of a lot.

Ricki's a realist enough to know she won't live happily ever after, but she is living happier ever after. There's a difference and she'll take the latter one any day.

As the saying goes, ain't life grand?